TALK

TALK

LAURA
Van Wormer

MIRA

MIRA

ISBN 1-55166-317-1

TALK

**For my friend
Jim Spada**

With gratitude and appreciation
to my agent, Loretta Barrett, and to Mollie Doyle,
and to my editor, Dianne Moggy, and the gang at MIRA.

And a very special thank-you
to Christine Robinson and Michael McCarthy,
whose colorful tour of their hometown gave me an idea....

The man roamed the office, eyes wide with wonder and happiness. He studied the photographs, and the artwork on the walls, the books in the shelves, the newspapers and magazines scattered all over, and he smiled at the unruly pile of highlighters on the coffee table. His eyes moved to the desk. He walked over, circled it and knelt down behind it. With his forearm he bumped the swivel chair to turn toward him. And then, sighing softly, the man lowered the side of his face to rest on the fabric of the seat. He closed his eyes, and slowly began to grind his cheek into the seat. "Jessica," he sighed. "Oh, yes, Jessica."

I

Celebrity

1

There had to be more to her secret admirer than they were telling her. Otherwise, everyone wouldn't be freaking out. As far as Jessica was concerned, he was harmless. He was just another terribly lonely fan who every once in a while sent her a gift and a polite note explaining how no one understood Jessica the way he did.

"Close," Cleo instructed her.

Jessica was sitting in makeup and hair, getting "poofed" before the evening taping of her show. She took one more look at Dirk Lawson, head of security at DBS, and obediently closed her eyes so Cleo could dab foundation around them. "What, exactly, is it you wish me to do, Dirk?"

"Be supportive of our security effort."

Jessica opened one eye. "Which means?"

"For one, not ditching your bodyguard and sneaking off somewhere."

"Where did you sneak to?" Cleo asked admiringly, tossing the sponge on the counter and picking up an eyeliner pencil.

"It wouldn't be sneaking if everyone knew."

"It's not funny," Dirk said sharply. "Your well-being is my responsibility. And this guy is a nut. And the fact that we can't trace his letters tells us he's a bright nut, exactly the kind of nut you should be nervous about."

"I'm not the nervous type," Jessica commented, automatically looking up to the right as Cleo applied liner around her left eye. After twelve years on television, seven of them nationally, she could do this makeup-and-hair routine in her sleep. "And it's not as if he's a stalker or anything."

"Oh, but he is," he assured her. "He's stalking you through the mail now, just warming up to the game. And with these guys, you've got to remember, his obsession's not only about you, Jessica, it's also about us—the people who stand between you and him."

"Perhaps you left the FBI a bit too hastily," Jessica said, looking up to the left now as Cleo ringed her right eye. "I'm not sure there's enough excitement here for you." It was against her nature to be rude, but Dirk Lawson had brought out the worst in her since the day he'd arrived three years ago. She could never get over the feeling that the security expert created panic on purpose every once in a while in order to make himself indispensable to the network. Besides that, he simply bugged her, his macho air of self-importance.

"Normal people don't wear gloves to write letters," Dirk said. "Normal people don't use false return addresses. Normal people don't write to strangers and make up imaginary bonds with them."

"Now take that guy that's always outside my apartment," Jessica said, closing her eyes again as Cleo brushed on some eye shadow. "I wish you'd do something about *him*."

"I've told you—as long as he's on public property, there's not much I can do."

"Wonderful," Jessica said, opening her eyes. "So he can just make obscene gestures and scream profanities at me for the rest of my life."

"Excuse me," Bea Blakely said, charging breathlessly into the room, "but we've got some changes." She shoved a number of index cards into Jessica's lap. "We lost the pretzel-maker but found a schoolteacher."

Jessica was staring into the mirror, openmouthed at the sight of her new secretary. Jessica was quite sure that Bea had possessed long light brown hair as recently as before lunch. Now she had shoulder-length auburn hair the exact color of Jessica's.

Bea beamed. "Don't you love it?" she asked, touching her hair, admiring herself. "Cleo did it for me. Well, gotta go!" And she ran out.

Jessica's eyes moved to Cleo, who was smiling nervously back at Jessica in the mirror. "It's hero worship," the hair-and-makeup artist hastily explained. "You should be flattered."

"It's not hero worship," Jessica said, "it's weird."

"Jessica," Dirk said, "we've got to talk about this."

"This, this, what *this?*" Jessica said, pushing Cleo's hand away to look at him. Cleo grabbed her chin and firmly yanked her face back into place to apply blush into the hollows of her cheeks.

"Your *stalker*," he answered. "This guy fits the pattern. And sooner or later he's going to try to get to you. To get near you."

"And do what?" Jessica wanted to know. "I've had every kind of crazy person pursuing me in the past and nobody ever really does anything. There was that guy who sent me a gun in the mail, that woman who insisted I was her reincarnated mother, that wacko who said he'd set West End on fire," she said, referring to the home of the DBS broadcast center.

"Ten minutes, Jess," her producer, Denny Ladler, said, poking his head around the doorway. "Did you get the new notes?"

"All set," she told him. "Not that anyone's going to give me time to go over them," she added to Dirk.

Denny was gone. Then he was back. "By the way, Jess,

the tabloids have you all over them next week again in some sort of lonely-hearts crisis."

"In a *what?*"

"Lonely-hearts crisis," Denny said. "'Talk-show host starved for love,' you know. We're getting copies tonight." He looked at his watch. "Seven minutes, Jess." And he was gone.

"Over here," Cleo directed, patting the next chair.

Jessica moved over and Cleo stuck a bucket of long-handled styling brushes in her lap. Cleo grabbed one, wound a lock of Jessica's thick hair around it, and then wound the brush to the top of Jessica's head where she clipped it. She took another brush and did the same. Then another and another until all the brushes in the bucket had been used and Jessica looked like a very pretty porcupine.

"Listen, Jessica," Dirk said, leaning forward as if to speak confidentially, "if you want to argue with anyone about this, then you're going to have to argue with Cassy." Cassy Cochran was the president of the network. "You know what she's like. Every time I tell her I've got this under control, she says, 'Last time security told me everything was under control, our anchorwoman was nearly killed.'"

The aforementioned anchorwoman happened to be Jessica's best friend, as well as a colleague here at the Darenbrook Broadcasting System. Alexandra Waring had been shot while touring for the network seven years before, this after having been stalked and shot by a crazed fan the year before she came to DBS.

Jessica gestured helplessly, indicating she couldn't respond until Cleo finished painting lipstick on her mouth. Finally Cleo backed off. "I won't ditch your bodyguard anymore, Dirk," Jessica said.

"You promise?"

Cleo snapped her fingers high in the air, signaling Jessica

to look up so she could apply a thick coating of mascara on her lashes. The makeup would be ridiculously heavy for real life, but would make Jessica look very natural on TV. It was meant to accentuate her features, not to change them. But then, as Cleo always nicely said, Jessica certainly had a lot to work with.

"I promise I won't ditch your bodyguard anymore," Jessica repeated.

"I may have to ask you to postpone Jessica's book," Cassy Cochran said. On the other end of the telephone was Kate Weston of Bennett, Fitzallen & Coe, the publishing house issuing Jessica's autobiography.

There was dead silence on Kate's end. Finally the publisher found her voice. "The finished books are due from the plant next week. I don't know how much you know about book publishing, Cassy, but books are literally dropped shipped across the country as they come off the press. To stop the process—"

"I thought the publication date wasn't until next month," Cassy said.

"We have to start shipping six weeks in advance," the publisher explained, "to make sure the books are in the stores when the pub date arrives and the promotion kicks in." She sighed. "Look, I'll give it to you straight. I came back to BFC to turn the company around, and I can't afford to sit on five million dollars' worth of inventory next week."

"Well, I can let you have Jessica here in New York, I suppose," Cassy said. "It's just that I have to go by what my security people tell me." Cassy had been very supportive of Jessica's eagerness to promote her autobiography. But now, with Dirk's urgent warnings about this potential stalker, the idea of Jessica doing what Bennett, Fitzallen &

Coe wanted her to do—a ten-day nonstop cross-country tour with signings in fourteen cities—seemed like running an unnecessary risk. Dirk was ex-FBI and knew this stuff; she had to heed his warnings. And when she stopped and thought about it, the idea of having Jessica sitting out there, surrounded by thousands of "fans," made her nervous, too. The problem was trying to alert Jessica to the danger without panicking her, which raised yet another pressing issue—should they show Jessica the new letters that had been sent to her?

"All right," Kate said, sounding as though she was making notes. "If we've only got New York, then we can do 'Today,' Rosie and Letterman. And then there's Montgomery Grant Smith's radio show. And the local news." A pause. "Now we just have commitments in thirteen other cities to honor."

"I'll let you do a satellite tour from DBS," Cassy offered.

A satellite tour was when the guest sat in a room in front of a single camera and participated in back-to-back interviews scheduled with local markets around the country. One could do as many as twelve decent interviews with morning shows in the eastern standard time zone, then six in central, and then twelve on the West Coast, overlapping with the noon news and local talk shows back in the East. It was exhausting, but a TV professional like Jessica could do it in a snap. In fact, she had done hundreds of such interviews to promote her talk show when it first went national.

The fact was, whether anyone wished to openly discuss it or not, the revenues from "The Jessica Wright Show" had launched DBS and still largely supported the network. Whatever it was that Jessica had that made TV viewers addicted to her—a mixture of warmth and wit, compassion and genuine curiosity—the young woman's gift had been so strong that the network had first signed her despite the knowledge of her drinking problem.

Happily, shortly after launching her show at DBS, Jessica had stopped drinking. That had been seven years ago and nothing could stop her climb in the ratings after that. She was truly a phenomenon unto herself. And Cassy, as the president of the network who had overseen Jessica's amazing growth, felt privileged to have been a part of it. Besides, Jessica was a joy to work with.

"So who would pay for this satellite tour?" the publisher wanted to know.

"Well, we'll have to talk about it."

"Right." A sigh. "Just remember, Cassy, will you? That I'm a book publisher—your poor cousin in communications?"

"A poor cousin about to make a fortune on *my* talk-show host." Cassy laughed. "I'm not running the Salvation Army here, but okay, I'll work on some do-able numbers."

"And what about the Barnes and Noble signing on Fifth Avenue?"

"For the moment, no way," Cassy said.

"Howard Stern can sign on Fifth Avenue, and so can Colin Powell. And they've been protected just fine."

"Look, we may very well find this guy tomorrow," Cassy told the publisher. "I really called only to warn you of the possibility, and give you time to make alternative plans. I suppose I must sound ridiculously paranoid to you—"

"No," Kate interrupted. "Trust me, you don't. Unfortunately this is getting to be a way of life with celebrity books. There are so many crazies out there these days. And I know you're particularly sensitive because of what happened to Alexandra Waring."

"Bingo, you've got it."

There was a quiet knock on Cassy's door and then it opened. Her boss, Langley Peterson, stepped in. He had his briefcase in hand, ready to go home. Cassy held up a hand to signal she'd be a minute.

"Kate, I've got to go, but I'll keep you posted." After a moment, she said goodbye and hung up the phone.

"What's up?" Langley asked, falling into one of the chairs.

Langley Peterson, co-CEO of Darenbrook Communications, the parent company of the Darenbrook Broadcasting System, was a longtime officer of the privately held company which was controlled by an extremely colorful southern family. The Darenbrooks' empire had begun with a single newspaper in Georgia that the old man, Elrod B. Darenbrook, won in a poker game. Big El, as he was known, would marry four times and have children with each wife, but it would be his dynamic youngest son, Jackson, who would grow the company into a multimedia conglomerate consisting of newspapers, printing plants, electronic information services, satellites and broadcasting. Jackson's right-hand man in this had been Langley—who had married a Darenbrook daughter along the way—and he now oversaw the electronic side of the company while Jackson focused on the printing and publishing side. Jackson had originally hired Cassy Cochran to be the executive producer of DBS News, but in short order, she had, for reasons of expediency as well as emergency, ended up launching not only Jessica's show but recruiting almost all the independent TV stations that affiliated with DBS. And thus when Jackson Darenbrook had later seen fit to marry the new president of DBS, Cassy—a second marriage for both of them—Langley had not been fazed in the least. He'd simply been grateful that the Darenbrook Communications empire had been reorganized so that Cassy would never report to her own husband, which meant Langley did not have to look for a new executive.

"Oh," Cassy said to Langley, "it's this letter-stalker of Jessica's. It's taken a turn for the worse and we can't seem to get her to take it very seriously."

"I'm still not clear on why we are," he admitted, pushing his glasses higher up on his nose and bringing one ankle up to rest on his knee.

"At first I didn't understand Dirk's alarm, either." She stood up and walked around her desk. "But then I took these home to read last night." She handed him some papers. They were photocopies of type-written notes. "The ones with the check marks are ones that Jessica has seen," she explained. "The ones without are the ones security intercepted."

Langley started to read.

Dear Jessica,
   I know how lonely you have been. I have been lonely too. But now we will have a chance to get to know each other and move on to the kind of intimate relationship I know you long for.
   If I may, I wish to suggest you wear less revealing clothing now.

Love,
Leopold

"Leopold?" Langley said. "Surely it wouldn't be hard to find some guy named Leopold in this day and age."

"If only we knew for sure that was his name," Cassy said. "But keep going."

Dear Jessica,
   You mentioned the other day you needed one of these. I hope you like it. I look forward to seeing you

wear it. Perhaps you will tuck it in your bosom. I do not like how much other men can see.

Ever yours,
Leopold

"What did he send her?" Langley asked.

"A scarf," Cassy said. "The creepy part was that she made the comment as a joke after a sex therapist on the show suggested using silk scarves in a bondage routine in bed."

Langley blinked, eyes still on Cassy. Then he winced slightly. "That's revolting."

"Well, keep reading."

"Can we trace the scarf somehow?"

"Dirk's trying." She paused. "It's a Versace."

"That guy who was murdered in Florida? The designer?"

Cassy nodded.

His lip curling in disgust, Langley went to the next page.

Dear Jessica,

I watch your eyes in those unguarded moments and I see the sadness there. You mustn't give up hope. It won't always be like this. We will be together and after that, happy always.

You will be able to wear sexy clothes with me. I do not want you to think I do not find you alluring.

Love,
Leopold

Dear Jessica,

It is with great joy I share with you that I am busy working on our future. After so many years of loneliness, the mere thought of you makes everything worthwhile, all pain merely a path to you. I watch you and revel in the love and warmth in my heart. I crave to cover your body with my own. Soon, Jessica, soon.

Love,
Leopold

P.S. Did you like my present? You have not worn it yet.

Cassy leaned closer to look over Langley's shoulder. As he turned to the next page, she said, "Jessica hasn't seen these. This one, the next one, is the one that set off the alarm bells with Dirk."

Darling Jessica,
    Beware, for there are enemies around you. But do not fear, love, for no one can keep me away. I will be there soon, love, so close you will feel my protection. I will not let anyone hurt you. I will not let anyone keep us apart.

Love,
Leopold

Dear Jessica,
    There are people who wish to hurt you. I will do my best to protect you, but you must be careful. Please, please, promise me you will keep a sharp eye out. I will be there as soon as I can be. Please do not wear revealing clothes. It makes it hard to control myself and yet I must until we are together.

Love,
Leopold

"And then we got this one yesterday," Cassy said, pointing.

Dearest Jessica,
    The time is drawing near for us to be together. I

am coming to get you very, very soon. Do not fear, my love, for no one can stop me. I tremble at the thought of your touch.

Love,
Leopold

"No, this isn't good," Langley sighed.

The band started, the cameras rolled and Jessica came striding into the studio from the back today, surprising the audience. They immediately rose to their feet, clapping and cheering the woman they had come to see.

Jessica walked down through the aisle, pausing to shake some hands, wave all around, slowly making her way to the front of the studio where she climbed up onto the set. She picked up a wireless microphone and turned to address the group.

"Thank you, thank you." No matter how many years she had done this, she still blushed when she got applause, a noticeable trait in an otherwise confident and fearless public face. "Thank you all. This is great. Boy am I glad I came tonight." When they kept clapping and cheering, Jessica squinted and looked offstage and said, "What did you do in the warm-up, Alicia? Give them laughing gas? Camera people, get Alicia, will you?"

The camera on the high boom swept down on Alicia Washington, the slim black woman who years ago had started as Jessica's secretary. Alicia hid her face behind a clipboard as Jessica said, "For our viewers, another peek at Alicia Washington, my producer and head writer who, before the show starts, comes out here and warms up my audience." In the control room, the director jumped back to another camera, and Jessica, seeing the red light come on, leaned confidentially toward it to say, "And you thought my audiences simply become instantly unglued the moment I appear." She straightened up, laughing, pushing her hair back off her shoulders.

"She's looking great," the assistant director commented in the control room.

Indeed she was. Tonight's outfit was a short navy blue skirt and a pale blue silk blouse with a V neck that was not terribly revealing, but nonetheless still proved that Jessica's ample cleavage did not need the assistance of any Miracle Bra.

Years of a healthy diet and hard exercise had only enhanced Jessica's looks. She had slimmed way down, but the camera distortion still made her look as voluptuous as any movie star, even when wearing her trademark cowgirl boots. She had a fast-moving line of them now with Garner's of Fort Worth. "All women wear cowgirl boots," the ads ran. Her green eyes blazed with excitement under the studio lights, and her teeth dazzled white, the combination making her smile utterly infectious—even to the gang in the control room. She moved with a style and grace now that had been lacking in her earliest years on TV. As *TV Guide* said, "Jessica Wright has grown into one of the most beautiful and charismatic personalities on the airwaves."

"Tonight's show," Jessica began, "is a bit different and rather fascinating, if I may say so myself. And if I may also suggest to viewers, I think you should get a pencil and piece of paper before we start. As you can see, we've given each of our studio-audience members paper and a pencil so they can make notes too."

She took a step forward to address the camera. "Tonight we're going to talk to 'ordinary millionaires,' a group of people who made over a million dollars by the time they retired. But these are not big movers and shakers on Wall Street, these are regular people with everyday jobs. One of our guests was a public-school teacher. Another was a short-order cook at a Howard Johnson's restaurant, and his wife, a secretary. Actually, this couple made over *two* million dollars. Another guest, ladies and gentlemen, another *millionaire*, was a cashier at a Wal-Mart store for thirty-one years."

A big smile. "Yep. Ordinary jobs, extraordinary savings. Ordinary Millionaires, that's our show. Also joining us will be *the* Mr. and Mrs. of money matters, Ken and Daria Dolan, who will help us to get our finances and savings on track so we can retire millionaires too." She pointed into the camera. "When we come back."

They faded into commercial.

The stagehands helped the guests take their seats on the set and get their microphones connected. The boom microphone swung in closer to augment the sound. Jessica gave each of the Dolans a kiss and a hug, as they were old friends and had been on several times, and quickly shook hands with the other guests, reminding them it was her job to run the show, so they should just sit back and relax and talk to her as if they were sitting in her living room at home.

"But I'd be a nervous wreck sitting in your living room too!" the schoolteacher blurted out.

They all laughed and Jessica gave the teacher a pat on the back before moving over to her chair. Facedown on the seat was another index card. A last-minute note from Bea or Denny, no doubt.

Wrong.

I am here, darling Jessica.

L.

2

"What the heck is going on, Cassy?" Will Rafferty demanded as the network president came striding into the newsroom. Will was the executive producer of "DBS News America Tonight," the programming that preceded "The Jessica Wright Show" live at 9:00 p.m. "They won't let the mobile unit through the front gate. They say the center is sealed off."

Heads turned in the newsroom but no one stopped working. That's what good newspeople did—they tried to live lives while continuing to work at the same time.

"It is closed, I'm afraid," Cassy acknowledged. "We've had a major security alert. I'm sorry for the disruption, but do the best you can. It may take a while."

"Charlie," Will said to a technician as he followed Cassy, "run out to the gate and get the video from the truck, will you?"

The guy took off.

When they reached the privacy of the hallway, Will asked, "Another bomb threat?"

Cassy looked around and then said quietly, "A stalker infiltration."

"Oh, no, not for Alexandra again."

"No," Cassy told him. "This time it's Jessica."

"*Jessica?*" He sighed. "Well, check in with Alexandra, will you? She'll want to know."

"I'm on my way."

"She's in editing bay two," he added. Then he hurried back into the newsroom. "Hey, Midge?"

"Yeah?" The assistant producer was sitting at a computer terminal scanning copy.

"When Charlie comes back with the video, make sure it gets to sports, okay? It's the Yankee stuff we need for tonight."

"Will do," she promised without looking from the computer screen.

"I'll be right back," Will said to no one in particular, walking quickly out of the newsroom, across Studio A, into the outside corridor, past the hubbub of Studio B where the taping of "The Jessica Wright Show" was breaking up, down another hall, through a doorway, past Makeup and Hair, past a blue door before stopping in front of a green one. He knocked and the door immediately swung open, held firmly in place by a huge fellow who squinted at him suspiciously.

"If it's my stalker," Jessica's voice merrily called, "tell him I'm not in."

Will popped his head in. "It's me."

Jessica was sitting in a bathrobe in front of the makeup mirror in her dressing room, wiping the worst of the makeup off her face. At the sight of Will in the mirror she beamed, threw down the cotton ball in her hand and turned around. "Hi," she said in that special voice one likes to save for special people. "Excuse me—um, hello?" she said, addressing the bodyguard now. "Mr. Terminator? You can step just outside the door, if you please. And close the door behind you, will you?"

The man moved past Will and closed the door behind him.

"Are you okay?" Will said, rushing over to kneel next to the bench she was sitting on. "What's this about a stalker?"

"Oh, I don't know, some guy who's been sending me love notes," she said, gesturing to indicate that the specifics weren't worth knowing about. "Dirk told me not to say anything to anyone because he wanted to check out the people here at West End. So anyway, now, this guy somehow got past security and left a note on the set."

"On the set!" Will almost roared.

"It wasn't a bad note," Jessica added quickly. "It just said he was here and—I don't know, Dirk freaked out." She kicked her head toward the door. "So I'm stuck with Mr. Terminator around the clock now." She smiled. "I promised I wouldn't ditch him, so you might as well introduce yourself to him."

Yesterday she had ducked the bodyguard to slip out to take a walk with Will. After working around each other for seven years, they had only recently begun to look at each other in a decidedly different way. As potential lovers. The feeling was strong, surprising and mutual, and both of them were excited and nervous about what the future might hold, since both had learned some pretty hard lessons in the past.

"Jessica, this is very serious," he said, gently touching her hand. "Remember what happened to Alexandra."

Will Rafferty wasn't the best-looking man she had ever been attracted to. In fact, if she took his features one by one—average brown hair, light brown eyes, a large nose, slightly uneven front teeth (otherwise unheard of in TV)— he should have appeared nondescript, if not plain. But he wasn't. There was a kind of gentle energy and youthful enthusiasm that coursed through Will—to say nothing of considerable intellect—and though he tended to be unobtrusive, that life force made him very attractive. And then there were those eyes, the eyes in which Jessica saw a quiet sadness, the kind of sadness of someone who had seen perhaps a little too much too soon.

"Don't worry, it's nothing, Will," Jessica murmured.

"I've got more whacked-out fans these days than 'The X-Files.'"

His gaze lowered to her mouth and stayed there a moment before he looked back into her eyes. "But you've got to be careful."

"Somehow I think you pose a far greater threat of distraction than anything or anybody else possibly could," she said, leaning to kiss him lightly on the mouth.

It had started a couple of months ago at the DBS affiliates convention in Palm Springs. The talent and producers were all shipped out there to schmooze with the management of the affiliates who were signed with DBS. Jessica had been talked into playing golf with the station owner from a key market, San Francisco, since his station was being seriously wooed by Fox to drop DBS and join them. Will had been playing in the foursome ahead with a group of affiliate news directors, and when that group reached the green, Jessica's impatient station owner told her to go ahead and tee off. "Go on," he said. "It's over two hundred yards. Just hit it."

Jessica dutifully stepped up and ran through her checklist from her twice-a-year lessons she always took before her twice-a-year golf ventures at convention time. This past year, however, her personal trainer had increased her weight training and these days she was amazingly strong and coordinated. So she stepped up to place her ball on the ladies' tee, took measure of the hole, addressed the ball, wound up and then gave the ball a great big wallop with her number-two driver. The ball soared, straight and true (for a change), and came down near the green, hitting Will on the back of the head.

"Holy crow, girl!" the station owner declared. "You're good!"

"Oh, no!" Jessica cried, running up the course with the murderous driver still in hand.

The group had gathered around Will, who had, by this time, slowly gotten up and was holding his hand over the back of his head where, Jessica could see, he already had a bump welling up.

"And people wonder why they called her the Terror of Tucson," Will joked to the news producers, referring to Jessica's nickname in her less stable days.

Jessica had insisted on driving Will to the clubhouse for first aid. Of course, since she had kept talking and looking at him, worried that she had seriously injured him, the golf cart had veered rather wildly this way and that, so that by the time they reached the clubhouse Will had been pretty much a basket case. "I've killed him," Jessica confessed to the club pro. "Why didn't you tell me I could hit the ball two hundred yards?"

"I didn't know you could," the pro said honestly, looking at the back of Will's head. "Ouch. Yeah, that hurts, I bet. Lie down here a minute, Mr.—"

"Rafferty," Jessica said, hovering. "Oh, Will, I'm so sorry."

"It's all right, Jessica," Will had said for the nineteenth time.

And thus had begun the first conversation the two had held by themselves in over seven years. Not since the time when Jessica, shortly after her arrival at West End, had been drunk one night after a company party and nearly had sex with an equally inebriated Will on a bunch of deflated cardboard boxes in the corner of Studio B, before Studio B was even finished.

Truth was, Jessica would have had sex with Will that night, had Will not—after some decidedly passionate foreplay—suddenly stopped and pulled away from her. In response to Jessica's drunken demands and ensuing tantrum, he had absolutely refused to touch her again, saying it wasn't right, she wouldn't feel the same way about it sober. And the next morning, of course, Jessica had found this to be absolutely true. In fact, she hadn't even remembered the incident until Will had come to her office to apologize. With a sickening thump of realization, Jessica had realized how close she had come to already dirtying her new nest at DBS.

The most painful irony of the incident had been Jessica's hunch that Will Rafferty was one of the few genuinely eligible men in New York. Certainly as Alexandra's longtime friend and right-hand producer he came with the kind of credentials no sane woman would dismiss.

But Jessica couldn't get past that night in Studio B and what she had done. And when Will had asked her a couple of months later, shortly after she had stopped drinking, to go out of the city for the weekend, to swim and play tennis with him and some friends, she had said no so quickly, she knew she had hurt his feelings. Later she realized he might have misinterpreted her refusal, believing that *she* thought he was good enough to sleep with, but not good enough to date. To the contrary! It was because she was so bitterly ashamed and embarrassed, and all she wanted to do was forget her drunken behavior. And on top of that, Will was so close to her new friend Alexandra that she dared not mess up with him. And so, Jessica had just stayed away.

And then later, Alexandra had told her that Will had a new girlfriend and that was that. A year later Will had another new girlfriend, another gorgeous young thing, and by that time, anyway, Jessica had gotten herself mixed up with Matthew, aka the Doc. The fact that the Doc turned out not to be the love of her life, but one of the more painful lessons of her life, made it all the more sad and embarrassing to look at Will walking around at West End and wonder what might have happened if only she had gone to swim and play tennis with him that weekend so long ago.

There had been at least two more knockout girlfriends for Will since that time. Alexandra told her once that if, after dating a while, Will didn't want to marry the woman, he only thought it fair to break it off then and there.

Yeah, well, Jessica had thought at the time, *that was some men all over, wasn't it? Once they had slept out their passion with one woman, it was time to move on with the next.*

But then, she didn't think so. Certainly Alexandra would have conveyed some kind of personal opinion along with her comment had she thought it was the case with Will. In fact, the more Jessica thought it over, and the better she got to know Alexandra, the more she sensed that Alexandra had been the one to ingrain the if - you - don't - want - to - marry - her - let - her - go - so - she - can - find - someone - who - does doctrine in him in the first place.

At any rate, the Palm Springs convention had set something in motion and Jessica and Will had been circling one another ever since. They had been taking their time, wary, at first merely making a point of chatting with each other a bit each day at West End. Soon they were rather like kids, when schoolkids were still innocent and optimistic, Will symbolically carrying her books and Jessica rewarding him with special smiles. They started having coffee, and then lunch, and then they were always having lunch. They felt as though they knew each other well and, indeed, perhaps they did. It was true, Jessica had found, that when two close friends of one person got together, there was usually a transfer of affection, and this they had already shared for years through Alexandra.

Only last week they had ventured to the occasional dry kiss. This should have seemed extraordinary for two people who had maintained only God knew how many lovers between them. Interestingly, for Jessica, it did not seem extraordinary; it seemed inordinately right.

There were three rapid knocks on the dressing-room door before Bea came bursting in. "Jessica—" She stopped when she saw Will down on his knee.

"Yes?" Jessica asked.

"Um—" She was looking at Will's hand on Jessica's. "They've sealed off West End and Dirk's going to frisk the audience or something."

"He's going to do *what?*"

Bea tore her eyes away from Will's hand to look at her. "Yeah. He says he's going to keep them in the cafeteria and screen them one by one."

"I'm beginning to think Dirk's a little whacked," Jessica muttered. "Okay. Let me hop in the shower and then I'll be up to see what's going on."

Bea backed out and closed the door.

Jessica smiled and looked into Will's eyes. "You realize that tongues are going to start wagging now. And we were doing so well."

He smiled back. "Are you sure you're all right?"

She nodded.

"Jess?"

"Hmm?"

"What's with your secretary's hair?"

She threw her head back and laughed. When she finished she looked back down at him, shaking her head and still chuckling. "I have no idea. When I first hired her, I thought she was pretty normal, but lately—"

He was kissing her.

Will was thirty-eight years old and had never been married. She was thirty-four and had been married once, disastrously and years ago. The kiss was wonderful, but what were the chances of this ever working out?

"What do you mean we can't get on the bus?" the old lady wanted to know. Jessica's studio audience had been ushered upstairs to the company cafeteria for the traditional buffet following the taping. (Jessica always preferred that her audience come hungry; she said it made them more alert.) "Last time I came to the show, you wouldn't let me finish my dessert before shoving me on the bus and shipping us out. Now I've had *two* desserts and I want to go home and you won't let me get on the bus!"

"I apologize for the delay, madam," the security guard blocking the door said. "If you'll just take a seat, I'm sure the buses will be ready soon."

"What's going on?" a man came up to ask. He looked at his watch. "It's getting late and I've got to drive back to Philly. And where did those other people go? Did they get to leave?"

"The president of the network is coming right up to explain the delay," another guard said, walking over. "If you will just take a seat—"

"I've been sitting for days!" complained a young woman. "I came here from Australia!"

"Jessica, damn it, come back here!" Dirk Lawson barked down the hall.

"If you're going to hold my audience captive," Jessica said as she followed Cassy toward the cafeteria, "then the least I can do is wait with them."

Cassy stopped and turned around. "Jessica, you can't."

"Why not?"

"Because your stalker's probably in there!" Dirk said, striding over to take hold of Jessica's arm.

"You put them through metal detectors when they got

here," Jessica said, exasperated. "What's he going to do, stab me with a plastic knife?" She shook Dirk's hand off and pushed past Cassy. "These people are *my* guests." And she banged her way through the doors—scaring the heck out of the security guys—and entered the cafeteria. The audience members looked up with interest. Jessica stepped on a chair to climb up on a table. She had showered, washing off all the gook on her face and in her hair, and then had hastily blow-dried her hair. She was in well-fitting jeans, blouse, hoop earrings and loafers and looked fantastic.

"Hi, everybody, I'm so sorry about the delay. I was downstairs taking a shower and I didn't hear about the bus problem until just now. So I wanted to tell you it won't be long, we're trying to board people one by one, and I'll be waiting right here with you until each and every one of you is on his or her way." She pointed across the cafeteria to Denny and Alicia, who had just come in carrying large cardboard boxes. "We've brought up some bound galleys of my book I thought you might find interesting. I'll sign them for you. It's not the finished book, but it is, technically, the first printing, and it just might be worth something someday. And of course you know there's lots of food and fruit and cheese and desserts and coffee and tea and juice and water and stuff over there, you are to just help yourselves."

People roared their approval.

"While we're trying to sort out the bus problem," she continued, having decided there was no need for her fans to know that they were being considered potential psycho stalkers, "we'll be taking your picture, and taking down your name and address, and we'll be asking you a few questions. This is so we can contact you about future shows that might be of interest to you."

An hour later, Cassy leaned heavily into Denny in the corner of the cafeteria. "Before, they were breaking the doors down to get out and now they won't leave," she groaned. The crowd was laughing and chatting with Jessica, who was still signing bound galleys of her book, publicity photos and DBS T-shirts, and handing out water bottles and coffee mugs and baseball hats and whatever old promotional goodies they had been able to find downstairs.

Finally, at almost midnight, every audience member had been screened and bused off. No stalker found. Jessica left West End for home, bodyguard in tow.

Cassy stood by the elevator, wearily preparing for the next phase. The West End Broadcasting Center was still sealed off and there was a lot more screening to do. There was the whole news group in Studio A and then the evening shift in the Darenbrook research group in another part of the complex.

This was the part she dreaded. She did not want to find out that Jessica's stalker was someone working right here at West End.

3

"If you must know," Jessica said, arriving the following day at her office with Cassy on her heels, "I'm more than a little annoyed that no one will do anything about that creep outside my apartment, but you'll shut down the whole complex and shake my audience down over the only polite stalker I've ever had."

"Jessica! This stalker has infiltrated security!"

"Careful," Jessica said, throwing her head in the direction of the hall, "you're blocking the view of my bodyguard. We mustn't have that. Good morning, Bea."

"Messages on your desk, Jessica, coffee on the way," her secretary said, standing up. "Hello, Ms. Cochran."

"Hi—" Cassy stopped for a moment, vaguely taken back. Then she recovered. "You've done something to your hair."

"Do you like it?" Bea asked, smiling, touching it.

"Sure," Cassy said helplessly, following Jessica into her office.

"Hi, Alexandra Eyes," Jessica hailed the anchorwoman sitting on her couch.

When Jessica had first arrived at DBS, she had not even met the star anchorwoman for the news division before deciding to hate her. All Jessica had heard was how great Alexandra was, how smart Alexandra was, how beautiful Alexandra was, how lucky DBS was to get her (as if *she* were chopped liver). The only problem was, after Jessica had gotten to know Alexandra, she found out that it was all true—Alexandra *was* smart and beautiful, and not only were they lucky to have her, Jessica was quickly ineffably grateful that Alexandra wanted to be her friend.

And thus the talk-show host and the anchorwoman had ended up becoming inseparable friends, and Jessica called her "Alexandra Eyes"—a reference to the anchorwoman's trademark, a set of positively mesmerizing blue-gray eyes—instead of "Queen of the Daisy Chain," which was how she had originally perceived her.

Whenever Cassy had a problem dealing with either Jessica or Alexandra, she would inevitably ask the other for assistance. Jessica assumed that this morning was no exception. She'd bet her bottom dollar that Cassy had coerced Alexandra into talking to her about the stalker.

"Hi, Jess," Alexandra said from behind a newspaper. "I was just reading an item in Liz Smith. 'Everyone who's anyone is clamoring to be invited to *the* party of the year to be given next month by mega–movie star Georgiana Hamilton-Ayres and DBS anchorwoman Alexandra Waring. It's being held in honor of their pal Jessica Wright and the publication of her autobiography. Yours truly is invited—of course!'"

Cassy closed the office door in the face of Jessica's bodyguard and came in, whispering, "Jessica, what in Sam Hill's with your secretary's hair?"

"Cleo did it," Jessica said, dropping her big leather satchel on the floor by her desk with a thud. "She says it's hero-worship."

Cassy and Alexandra exchanged looks—which Jessica caught. "Leave the kid alone. She's quick, and great on the phone." She picked up the pile of messages on her desk, started to scan them and then paused, looking up. "Not that you aren't two of my favorite people in the whole wide world, but what do you want? I've got a ton of reading to do before today's show." She reached for the telephone and started punching in numbers while waiting for their answer. Neither woman would take offense, Jessica knew; it was just how one had to proceed in TV in order to get everything done.

"It's about your stalker," Alexandra began.

"I've got a bodyguard with me twenty-four hours a day, what more do you want?" Jessica demanded. Into the phone, "Hi, is Kate there, please? It's Jessica Wright returning her phone call."

"Dirk thinks—" Cassy began.

"Dirk is a jerk, Cassy," Jessica said. "I'm sorry, but he is, and this macho power trip he's on with me has got to stop. I've got his bodyguard—" She spoke into the phone, her voice immediately softening. "Hi."

Cassy looked at Alexandra and rolled her eyes.

"Dirk is a little heavy-handed," Alexandra said.

Jessica was smiling now, listening into the phone. And then she said, "Really? It is?" To Alexandra, "Could you go out and tell Bea to stand by the fax machine? There's a fax coming in from Kate."

Alexandra did as she asked.

"We'll need to make this fast, Kate," Jessica said into the phone, "because the big boss is sitting here." There was silence for a moment while Jessica listened, then suddenly, she looked surprised. To Cassy, "I'm talking to Kate Weston and she says you've been talking to her."

"And I'll be talking to her again later today."

"It's coming through," Alexandra reported, returning to her spot on the couch.

"Okay, it's coming through," Jessica said into the phone. "Thanks a lot. I'll call you later." Jessica jumped out of her chair. "It's a review from some magazine that all the booksellers and librarians read before the book comes out." As Jessica reached the door, Bea was on the way in with the fax. Jessica quickly took it from her, walking back slowly as she read, then stopping altogether, allowing Alexandra a chance to jump up and read over her shoulder.

> TALK *by Jessica Wright*
> Bennett, Fitzallen & Coe 232pp.
> $22
> The autobiography of the TV talk-show host makes for terrific reading. Born a child of privilege in suburban New Jersey, Wright was known for her brains, wit, charm and physical attractiveness even as an adolescent. However, hers is a tale of gifts gone awry, a young life turned to sex and excess, of harrowing adventures and narrow escapes, including a marriage to a violent drug dealer. Ultimately it's the story of an immensely talented young woman whose accidental discovery on a public-access TV show in Tucson set her on the road to overcoming first her drug addiction and then later her alcoholism, and blossoming into the most beloved talk-show host since Oprah. At turns saucy, sassy, intelligent, and hilarious (much like Wright herself), this memoir is surprisingly moving. An introduction by Wright's friend and fellow DBS star, anchorwoman Alexandra Waring, is a bonus. Fans will eat this up. (June) *250,000 first printing. $200,000 ad/promo. Author Tour. 1st Serial to McCall's; Featured Selection Literary Guild and Doubleday Book Club, TV Rights to Strenn Productions.*

"Wow, Jessica," Alexandra said, patting her back. "This is unbelievable. This is wonderful!"

"Of course *you'd* think it's wonderful," Jessica said modestly. "You only rewrote every sentence in the book for me."

"I did not," Alexandra said.

"Yes, you did, Alexandra Eyes, but who cares? They like it!" Jessica waltzed around her office and then she stopped to strike a mockingly seductive pose. "Please note the physical attractiveness for which I have always been famous."

All three laughed. While it was true that Jessica had become a beautiful woman, it was equally true that until very recently no one could convince her of that fact. Since coming to DBS she had always compared herself to Alexandra, the dark-haired "intelligent beauty" of the airwaves, who had always used those blue-gray eyes the way a master carpenter wielded a hammer. And then there was Cassy, the most classically beautiful of the three—with blue eyes and long blond hair, streaked now with ash gray, still wound around up on the back of her head in a style reminiscent of the seventies—who had run away from her looks all her life and so had insisted on the production side of the industry. Even now that she was closing in fast on fifty, while she might not stop people dead in their tracks the way she used to, Cassy still turned heads wherever she went.

People around West End had nicknamed the women "Charlie's Angels." (Jessica was always quick to insist that no matter what anybody thought, *she* was the smart one.)

"Come here, sweetie, and sit down," Cassy said to Jessica, pointing to the couch. "We need to talk about this stalker business."

"How many network presidents call the help 'sweetie,' I wonder," Jessica remarked to Alexandra, sitting down. "May it be duly recorded in the notes that 'sweetie' is now seated."

"Okay, first, we need a list of who you think your stalker might be."

"How would I know?" Jessica said. "I don't know anyone named *Leopold*."

"I told Cassy to put the Doc on the list," Alexandra said. Jessica hesitated.

Matthew, aka the Doc, had been Jessica's one almost-significant relationship since she had stopped drinking. He had been a doctor, divorced, with two kids living nearby in Manhattan, and while Jessica thought her prayers had been answered, her friend Alexandra had been (a pain in the neck and) less enthusiastic about him. As it turned out, about ten months later, Jessica finally had to admit that she could not ignore that her boyfriend was self-medicating with highly addictive drugs and that his mood changes were unbearable. And no matter how many times the Doc told her differently, Jessica knew darn well that a shot of Demerol was not like a shot of penicillin and Valium was not in the least like Prozac.

It had been the Doc's lack of interest in his children that had gotten to her most, though. It had now been two years since Jessica had broken up with the Doc, but she still saw his children occasionally. Even his ex-wife had come to like her and vice versa. It was through the ex-wife, in fact, that Jessica had recently learned the Doc had crashed into a rehab upstate, an institution especially set up for doctors so they wouldn't lose their license to practice. The Doc had not gone for the usual twenty-eight days, but for three months, and Jessica knew there was a good chance he might be truly clean for the first time in years.

And it had, admittedly, crossed her mind at one point that the Doc might have something to do with these letters. That he might still hold a grudge and wanted to scare her.

"Okay, put the Doc down," Jessica finally said. "I'll give

you his ex-wife's number. She can tell you where he is these days."

"Good," Cassy said. "Who else?"

"I gave her the name of that guy in the Nerd Brigade," Alexandra said.

The Nerd Brigade was the generic term for the electronic research and development staff under Dr. Irwin Kessler in another part of the complex.

"Oh, come on, Alexandra, no way he's a stalker. Leave him alone. Just putting his name on that list is going to hurt his career."

"No, no." Cassy was shaking her head. "Absolutely not. This is completely confidential."

"Yeah, right," Jessica said skeptically. "If it's in a file somewhere…"

"Jessica, get it through your head," Cassy said sharply. "Whoever this is, is playing a very serious game. And if it's one of our people, then he is a person we do not want here."

Alexandra withdrew a folded sheet of paper from her blazer pocket. "Cassy." She handed her the paper. "This is a list of the people around here who I know are smitten with Jessica."

"Let me see that," Jessica said, snatching the paper out of Cassy's hands. "What is this? You've got Will on this list!" She looked at Alexandra. "What are you, nuts? You write down your own friend and producer as a possible stalker!"

"This is not a—" Alexandra started to protest.

"The woman in the cafeteria!" Jessica nearly yelled, looking back at the list. "You mean that fat lady who's always yakking at me over the desserts?"

"Jessica," Alexandra admonished. (Cassy was laughing.)

"Well, this is weird! *Will?* The lady at the dessert wagon?

You've got my cue-card holder on here! And look—*your* news intern, *your* graphic designer, *your* soundman. What the hell are you doing wrong over there, Alexandra, if your whole staff's obsessed with *me?*"

They were laughing, all of them now.

"Jessica, this is not a list of people I think are your stalker," Alexandra said, laughing still, trying again. "It's a list of people at West End I know that—well, admire you—"

More laughter.

"And who I can personally vouch for," the anchor-woman finished. "The purpose of this list precisely is to avoid having Dirk harass them."

"Oh, brother, Dirk the Jerk," Jessica groaned. "I tell you, he'll wreck your life with paranoia if you listen to him. I mean, did it ever occur to you, Cassy, that he'd never get a raise unless he periodically sounds the alarm around here?" She handed the list back to Cassy.

"What about it, Jessica?" Cassy persisted. "Is there any-body here at West End we should check out?"

After a moment, Jessica nodded. "Actually, there are a couple of names you should add to that—what shall we call it?—smitten-but-not-psycho list?"

At this they all broke up again, they couldn't help it. But once they pulled themselves together and Cassy got her pen out, Jessica started to list the workers at West End she knew liked her, but who she also knew should not be ha-rassed. "Jeff, Brad and Steve in the Nerd Brigade—"

"Good," Cassy said, writing.

"Langley," Jessica continued.

Cassy didn't flinch. Although now—after a great deal of work—Langley and his wife, the former Belinda Daren-brook, were happily married, with twin four-year-olds, his admiration of Jessica was no secret around West End.

Years ago, it had almost resulted in something. Of course, that had been back in Jessica's drinking days, too.

"Um, not really anybody else, I don't think," Jessica said. "But I have to admit, I do have a couple of guys around here that maybe Dirk should check out. *Discreetly.*"

"Who?" Cassy said, ready to write.

"The new guy who delivers our cleaning downstairs. He is just a friggin' creep."

"Oh, him," Alexandra said, nodding. "He is kind of..."

"Really?" Cassy asked. "They've always been so good about their delivery people in the past."

"That gal got pregnant and quit. We loved her," Jessica said. "And then there's that strange guy who's been working outside—you know, doing the cleanup in the square? He never did anything weird to me, not directly, but I sure don't like the way he watches me or those kids from the day-care center."

"The blond guy?" Alexandra asked her. "With the eternal five o'clock shadow?"

"Yeah. And his sleeves are always torn off?" Jessica said.

"I've noticed him too," Alexandra said to Cassy. "I have no idea what his name is."

Cassy nodded, writing.

"And then there's creepy Stevie in the mail room," Jessica said.

Cassy looked up.

"I know, I know," Jessica said quickly, holding her hand up in defense. "The guy lost his arm in Vietnam and all that, but there is something very—" she gestured with her hand "—*strange* going on in his head. If Dirk's going to be keeping an eye on people, I'd keep an eye on him. He may not be my stalker, but I'll bet he's up to something down there."

Cassy was studying her carefully. "What are you trying to tell me?"

Jessica stood up. "Look, I'm only the hired help. You wanted to know some strange people around here, I've given you three strange people. So now, please," she finished, walking toward her desk, "let me get back to work."

Cassy looked to Alexandra, who nodded slightly, and they got up.

Jessica patted her hair in mock provocativeness. "Do give my regards to my fans in the news division, won't you, Alexandra?"

The show, frankly, turned out great. And how could it be otherwise—a celebration of Mother's Day by having mothers like Janet Leigh, Debbie Reynolds and Tippi Hedren on, appearing with daughters Jamie Lee Curtis, Carrie Fisher and Melanie Griffith.

The ladies were great and the audience enthralled and Jessica earned her salary by keeping her personality out of it. One of her greatest strengths as a talk-show host, Jessica knew, was that she never confused the stars with the host. Her job was to be the eternal background, the constant against which the universe was to shine.

After the taping, the ladies were gracious enough to stay and sign autographs and spend some time with the audience before leaving. As soon as they were on their way, Jessica went to her dressing room and hit the shower. She changed into blue jeans, a blouse, sweater and sneakers, and with her hair still wet and her bodyguard following behind, checked out of West End and met her driver outside. She had had the same driver for two years now, Abdul, an exchange student from Egypt who was working his way through Columbia Medical School.

They chatted while heading over to Broadway and then

uptown. He let her off at Ninety-sixth Street and she walked a few blocks before turning down a side street and entering a stone parish house. "You have to stay out here," she told her bodyguard in the hallway, pointing to a bench. "You can see me through that window in the door, but otherwise, you have no eyes, no ears, got it?" When he nodded, she went through the swinging doors and took a seat. She was a few minutes late; the meeting had already begun.

A man was telling his story. Jessica had heard him before. He had been sober about three years, she knew, and was what they called a "high bottom" drunk, in that he had not lost his job or his family before finding his way to Alcoholics Anonymous and getting sober. Jessica's had been a high bottom too. A very high bottom, some would say, since her getting sober had been simultaneous with launching her national TV show.

After the man told his story they had announcements. Then the meeting chairperson asked if there were any anniversaries. In less than a month, God willing, Jessica would be able to raise her hand and say, "My name's Jessica and I'm an alcoholic and today I'm celebrating seven years," but tonight she said nothing, but applauded other people who announced they had everything from three days to twenty-one years of not drinking.

Seven *years*.

It was a cliché, certainly, but time *had* flown. On one hand, it seemed like another lifetime when she had been drinking; on the other, she could remember sleeping in Alexandra's guest room as though it were yesterday, sleeping there because she was too scared to be alone. Too scared that if she were by herself she'd pick up a drink again. Scared that after the success of one whole day of not drinking, she might not be able to make it through another.

And now it was seven years later.

She saw Mr. Terminator watching her through the window and tried to ignore him.

This was her "home" group in AA, the one meeting she always tried to make, where people knew her and she knew them, so that if any of them disappeared for a while, someone would give a call to make sure they were all right. It wasn't nosy, it wasn't pushy, it was simply the loosely constructed camaraderie of people who might otherwise be drinking themselves to death.

After the meeting, a tall black man of about sixty came over to her. Sam Wyatt was her friend, and, actually, sort of her sponsor all these years. She had never asked him to be her sponsor and he had never brought it up, but since he had taken her to her very first meeting, he had always been there for her in that function whenever she needed him. While AA strongly encouraged sponsors and sponsees to be in an impossible-to-be-sexually-attracted matchup—heterosexuals with sponsors of the same sex, gays with the opposite—Sam was so very sober and so very committed to his wife and family, it had never been a concern, not even in passing. He had a big-shot job at Elektronica International and Jessica had met him through Cassy; Cassy and Sam were neighbors on Riverside Drive.

They walked down Broadway to have a cup of coffee in the cheerful Key West Diner. They said hi to the waiters and sat in back and drank decaf and caught up on his family news: his wife, Harriet, had a big new promotion, his daughter Althea was working at Warner Records in Los Angeles, his youngest, the "reconciliation" child, Samantha, was a tenth-grader at the Gregory School.

"So," Sam said, turning the conversation around, "are you feeling a little nervous with your anniversary coming up?"

She shrugged. "Not really. But I'll tell you what is making me nervous—that stupid book I wrote. I got a fantastic review today."

He smiled. "This is a problem?"

She sighed. "Why do I still feel so guilty about everything?"

"Maybe because millions of other people do the right thing just about every day of their lives and they don't end up millionaires and television stars and writing bestselling books." He patted her hand. "Got to take the good with the bad, my friend."

"I didn't realize how much all this book stuff meant to me until I got that review this morning. And then I realized how upset I would have been if it had been bad."

"A lot of the authors Harriet works with don't read their reviews at all."

"I think my problem is that this whole publishing process feels so out of my control."

"It *is* out of your control," Sam observed. "Which can't help but be a good thing. So be grateful, stay humble, ask your Higher Power every morning to help you stay sober and thank him at night."

"Maybe it's a her," she said, smiling.

"Whomever," he told her, "capital *W*."

"By the way," she said, "did you notice? I've got a bodyguard."

"I was too polite to mention it," he said, eyes shifting to Mr. Terminator, sitting at the counter, periodically looking back at them.

"Cassy didn't happen to call you today, did she?"

"As a matter of fact, I think I did hear from the great lady herself."

"Did she tell you about my stalker?"

"Uh-huh." He lifted his eyebrows. "Interesting how you

talked about your book. No, 'Oh, by the way, Sam, I've got a stalker who's penetrated security at West End.'"

"Don't be too sarcastic," Jessica warned him, winking, "or I might have you wrestled to the ground and cuffed."

"Naaa, not me," Sam pooh-poohed, stretching back to yawn and then hitting his abdomen with a fist. "Harriet's got me doing double time at the gym."

Jessica smiled. It was so interesting. Everything she had always thought made boring people boring—like eating and sleeping regularly, getting exercise, building a spiritual life and a sense of community, and trying to maintain a sense of wonderment, curiosity and gratitude about life—had become the mainstays of her life. Was she boring? She thought Sam kind of was, sometimes. Interesting people, in the old days, had always been the spiritually distressed, those made so recognizable by their chronic intake of junk food, alcohol, cigarettes or drugs, their aversion to exercise and devotion to weird hours and a tendency to blame all their troubles on everyone else but themselves. Such people almost always had some interesting daily catastrophe going on of one kind or another.

And now that she was no longer one of those "interesting" people, Jessica had finally figured out that the only reason anyone ever hung out with spiritually distressed people was not because they were "interesting," but because there was sex, money or drugs to be had from them. Otherwise, no one put up with them.

It had come as a tremendous shock to Jessica to realize that sickness only attracted sickness, and never did the rule break. And it was only after coming to this realization that it had finally made sense to her why certain men and women, no matter how much they had cared for her in her drinking days, had ultimately fled.

"Jessica," Sam said, "Cassy did bring up something I think we need to talk about."

"What's that?"

"The possibility your stalker could be someone who knows you from AA."

She was dumbfounded. And disturbed. To drag AA into this paranoia... And yet, it was true, there was every kind of person in attendance and this was New York City and, indeed, some were sicker than others. And it was perfectly reasonable to wonder if in all the meetings Jessica went to, there wasn't a deeply disturbed individual who had fixated on her. It was an anonymous program with no requirement to speak, and many chose not to, so how would she know if someone was a nut unless he raised his hand and outright said it?

"Let's just think a moment if it could be possible," Sam said.

"We both know it's possible," Jessica said, "but I think it's highly improbable. And since AA is the best and purest thing I've ever had in my life, I have absolutely no desire to mess with it, or to have anyone at West End mess with it, either."

"I agree," he told her. "But still, keep your eyes open."

Jessica went into her apartment and closed and locked the front door. Then she sighed, dropped her bag, unchained the door, flipped the locks back and opened it again. "Hey." She was talking to the bodyguard. "What's your name, anyway?"

"Slim," the big man answered.

"Ah, yes, of course. Slim what?"

"Karlzycki."

"Okay, Slim Karlzycki, why don't you come inside? It's going to be another long night out there."

He looked heartbreakingly grateful. Like a big old stray dog longing to come in from the rain.

She led him into the apartment and showed him around: bedroom, guest room, exercise room, living room, guest bathroom, dining room, kitchen, pantry. She got him settled on the living-room couch with the TV and even fixed him a couple of tuna-fish sandwiches.

Jessica washed up in her bathroom and changed into a New Jersey Giants T-shirt. She crawled into bed with piles of stuff to read for tomorrow's show. She clicked on the TV with the remote and flicked through stations, looking to see what was on—Letterman, Jay Leno, Charlie Rose, "Prime-Time Justice"...

She dialed Alexandra's apartment farther up the block on Central Park West.

"I feel like a bird sitting in a cat house," Jessica announced.

"Funny, I thought it was only me that felt that way." Alexandra had struggled valiantly to maintain a veil of privacy around her personal life. To a degree she had succeeded, but not without having to spend a fortune on security measures. "Are you still coming out tomorrow?" Jessica was supposed to go to the anchorwoman's farm in New Jersey for the weekend.

"The question is," Jessica sighed, "am I allowed to?"

"Oh, you're allowed, and Delta Force can camp out in the barn."

"Delta Force?"

"They'll assign at least two bodyguards to cover you over the weekend. At least that's what they've done with me. And I just stick them out in the barn."

What kind of world was it that bodyguards had to be a part of the household planning? Jessica hated to think about it. The last time she had seriously considered buying her own home in the country (instead of crashing at Alexandra's farm, which she had done with amazing regularity for the past seven years), she had been aghast at what it would cost to insure her safety.

Her eyes had blurred over on the "Nightline" screen in front of her.

"Are you watching 'Nightline'?" Alexandra asked her.

"Yes." Long ago Jessica had given up trying to figure out how Alexandra's ESP worked.

"Me, too. I'm sort of interested in it tonight." Translation, *If you need to talk, get to it, please, or otherwise let me get off.*

So Jessica said her good-nights and hung up. But during the next commercial the phone rang. "I meant to tell you, pack nice for this weekend. I have a little surprise for you on Saturday."

"Coming from a girl from Kansas, one wonders what 'pack nice' means," Jessica said, mulling it over. "Gingham, perhaps?"

"How about one of those dirty black T-shirts with a pack of Camels rolled up in the sleeve you girls from Jersey favor?" Alexandra said.

"Ha-ha. As a matter of fact," Jessica countered, "I'll have you know that all girls from New Jersey dress just like Christine Todd Whitman from birth. Go to any hospital and you'll see—there they are, every baby in pearls and Topsiders, no exceptions, that's always the rule."

"Right. Anyway, very casual, but picnic casual," Alexandra said. "Shorts and a T-shirt you feel great in."

"This little surprise sounds absolutely horrible," Jessica told her. "I don't like potato-sack races."

After they hung up again, Jessica tried to settle down and read a book for tomorrow's show, but then she got curious about her bodyguard. She went to peek into the living room to see what he was doing.

He was watching the Cartoon Network.

Hmm.

She climbed back into bed and started reading. The phone rang again and she assumed it was Alexandra. When they were both home alone like this late at night, they often called back and forth. "I want to know what the little surprise is," Jessica said, picking up the phone, "or I'm not coming."

"I don't know," Will's voice said. "Meat loaf maybe."

"Oh, it's you. What are you doing on my phone?"

"Wanting to see if we can move lunch up a half hour tomorrow."

"Sure," she said, reaching to reset her alarm for a half hour earlier. As disorganized as some people thought she was, she really did have maintaining her schedule down to a science, knowing exactly how much time she needed for each segment of her day and night in order to get everything in. Strange, but effective. After all, no matter what, the show had to go on, at least Monday through Friday.

"Oh, that's great," Will said. "Thanks."

"How was your day?"

"Okay. Busy." He sounded tired.

She looked at the clock. "What's wrong?"

"Oh, I don't know. I've just got a lot on my plate, I guess." There was a hesitation in his voice.

"Come on, out with it, Rafferty. You've never called me at home."

"Well, actually, there is something. But I'm not supposed to tell you about it—but I'm not very sure about it, either, and I think I should tell you about it to make sure it's okay with you."

She thought it might be something to do with the stalker, but she admonished herself to banish *that* from her mind.

"Alexandra wants me to rent the cabin on her farm this summer."

Relief—and then interest. "Really. Do you think you might do it?"

"Well, I'd like to, but on the other hand, I, uh—well, you know, I don't want to intrude."

"The cabin's miles from her house," she said, exaggerating, but in the crowded Northeast, it did seem as though it were. Realistically it was more like half a mile. "And Alexandra would never suggest it if she thought you being there might bother her. Come on, Will, you know how she is about her privacy."

Of course he did. He and Alexandra had been friends and colleagues for ten years.

"Actually, it wasn't her privacy I was worried about," he continued. "It was yours. You're out there a lot."

"Oh," Jessica said, feeling funny inside, but determined to keep this light. "You mean that you won't be able to date anybody this summer without having me hanging around."

"What?" He sounded genuinely baffled.

"Well, I was thinking about renting a place myself this summer," she lied. She felt very nearly as attached to Alexandra's farm as the anchorwoman did, particularly since she had been there for all the renovations and improvements over the years. But the idea of having to see Will with another woman made her willing to rent on the moon if only to be spared the sight.

"I didn't know," he said quietly. "I mean, I don't *know*, Jessica, for sure what's going on with you."

"Nothing's going on with me." She gestured, as if he could see her. "Look, if you want to rent the cabin, that's fine with me. Even if I was out there, you'd never see me—unless you wanted to. So if you wanted to bring someone out—"

"Jessica," he interrupted. "The thing is, what I'm trying to say is, I don't want to date anybody else this summer but you."

Jessica blinked. "Oh."

"I mean, I don't know what's going to happen. I mean, we've been having great lunches and walks and stuff—"

And kisses, she thought.

"And you seem to like me pretty well—"

Like him pretty well? Was he brain-damaged?

"And while I would like nothing better than to be out there this summer, it seemed as though I should ask you before I said yes."

"You're not staying in the cabin this weekend, by chance, are you?"

"Yeah. That's the other reason I called. I felt awkward about it."

"And what did Alexandra Eyes say to you about all this? I'm curious."

He laughed. "She said, 'Why would I offer you the cabin unless I thought it would be a good thing all round?'"

"My, somewhat controlling our personal lives, isn't she?" Jessica said.

"She said you pushed someone you thought was good for her into her lap, and now she's merely doing a little steering in return."

Jessica flushed with pleasure. This was so wonderful. He really cared for her, wanted to do this dating thing, the whole nine yards. The prospect of the summer loomed now like paradise and she wished she could cancel the book tour and spend her vacation with him. She quickly reined in her thoughts, though. *Come on, no tricking, no trapping, take it slow.*

"I can think of nothing nicer than to have you out there," Jessica told him.

He gave a happy sigh. "Phew. Okay. Great. Then it's a go."

"And if you change your mind later this summer, you know, and want to date other people—"

"Why? Do you?" he asked quickly. "I mean, is there—"

"No, no," she said quickly. "There's no one else, Will. What I was going to say was that if, you know, later, you do want to date someone else, I'd understand."

There was a long pause. And then, finally, "Jessica," he said, "don't you get it? I've been waiting to go out with you for years."

4

"And here, ladies and gentlemen," Langley Peterson said late Friday morning to the group following him into Studio B, "is our one and only Jessica Wright."

"Better known, actually," Jessica added, looking up from the notebook in her lap, "as the jewel in the crown." She smiled. "But seeing as you're friends, you may call me Miss Crown for short."

After a moment's hesitation, the tour group behind Langley burst into laughter, realizing that Jessica was mocking the latest annual report that described her as the jewel in the DBS crown, since "The Jessica Wright Show" was the biggest moneymaker for the network.

Everyone in the tour group was very important to DBS. There were executives from Procter & Gamble, IBM, Ford, Pillsbury, Fidelity, Travelers, Time Warner, Microsoft, Revlon, General Electric, Staples, Sony, Pepsi, Exxon, Purina and American Airlines. The group represented the largest part of the network's bread-and-butter advertising and it was particularly important they continued to like Jessica, since hers was the only DBS show that was ever boycotted by consumer groups. Nobody ever cared when the boycotting group was something like the Cross-Dressers of America, but boy oh boy had they cared when it was the Christian Coalition not so long ago. Happily, the sponsors had stood by "The Jessica Wright Show," and as it turned out, no real Christians had agreed with the boycott—it had only been the bodies politic within the coalition seeking personal publicity—and the boycott had been quickly rescinded.

Also in today's group were New York City trade and commerce officers from Mayor Guiliani's office, a business-affairs liaison from Governor Pataki's office and an official from the New York State Energy Commission.

"Langley was just explaining," Cassy said, stepping forward, "that 'The Jessica Wright Show' has been on the air now for seven years—with at least a twenty percent ratings increase every single year. Jessica currently has an average of seven and a half million viewers every night, translating into a prime-time Nielsen's rating of eleven point five, which, as you know, is pretty darn good for a show on the youngest of the five broadcast networks. Certainly it's encouraging that as the big three continue to lose viewers in prime time, Jessica continues to find them."

"Hi, Miss Crown here," Jessica said, winking at, and shaking hands with, the tallest man in the group. "Aren't you Greg something? Greg—"

"Roth."

"I've met you before," Jessica told him.

The man was elated. "Yes, I can't believe you remember. It's been a while."

"And Ms. Gallagher, isn't it?" Jessica said smoothly, reaching her hand out to another executive. "It's very nice to see you again. I certainly appreciate your support."

The woman positively beamed.

There was no need for them to know about the sponsor cards Cassy maintained on behalf of the DBS talent, expressly for these kinds of events. On the cards were the names of sponsor representatives, the dates and who they had met from DBS, and, if a photo was not available, a description of the executive. Before these kinds of meetings, Cassy would send copies of the cards to prep everyone.

For ten minutes Jessica shook hands and chatted with every member of the group. She and Alexandra called these the Annual Dog and Pony Shows. (Jessica complained she was always the dog.)

When she had finished shaking everyone's hand, Jessica said she wanted to introduce the brains behind the show, her executive producer, Dennis Ladler. "Although Denny and I have been working together for almost fourteen years—since the very, *very* beginning, before we were syndicated and ours was just a little show on a UHF station in Tucson—I'm still only twenty-seven years old. Got it, everyone?"

"It's like the picture of Dorian Gray," Denny explained, coming forward and pointing to his head. "Her sins graying my hair."

There was some polite laughter.

"I also want to introduce you to the creative brains behind the show," Jessica continued. "The woman who keeps us fresh and entertaining and informative, Alicia Washington." Alicia stepped forward and murmured a shy hello.

"For those of you with kids who want to know how Alicia got started in the business," Jessica said, moving over to put her arm around Alicia, "I've got six words of advice— type fast and give good phone."

People chuckled.

"You think I'm kidding. Well, I'm not. And you can save your kids a lot of disappointment if you set them straight right from the beginning. Alicia graduated from NYU with all kinds of fancy awards, but she started here at DBS as my secretary—as almost every other successful media person in the business did and does. Communications and mass media are apprenticeship businesses. When you go next door, ask Alexandra how she started her brilliant career. Which was, incidentally," she added, leaning forward, "mopping floors at a California radio station."

People laughed, but Jessica only smiled. "Oh, you'll see," she told them. "Just don't be shocked when your kid's first job pays less than one semester's tuition at that fancy school you sent him or her to."

"How about you, Jessica?" someone asked. "How did you get started?"

"Oh, man, I knew someone was going to ask me that," she groaned, provoking more laughter. "Actually, I got my start because Denny here asked me to fill in as a host on a public affairs TV show in Tucson. I was twenty-one years old and as crazy as a loon and I was an undergraduate at the U of A—that's University of Arizona. No one watched this public affairs show. No one. It was on UHF, and the only reason anyone could get the station in the first place was because they had to have cable in the valley—they couldn't get TV signals over the mountains otherwise— and so the UHF station was thrown into the package. Anyway, we soon found out that at least *one* person had been watching that particular night, the night I was substituting—" She squinted and looked at Denny. "Wasn't that the night I fell backward off the set in my chair?"

Laughter.

"Almost," Denny said, increasing the laughter.

"Yeah, I thought so." To the group, "Seriously, this was a major problem for me in those days, not falling off the set. I was crocked. I mean, most everybody knows—it's no secret—I don't drink at all anymore, and haven't for several years. But back then those high ratings were coming at a high price—" She rolled her eyes.

Alicia whispered something in Jessica's ear.

"Oh, gosh, you're right," Jessica said, turning back to the group. "Listen, my autobiography is being published in a few weeks and the whole sordid story is in there. The nice part is, it is a story of recovery, so your customers will like it. No boycotts because of it, I promise."

Nervous laughter this time.

"We'll be sending each of you a complimentary copy," Langley added.

"Hey! No way!" Jessica said. "Everybody's got to buy it. These guys make lots of money!"

"*We're* buying copies," Langley told her. "DBS is."

"Oh, well, that's all right then." To the group, "Okay, so you've got your beach reading all lined up for you. And by the way, there is an appendix in the book—it's called, 'So You Want To Work In TV' and I give every piece of advice I know that works. So, if you know anybody that wants to work in TV, you can loan them your copy."

"Don't you want those people to buy the book too?" someone asked.

"Are you kidding?" Jessica asked. "Nobody starting out in television has any money! Later, maybe, but certainly not in the beginning." She turned to Denny. "What did you pay me in the early days? Wampum and firewater, wasn't it?"

Cassy climbed up on the set. "Okay, everyone, Langley and I are going to take you on to Studio A now, to the set of 'DBS News America Tonight.'"

"But just remember, people," Jessica said, "*I* am the jewel in the crown." To Cassy, "They'll take one look at old Alexandra Eyes and forget all about me."

The group laughed.

"Hardly," the man from P&G said.

More laughter.

"At any rate," Cassy said, "after we visit DBS News, we'll be heading upstairs to the corporate dining room where Jessica and Alexandra will be joining us for lunch.

So if you have any more questions for Jessica, you'll have an opportunity to talk with her then."

The group moved on, though many reluctantly; they wanted to stay and chat with Jessica, sit on her set, just hang out, she could tell. Good sign.

Once the executives were out of the studio and the doors were closed behind them, Jessica let out a sigh of relief and plunked down to sit on the edge of the set. "Air-raid sirens off."

"That went very well," Denny said.

"I don't know why I have to be introduced," Alicia sighed, sitting down next to Jessica. "They could care less about me."

Jessica looked at her. "Because you're the heart of the show, doll-face. And I'm the soul. Get it?"

"So what does that make me?" Denny wanted to know.

"Management, baby, always and forever management," Jessica answered, and they laughed.

"Hey, while I've got both of you here," Denny said, "I want you to see the tape on Roger Jard."

"I don't care what you guys say," Jessica said, getting up, "I don't want to have that sleazebag on."

Today's guest, said sleazebag in question, was a popular actor making his first appearance since being caught on video slugging a woman in the face.

"He's not really such a sleaze, though," Alicia said. "I keep telling you, he's been in a rehab kicking booze and drugs ever since he hit that woman."

"All the more reason not to have him on," Jessica said. "What the hell does he know about staying sober yet?"

"Well, that's just the point," Alicia said quickly. "You do. So who better to guide him through his first public interview? And make sure audiences get it?"

Jessica smiled suddenly, and threw her arms around Alicia, giving her a hug. "I love you, you know that?" she asked her as they followed Denny across the studio toward the control room. "You are so smart. That never occurred to me. Finally I can straighten out one of these guys on the air, instead of sitting there wanting to throw a shoe through the screen at their b.s. on another talk show."

"I've got it cued up," Denny began as he pushed the control-room door open. But then he stopped suddenly, making the women nearly pile into him. "What the hell?"

"What?" Jessica said, peering past him.

It was the weirdest thing. In the control room, in back of the director's chair at the console, there was a small oblong gift-wrapped package—hanging in midair.

"Is it on a string?" Alicia said as the three slowly approached it.

"I don't think so," Denny said, drawing closer.

It looked as though it might be a jeweler's box, containing a bracelet or watch. There was a tiny gift card dangling from the ribbon, turning in the air current they had created by opening the door from the studio.

Denny turned around. "Jessica, Alicia, both of you, stay back there."

"Why?"

"Just stand back, Jess, out the door. Just for a minute."

Jessica and Alicia moved just outside the control room, but Jessica kept the door open to watch. "It must be on a thread, how can it just hang in the air like that?"

Denny reached toward the present, hesitated and then took hold of it. Effortlessly he brought it back to him. "No string, no thread. Just a gentle pull. It must be—"

"Trying putting it back," Jessica said.

He did. And when he released the box, it dipped an inch or two in the air, bobbed a bit, steadied and hung there, in the air, slowly turning.

"Welcome to 'Star Trek Voyager,'" Jessica muttered, coming back into the control room.

"Or 'Bewitched,'" Alicia said.

Denny pulled the package back to hold it in his hand and then put it back again. It did the same thing, bouncing down and up and settling, finally, still, in midair. He looked up at the ceiling and down at the floor. He squatted and held his hand under the package—almost immediately it dropped to the floor. "It's some sort of magnetic field."

"What does the tag say?" Jessica asked.

Denny read it, and then abruptly stood up, leaving the package on the floor. "I'm calling Dirk."

Jessica bent over to reach for it.

"No!" Denny shouted, lunging back to prevent her from touching the package. "Just leave it there until we know what's in it."

While Denny called Dirk, Jessica turned her head so she could read what was on the enclosure card.

**For my precious Jessica,
with all my love,
Leopold**

5

"And where the hell were *you?*" Dirk yelled at Slim, Jessica's bodyguard.

"He was waiting in my dressing room where we told him to wait because we didn't want bodyguards scaring away our sponsors!" Jessica snapped. Actually, she had no idea what had happened to Slim, but she had gotten kind of attached to the guy and didn't want him to lose his job.

"I wasn't talking to you, Jessica," Dirk said.

"I *am* speaking to you," she said, "so lay off him. If you've got a problem, your problem's with me—and the job I have to do so DBS can pay your stupid paycheck. Got it?"

"I'm trying to protect your life so I can get that stupid paycheck," he snarled back. "Got it?"

"Hey, hey, let's turn the volume down a bit, shall we?" Langley suggested. The package left in the control room of Studio B now lay disassembled on his desk. Cassy was standing by the window, silent, arms crossed over her chest. "And Jessica," he began.

"Yeah, yeah, yeah," Jessica muttered, throwing herself down in a chair and crossing her legs. "He's just doing his job." She sighed heavily and turned around. "Dirk, I apologize for speaking to you that way. I just want you to stop picking on Slim. I haven't been out of his sight in twenty-four hours. He's doing a fabulous job—and there was no reason for him to be in the control room because even I didn't know I was going in there."

"And that was my fault," Denny offered. "It never occurred to me anyone had been in there. I mean—how?"

That's what they were all wondering. How the heck had the stalker not only gotten into West End again, but down below ground level into the control room?

"Look, Jessica," Dirk said, stepping closer to her, "I am frankly scared about what can happen to you." He paused for effect. "And Slim knows that he could have cost you your life by not being there."

Jessica rolled her eyes; she couldn't help it. "Right, my stalker's a vice president at Procter & Gamble."

"He very well could be."

"Get a life, Dirk," Jessica said, grimacing. "I've been dealing with stalkers for a lot longer than you've been here."

"Oh yeah? Well, I was dealing with stalkers who killed their victims long before you blew into town, babe. So if you're content to just let this guy waltz in and out of West End, until you displease him and he kills you, then fine, I'm all for it. Just as long as I get my paycheck."

Jessica looked at Langley. "I think Dirk's the stalker."

"That's it, Langley!" the security expert yelled, throwing his hands in the air. "How can I possibly work with her!"

As the argument escalated, Langley looked down at the enclosure card that lay on his desk in a plastic bag.

For my precious Jessica,
With all my love,
Leopold

In another plastic bag was an oblong ornate silver case, in another, a box from Tiffany's. In a fourth bag was the wrapping paper, in the fifth, the ribbon. Langley picked up the bag with the silver case to examine it.

Jessica turned from yelling at Dirk to comment to Langley, in a perfectly normal tone of voice, "It holds a high-lighter pen. I've seen them at Tiffany's, but I've never seen anything like that one. I don't think it's from there."

"It looks old," Langley commented.

"It's from someone who certainly knows me well," Jessica said. She went through hundreds of markers a year, highlighting her notes, in books, magazines and scripts, newspapers, faxes and E-mail.

"And doesn't the fact he knows your habits worry you?" Dirk wanted to know. "Because it does me."

"Anybody who reads *People* knows about Jessica and her highlighters," Cassy said quietly, speaking for the first time. "They ran that picture of her with all of them on her desk."

"And what about her real name, Cassy?" Dirk said. "Look at the initials engraved on that thing."

Langley looked at the ornate monogram, unusual because it was four letters, even odder since there was no *J* to be found in it. SEHW.

"Sarah Elizabeth Hollingstown Wright," Dirk said. "How would whoever it is know that? It's not even in the almanac."

"He may have gotten a copy of her book," Cassy said.

"Damn it," Dirk said, rubbing his eyes. "So he could have been in that audience last night." He looked at Jessica. "You gave each one of them a galley, didn't you?"

"Look, I'd love to stay and chat some more," Jessica said, slapping the arms of her chair and standing up, "but I've got work to do. In case you've forgotten, Alexandra's out there entertaining half the Dow Jones Industrial Average by herself. Come on, Slim. If he fires you, I'll hire you as my administrative assistant."

Slim looked to Dirk as Jessica started pulling him toward the door.

Dirk waved him off. "Go on."

When the door closed behind them, Cassy said, "You don't really think one of our sponsors could be the stalker, do you?"

"Honest to God, one of them could be."

Cassy and Langley looked at each other and, without speaking further, fell in line to follow Dirk into the corporate dining room.

6

—▶ ◀—

"Hi," Bea said to Jessica later that evening, following the taping with Roger Jard. "I saw part of the interview and you handled him very well."

"Thanks," Jessica said, looking through the in-box on Bea's desk. She had come back up to the office to get the stuff she needed to review over the weekend.

"Alexandra wants you to call her in the newsroom," Bea continued, "I put that book you wanted on your chair, your dentist confirmed your appointment for next week, Sotheby's wants to know if you'll do the celebrity auction again, and you've got another bodyguard waiting for you in your office."

"Uh-oh, Slim," Jessica said over her shoulder to her bodyguard. "Competition. But I guess that's showbiz, my friend." She looked at Bea. "Thanks for all your help. Now go home, get out of here, have a life. There's no need for you to wait around." She started toward her office. "And have a nice weekend, okay?" she added, turning around. "Sleep, eat and be irresponsible for a change."

"Thanks." Her secretary laughed. "You have a nice weekend, too."

"Come on, Slim." Jessica waved on her bodyguard. "I've got some sodas in my fridge. Let's check out the new terminator."

As Jessica walked in, a tall, slim, young, very Waspy-looking woman stood up. In her hand were several supermarket tabloids.

"There must be some mistake," Jessica told her. "I was

told there was a bodyguard in here, not a recruiter for the Seven Sister schools with a closet addiction to *The Inquiring Eye.*"

The young woman smiled good-naturedly. "Wendy Mitchell, Ms. Wright, and I *am* your new bodyguard." She extended her hand, which Jessica briefly shook before continuing to her desk.

"I didn't know you were coming on board, Wendy," Slim said, somewhat startling Jessica because he hadn't uttered more than two consecutive words since she had met him. To Jessica's look of surprise, he added, "Wendy's a private investigator."

"And bodyguard," Wendy said. "And if I may say so, Ms. Wright, you sure seem to be a hot topic in the tabloids." She held up the papers. "Did something happen recently? Did someone go through your apartment or steal a cache of letters from you?"

Jessica felt vaguely ill. "No."

"*Did* you ever go out with a drug-addicted doctor? Because if you did," the new bodyguard said, "then I'm afraid you've got someone spying on you."

"No, someone's *stalking* me, get it right," Jessica said irritably, sitting down in her chair with a thump. "So who hired you?"

"Mrs. Cochran?" she said with a question in her voice.

"She's president of the network, it's okay, I've heard of her," Jessica said. "Sit down. You too, Slim." She riffled through some papers, pretending she was looking for something when actually she was freaking out over what Wendy Mitchell had told her about the tabloids. "All right, then," she said as if just refocusing on Wendy, "what's this about someone spying on me?"

"It's these," Wendy said, gesturing to the tabloids. "I've done enough work for enough celebrities to know when an insider's selling information. Of course, it could be that they've gotten their hands on an early copy of your autobiography."

"There is no doctor mentioned in my book," Jessica told her.

"There it is then, I'm afraid," Wendy said quietly, thumbing through another paper.

Jessica shifted her eyes to Slim. "So is this person any good?"

He nodded.

Wendy glanced up from the paper with a furrowed brow and then got up to bring it over to show Jessica. "This photograph... Do you know who took it?"

"How did they get that!" Jessica nearly squeaked. It was a snapshot of her crying on the set. Only she hadn't been crying.

"That's what I wanted to ask you."

"Oh, man. What is this?" She studied the picture for a moment longer. "Anybody could have given them this. It was on the bulletin board in the company cafeteria for a while, but this is just one little part of the whole picture that was taken. It was my cameraman's birthday and we threw a party on the set. We had trick candles on the cake, so when he tried to blow them out, they blew up and we got all this junk in our eyes, so it looked like we were all crying and wailing. And somebody's cut out this little part of that picture."

Wendy was nodding. "So your spy's right here at West End."

"What do you mean, spy?"

"Whoever it is made a thousand at least on that picture, I should think," Wendy told her. "Look, Ms. Wright, it's nothing to worry about. It's just that if I can clear up this little problem too while I'm here—"

"You certainly don't sound like anyone Cassy would willingly know," Jessica said suspiciously.

"I've done some work for Alexandra Waring too, in the past."

"And how do you know Slim?"

"He used to work in my mother's courthouse," Wendy said. "My mom's a D.A. in Delaware, Slim used to be a courthouse sheriff."

"Ah. I see. Happy hands at home. You hunt the people down, Slim stomps 'em and Mama throws them in the slammer."

"In a more perfect world, yes." Wendy laughed. "When I came up to New York and I met Dirk, I gave Slim's name to him."

"Ouch!" Jessica said, looking under her desk. "Oh, rats. If either one of you happen to run into my stalker," she said, straightening up, "tell him I need new panty hose, will you? I keep getting holes in these." She reached ahead to grab her in-box and pull it near so she could start stuffing the papers in it into her big leather bag. "I'm going away for the weekend," she told Wendy.

"Yes, I know," Wendy said. "To Alexandra's farm. I did some surveillance there last year. When she had that photographer problem."

"Charming business we're in, isn't it?" Jessica muttered. She looked at Wendy. "So you're coming with me?"

She nodded.

Jessica looked at Slim. "And you?"

"Yes," he said. "But I'm outside. Wendy's inside. She rides with you. I ride behind in another car."

"Oh, I see, upstairs downstairs, you're still indentured and she's like a nanny, elevated to the family quarters."

"Kind of."

Jessica finished stowing stuff in her bag and stood up. "Okay, I'm the Pied Piper, follow me."

Jessica led her entourage home to her apartment, Slim riding in the front seat with Abdul, and Wendy in the seat beside her. Upstairs in her apartment she read the menu from an Indian restaurant on Columbus Avenue and took orders. Then she called in the order, showered, changed, packed, and the three of them sat down in the kitchen to eat.

"It's awfully nice of you to give us dinner," Wendy said.

"Yeah, well, just catch the spy and get rid of my stalker." Truth was, she'd sooner die than admit it to Dirk, but this stalker was starting to get on her nerves.

Slim carried Jessica's weekend bag downstairs and Abdul drove them back to West End, but not before Jessica's daily neighborhood harasser came over to lean near the car window and let out a stream of vile language. Wendy tapped Slim on the shoulder, said something, and simultaneously they jumped out of the car. Jessica watched in astonishment as the two pushed their faces into her harasser's face, saying something Jessica couldn't hear. They didn't touch him, just surrounded him, talking at him, crowding him, and as he backed off, they got louder and more aggressive, picking up their pace. Now the creep was half running down the block and yet Wendy and Slim kept at him, invading his space, yelling. And then suddenly they stopped, trotted back and jumped in the car.

Jessica smiled. "Hey, I like that. Are you guys going to do that every time you see him?"

"You bet we will," Wendy promised.

"You're my kind of guys," Jessica said happily.

At West End, Jessica had Slim put her bag in her dressing room while she and Wendy took seats in the control room of Studio A to watch the newscast. She smiled at Will on her way in. He was sitting next to the director at the console, headset on, talking to someone in his mouthpiece. Still, he spotted her and waved.

Out in the darkened studio, the newscasters were at their respective desks, bright lights glaring down on them. In the control room, rows of monitors were ablaze with cued film clips, video feeds, graphics and commercials, but Jessica focused on the "out" monitor, which showed what was actually going out over the air. For a moment the screen was utterly black. And then a blue dot appeared, growing brighter, which then started to move as a line, quickly outlining the continental United States, Hawaii and Alaska. Two hundred and six red dots then appeared within the shapes and then suddenly each red dot sent a white line streaking toward New York where they met in a flash of white light, clearing to show the full-color "DBS News America Tonight" lettering and logo. The glow of letters grew bright and the screen flashed out in a blaze of blue light, clearing again to show "With Alexandra Waring."

"Ten, nine, eight..." the assistant director called.

The screen blazed white again and then faded to the original map of the United States, outlined in blue upon black, red affiliate points twinkling, white lines leading to New York.

"Ready to take camera two," the director said. "Fade out video, fade up on camera two. Bring up sound. Cue Alexandra."

In the studio, the red light on top of camera two came on and the floor manager's right hand came down to point at Alexandra.

In the monitor, Alexandra's eyes were sparkling. "This is 'DBS News America Tonight' in New York City, I'm Alexandra Waring, and this is the news."

The format of the newscast had changed little over the years: headline hard news by Alexandra at the top of the hour and the half hour, national and local weather updates at quarter after and quarter to, the rest of the hour filled with regular reports from the science, politics, money, health, sports and entertainment editors and special correspondents.

Alexandra was looking great, as usual. While she was a striking woman in person, she was positively blessed by the slight distortion of the camera. Even when, at times, in real life she could look tired and thin and slightly haggard, on camera she always looked vibrant and beautiful. Her keen intelligence, however, never faltered, on or off the air. Though she was still only thirty-eight years old, few in the news-gathering industry begrudged Alexandra's extraordinary success anymore. She had paid her dues. More than that, she was one of the few who had stayed in hard news and had a growing audience when everyone else's was slipping away.

In the course of the hour, Will jumped up from the console and ran off somewhere three times—standard procedure for a news producer. His job was essentially to make sure everyone had everything they needed—including an audience for the broadcast—or he was history. Thus far, he had done very well. From a local news production assistant, to field producer, producer and then executive producer, his career had risen side by side with Alexandra's.

"And from everyone at DBS News, here and around the world," Alexandra told the camera at the end of the hour, "we wish you a very good night—and an even better tomorrow."

A few moments later, the floor manager called, "All clear!"

"And we're out of here!" Alexandra declared, jumping up from the anchor desk.

A year ago a comment like "We're out of here!" from Alexandra would have been unheard of. But the wear and tear of nightly television had even gotten to Alexandra these days. She and Jessica and people like them in television were extremely well paid not only for their talent and audience appeal, but also for their ability to fight the boredom and sense of imprisonment that a never-altering schedule produced. Day in, day out, feeling good or bad, it made no difference as they *had* to show up for a routine that never changed, unless to accommodate an emergency, which only doubled the workload.

Day in, day out, week in, week out, year after year...

Alexandra claimed that in recent months she could actually feel herself aging in front of the camera.

Monday, Tuesday, Wednesday, Thursday, Friday, another week gone, another week older in another year passing too quickly. Did Jessica remember when they were in their twenties? Alexandra would ask. How exhilarated they had been by their climb, knowing but not caring that everybody else their age was out there creating a life for themselves, establishing homes and families, while they were channeling their all into creating ratings? Then came their thirties, mid-thirties, and now, for Alexandra, her late thirties, when she had to start looking back over her shoulder at the younger people who were determined to have her job. She had begun to wonder aloud that if it was this bad at thirty-eight, how would it be at forty-eight, fifty-eight? And just when was it she was supposed to have a life outside of DBS News?

What was it that Jane Smiley had called it in her first book of short stories? *The Age of Grief?* When lifelong dreams crashed with startling velocity as the realities of reasonable expectations came so dreadfully into focus.

Jessica understood what Alexandra was feeling. She was just four years behind her in the intensity of it.

She wanted to say something to Will before leaving, but there was a problem in the satellite room and he had run off, unlikely to return anytime soon. And Alexandra was itching to get out of there. So Jessica left the control room, knowing that she would see Will tomorrow, and on her way out, she saw the opening of her show rolling on the out-going monitor. News at nine with Alexandra Waring, Jessica at ten with heaven only knew what. That was the linchpin of DBS programming, Monday through Friday. A whole different prime-time programming approach that, thankfully, still worked.

"One good thing about my hours," Alexandra said to Wendy in the limousine as they flew out the Holland Tunnel toward New Jersey, "is that I get to miss the traffic. We leave the city around ten-thirty or eleven on Friday nights and come in at noon on Monday." She was leaning into a portable mirror, wiping the worst of her studio makeup off with specially treated towelettes.

"Where's Slim, do you suppose?" Jessica asked, looking out the back window.

"Over there," Wendy said from the front seat, pointing to the lane next to them.

Sure enough, there was Slim in a dark Ford Crown Victoria about half a car length behind them.

"Who wants something to drink?" Alexandra asked, still bending into the mirror. She glanced over. "Do you mind playing bartender?"

Just because Jessica was a recovering alcoholic didn't mean she had stopped drinking more than everybody else. Only it wasn't booze anymore. While some people reached for food or tobacco or alcohol in times of stress or in search of relaxation, Jessica reached for water or juice, or, if she had a craving for a *real* drink, something loaded with sugar like a Coke or tonic water.

So as they drove along, Jessica took orders and played bartender, although there really wasn't much to bartend since Alexandra only kept Perrier, orange juice and Diet Pepsi in her limo bar.

They drove west across New Jersey on 78, listening to Jewel's new album that Jessica had just received from the singer's publicist, took exit 18 and headed north on 206, then west on 512 toward Pottersville. By now Alexandra was unwinding as an anchorwoman and winding back up as a born-and-raised farm girl who was excited to be nearing home. Bonner Farm was small by Kansas standards (her family's farm was some fifteen times the size), but huge by suburban New Jersey's. It was a gorgeous property, one that Alexandra had added parcels to as adjacent land had come up for sale. It was now nearly one hundred twenty-six acres and, because it bordered on Hacklebarney State Park, seemed to stretch on forever.

Alexandra did not farm the land herself, but allowed two local families to farm sixty-eight acres of it. One family also kept livestock there. The state and town, in gratitude to Alexandra—and people like her who could afford to protect the land from real estate developers—gave her a significant tax break on those acres dedicated to maintaining the state's agricultural heritage. On the house and immediate grounds, however, they taxed the hell out of Alexandra in the way only the tristate area could.

The families who worked the fields of Bonner Farm kept the proceeds for themselves, but in return gave daily care—feeding, exercising, grooming, cleaning the stalls—to the three horses in Alexandra's stable. They also main-

tained the access road and riding trails, plowed the driveway in the winter, in summer allowed Alexandra to pick
fresh vegetables and fruits and gave her a year-round pass
to the dairy down the road where she could pick up dairy
products made from the milk of the cows and goats that
grazed on her land.

Still, as a financial investment, the farm was a fiasco. Fortunately for the community, Alexandra was in a financial
position that meant she could afford the losses. The area
was swarming with developers dying to get their hands on
any part of her land, but Alexandra was going to do her
best, at least in her lifetime, to preserve the tract. It wasn't a
case of not wanting people to have a nice place to live, it
was a case of her wanting northern New Jersey to rehab the
masses of existing housing they had already abandoned
for easier schemes. The state, too, was not particularly
thrilled with the prospect of seeing Bonner Farm falling
anytime soon; they didn't want to see condos thrown up
there, with sewage leakage spilling into the park reserve
and bulldozers tearing down the trees and eroding the
banks of an already fragile flood zone.

No, the developers were going to have to take Alexandra
off Bonner Farm feetfirst, and until that time, she seemed
quite content to spend whatever fortune it would take to
preserve this little part of God's green earth in the New
York City metropolitan area.

Jessica had been at the farm since day one. In fact, she
had seen it before Alexandra had, doing her friend a favor
by scouting it out while Alexandra had been covering a
presidential visit to Helsinki. And then there had been all
the time she'd spent there, helping Alexandra paint and
wallpaper in the earliest days (which happened to be, not
coincidentally, the days when Jessica had desperately

needed something to do on weekends to keep her out of trouble).

Jessica had spent so much time there, in fact, that when Alexandra renovated the house, the anchorwoman had added a one-bedroom suite on the far side expressly for Jessica. It had a full bath, kitchenette and a small sitting room. In return, Jessica had insisted on paying the bill for a gorgeously large and beautifully landscaped pool in the back. If the truth be known, Alexandra was not much of a swimmer, and so it was not a big surprise who used the pool the most.

At any rate, when Alexandra had fallen in love a few years before—in a match engineered by Jessica—and the anchorwoman no longer slept alone at the farm, Jessica had known that Alexandra had meant it when she'd said nothing should change, that there was plenty of privacy in the house and Jessica's rooms were always waiting for her.

The access road to Bonner Farm was three-quarters of a mile long. It bounced past split-rail fences holding in cattle, past bean and strawberry fields already in full offering, past apple and pear and plum orchards, and past the fields that would bear sweet corn and cattle corn, clover, tomatoes, cucumbers, cauliflower, snow peas, eggplant, acorn and butternut squash, cantaloupes and pumpkins. And then suddenly the drive swung into a wood of tall oaks, and when the car emerged on the other side, the house magically appeared in full view, there on the rise, with the lush green lawn spreading down below it. In the daytime, one could see, down behind the house, the barn, the stable, the potting shed and other outbuildings.

It seemed that just about every light of the big old farmhouse was on tonight. The car drove up and around the circular driveway and stopped at the stairs of the massive front porch. Slim, in the Crown Victoria, pulled up behind them. Alexandra's studio driver popped the trunk and brought their bags up onto the porch. Wendy left them, to show Slim to his quarters in the barn. Alexandra unlocked the front door, thanked the driver and then went inside to turn off the alarm.

They brought their bags in. The house was quiet. But then Alexandra spotted another suitcase at the foot of the stairs and she was up to the second floor in a shot.

Jessica smiled, carrying her bag and taking the stairs at a much slower pace. She went down the opposite end of the hall to her room and tossed the bag on the bed. Wendy, she assumed, would be taking the guest room next door. Jessica went to the window and watched Wendy and Slim go into the barn. She frowned slightly and drew the drapes closed. Somehow it wasn't going to be quite the same relaxing weekend knowing they would be watching her. Or that so many people felt the need for the bodyguards to do so.

She was more concerned than they knew. She didn't like living this way.

She also absolutely hated the thought that some wacko stranger could penetrate her life and alter not only her routine, but her very peace of mind.

Well, she would try to relax. The security at Bonner Farm was elaborate.

"Jessica," came a sleepy voice from the doorway. "I wanted to say hello."

Jessica turned around. And smiled. There, standing in the doorway, with one arm draped around Alexandra and the other reaching out to her, was Jessica's old friend and the love of Alexandra Waring's life.

The actress Georgiana Hamilton-Ayres.

7

Lured by the smell of bacon cooking and coffee percolating on Saturday morning, Jessica went downstairs, confident that Alexandra had made the successful transition from health-conscious overworked city slicker to farm girl who served great breakfasts. Her hostess was dressed in a short-sleeved polo shirt, skintight denim jodhpurs and socks. There were telltale smudges of mud on her thighs, confirming that she'd been up and out riding already.

Happily, upon further investigation, Jessica could see that Alexandra was not only making eggs and bacon this morning, but homemade biscuits and white gravy—a meal that contained about ten zillion grams of fat and cholesterol.

"Oh my," Jessica told her friend, yawning. "You've gone completely mad I see."

Alexandra glanced over to smile and Jessica spotted that wondrous glow in her friend's cheeks that came only from one thing. Making love.

"Better enjoy it," Alexandra told her, "because tomorrow it's back to cereal and skim milk." She glanced at Jessica's robe and looked vaguely distressed. "You're not getting dressed? It's almost eleven."

"You mean in my 'dress nicely' clothes?" Jessica asked, snatching a piece of bacon from the bed of paper towels it was on.

"I told you, I have a surprise for you." She looked at her watch. "Which is arriving very soon."

"I'm up for any surprise," Jessica said, coyly turning her

back on Alexandra so her friend could not see her face, "as long as it has nothing to do with Will Rafferty." She moved toward the large oak table. "I know he's your friend and everything, but I had a horrendous argument with him yesterday and I think he's a complete jerk." Keeping a straight face, she sat down at the table and reached for the newspaper.

Finally Alexandra spoke. "You had an argument?"

"I told him to go to hell," Jessica said, scanning the front page of the *Times.*

She hazarded a peek. Alexandra was stirring the gravy in an iron skillet, frowning, looking very disturbed indeed.

"As I say, I know you're tight friends and everything," Jessica continued, "and I respect that. Just don't make me ever have to see him again if you can avoid it."

Oh, this was mean. She could see the panic rising in her friend.

"Jessica," Alexandra said, sounding uncharacteristically unsure of herself. "I really thought you and Will were hitting it off."

"Yeah, well, about the only thing I want to hit off is his conceited head." The expression on Alexandra's face at this comment told Jessica she could not go on with the charade. "Oh, Alexandra Eyes," she cried, jumping up. "I'm pulling your leg! Will called me the other night about the cabin and I just wanted to make you sweat a little."

"You didn't have a fight with him?"

"*Fight* with him?" Jessica said, approaching her. "The only fighting I'm doing is fighting to maintain control of myself." She drew up next to her friend and lowered her voice in genuine awe. "He's wonderful. Absolutely wonderful."

Alexandra smiled, visibly relieved. And then she

frowned again, elbowing Jessica in the side. "Rotten kid. I believed you."

There was a sprightly knock on the door.

"Speak of the devil," Alexandra said. "Let him in, will you, please?"

Will was smiling and waving through the door window. Jessica let him in and there was a lot of laughter in the kitchen as Jessica brought him up to speed on what had just transpired.

"And see how I dressed up for you?" she asked, modeling her unbrushed hair and massive terry-cloth robe.

"You look great." He pulled a chair out at the table for Jessica, and he sat down in the one next to her.

"So," she began, reaching for the pitcher of orange juice and pouring him a glass, "you guys are prepared to work together all week and then see each other every weekend?"

"We're just seeing each other today because you're here," Will explained.

It really was a disgrace, what Jessica felt between her legs in that moment. If she ever fully remembered what had happened between her and Will that night in the studio so long ago, perhaps the answer would be clear as to why and how he could have such a dramatic physical effect on her now.

What she did remember was seeing him at a party at West End that night and flirting with him, and feeling increasingly excited by his attention. When she had crossed that line—that drinking line where suddenly she cared about nothing but feeling alive, and then acting out in order to do so—she had casually sauntered over to him and said, "Why don't you come and see my studio sometime?"

At that point, the DBS news operation had been built in Studio A, but Studio B was barely beyond the planning stages. When Will accepted her invitation by saying, "Why not now?" they had slipped out of the party and into what could best be described as a massive indoor construction site.

They had barely closed the studio doors behind them when they had fallen into each other's arms and started making out.

It had been great. She remembered that much. How fantastic a kisser he was, how attractive and strong and sure of himself as a lover. There had been warnings flashing across her mind at the time—"Not with someone from DBS!"— but Will was not just anyone, this guy was *it*. He was not married, he was immensely attractive, and she wanted so badly to—

She remembered moving to a dark corner, working their way toward a storage room. She remembered his hands on her breasts, his mouth on her neck; she remembered lying down, feeling his excitement pressing into her thigh, the sound of his belt buckle being undone.

And then she remembered suddenly arguing with Will, and how upset he was, saying something about it not being right, she was too drunk.

The last part of this memory she had tried not to think about. The first part she had thought about many, many times over the years in the form of a most pleasant sexual fantasy, and it was that, she finally decided, that her body was responding to.

"And where might be the lovely Lady Hamilton-Ayres?" Will asked Alexandra.

"Still in bed," Alexandra reported. She came over to place a platter of bacon and scrambled eggs on the table and a basket of biscuits wrapped in a linen napkin. "They've been shooting at night all week, so her internal clock's all messed up."

Georgiana was finishing a movie in Canada. She and Jessica had first met several years ago out West, when the actress had appeared on "The Jessica Wright Show" to promote a film. At the time, Georgiana had been married and her life was just about as messy as Jessica's had been and so the two had hit it off and become friends. As the years had bumped along, Jessica had heard rumors about Georgiana and a lesbian affair, and then a few years later, after Georgiana had divorced her husband, she had come right out and told Jessica she wasn't really sure what she was anymore, straight or gay or bisexual.

"As I understand it," Jessica had told the actress at the time, "the term *bisexual* simply means you're unable to have a committed relationship with anyone."

"You've been watching your own show too much," Georgiana had scoffed, clearly irritated. "You don't understand."

"Okay, I don't understand." And in that moment Jessica had been reminded very much of someone else in her life who happened to be her very best friend. Good old Alexandra Eyes, who seemed to have made a lifetime habit of getting engaged and then breaking it off to have an affair with a woman. Not that it had happened that many times, really only twice. But that was enough, wasn't it, for even Alexandra to know that she was not, perhaps, the best candidate for marriage? And the last engagement Alexandra had broken off had not only been wise but kind; the man had gone on to marry someone else who loved him totally. As for Alexandra, she had rather listlessly dated men after that, and Jessica had often wondered if she did it only for the sake of her career.

And so Jessica had then engineered a party at which she had very nearly thrown Georgiana Hamilton-Ayres into Alexandra's lap. Although Georgiana divided her time between L.A. and New York, the women had essentially been together ever since.

"So is your security entourage out here?" Will asked Jessica.

"I haven't seen either one of them this morning."

"You're not supposed to see me," Wendy's voice said from behind the swinging door leading into the dining room.

Silence.

And then Jessica, Will and Alexandra broke up into laughter. "She's in there?" Jessica finally said.

"Come and get it, Wendy," Alexandra called, placing a bowl of steaming white gravy on the table. "Breakfast is served."

As the four settled in to eat, and Jessica tasted her eggs, she looked at Will and smiled. "Are these the good old days or what?"

It was an incredibly gorgeous day. The air was unseasonably cool but the sun shone bright and the sky was so clear that Jessica knew her freckles would be coming out this day. She and Will walked by themselves to see his cabin, and halfway there they rather naturally joined hands and fell into step.

Years ago the cabin had been a hunting lodge. It was a rough saw-board dwelling, now with a nice cedar shingle roof. The cabin's best feature was a covered porch that wrapped around three sides. There were a couple of rocking chairs outside and a pond nearby, which Alexandra claimed had largemouth bass in it. Inside, the cabin had one open room, paneled in cedar, with a big stone fireplace at one end and a kitchenette and closet of a bathroom at the other. There was a couch, chairs and coffee table, a comfy double bed in the corner, and a table and four chairs by the kitchenette.

"There's a little loft up there," he said, pointing up into the eaves. "I was thinking about bringing my sister's kids out. They'd love to sleep up there."

"How old are they?"

"Seven and nine."

"Nice ages," Jessica murmured, admiring the large braided rug in front of the fireplace.

"Are you cold, Jessica? I can light a fire."

"No, I'm fine. Thank you." She looked around. "No TV?"

"Well..." He walked over to the bed, reached under, groped around a bit and came back up holding a mini-TV.

"We never quite get away from it, do we?" she mused, walking to stand in front of the largest window, looking out at the new growth on the trees.

"I think it might get pretty buggy around here later in the season," Will said, coming over to stand next to her, "but Alexandra had all the screens replaced."

"Is there even electricity out here?" Jessica asked, peering around. "Oh, right. You have the TV. When did the electricity get hooked up?"

"A month ago."

She looked at him. "Alexandra knew you were coming a month ago?"

He laughed. "Who ever knows what she knows or doesn't know?"

Jessica smiled, moving across the room. "Mind if I peek at your bathroom?"

"Sure."

She poked her head in. A small, square bathroom, wood-paneled, with a proper john and sink and shower. Nice— for an outdoorsy kind of guy. She herself thought any place without a bathtub utterly intolerable, but guys usually preferred showers anyway.

"My dad and his brothers had a place like this when I was a kid," Will said when she came back out.

Her ears perked up. Will had never spoken of his father before. And instinctively she had known not to ask about him.

"They built it themselves on some land their grandfather gave them in upstate Connecticut," he said, walking over to run his hand over the mantelpiece. "They were young and single. They used it as a fishing lodge. Later, when they had families, they'd sneak off to—" He turned around, resting his arm on the mantel. "I don't know, be a man or something, I guess."

"Did you go there with your father?"

"Once." The way he said this did not inspire Jessica to ask for details. Will absently touched his chin and then dropped his hand. "I think I told you about my father being a pretty mean alcoholic."

"Actually, no," she said softly.

He hitched up one side of his mouth and squinted, as if glaring into the sun. "Oh."

"You did tell me once," Jessica offered, "that some drunk guy broke your elbow."

"Oh, right. I knew I had said something," Will said, nodding, pushing off the mantel. "That was Dad. I guess I just didn't mention which drunk guy it was." He laughed nervously. "We've had quite a few in our family line."

"That's pretty rough."

He shrugged. "It was worse for my younger brother. But then Mom finally threw my father out, so he got back on track." He toed the rug with the end of his Bean Brother boot. "For whatever reasons, he left my sisters alone—well, you know what I mean. So that was good."

She felt awkward standing there, but it didn't seem appropriate to sit. "Is he still around? Your father?"

"Oh, he's still alive. Somewhere. He was sober for a while, but then he started drinking again, who knows why." He looked at her. "Do you think I should go to Al-Anon or something? I mean, isn't that what people are supposed to do if they're interested in someone who's—you know—"

"An alcoholic?"

He nodded.

"Well, it depends," Jessica told him. "For someone who chooses to live with an active alcoholic, I should think definitely yes. And I think someone who's having problems with a sober alcoholic might want to, too. Need to. I mean, Al-Anon never hurts, and it really helps if a situation's out of whack."

"So what if you're with a recovering alcoholic and things are good?"

"I'm not sure I know anyone who's gone for that reason," she admitted. "But you shouldn't have to wait for a crisis in the relationship to find out what it's about."

He came over to stand before her. "I swore, since I was a little kid, that I'd never have anything to do with an alcoholic ever again."

She smiled slightly. "Makes for a mighty small world to live in, doesn't it?"

"In TV news?" He laughed. "Tell me about it!" After a moment, he reached to take her hands into his own. "I couldn't believe it when you first came to West End. How attracted I was to you, how terrific I thought you were— even though you were—um, you know."

"An alcoholic."

"Yeah. And then you stopped drinking." He paused. "And I've watched you, Jessica. And it's been incredible."

The last was said somewhat breathlessly. "You've changed so much, and you're so much stronger, and yet, you're also much softer." He seemed a little embarrassed and looked to the ground for a moment before continuing. "I guess I just want to say that I would be more than happy to do anything, or go to any meetings, if you thought it was the right thing. For us."

She was moved beyond words.

He hesitated and then said, "What do you want, Jessica?"

She smiled slightly. "To find out what love really is. Romantic love, I mean."

He nodded slowly. "Me, too." He squeezed her hands. "That's why I chose you."

She closed her eyes and moved forward into his arms.

"Hey, guys!" Georgiana's voice called from outside.

They separated, reluctant to let go of each other, and moved to the door. Georgiana was outside on horseback, looking ridiculously glamorous though she had no makeup on. She wore faded jeans and riding boots, and her long blond hair was blowing free.

"Good afternoon, Lady Hamilton-Ayres," Jessica called. "It's about time you got up."

Georgiana reined in her horse as it tried to shy away. "It's all right, boy," she murmured, patting it. "You wouldn't believe the schedule they had us on this week. I only got away because I shoved my contract in the producer's face." She smiled. "Hello, Will, congratulations on your new summer digs."

"Thank you," he said with a sweeping bow.

"You're looking very well, Jessica."

"Thank you, Lady Georgiana," she said, curtsying. Georgiana really did hold the title of Lady. Although her mother was a very famous—if not notorious—American screen siren of the 1950s and 1960s, her father was a genuine Scottish peer. There was even a family castle into which Georgiana had been pouring money on behalf of her aging, if not downright batty, father, for years.

"I came by to warn you that Alexandra's organizing a bridge game for tonight."

"Oh no," Jessica said, slapping a hand over her eyes.

"I've already recruited a replacement for me," the actress said. "And if I were you, Jessica, I'd do the same."

"Wendy!" Jessica called.

After a moment, a deeply masculine voice said, "Wendy's not on. It's me." Sheepishly, Slim, the massive bodyguard, came around the side of the cabin.

"Hey," Jessica said, "you don't happen to play bridge, do you?"

"What good are bodyguards if they can't protect me from the likes of you?" Jessica asked Alexandra and Will after dinner at the bridge table.

Alexandra and Will were horribly competitive bridge players, due in large part to years of being out on assignment together, killing time by playing guys from other news organizations until something either happened or it was time to beam a report back home. They hadn't been out of the studio for a while, and thus on their last long trip—to Hong Kong—they had been beaten badly by a pair from CBS and the duo hadn't been the same since.

Georgiana had recruited a neighbor from down the road to take her place as Jessica's partner. "Will plays bridge like a contact sport and Alexandra's smugness makes me simply want to smack her," Georgiana had said. Jacques, a transplanted Frenchman and weekender from New York whose wife was away, was eager to prove himself to Jessica. "I am a superb player of cards," he told her.

"One club," Jessica announced to the superb player of cards, keeping her eyes purposely fixed on her hand. She had a fantastic hand and thought she'd throw Will and Alexandra off by bidding the lowest bid on the lowest suit. Unfortunately, old Alexandra Eyes seemed to catch on to this trick, for she was smiling sweetly at Jessica. "Going to sock you, Waring, if you don't cut it out," Jessica growled.

Across the table Jacques had come to attention, raising one eyebrow in response to Jessica's bid. Jessica had met the antique dealer before in Manhattan. She had purchased a buffet table from him. She didn't know how, frankly, his very American wife—an investment banker—could stand being married to him. He was *so* laid-back, Jessica imagined the wife would have to burn down the house before getting a reaction out of Jacques. But maybe all French guys were like Jacques, she didn't know. They still took long lunches over there, didn't they? Naps in the afternoon and the summers off?

She herself preferred a man who ate quickly, rarely slept, worked hard and adored the ground she walked on. She smiled, sneaking a look at Will. Could it get any better than this? The closeness, the knowledge of how he felt about her, the anticipation of what was to come?

"Refreshments, ladies and gentlemen," Georgiana announced, swinging into the living room with a tray of drinks: a glass of wine for Jacques, Perrier for Alexandra, a Coors' Light for Will, iced tea for Jessica.

"Jessica," Will said, passing her iced tea to her.

"Thank you." She put the glass down and glanced up. Will was openly looking at her, deliberately enticing her to do the same. It made her feel a little weak.

She caught her breath and tried to focus on the game— the game in which she realized she had already badly misbid.

Jessica looked across the table to Jacques and arched her eyebrows, hoping that he would take the hint that he was to bid up, and bid big.

"One diamond," Will said, leaning forward as he did so, as if, as Georgiana claimed, bridge was a game requiring physical prowess.

"One heart," Jacques bid.

Hearts. Jacques had hearts. Jessica had none. Uh-oh.

"Two hearts," Alexandra bid.

Okay, so that's where the rest of the hearts were.

"Three clubs," Jessica insisted, letting Jacques know she had clubs and no diamonds, and opening the way for him to tell her what else he had.

Will slumped violently back in his chair. "Pass."

"Three diamonds," Jacques said.

Three diamonds! What the heck was *that* about? Okay, *think*—she had clubs, Jacques had hearts and diamonds. Alexandra had hearts and Will had a little of everything.

"Pass," Alexandra said, smirking.

Jessica had two diamonds, but was still trying to figure out her partner's hand. She had made an obvious play for the clubs and indicated she had no hearts, so he had to be pretty confident of the diamonds in his hand. She should let him have it. "Pass," Jessica said.

So he played it for three diamonds and they actually ended up getting a little slam.

"Ha!" Jessica cried triumphantly to Alexandra as they finished the hand.

Alexandra looked coolly across the table at Will. "Sounds like one of those guys from CBS, doesn't she?"

"Oh, shove off, Waring. You were positively gloating when you thought I'd messed up."

"True," Alexandra said, smiling slightly. To Will, "Okay, Raff, now we play."

"Come on, Jacques! *Vive la France!*" Jessica cheered.

Jessica and Jacques did not win another hand and went down by over one thousand points.

"I'm really sorry, Jacques," Jessica said to her bridge partner, walking him to the front door when they were finished. "I don't know what happened to my concentration."

"These things happen," he sighed, "even to the most excellent player of cards."

"Hey, is that the new Jag?" Jessica asked, looking past him to the circular driveway.

"Last week, right off the line."

"Nice car," Jessica said admiringly, following him outside. She went down the porch stairs with him to look at it. It was a black convertible. "Where do you get to drive it around here? Doesn't it wreck the engine to never open it up?"

"Oh, I find places," he assured her.

As Jessica peered around at the back of the car, Jacques moved in behind her, slipping his arms around her waist and pressing his lower body into her derriere. "You are a marvelous woman," he murmured, nuzzling her neck.

Shocked, Jessica straightened up and tried to turn around while simultaneously easing him off her. "Thank you, Jacques, but—"

He was kissing her.

Jessica broke it off. "Jacques, stop it."

"Come to my house," he urged. She could see his confident smile in the moonlight. "You are a very sexual, sensual woman. I know. I felt it. And I want to make love with you, too."

Evidently Jacques had picked up the signals Jessica had been exchanging with Will. "No, Jacques," she said firmly, pushing him away—trying to push him away, but he wasn't yet convinced of her refusal.

No matter, though, because Slim came crashing through the bushes a moment later to grab Jacques and slam him backward to the ground, while Wendy jumped out from somewhere and stood over the Frenchman with a small pistol pointed in his face.

"They've got this thing about married men cheating on their wives," Jessica explained.

After they sorted out the misunderstanding, Jacques was dusted off and escorted to his Jaguar by Slim. Jessica went up the porch stairs to find Alexandra standing in the doorway. "I guess we'll have to find a new fourth for bridge," sighed her hostess.

They went back into the den where Alexandra, yawning, said she was going to turn in. Georgiana echoed the same. Jessica said she would be up soon. "Anybody know where Steed and Mrs. Peel are?"

"Wendy's around here somewhere," Will said.

"I think Slim's going to the barn," Alexandra said, leaving the room.

"Sleep well, everybody," Georgiana said, waving goodnight.

"Oh, Will," Alexandra said, backtracking around the corner. "Remember to take the flashlight in the kitchen. The trail to the cabin isn't the greatest."

"Okay, thanks. Good night."

Jessica and Will sat in quiet a while as the sounds of the women faded upstairs. Then Will reached to put his arm around Jessica's shoulder, settling in closer. He whispered, "I feel like we're being watched."

"We are," she whispered back, giggling, luxuriating in his warmth, the coolness of the night, the farm smells that were wafting in through the window. They sat like that for several minutes until a telltale snore let Jessica know that while she had been plotting romance and sexual intrigue for them this night, Will had fallen asleep.

She smiled. Well, that decided that.

"Will," she whispered.

He awakened with a start, at first not knowing where he was. "Oh, sorry. I fell asleep, didn't I?"

"You're tired."

"Mmm, yeah, I guess." He turned to her, regripping her shoulder. "Sleeping, frankly, is not what I had in mind." Before she could respond, he added, "But I think, under the circumstances, it's best if I go to the cabin."

"It's hard to let you go."

He smiled, sleepy.

He went into the kitchen to get the flashlight while Jessica went out on the front porch. "Psst! Wendy! Wendy!"

"What?" came a voice from behind her, scaring the heck out of Jessica. "Sorry," Wendy said, appearing out of the shadows on the porch. "I didn't mean to sneak up on you."

"Listen, Mrs. Peel, Will's going to his cabin, so don't shoot him or anything, okay?"

"Okay."

Jessica whispered, "But shoo, will you? Just beat it for a minute or two?"

"Sure." As Wendy went skipping down the steps and off into the night, Will came out onto the porch and almost immediately took Jessica into his arms. She slid her hands around his waist and they kissed. But not for long, because they wouldn't be able to stay in control for long. The kind of sexual desire she felt for Will was new to Jessica in sobriety. It wasn't a tide; it felt more like a tidal wave of sensation.

"After they catch this stalker of yours," Will murmured, kissing her forehead, her eyes and then her neck. "You and I, Jessica Wright," he continued, kissing her ear, her cheek and then bringing his head back up to look at her, "are going to spend days and days and days getting to know each other."

She knew exactly what he had in mind, for their lower bodies were already working their way toward the un-stated goal.

"I'll see you tomorrow," he said after kissing her briefly once more and breaking away.

"Sleep tight," she called softly.

At the bottom of the stairs he stopped. "You do know that I'm falling in love with you, don't you? And that it started a long, long time ago? Like maybe seven years ago, the very first moment I saw you?"

After a moment, she said, "I know." She didn't know what else to say because she didn't know what it was, ex-actly, that she felt. Other than physically, that was. Not yet. "Good night."

She went back inside and locked the front door. She stood in the front foyer, feeling very wide-awake. Now what?

Hot chocolate and something to read for fun. She went into the kitchen and heated some skim milk, stirring some Nestlé's Quik into it. Then she went into Alexandra's li-brary and looked around on the shelves. Ah, *Vanity Fair*. Surely Thackeray had been dead long enough that no pub-licist would be trying to book him on her show.

Jessica poured her hot chocolate in a mug, set the sauce-pan in the sink with some water in it, picked up her book, turned out the lights and went upstairs to her room.

She turned on the bedside lamp, put down the mug of hot chocolate and went back to the door to turn off the overhead light. She closed the drapes, went into the bath-room and washed up, slipped into her nightie and came back to slide under the sheets. As she was puffing up the pillows, her hand felt something underneath. She closed her fingers around it and pulled. It was a foil packet of hot chocolate and a note.

Dear Jessica,
Sleep well, my precious. I hold the vision of you in my heart, of your body against mine.

Love,
Leopold

Jessica cried out, clawing her way out of the bedcovers and flying out of the bedroom, nearly falling over Wendy in the hall. "How the hell did he get *in* here?" she asked as Wendy rushed into her room.

Alexandra came running down the hall, hastily tying a silk robe around her.

Wendy came back out of Jessica's bedroom, barking into a walkie-talkie.

Georgiana appeared next, knotting her robe securely around her waist. "What's happened?" she asked, taking Jessica's elbow in hand.

"That freak's been in my room!" Jessica said. "God damn it!" she cried, slapping her hand against the wall. "The son of a bitch has been in my bed!" A stalker was one thing, but a creep actually touching her things, her private places. Her bed! Here!

The front door opened and Slim came barreling up the stairs. "Are you all right?"

"Find him!" Jessica yelled, crossing her arms over her chest. "Shoot the son of a bitch, I don't care, just get this guy out of my life and out of my stuff!"

Slim went into the bedroom with Wendy. Alexandra went in, too. When she came back out she handed Jessica's robe to her. "Come on, come downstairs to the kitchen. They're going to be a while."

"I'm not going back in that bedroom, Alexandra. I'm sorry, but there's no way until you fumigate it!"

"No, no, of course not," the anchorwoman said, leading her friend downstairs. "We'll go back to New York. We'll have some hot chocolate—"

"That's what he left me under my pillow!" Jessica shrieked. "I'm never having hot chocolate again!"

"Come downstairs, Jessica," Alexandra urged, pulling her along.

"I'm telling you, I'm getting a gun," Jessica declared. "And if that guy comes near me, I swear I'm blowing his head off. How *dare* he trespass on my private life!"

Alexandra left Jessica under Georgiana's care in the kitchen and returned to Jessica's room. "How is she?" Wendy asked her.

"Furious. She says she's going to get a gun and blow his head off."

"Scared to death, then," Wendy said. "It gets real when it gets personal." She turned to Slim, who was bagging the note. "So what do you think?"

"I think we better bring her back to New York."

"That's what I think, too," Alexandra said. She drew her robe closer around her, giving a slight shiver, and looked to Wendy. "You know how this house is wired. How did he do it? How did he get in here?" She noticed something funny in Wendy's expression and asked, "What? What's wrong?"

"It's just that Slim got some news," Wendy said. "He was on the phone when he heard Jessica scream."

Alexandra turned. "What news?"

"It's about Jessica's secretary," he said solemnly.

"Bea? What about her?"

"They just found her body," he said. "At West End. She's been murdered."

II

Death

8

Jessica, Alexandra, Will and Jessica's bodyguards were back at West End on Sunday morning to meet with police. "I'm fine, just numb," Jessica said to Cassy on her way into the network president's office. "Tell me what to do and I'll do it."

"If you're up to it," Cassy said gently, "the police would like to ask you some questions."

"Sure." Jessica looked to Alexandra.

"I'll stay with you," Alexandra told her.

"Mr. Rafferty?" a man said. "I was wondering if you could come with me into the next office?"

"Sure." Then to Jessica, "I'll be right next door if you need me."

Jessica nodded and, head slightly bowed, walked over to take a seat on the couch.

"Jessica," Cassy said as the rest seated themselves around Jessica, "this is Detective Jefferson Hepplewhite from the New York Police Department."

"And my associate," the black detective said, nodding to a big white guy in the chair across from him who had taken out a pen and pad, "Detective Richard O'Neal."

"How do you do?" Jessica said mechanically.

"As you know, Ms. Wright, your secretary, Bea Blakely, was found here at West End last night."

Jessica felt a blanket of dread and fear descending on her, and the gnawings of pent-up grief. "How was she killed?"

"I'm afraid we can't discuss the specifics right now."

Jessica stared at him. Finally she said, "Could it have been an accident?"

The detective shook his head. "No."

"Wonderful," Jessica muttered. "A murderer's running around here and you can't discuss it." She glared at him. "How are we supposed to help if we don't even know what happened?"

Cassy and the detective exchanged looks. "Let me get you some water, Jessica," Cassy said, rising from her chair.

"Thank you, that won't be necessary," Jessica said sharply, prompting Cassy to sit down again. "Okay, Detective, you've got me here, you won't tell me anything except that someone murdered my secretary. So what do you want to know?"

"Do you know why your secretary was here last night?"

"Oh, God," Jessica said, crashing in an instant and dropping her face into her hands. "Poor Bea."

"It's possible she could have been trying to get a jump on this week's shows," Cassy said.

"So it was not unusual for her to be here on a weekend."

"It wasn't usual," Jessica said, dropping her hands and sniffing. She took a Kleenex from Alexandra. "As a matter of fact, I made a point of telling her not to do any work this weekend." She blew her nose. "I wish you'd tell me how she was killed."

"It's not for public knowledge at this time," Detective Hepplewhite said, glancing at Alexandra.

Jessica followed his eyes. "Oh for God's sake, you aren't reporting this, are you?" Jessica nearly shrieked at the anchorwoman.

"Not who or how the murder occurred," Cassy said quickly. "But of course DBS News has to report the incident, Jessica, you know that."

"That's sick," Jessica said. "She worked here. You knew her."

"We have an obligation to report the news as it happens," Alexandra said quietly.

Jessica stared at her and then turned to the detective. "Could we please continue this conversation in private, please?"

"Jessica," Alexandra protested, "you don't think I'd—"

"I'm not about to talk about Bea in front of the press, that's for damn sure!" Jessica told her. "She wasn't here long, but I don't want her corpse winning anybody a raise around here."

"Jessica!" This was from Cassy.

"It's okay," Alexandra said, getting up to leave. "I know how she feels."

"Why don't you use your vultures downstairs to find the murderer?" Jessica wanted to know.

"I will," Alexandra told her, leaving the office and closing the door perhaps a degree or two harder than was required.

Jessica turned her eyes on Cassy then, as though she might throw her out, too.

"So Miss Blakely had a set of keys to your office," Detective Hepplewhite continued.

"Yes, of course she did."

"Did she have keys to your apartment?" he asked next.

"No."

"Have you ever kept keys to your apartment here at West End?" he asked next. "In your office, perhaps?"

"Why do you want to know?"

"Jessica," Cassy said.

"All right. Yes, I keep a set of keys to my apartment hidden in my desk."

"So Miss Blakely had access to them."

"Yes."

"To your knowledge, has she ever been in your apartment?"

"Sure. At least twice, maybe three times. We did some tapings there and she came over with the crew. And then another time, she came for dinner, with the rest of my staff."

The cop nodded. "Good. Now, what can you tell me about Bea? Miss Blakely, rather."

"I've already given them her personnel file, Jessica," Cassy said. "And I called Bea's family myself."

"Oh, God, those poor people," Jessica said, tears welling up. "Geez, their daughter..."

The detective politely waited for Jessica to pull herself together.

"Bea was not an easy person to know," Jessica finally said. "She was very young, green, but a good secretary. Very good on the phone, with messages, typing, organizing me."

"What about friends?"

Jessica shook her head. "She never talked about her personal life."

"Boyfriends?"

"She never said anything," Jessica said. "But it's not as if I encouraged her to talk about her personal life. Frankly, until someone's here for six months, I try not to invest too much time emotionally in getting to know them. It's age, I guess. So many of the younger people come and go so fast, you get kind of jaded."

"What about time off? Did she ever say how she spent it?"

"She was into astrology, I know," Jessica said. "She did my chart once."

"Did you trust her?"

Jessica shrugged. "No reason not to. But then again, I had no particular reason to have to. As I said, she hadn't been here very long."

"Miss Wright, did it ever occur to you that Miss Blakely might have been supplying information to the tabloids about you?"

Jessica was dumbfounded. "No. It didn't."

"There have been some stories recently," Cassy said.

"So we hear," the cop said.

"You think Bea was feeding information to the tabloids?"

"Selling information," the detective corrected her. "And we don't think, Miss Wright, we know without a doubt that she was."

Jessica walked out of Cassy's office shell-shocked. Will was waiting outside, and jumped up when the door opened. "Are you all right?"

"Yeah," she said vaguely. Automatically she looked for Slim and Wendy and felt better when she saw them.

"Nobody's going to get near you, Miss Wright," Slim promised.

"Jessica," Will said, "please don't be angry about DBS breaking the news about Bea."

She looked at him, not fully registering what he had said, which he mistook for anger.

"Alexandra had to call it into the newsroom," Will continued. "She didn't give any name or details, but she had to call it in, Jessica. NBC already had it off the police scanner."

"I'm not mad," she said weakly. She looked at Will. "I just don't know what I'm supposed to do now."

"We'll go home, Jess."

"But I don't want to go to my house," Jessica said, starting to cry. "I'm scared to go there."

* * *

"Will's taking her to my place as we speak," Alexandra told Cassy a little while later. "Wendy's with them and Slim's nearby."

"Good," Cassy said. "I frankly don't know where else to put her at the moment."

"Where's Dirk?" Alexandra asked. "What's his take on this?"

"He's trying to bring the FBI in, which of course has already ticked off the NYPD." Cassy slid down heavily to her chair behind her desk and rubbed her eyes. "I just flew up from Hilleanderville," she said, referring to her husband's hometown in Georgia. "Jackson's still there. His brother's ill. He'll come up as soon as he can."

"Cassy," Alexandra said, drawing a chair to Cassy's desk, "tell me what you know."

"No can do, sorry. I gave my word. No press statements."

"Cassy—" Alexandra waited for the network president to meet her eyes. "I swear I won't use any of it. Not until you tell me I can."

"And if I don't believe you?"

The question hung in the air a moment.

"If you don't believe in me, Cassy, frankly I don't know who you can."

Cassy nodded, biting her lower lip. "She was electrocuted over the telephone in property room three."

Alexandra closed her eyes.

"How she got in there or why she was there, we don't know. But we do know that someone diverted over a thousand volts from a main power cable into that phone line to kill her instantly."

"At least that's something," Alexandra said, reopening

her eyes. "She didn't know it was going to happen and she didn't suffer."

Cassy looked miserable. "The body was horrible, Alexandra. I didn't even know it was Bea at first, she was so badly burnt."

"I'm sorry."

"So am I." Cassy shoved a photocopy across her desk. "And look at this. They found it upstairs in Jessica's office."

Alexandra picked up the sheet of paper.

Dearest Jessica,
    She won't hurt you anymore. I'll see that no one else does, either.

All my love,
Leopold

9

The first black limousine to turn into the church parking lot in Huntington, Long Island, carried Jessica Wright, Denny Ladler, Alicia Washington, Langley Peterson, his wife, Belinda Darenbrook Peterson, and Jessica's bodyguard, Wendy Mitchell. The second limousine carried Cassy Cochran, her husband, Jackson Darenbrook, Alexandra Waring and Will Rafferty. The next six limos carried the rest of the production staff and crew for "The Jessica Wright Show."

When Jessica emerged from her limo she felt very shaky. She hadn't known Bea at all well, but she did know that the twenty-three-year-old woman should not be dead, and that she was dead only because Jessica had hired her.

DBS was taking care of everything on behalf of Bea's parents. The Blakelys had divorced several years ago, Bea's mother moving to Florida and her father to Los Angeles, and the funeral was being held here in Huntington because it was where Bea had spent her early childhood—the happy years, as her mother called them—and because the grandmother Bea had been close to was buried in a cemetery here. Bea's mother had been Jewish, but later converted to some sort of New Age discipline, and her father was a lapsed Catholic, and so the parents had compromised and chosen a Congregational church that, Mrs. Blakely said, would take anybody.

Jessica led the way up the stairs into the church. When a reporter shoved forward to ask, "Jessica, do you blame yourself for Bea Blakely's murder?" Jessica only looked at him, tears springing to her eyes. "No," she finally whispered. And she pushed past him into the church.

Back several yards, just outside her limousine, Cassy was saying a forceful, "No," to Alexandra.

"But—" the anchorwoman started.

"*No*," Cassy repeated. "Will cannot take a leave, you cannot—"

"Fine, I'll finance it myself," Alexandra declared.

"Alexandra," Jackson Darenbrook urged, "just let her finish, will you?"

"I've already made a deal with the NYPD and the feds," Cassy said under her breath, looking around to make sure no one could hear. She looked at Alexandra. "The deal is, you work *with* them—and we get the scoop, hands down. They owe me, and they'll do it. All right?"

The church was very nearly empty. The organ was playing softly. The gleaming coffin was on the altar, closed, with a blanket of roses over it. Jessica walked down the aisle and took a seat in a pew on the left, in the fifth row, so she would not be confused with family, but would be close enough to let others know that everyone around her had known Bea. She was joined by Denny, Alicia, Langley and Belinda. Wendy sat directly behind her and Slim stood in the very back of the church. Cassy led the way into the pew directly across the aisle, with Jackson, Alexandra and Will. The rest of the DBS employees scattered behind them on either side.

At noon, a door to the side of the altar opened and a woman was led out, leaning heavily on the arm of a solemn-faced man. The woman was older, in her sixties perhaps, and she appeared slightly unsteady on her feet. She looked at Jessica and nodded slightly, and then was seated in the first row, the man easing down beside her.

Bea's mother.

An older man, in his sixties, too, surely, came striding quickly down the aisle and threw himself down in the front row on the other side. Alone. In contrast to the mother, however, he was deeply tanned and had a scraggly ponytail below the back of his balding head.

Bea's father.

Jessica turned around. Other than the DBS crew, maybe five other people had come. She turned quickly back around and bowed her head, tears squeezing out from under her lids as she prayed and prayed and prayed that God watch over Bea and her parents. *Please, God, take care of her and tell her we'll miss her. We didn't know her very well yet, but she counted and she mattered and that's why we're all here today. Bea, we'll miss you. I'll miss you. I miss you now.* Through her tears, head still bowed, Jessica smiled. *I miss your hair.*

As Jessica wept, she blindly accepted the handkerchief Denny was pressing into her hand and held it against her mouth. It kept crossing her mind that Bea had betrayed her, sold information and pictures to the tabloids, but whatever anger she felt was far outweighed by the fact that Bea had died while working for her, and it had clearly been Jessica's stalker who had killed her. Although death would have been instantaneous, being electrocuted was too horrible (for Alexandra had told her how Bea had died). The sick son of a bitch, Dirk had explained, somehow knew that Bea was selling Jessica out to the tabloids and had executed her at eleven thirty-five on Saturday night. What exactly Bea had been doing at West End was still a mystery. Probably, Dirk said, she had been looking for more stuff to pass along to *The Inquiring Eye. In the property room?* Jessica wondered.

The service was perfectly adequate except the minister kept calling Bea "Beatrice," a slip that only Jessica and

Bea's parents would catch, since they were the only ones who knew her full name was Bea. In the minister's defense, not knowing the deceased or her family, he had simply, Jessica assumed, elongated her name to add more dignity to the proceedings.

At the conclusion of the service Bea's mother was hustled out the front again. Jessica slipped out the far side of the pew and went after her.

"Mrs. Blakely," she called softly, closing the door behind her.

The woman stopped and turned around, and the man with her looked angrily at Jessica. It was only when Jessica had reached Bea's mother and had taken her hand that she realized that Mrs. Blakely was slightly drunk. "I wanted to tell you that your daughter was a very special young woman. And that she did a wonderful job and I was extremely fond of her. There are no words that can express how terrible I feel." Tears sprang into her eyes again. "All I can do is pray for Bea and for you—"

And then Jessica threw her arms around the woman and hugged her, because she had lost her daughter, because she was drunk, Jessica didn't know, but it was all so awful and lonely and terrible and she knew this woman desperately needed love and warmth from somewhere.

Bea's mother remained dry-eyed, though. "Thank you," she said.

Jessica turned around and went back out to the church. It was empty. Everyone was out front, on the steps now, the DBS group milling around, some of the crew chatting to the press standing behind the ropes. Jessica was looking for Bea's father when Cassy and Belinda Darenbrook Peterson approached. "Did you see where the father went?" she asked them.

"Oh," Cassy said, "he's already left."

"Apparently," Belinda said to Jessica in her lilting southern drawl, putting a hand on her shoulder, "Bea had been estranged from her parents for quite some time."

"She's still their daughter," Jessica said. "Aren't they going to the cemetery? Isn't anybody going to be there to bury her?"

"The minister's going over," Belinda said. "Langley and Cassy and Jackson and the rest need to get back to Manhattan. But I'll be happy to go with you, Jessica, if you'd like to go."

"I don't want Bea to be buried all by herself," Jessica said, starting to cry again. "We can't just *leave* her."

"Jess, we'll go to the cemetery," Denny said quickly, moving next to her and putting his arm around her. "You and me and Alicia—"

"We're coming too," Alexandra called, standing nearby with Will.

And so, when the coffin of Bea Blakely, age twenty-three, was lowered into the grave next to her grandmother's, Jessica and Denny and Alicia and Alexandra and Belinda and Will each dropped a rose on her coffin and said a prayer with the minister.

Afterward, Jessica felt a little bit better. "What are you going to do now?" Will asked, walking alongside her back to the limo.

"Oh, I don't know, go to an AA meeting, I guess," she sighed.

"If it's an open meeting, maybe I could go with you."

She took his hand and kept walking, looking at the blue sky, the rolling green hills of the cemetery and thanking God that Bea's spot next to her grandmother was so pretty, and that they were nestled together in the shade of a big old maple.

They reached the limo, but she pulled Will on a little ways so they could talk in private.

"What is it?" Will asked softly.

"I don't know," she said, brushing a piece of hair back off his face. "I guess I'm feeling incredibly grateful. Grateful that you're here, that they're here—" She nodded to the gang. "It's funny, isn't it? How family is what you make of it. I mean," she said, turning back to look into his eyes, "this *is* my family in so many ways. And I am so grateful to feel so loved, so cared for."

He raised her hand to kiss it.

A twitch of a smile. "Would you really like to come with me to a meeting?" She checked her watch. "There's one on the Upper West Side at four-thirty I think we could make."

He held his arm out to her.

The meeting had been canceled for room-renovation reasons, the note on the church door said, which probably was just as well since reporters from the cemetery had followed them there. And so Jessica, Will and Wendy climbed back into the limo and Slim jumped back into the Crown Victoria and they all drove to Central Park West to Alexandra's building, The Roehampton.

"You must be exhausted," Jessica said to Wendy as the woman unlocked the door for her.

"Not yet."

"Well, I am," Jessica said.

"Actually," Wendy said, preceding Jessica into the apartment to turn off the alarm system and look around, "if you're going to stay here a while, I would like to put in an hour on Alexandra's StairMaster."

"Be my guest," Jessica said, poking her head back out the front door. "Come on, Slim, we're going to order in from a great coffee shop I know. I'll buy you a cheese-burger."

While they had been in Long Island, Alexandra's house-keeper, the infamous Mrs. Roberts, had visited, for all the suitcases and clothes that had been strewn all over the guest room and in Alexandra's study had been carefully unpacked and organized.

"I have got to get these shoes off," Jessica said, slipping off the black high heels she had never worn before. She had dressed respectfully for Bea: a simple black dress, a single strand of pearls, pearl earrings, black stockings. No one wore black to funerals anymore, her mother always told her, but Jessica didn't care. To wear this getup was paying the highest compliment she could.

"Okay, who wants what?" she asked, picking up the pad and pen on the telephone table and throwing herself down on the couch. They had all missed lunch in order to get out to Long Island in time for the funeral.

"What are you having?" Slim asked.

"Park Burger, well done—that's got bacon, cheese, let-tuce, tomato, onion, mayo, catsup and mustard, and pick-les, too, I think—and, let's see...onion rings. And a Pepsi." She looked at Wendy. "What about you?"

"Plain hamburger—no bun—with lettuce, tomato and onion, cottage cheese and fruit salad, if they have it."

"What to drink?"

"Water's fine," Wendy said, going into the guest room.

"The woman's sick," Jessica said, looking to Slim. "You like Park Burgers," she reminded him.

"Yeah. That would be good."

"Okay, three Park Burgers for Slim," Jessica said, mark-ing this down, "an order of fries and onion rings, and a manhandler Pepsi." She looked to Will.

"One Park Burger and I'll share your onion rings," he said.

Jessica frowned. "Who said I wanted to share?" She winked. "To drink?"

"I'll have water, too."

Jessica studied the list and then sighed. "Okay, I guess I'll have water, too. Not that grease is water soluble."

The food came and was eaten and soon they were all yawning. Wendy ended up passing on the StairMaster and went into the guest room to take a nap, Slim stretched out on the couch in the living room, and Jessica and Will went into Alexandra's bedroom ostensibly to watch TV.

As soon as she closed the door behind them, however, Jessica knew darn well what she wanted to do. And judging from Will's expression, she knew he did, too.

Without a word they went to each other and started kissing. The kissing gave way to moving onto the bed, lying across it, kissing each other's faces and eyes and ears, necks and throats. In very short time they had taken Jessica's stockings off, and her dress, and Will's shirt and pants—for the first time there was contact of skin that left Jessica breathless.

There was nothing remarkable about Will's body, at least not from Jessica's experience. He was neither particularly muscular nor remarkably endowed. He was simply fit and healthy and desperate in his desire for her. On her part, it was impossible to pretend that her chest was normal—it simply wasn't, but rather, an embarrassment of riches for those so inclined to enjoy. Not everyone was so inclined, Jessica knew.

But Will was. And it did not take long for her brassiere to be off, and then her panties, and then his underpants, though they only continued to roll around, kissing each other, exploring each other with their hands and mouths, prolonging release and reveling in the obvious joy of their bodies. But then it became time critical. His erection was impossible to ignore, the sleek dampness between her legs extreme.

"Do you—I mean—do *we* have any birth control?" he murmured into her ear.

Jessica froze. Of all the times in her life *not* to be on the Pill. Of all the times in her life *not* to have condoms. After all these years she was finally with a man she knew to be a good man, through and through, and instead of running from him, she had embraced him, gotten to know him, let their emotions and attachment develop, and now that she wanted this man inside her more than she had darn near ever wanted anything in her life, she had no birth control on hand. She wanted to feel him inside her so badly she considered lying. But that was not to be the game in this relationship. In fact, there were to be no games at all. No lies. No gambling with pregnancy.

Although she frankly couldn't imagine any child nicer than one fathered by this man.

Jessica loudly sighed. "I don't."

She wondered if she should ask him if he had a condom or two in his wallet. Surely a former playboy would. But if he did and he brought them forth, would he think she'd think less of him? That he carried them around just in case he got lucky and had a chance to sleep with somebody?

"I don't, either," he said through clenched teeth.

Was he thinking now, as she was now, that he should go out and ask Slim if he had anything on him? (Good grief, Jessica thought, Slim's weight was one of the best birth control measures she had ever seen. He'd kill anybody he lay on.)

Alexandra certainly wouldn't have anything around. Although, wait a minute...

"You don't suppose there's anything left around from Gordon, do you?" Will asked, reading Jessica's mind. Gordon had been Alexandra's last fiancé. But in the next moment he said, "They'd be too old, though, wouldn't they?"

"He wasn't the last guy," Jessica blurted out. Nice. Blabbing her friend's secrets—Alexandra's halfhearted sexual attempt with another man before Georgiana had come into her life. "I could look around in the bathroom. Oh, God, no, I couldn't do that. I can't snoop in her private stuff."

He chuckled into the side of her neck and then sighed a big sigh of frustration. "Oh, we're a pair, aren't we?"

"I suppose you could," Jessica began, "well, you know, if you pulled out in time—"

"Sorry, darling, but it's too dangerous," he said. "Not with how worked up you've got me." He raised himself on one elbow to look at her. "But I know what I'd really, really like to do, at least *for* you, to compensate..."

"What's that?" Then she sat up, getting it. He meant oral sex. "But I haven't even showered or anything."

"Well, we could take a shower or something," he said, smiling.

"You are brilliant," she told him, kissing him.

And so they scrambled off the bed and into the bathroom and ran water into the tub, and poured in bubble bath.

The bath was delicious. Jessica sat in front, Will in back, and he bathed her from behind. And then she turned around to face him—the faucet pressing into her spine like a gun—and she bathed him, taking extra care with the soap below. His eyes closed, desire rendering him helpless.

Jessica simply continued, stroking, soaping, gently increasing speed and pressure until Will's eyes flew open and he covered her hand with his own. "Shh, it's okay, close your eyes," she whispered, now on her knees in the tub, leaning forward to kiss him, and then resting the side of her face on his shoulder. It was a very awkward position, but it made him obey and Jessica's excitement grew as she realized he was going to let her do it, let her stroke him, faster and faster in the warm soapy water, until beneath her hand she felt the telltale movement of his gland saying it was coming, he was coming, and...

Indeed, he did, with a quiet moan and sigh.

Now the awkwardness of the situation. Of Jessica's position.

But Will was kissing her face, holding her, and then lifting her to an upright position and then he got up, water streaming from him, and pulled her up to her feet so that he could hold her fully against him and kiss her. Then he stepped out of the tub, led her out, toweled them both off and took her into the bedroom. He helped her onto the bed, onto her back, closed her eyes with his hand, and then she felt him lift her up to slide a pillow beneath her. And moments later, his movements so smooth she hadn't even realized he was down there, had eased her legs apart and—

Jessica took a sharp breath as she felt his mouth on her.

Oh, he was no novice at this. And she let him, as he had let her, and let herself slide away into the sensation, something that had been impossible forever and ever it seemed, since she had stopped drinking. But it was happening, she was letting go, and he was taking her very far, very deep down inside herself, and it took a while, too long, she thought—poor Will—but she didn't care because it was as if she had turned a corner, the sudden plunge down inside herself, the feeling that she couldn't stop it now if she tried, and then she was pulling down hard on the sensation, crying out, feeling her body plunge and then surge against him, helpless, until that rolling energy broke to skitter into nerves, and she grabbed his head to stop him.

"Oh my," she said, relaxing, looking up at the ceiling. And then she laughed. "Oh my." And she reached down for him. "Come up here this minute." And he climbed up to hold her in his arms, and they lay there, kissing. And talking. And kissing. And feeling each other until it was time to help him out again.

And he helped her out again.

And then they fell asleep.

The next thing Jessica knew, Alexandra was standing in the doorway, blinking at the sight of her and Will intertwined in the mess of sheets that had once been her neatly made bed.

"Oh, good," the anchorwoman said. "I was hoping you'd find something that might take your mind off things."

III

The Trap

10

It had been two weeks since the murder of Bea Blakely and things had, as much as possible, returned to normal at the West End Broadcasting Center. Jessica had a new temporary secretary, a man this time—who also happened to double as another bodyguard—and much had been discovered about the double life that Bea Blakely had led.

The NYPD found that in the seven weeks prior to Bea's death, she had made three separate deposits of five thousand dollars into her bank account, and a final one of ten thousand dollars. The first three were payments accounted for by *The Inquiring Eye* tabloid magazine, payments they made to Ms. Blakely for "Information regarding the personal life of the talk-show host Jessica Wright." The information supplied had been copies of letters sent to Jessica by the Doc after she dumped him—which the tabloid had wisely paraphrased so as to avoid prosecution for copyright violation. The letters had described Jessica as "a coldhearted, self-centered bitch" who had no mind of her own and was incapable of any relationship beyond "the cold, calculating standards of a prostitute."

Bea had also supplied the tabloid with a sketch of Jessica's day-to-day life, including work, AA meetings and "hours of crying from loneliness because of her inability to sustain relationships."

Bea had also told them that Jessica was no longer taking birth control pills, that she had seen a psychotherapist for five years and was prone to melancholy blues.

The ten-thousand-dollar deposit, however, had police

baffled. It had come from a cashier's check, made out to Bea Blakely, issued from the First Bank of Las Vegas in Nevada. What this check had been for, or who had issued it was unknown. The only thing the teller could remember about the person purchasing the cashier's check was that it had been a polite man who had paid in cash. "One of those nice nerdy guys," the teller explained. "He said he had won big in the casino the night before."

Trying to find a nice nerdy guy who had won ten thousand dollars or more in a nameless casino somewhere in Las Vegas several months before seemed like an impossible task. The FBI, however, was studiously cross-checking the IRS forms submitted by every casino for the three nights prior to the purchase of the bank check. The problem was, the NYPD or the FBI didn't really know who or what they were looking for. Bea's parents had no idea who might have given their daughter ten thousand dollars. And no, they couldn't remember Bea ever mentioning a boyfriend, or really any kind of a friend for years.

The NYPD was openly working with the FBI to track down Jessica's stalker-turned-murderer. Less openly, Cassy and Dirk and members of DBS News were in full cooperation. The FBI agent in charge, Norman Kunsa, had not only worked with Dirk before, when the security expert had been an active agent, but with Cassy herself, years ago when she had tipped him off to a major inside-trading scam at a Fortune 500 company.

"It was him, I feel sure of it," Dirk was saying to Cassy and Detective Hepplewhite and Agent Kunsa who had gathered in her office. "Leopold, the stalker," Dirk continued. "He paid Bea the ten thousand. For information, or for—" He looked at Agent Kunsa. "Maybe you should explain."

"Stalkers like this Leopold almost always work alone,"

Agent Kunsa said. "Carefully premeditated murders, like the one of Bea Blakely, are most often carried out alone. However, to penetrate West End security, we're convinced Leopold had to have the help of someone on the inside."

"So you believe Bea was helping the stalker," Cassy said.

"Yes."

Cassy stared down at her legal pad for a moment. "It would help explain how he got into West End," she finally said. "And why he hasn't appeared at West End since her murder." She looked up. "But what about Alexandra's farm? How the hell did he get through there?"

"We're working on it," the agent promised.

"Well, where are we now? I mean, what *do* you have?" Cassy wanted to know. "Definitively, what can I pass on to my people?"

Detective Hepplewhite flipped open a notebook. "Bea Blakely was electrocuted at 11:35 p.m. on Saturday night. The method of execution was the diversion of eleven hundred volts from a power cable in the wall into the telephone wire leading to the in-house phone in property room three. We know the perp got access to that wall unit from the ventilation shaft leading from the storage room next door, property room two. We believe he placed a splice that was activated by timer or remote control, but we can't be positive because the resulting fire in the wall melted just about everything."

"So," Cassy interjected, "that means he wasn't necessarily here, physically, at West End, to commit the murder."

"We're not sure," Hepplewhite said. "On one hand, if he had been anywhere near the splice he would have died in the fire—or been electrocuted himself. On the other hand, we believe the victim was expecting his call, or he was actually speaking with her, when the splice relayed the power. It was an in-house phone, but it could receive calls from outside the complex."

"So even if he wasn't here when she died, he did have to be here at some point, in West End, to set up that splice and relay," Cassy said.

"Yes."

Cassy's jaw visibly tensed. "What kind of sick creature could do this?"

"One who thinks this is a game," Kunsa said.

"A *game?*"

Dirk was nodding. "Stalkers, or murderers like this, are always playing a game. It's him against us, and for him, every successful contact is a round won. He wants us to feel like he's been everywhere, like he's a phantom, and he's daring us to catch him."

"And how does he win this game?" Cassy asked impatiently. "Exactly what does he have to do to Jessica?" She held her hand up to block an answer. "Never mind." She paused, thinking, and then looked at Agent Kunsa. "So how do we find him? It sounds like you've got next to nothing to go on."

"That's not true," the agent said. "We've got a general profile on this guy already. Our people say he's probably a white male, in his thirties, a loner who's incapable of sustaining a normal relationship with a woman. He's very bright, socially backward and has extensive training and experience in electricity, electronics and probably computers. He's very insecure, has a tendency toward depression and might live with his mother or another dominating female. And although he's very bright and highly skilled, he probably has a low-level job due to his difficulty relating to people. His job is definitely connected with electricity in some way, probably in construction or with one of the power companies here in the city. The fact he is familiar with West End tells us that he is—or has in the past—probably worked here in some capacity. Maybe in the building of the complex, or in connection with its maintenance, repairs or upgrade of its equipment."

"But the whole *complex* is in the business of electronics!" Cassy said. "The electronic retrieval companies, the research labs, TV broadcasting, our satellite hookup with the affiliates, the Darenbrook printing plants and newspaper-distribution centers—good Lord, that's all that we do here. Maintain, repair and upgrade systems that run on electricity." She turned to Dirk. "Do we know how many outside maintenance and technical people we've had in here the last couple of months?"

"About three hundred."

"About three hundred," Cassy repeated, not looking terribly happy.

"We've got a lot more to work with than you think," Agent Kunsa told her.

"But it's been two weeks!"

"We'll get him," the FBI agent said.

Cassy sat back in her chair, ran her hands over her hair and then dropped her hands on the desk with a thud. "Maybe what I don't understand is what this guy is getting out of this. Why he's stalking Jessica in the first place."

"His need to do it," Kunsa said, "is based on his need to feel alive, and it's the kick he gets from this that makes him feel alive."

"What kind of kick could anyone possibly get from murdering someone in cold blood?" Cassy demanded.

"Sexual." The tone Kunsa used was chilling. "He jerks off over it. I apologize for being so crude, but there it is. When he stalked Jessica through the mail, he jerked off over it. When that wasn't enough, he penetrated West End security and starting jerking off over that. And when that wasn't enough, the stakes of the game rose to something that would really get him sexually excited—murder. And now that the heat's on and he feels he has to cool it, the only way he can masturbate successfully will be to relive the murder somehow, the chase, his obsession with Jessica, the whole game."

Cassy's expression was one of utter revulsion. She looked away, pressing her hand over her eyes for a moment. She lowered her hand. "I think we're insane to even consider holding Jessica's book party."

"But that's how we're going to get him," Kunsa said. "Predators like this will generally do anything to stay near the investigation, to stay near their prey. Often they try to inject themselves into the investigation, trying to be helpful."

"Why?"

"Partly to eliminate themselves from suspicion, but mostly to—"

"Jerk off over it," Cassy finished for him, grimacing. "I understand. But, Agent Kunsa, you also said that about Bea's funeral. You've gone over and over those videotapes of everyone who came near the church or the grave—"

"We're still watching the grave," Kunsa reminded her. "He may come yet."

"Okay, fine, but what's it gotten you?" Cassy asked. "Nothing."

"We'll get him at the party," Kunsa said. "Don't kid yourself, he'll be there. He won't be able to stay away. He has this fantasy of not only being Jessica's soul mate, but her protector. He will have to be there."

"We'll have a very tight net around her," Detective Hepplewhite said. "And around the other guests. Miss Wright's self-defense skills are pretty good and Wendy and Slim are excellent at what they do."

Cassy's eyes moved to Dirk. "What do you think?"

"I think it may be our best chance of catching the guy," he answered. "But I have to admit, I hate the idea of risking it. Not with so many big names there." He turned to Agent Kunsa. "If we do it, I'd want to change the locale at the last minute."

"Of course," Kunsa said.

Dirk turned back to Cassy. "If we get final approval over the security arrangements, it should be okay."

After the meeting broke, Agent Kunsa asked Cassy for a private word, outside the facility; perhaps they could take a stroll in the square. Cassy said sure, told her longtime secretary, Chi Chi, to hold off anybody and everything, and took the elevator down to the ground floor with the agent. As they walked outside, she looked up at the three buildings that surrounded the square, the endless line of office windows facing them.

"Yep," Agent Kunsa confirmed, "he could be up there watching us this second."

Cassy frowned slightly, but walked on. "You seem pretty confident of catching him."

"I am. The trick is to do it without him hurting anyone else before we get to him." They walked a few steps, heading toward the thick line of fir trees that blocked the sight of the West Side Highway, but allowed a view of the Hudson River. They stopped under a shady elm and sat on the bench there.

"I hear Jessica's pretty heavily involved with Will Rafferty," Agent Kunsa said. "Is that right?"

"Yes," Cassy confirmed.

"I don't know how you can manage it," he continued, looking straight out at the water, "but I think it would be a good idea if you see that she's not left alone with him anymore. Not until our investigation is concluded."

For a moment Cassy was confused and then she caught the look in the agent's eyes and recoiled. "No. Oh, no—no way. You're way off base."

"It's only a precaution," he said, "until we finish checking him out." He paused a moment and then looked at her. "It could be coincidental, but the fact remains, Rafferty's either been right at the scene of Leopold's visits, or has been free and able to leave the notes and presents for Jessica."

"That's absolutely ridiculous," Cassy told him. "And may I remind you that he was with Jessica in New Jersey when Bea was killed."

"He was not *with* Jessica at the time of the murder. He was somewhere outside on the farm, and Rafferty's no stranger to electronics, as you know."

"Agent Kunsa!"

"We also know," he continued in a low voice, "that the stalker somehow penetrated security at Bonner Farm to leave the note and hot chocolate for Jessica under her pillow. And the easiest way, obviously, maybe the only way to do that would have been to have had access to the house earlier in the day."

"So what about Jessica's bridge partner, that French guy?"

"We've checked him out and he's not in the running. Rafferty is, that's all I'm telling you. And I'm also telling you that you better keep them apart until we finish checking him out."

From what Cassy had gleaned from Alexandra, Will and Jessica had been seeing a lot of each other since Bea's funeral, and the anchorwoman had intimated there was a sexual relationship going on, too. And Alexandra should know; Jessica was still staying at her apartment.

"Will hardly fits your profile. He's one of the most successful news producers in the world. He's *not* insecure.

And he certainly doesn't live with his mother." The idea
that Will Rafferty... It was ludicrous. She had known him
for years, Alexandra had known him for years. But the FBI
obviously knew Will's background, his engineer's license,
his days in the field, of power packs, splicing power lines
to run cameras, jerry-rigging lines off generators during
power outages, his visits to nonunion affiliates where he
easily pinch-hit as anything from lighting director to engineer.... And electrician.

No, no doubt about it. Will knew a hell of a lot about
electronics and electricity and gadgets and gizmos.

"It's been my experience that stalkers try to engineer a
crisis in hopes the subject will be drawn closer to him,"
Kunsa said. "Send her flying into his arms. And in this
case, it certainly seems to have worked."

Cassy looked past the agent to where the TV offices were
in Darenbrook III, trying to regain her cool. "How many of
our people—Darenbrook employees—are on this list of
yours? Besides Will?"

"At the moment, thirty-four."

"*Thirty-four?* Good grief, I suppose you're investigating
my husband, as well?"

"No, we're not. Because, for a start, your husband's happily married."

"So you've been checking on me, too."

"We're checking on everyone, and I think that's exactly
what you'd want us to do."

He was right.

"So on this list of yours, it's all unmarried men."

"Let me put it this way," Kunsa said. "If a guy has active, healthy relationships and a sex life, they move off the
list very quickly."

"And if Will has an active, healthy relationship and sex
life? That will get him off the list?"

"But that's just the point, Mrs. Cochran. He hasn't had any lasting relationships with women that we can find. And the happy, healthy sex life you speak of seems to have commenced only with the death of Bea Blakely. Which also happens to be the last time that Leopold made contact."

Later in the afternoon the intercom buzzed in Cassy's office.

"Alexandra wants to see you," Chi Chi said.

"I bet she does," Cassy sighed before telling her secretary to send Alexandra in.

At least Alexandra closed the door behind her before she blew up. "What do you mean by sending Will to *Moscow?* Not only do I need him here, but we have a little problem of a murdering stalker running around, and Will is just about the only thing that is taking Jessica's mind off it."

"I'm sorry, but he's got to go," Cassy said calmly. "There's no one else. Langley can't get there, I can't leave, and someone has to finalize the collaboration agreement for the Olympics coverage."

Alexandra's mouth fell open. Then she screwed up her face in disbelief. *"What?"*

"I just told you," Cassy said evenly.

Alexandra stepped forward to lean on Cassy's desk with both hands. Very carefully, very slowly, she said, "What the hell is going on?"

Cassy met her eyes. "I promised Kunsa I would keep Will away from Jessica until Will was completely cleared in the investigation."

Alexandra looked as though she might be sick, and couldn't speak for several moments. When she did, it came out as a whisper. "How could you?"

"I have to," Cassy said. "I have no choice. And I'm asking you to support me in my story and get him on a plane tonight. Besides," she looked away, messing with some papers on her desk, "we need that agreement finalized anyway."

Alexandra slammed the door on her way out.

"You'd better come back in one piece," Jessica said, coming around her desk to be held by Will. "Because I only just found you, you know. And this isn't fair."

"Darling, I'm so sorry, but I can't seem to get out of this. And the sooner I go, the sooner I'll get back. And Cassy swears that somehow she'll get me back here in time for your party."

"I know, I know," Jessica murmured, resting the side of her face on his shoulder.

"Wendy and Slim and Alexandra will take good care of you," he said.

"Hardly the kind of care I want." She sighed, smiling, bringing her head up to look at him. They kissed.

"I love you," he said.

"Yes, I know," she murmured back.

He smiled. "Jess, you're supposed to say, 'I love you, too.'"

"Okay. I love you, too."

He shook his head, still smiling. "You just don't get it, do you? How much you mean to me?"

She kissed him again and said, "I think you'll just have to come home and show me."

11

Jessica frankly didn't know how to feel tonight. Any joy and satisfaction from having written a book—holding it in her hands, seeing her photograph on the jacket, reading the finished book from cover to cover, seeing it in a bookstore window—had been quickly robbed from her. There was something positively ghastly about an autobiography that ended on such a positive note when Jessica, in fact, was being stalked by a psycho who had murdered her secretary. The same secretary, incidentally, who had stolen letters and journals from Jessica's apartment in order to sell morbid tidbits about her boss's personal life to the tabloids. ("Despite what she writes in her book," *The Inquiring Eye* said, "friends say Jessica lies alone in her apartment, sobbing, night after night from loneliness and regret.")

On the other hand, she had written the book and it was being received very well and it looked as if it was going to make a lot of money. And once Jessica had made arrangements to donate all monies earned by the book to various causes in Bea's name, she felt a good deal better about the whole thing.

And then, of course, there was how she felt about Will.

Although she missed him terribly, she thought it had perhaps been a good thing that he had gone away. Had he stayed, they might well have ended up doing something rash, like going down to City Hall and getting married in order to prove to each other and to themselves that this relationship was indeed different from all the rest. And how could anyone know something like that in such a short period of time? She knew better. He knew better. And yet they both felt overwhelmed by finding each other, particularly after knowing each other platonically for so many years.

"You've got that goofy expression on your face again," Alicia said to Jessica. "You're supposed to be memorizing names, not daydreaming about Sir Lancelot."

They were sitting in the back seat of a limousine, on the way to Jessica's publication party. Jessica had made Alicia ride with her, since *The Inquiring Eye* had already linked her romantically to Slim this week in an article entitled "Jessica Succumbing to Bodyguard's Boyish Charm." The last thing she wanted was the press to see her emerging alone with Slim from the back seat of a darkened limo. Wendy had gone ahead to go over the party site before Jessica's arrival.

"So where are we going?" Jessica asked.

"Rockefeller Center," her head writer said.

"And we're sure everyone was notified of the switch?"

"Believe me," Alicia assured her, "your publicist at Bennett, Fitzallen & Coe made sure. The woman is a tyrant."

Jessica burst out laughing. Talk about tyrants! If a guest missed a taping or jerked them around at the show, Alicia was famous for making the responsible party or parties suffer for *years* until they formally apologized and made amends. No one had ever jerked them around—no star, no publicist, politician, *nobody*—and gotten away with it without, sooner or later, having to ask for forgiveness.

At any rate, after the original party date had been postponed, new invitations had been sent out:

Alexandra Waring
Georgiana Hamilton-Ayres
Bennett, Fitzallen & Coe
&
the Darenbrook Broadcasting System
invite you to celebrate the publication of
TALK
by
Jessica Wright
5:30-7:30
The Starlight Room
St. Regis Hotel
2 East 57th Street
all royalties from the publication of TALK will be donated
to the National Task Force To End Violence Against Women,
the Women's Defense Fund, and The Coalition for Safe Families

This morning, however, the very day of the party, as part of the extreme security measures, guests were notified by phone, fax and messenger that they were not to go to the St. Regis Hotel, but to the All Nations Café at Rockefeller Center instead. At four o'clock, customers and tourists had been shooed out of the popular eatery and off its terrace (that, in winter, was the skating rink). Large tents were erected outside so that no one walking around the courtyard could see what was going on below. Jessica had already been told she was not allowed on the terrace at all, but had a fifty-by-fifty-foot designated area inside where she had to stay. Security cameras were mounted everywhere. "Normal" guests were notified to expect security delays as they entered through the elevator bank on Forty-third Street. Celebrity guests were to use the Fifth Avenue entrance and would be led through the underground tunnel to the café.

As for the press, only those personally known by DBS were allowed to photograph guests as they arrived.

Jessica's limo pulled up on the Fifth Avenue side of Rockefeller Center. Rush-hour crowds, walking around the police blockades, spotted her and stopped to wave and cheer. She was wearing a stunning navy silk minidress with rhinestones and matching navy and rhinestone cowgirl boots. She was also wearing Alicia's contribution to the evening, a big rhinestone tiara which, while hilariously funny, was also extremely flattering. She looked like Miss America or something. She smiled and waved to people and the press, and Wendy was suddenly there, too, saying hi, showing Jessica the way in as Slim followed the women.

There was quite a crowd assembled in the café already, mostly the book-publishing and DBS staffs, plus a number of plainclothes security people. The DBS and Bennett, Fitzallen & Coe publicists were standing at the door to the café; Cassy, Langley and Kate Weston came next, followed by Alexandra and Georgiana to round out representation of the party hosts. The café tables were covered in white linen tablecloths with elaborate floral centerpieces. Copies of *Talk* were prominently displayed. A blowup of the book jacket was at one end of the café, a blowup of Jessica at the other. A scaled-back version of Jessica's band from the show was set up by the bar, a foursome playing jazz. Through the plate-glass windows, Jessica could see the lovely table settings outside on the terrace and the livery for the occasion in white jackets and black-tie.

Jessica greeted all she knew and took her designated position in the middle of the café with Cassy's husband, Jackson Darenbrook.

Jessica's literary agent was there, Howard Stewart, and his wife, Amanda Miller. Her AA sponsor and friend, Sam Wyatt, appeared a short time later with his wife, Harriet.

People in the book business had come early so as not to miss the celebrity glitter, and Jessica was introduced to buyers and executives from a number of chains with bookstores in the East: Borders and Waldenbooks, Lauriet's-Encore, B. Dalton, Little Professor and others. They were not to be confused with, she was told, the wholesalers like Baker & Taylor and Ingram's, or distributors like Anderson's or Levy or Kroger, who were certainly not to be confused with people like Arthur Loeb and Perry Haberman of a splendid independent store like Madison Avenue Books.

Everyone invited to this party had been warned of Jessica's current security risk, which, surprisingly, seemed only to inspire greater determination on the part of celebrities to attend. To the TV newspeople, the security risk was nothing, since people like "60 Minutes'" Ed Bradley and "PrimeTime's" Diane Sawyer had regularly risked their lives in dangerous, godforsaken pockets of the world to cover stories, and then there was Barbara Walters, who had journeyed overseas many times to interview people who had entire countries trying to kill them. All three of the aforementioned news giants congratulated Jessica and circulated in the café with the easy grace of guests at a garden party.

Donna Mills and Madonna arrived at almost the same time, meaningful perhaps because of their own stalker problems in the past. (Dave Letterman was taping his show, otherwise he'd have been there, too.)

Linda Ellerbee, Rush Limbaugh and Kathie Lee Gifford were there, congratulating Jessica on the book and receiving hugs of gratitude from her. Rosie O'Donnell swept in, and Mary Higgins Clark arrived full of sparkle and pizzazz. It was the New York crowd for real, with Joan Hamburg, Liz Smith, Dominick Dunne, prosecutor-turned-novelist Linda Fairstein, "Saturday Night Live's" Molly Shannon, and a wisecracking Charles Grodin swirling by. Judy Collins appeared then, and in the next moment Jessica greeted Faye Dunaway. Queen Latifa was suddenly there, and then it seemed as though the theater had taken over as Betty Buckley, Patricia Elliot and Julie Harris arrived within moments of each other.

Jessica's mother and father and her brother and his family were there, too. ("Well," Jessica heard her mother say to Barbara Walters, "she was always a bit of a nut.")

Jessica worked hard hugging, kissing, thanking people for coming—Sam Waterston, Rona Jaffe, Deborah Norville, Joan Rivers—getting her photograph taken, and, most of all, never moving out of her designated box. She was introduced to Michael Anderson of the *New York Times Book Review*, and then to Len Riggio, CEO of Barnes and Noble, who she, in turn, introduced to Otto Penzler, owner of the Mysterious Bookshop in New York (and L.A. and London) where Jessica regularly shopped for mysteries. ("You are a bit of a puzzle," Otto told her. "I suppose we could use that angle to sell your autobiography to our customers.")

Madonna left, but Glen Close arrived, and Jessica kept going. Periodically, Alexandra would come over to shove a glass of Perrier into Jessica's hand and take away the empty.

"The food's pretty good," Alexandra said to Jessica, muscling in through the crowd again. "Have you had any? There's a great dip and some cheese-pastry thing."

"I couldn't possibly eat," Jessica said, handing her empty glass back to Alexandra and extending her arms out to radio talk-show host Montgomery Grant Smith. "Hey, Big Mont, you came!"

"How could I pass up a den of left-wing liberalism like

this," he said. He pulled a woman up next to him. "You remember my wife, Elizabeth Robinson?"

"I was only at your wedding, blockhead," Jessica told him, kissing Elizabeth on the cheek.

"Congratulations on your book," Elizabeth said. "It's very well written. I enjoyed it immensely."

"See that?" Jessica said to no one in particular. "A professor at Columbia University says I'm a literary sensation. By the way, Elizabeth, Ann Douglas is coming."

"She is? Wonderful!" the historian exclaimed. "Then, not only are you a literary sensation, but a major cultural event!"

"Elizabeth, hi," Alexandra said, giving the professor a big hug. "Georgiana's dying to see you."

"Where is she?"

Alexandra pointed. "Take a right at Jane Pauley."

"So, how are you?" Big Mont asked Jessica seriously. "This thing with your assistant has got to have been a nightmare."

"Yes, it has been. Oh, and Monty, thanks for the note you sent over. It's been—well, whatever it's been means nothing, does it, compared to what happened to poor Bea."

"They have any leads on this guy?"

"They're working—" Her heart swelled as she spotted Will across the room. She gave a little shout and waved.

Will was making his way through the crowd, trying to hurry. He was showered and shaved and dressed in a fabulous pale gray Armani suit, but Jessica could tell he was absolutely exhausted, knowing that he had worked practically round the clock these past three days so he could get back in time for her party. He gave her only a brief hug, but Jessica didn't care who saw and pulled Will back to her to kiss him big-time on the mouth and throw her arms around him. He broke down then and hugged her back, lifting her from the floor, then gently lowering her and kissing her again on the mouth.

There were several catcalls and whistles.

"Hi," he said.

"Hi," she said.

Jessica took Will's hand and refused to let go of it. While Denny offered Will a cocktail napkin to get Jessica's lipstick off his face, Jessica began introducing Will all around, starting with Montgomery Grant Smith, who, it turned out, knew Will already.

"Will's been in Russia to form a coverage pool on the Olympics," Jessica explained.

"Good luck," Monty said. "They'll steal your equipment and sell it to feed their families."

"Jessica," her agent, Howard, said, tugging on her arm. "Sorry to interrupt, but I need you to meet your paperback publisher."

"Yeah, yeah, all right." Jessica took Alexandra's hand and placed it firmly on Will's arm. "Don't lose him," she instructed her friend, waving to Robin Quivers who had just come in.

By seven o'clock, mercifully, all the big names had left, leaving a half hour to finish feeding and inebriating the press and the publishing people. Jessica started to unwind and enjoy herself. At seven-forty, the restaurant staff began physically moving tables in hopes of still having time to accommodate a dinner crowd, and the partyers took the hint. Alexandra and Georgiana, true hostesses, stayed on to the bitter end, and Georgiana ended up signing autographs for the entire restaurant staff.

Finally it was time to go. It had been a great party. Now it was time to move on to Cassy and Jackson's apartment on Riverside Drive for dinner. Wendy led the way out of the café, Slim followed up the rear with a building security guard, and Dirk walked alongside Jessica and Will, with Alexandra and Georgiana following. They turned down the passageway that led to the Fifth Avenue exit, where Jessica's and Alexandra's cars were waiting.

Their talk and laughter reverberated over the linoleum floor, and Jessica was just trying to put her tiara on Georgiana's head, naming her Miss Rockefeller Center, when there was a horrible searing sound and then a series of muffled pops and showers of sparks as the overhead lights literally exploded, showering the group with glass and filaments. The emergency light in the corner immediately came on, but the smoke and smell of burning rubber and chemicals was terrible.

Jessica felt two hands pull her abruptly away, into a doorway, and heard a male voice say, "Careful, Jessica, follow me."

In the next minute, Wendy was screaming, "Get this door open! Somebody grabbed Jessica!" She banged and kicked at the steel door and then there was a sudden burst of blue sparks and Wendy fell backward to the ground.

"Jessica!" Will cried, running to the door. But when he touched the door, he too was thrown backward in a blaze of sparks and fell to the ground.

"Christ, it's electrified," Dirk yelled. "Stand back!" He was whipping off his belt.

"Will!" Alexandra was down on her knees. She opened his eye and then grabbed his wrist to take his pulse. "He's alive, but we need an ambulance, call for an ambulance!"

Slim was already on his walkie-talkie; Dirk was trying to short out the door with the metal end of his belt "Where does this lead to?"

"It's a maintenance tunnel," the building guard said.

"I can't short it out," Dirk said, throwing the belt down

and grabbing at his walkie-talkie. "This is Lawson. Close the whole center down—*now!*"

"It was a nice party," Cassy agreed, sitting in the back seat of their limousine, resting her head against her husband's shoulder.

"They had a lot of cameras," Jackson said. "If that guy was there, he'll be on tape."

"Good Lord, I hope so," Cassy sighed.

As the Darenbrooks' limousine approached their building, the telephone rang. Cassy reached forward, beating her husband to it. "Hello?"

"*What?*" she said a moment later. She looked to the driver. "Harry, back to Rockefeller Center immediately— as fast as you can." Then she looked to her husband. "He's got Jessica."

12

At seven o'clock the following morning, Cassy Cochran, showing every minute of her forty-nine years, solemnly turned the corner into the outer area of her office. All the phone lines in Chi Chi's work area were lit.

"Good morning," she said.

"Oh, God, Cassy!" Chi Chi cried, jamming a call on hold and jumping up. Her eyes looked as though they were cried out. A great many people at West End were extremely fond of Jessica and Chi Chi was near the top of the list. Chi Chi had been Cassy's secretary for over twenty years, and Cassy knew firsthand that the woman did not give her loyalty—or her friendship—easily.

On Chi Chi's desk lay the morning's newspapers, on top the *New York Post* headline screamed:

JESSICA
KIDNAPPED!

"Forward the calls and come in, please," Cassy said, going into her office. Inside, she turned around and placed her hand on Chi Chi's arm. "We're going to find her. We will."

Chi Chi nodded, tears threatening.

"We'll find her," Cassy said again. And then she turned back around, threw her briefcase in a chair and circled her desk. "I want you to locate Alexandra, Will, Denny, Alicia and Dirk and get them here in my office by ten o'clock. I don't care what it takes, they have to be here. Tell them

I—" She stopped midsentence as she pulled her chair out from her desk. "Chi Chi," she said quietly, never taking her eyes from the seat of her chair, "do we have any gloves?"

"I've got the disposable gloves I use to refill the printing cartridge on the copying machine," she answered, not bothering to ask if Cassy wanted them, but simply running out to her area to retrieve a pair and bring them back to her boss. Staring down at the seat, Cassy snapped the gloves on like an emergency-room surgeon and leaned over to pick up the envelope that was lying there. **Cassy Cochran** it said in that now horribly familiar typeface.

"Do you know what's going on?" Alicia Washington asked Alexandra as she came into Cassy's office.

"No more than you," the anchorwoman answered. She was sitting on the couch, Will next to her, his face in his hands. Denny arrived, his eyes ringed with red. Dirk was the last to arrive, looking as tired and dreadful as the rest of them. When Will raised his head, however, it was clear who looked the worst. Much of his right eyebrow had been singed off and he had also lost a whole hank of hair in front. The electrical charge on the door at Rockefeller Center had been set to stun, not to kill, otherwise he would have been badly burnt. Nonetheless, the bodyguard, Wendy Mitchell, had to be hospitalized for an irregular heartbeat after the incident.

"Any news, Dirk?" Alexandra asked.

"Hell if I know," he said. "Cassy's cut me out completely." Dirk dropped into a chair, leaning forward, running his hands through his hair and avoiding the others' eyes.

Will was looking at the security expert with cold fury. Alexandra reached over to lightly rub his back and murmur, "We need him."

Cassy came striding in moments later, introducing FBI agents Norman Kunsa and Debbie Cole, and NYPD detectives Jefferson Hepplewhite and Richard O'Neal. Chi Chi arrived a moment later, closed the door behind her and sat down with a notepad. Cassy walked over to stand in front of her desk, and then leaned back against it, crossing her arms over her chest.

"First off, I want to reassure you that we have every reason to believe Jessica's all right, and that she will not be harmed."

The DBS gang looked at each other.

"Secondly, I've called you here to give you our official position on this, and to tell you how things will proceed from this moment on. I'm making Kate Benedict acting executive producer of DBS News, and we are immediately going into anchor rotation. Will and Alexandra, as of now I'm assigning you to a special investigative task force with access to every resource Darenbrook Communications has, or our affiliates have, that can help locate Jessica. This includes all the Darenbrook electronic retrieval systems, and Dr. Kessler will be working with you personally. Detective O'Neal and Agent Cole are to be given complete access to these resources. I've also got Craig Scholer coming up from D.C."

Scholer was a prize-winning crime-beat investigative journalist for the Darenbrook newspaper chain.

"The deal is," Cassy continued, "DBS and the *Sentinel* get the scoop when we bring Jessica home. Until then, no one—*no one*—but myself may convey information concerning our investigation to the DBS News staff or to the *Sentinel*. Is that understood? Alexandra?"

The anchorwoman nodded.

"Denny, Alicia—until Jessica gets back, we'll be running 'best-of' shows, so I want you working with Dirk to amass a database. We need everything you can remember about the guests and studio audiences—and anything and everything, personally and professionally, that you know about Jessica and anyone who has ever been anywhere near her at any time since you began working with her. This includes going through the fan mail." Denny and Alicia were nodding.

"Dirk, you'll be working with Dr. Kessler to determine the best way to process this information. You are not to talk to anyone else about it, or use anybody in the research department unless Dr. Kessler is physically present. Do you understand?"

Dirk, looking as though he wished to say something—but didn't—nodded.

"And now I'll let Jeff—Detective Hepplewhite—explain what we know thus far. We'll be giving out fact sheets at the end, so you don't need to take notes."

Alexandra reached into her blazer pocket to take out a pad and pen anyway.

There was a knock and then the door opened and Wendy Mitchell was standing there, with a scarf tied over her head and salve over dreadful-looking burns on one side of her face. "I'd like to help," she said.

After a moment, Cassy said, "Absolutely. Alexandra, Wendy's going to work with you and Will. You'll fill her in. Wendy, have a seat."

The bodyguard took the seat Alexandra offered her on the couch.

"That reminds me," Cassy said, turning to Dirk. "I'd feel better if we got Slim to work security here too, until we clear this up."

"Fine," Dirk said. "Consider it done."

Cassy turned around. "Okay, go ahead, Jeff."

"This is what we know," Detective Hepplewhite said,

standing up in front of Cassy's desk. "As Jessica Wright was exiting the party, the lights in the corridor leading to Fifth Avenue were blown out by a power surge of two thousand volts, at which time Jessica was pulled through a steel door off the hall—a building-maintenance passageway. Seconds later, the door was not only locked, but electrified with two hundred and forty volts, preventing pursuit.

"The electric current in the door was deactivated at 8:07 and the door was opened at 8:10, and two things were found—a power-pack battery that had electrified the door and a bomb. At 8:12 a security alert was issued and all of Rockefeller Center was evacuated because of the structural damage such a strategically placed bomb could cause. The bomb squad arrived at 8:26 and defused what turned out to be a cleverly constructed fake at 8:59." He paused. "Obviously, by that time, the kidnapper had a lead on us.

"We're assuming," Hepplewhite continued, "the kidnapper used the dummy bomb as a means to threaten Jessica into cooperating. We're assuming Jessica did cooperate, but she also did her best to leave a trail. The kidnapper's escape route ran through several underground maintenance tunnels and passageways that snake through the Rockefeller Center complex and ultimately feed into the central furnace room."

"Are you trying to tell us there is only one furnace room for all of Rockefeller Center?" Alexandra asked.

"Yes," the detective answered.

"One furnace for all those skyscrapers, the restaurants, the rink, all of it?" Will said skeptically.

Detective Hepplewhite nodded. "And the kidnapper not only knew this, but knew the corridors like the back of his hand."

"But we changed the locale of the party at the last minute," Alexandra said. "How did—"

"We'll get to that," Cassy promised. She looked to Hepplewhite to continue.

"We found Jessica's boots in a maintenance passage off the lobby of the NBC building at 30 Rock. Based on what witnesses have told us, we believe Jessica and the kidnapper put on Con Edison hard hats, ponchos and boots and drove off in a Con Ed vehicle that was parked at a work site outside the Avenue of the Americas entrance."

"So the guy must work for Con Edison, now or in the past," Alexandra said. "That's how he would know the layout of Rockefeller Center. Or West End. They'd have the building plans on file, wouldn't they?"

"We'll get to that in a second," the detective promised. "Back to the witnesses—we have several who say two Con Ed workers in hard hats and ponchos climbed into the truck and drove away."

Will dropped his face into his hands again.

"What time was that?" Alexandra asked.

"About 8:09. And at 1:30 a.m. we found the truck in a city maintenance lot down on Twelfth Avenue at Twenty-third Street. We also found several bloodstains at the site—" He quickly held up his hand in anticipation as Will's head snapped up. "Bloodstains that do not, I repeat, do *not* belong to Jessica Wright—we've already run the test. We're trying to figure out now if they were from something else, something unrelated to the kidnapping."

A moment later, Will said, "And?"

"And that's where we are," Hepplewhite told him.

"You mean that's where you've lost the trail," Will said, his voice breaking.

"I mean, that's where we are," Hepplewhite insisted. "More information is coming in every ten minutes."

"This is a summary of the specifics we know right at this moment," Cassy said, passing out sheets to the group. "Description of Jessica, the outfit she was wearing, witness statements, photos of the bomb, of the power pack, Xeroxes of all the notes from the stalker, including one that was found this morning."

"One this morning?" Alexandra said in surprise.

"You received a note?" Will asked, jumping up.

"Yes, I did—"

"You did?" Alexandra said.

"I did," Cassy confirmed. "And I'm personally taking it as a very good sign. And I think you should too. This is it," she added, quickly passing out the photocopy.

Dear Mrs. Cochran,

Do not fear, Jessica will be safe with me. I can and will look after her far better than you can. The danger is there.

Sincerely,
Leopold

"'The danger is there'?" Alexandra quoted. "He means *here?*"

"The guy is a wacko," Dirk reminded the group.

"We believe it's part of the game," Agent Kunsa said, speaking up for the first time, "to make us focus on things close to home while he's spiriting her off."

The room fell silent.

"But it could be someone here, couldn't it?" Alexandra said.

13

For a stalker and a kidnapper, he was very thoughtful.

He never raised his voice, but spoke to her in direct, clear sentences. One minute she had been walking down the hall in Rockefeller Center, the next the lights had exploded and in the next, she had felt two strong hands guiding her while in her ear she had heard, "Careful, Jessica, follow me."

So she had. Idiot. She had thought her kidnapper was one of the security guys.

By the time the steel door had clanged shut behind them and her abductor had turned on a flashlight, it was too late. In fact, if she remembered correctly, she had even said, "Oh, man, am I stupid," when she realized she had just been separated from her protection. The man had quickly moved toward the door to flick a switch attached to a mass that looked something like an electrical octopus. Then he'd stepped back and shone the flashlight beam on something hanging above them—a bomb with eight sticks of dynamite. "I will not hurt your friends if you cooperate, Jessica. But please remember, I can detonate this at any time."

"I'm not going to argue with you," she said. They had warned her that if something like this were ever to happen, she was to go along with it, and essentially do anything he asked, to spare her life. But in this case, it was the life of a lot of other people, too.

"This way, quickly please," he said, guiding her from behind.

Jessica felt she had no choice but to do as he said. They

only had to walk through two more short passageways before they reached a corridor where the lights were still working. At this point he urged her to move faster and faster, dictating "left," "right," "that door," until they were practically jogging through what seemed to be a labyrinth of concrete passageways beneath Rockefeller Center. When they entered an enormous room with the biggest furnace boiler she had ever seen in her life, she purposely dropped her bracelet to leave a trail. Unfortunately the bracelet clanked when it fell and then rolled over the concrete, and her abductor saw it. Urging her on, he said, "I suppose it will make you feel better that you tried."

"Don't make me want to punch you," she told him automatically, thinking in the next moment, *This is not a friend, Jessica! Well, he better be your friend,* she thought in the next instant. *You better make him your friend and keep him as your friend or you'll end up like Bea.*

What amazed her was that her kidnapper was such a pleasant-looking fellow. Dressed in a blue blazer and Dockers and loafers, no less, as though he had just hurried over from his Princeton reunion-committee meeting to kidnap her.

"Please hurry," he said, nodding to the next door.

The next door took them to a long corridor. Then they took a right, another right, and when they reached a dank little room, he stopped and told her to take off her cowboy boots and put on a pair of black rubber boots. They fit. Then she had to put on a big orange slicker, and finally he plopped a white hard hat on her head that was so big it nearly sat on her nose. He put on a Con Edison jacket and hard hat too and then said, "When we go out, you're going to turn right and head straight out to the street where the Con Ed truck is parked. Get directly into the passenger's-side seat." He blinked and extracted a device from his pocket that looked like some sort of electronic remote control. "Remember—"

"You won't have to set that off," Jessica told him. "Really. You've got me—just leave my friends alone."

It was strange how calm she felt, how clear her mind was. She was carefully making mental notes. Her kidnapper was approximately six foot one, about one hundred eighty pounds. Dark brown hair. Brown eyes. Dark mustache. Horn-rimmed glasses. Thin lips. White teeth, a bit crowded on the bottom. A chicken-pock mark or acne scar high on his left cheek. Large hands, thick wrists.

They came out a door to find themselves crossing a marble lobby. But before she could do anything to attract attention, she was guided through a brass revolving door onto what Jessica figured must be Avenue of the Americas. Just as she spotted the Con Edison truck, she managed to drop an earring, then headed straight toward the vehicle and, looking neither right nor left, opened the passenger's-side door and got in.

"You dropped this," her kidnapper said as he got in next to her, placing her diamond earring into her hand.

"Thanks," she said, reaching up to take her hard hat off.

"Leave it on," he told her. "And put on your seat belt."

She complied. Then she looked out her window, hoping to catch the look of a passerby. There were lots of them, only no one seemed terribly interested in peering inside a Con Ed truck. "Look straight ahead, please," he said. She did.

He drove across Forty-ninth Street to the West Side Highway extension and turned south. They went about twenty blocks and he turned into some sort of city parking facility on the Hudson River. No one appeared to be around. "Okay, we get out here," he said. She got out. "Over there." They walked toward a small, square brick utility building. He unlocked the door and held it open for her. It was a shack with a lot of tools and junk in it. He took the hard hat from Jessica, helped her off with the poncho and pointed to a battered wooden door. "You may want to use the bathroom before we make the next leg of our trip."

Wordlessly she went to the door and opened it. It was a bathroom that her kidnapper must have prepared for her, because while the john was clean and there was a roll of toilet paper, a bar of soap and a new roll of paper towels, it was the filthiest rat hole of a bathroom she had ever seen. But she used it. Heaven only knew what was next. But she also stuck the earring he had returned to her inside the toilet-paper roll. Since it was a diamond, she was pretty sure someone would pay attention. Try to pawn it, at least.

And then suddenly panic gripped her. He wasn't going to put her in a storage locker like those people did to that Exxon executive, was he? Or put her in a box like those guys who had buried that man alongside the West Side Highway? Dear God, he wouldn't bury her in something, would he?

As long as his fantasy remains intact, she had been told, *he probably won't hurt you.*

"Please, God," she thought, closing her eyes, "help me to remain calm. Help me to do your will. Please help me, God." And then she opened the door and found her kidnapper standing there, holding a bottle of water and a tissue with three pills on it.

"You need to take these, Jessica," he said quietly. "They will make you sleep. They won't hurt you, they won't threaten your sobriety."

"I'd rather not," she told him.

"It will be easier on you," he told her.

"You're not going to bury me in a box, are you?" she blurted out. "Because if you are, you might as well kill me right here and now because I'm claustrophobic and I will kill myself before getting into a box underground."

He looked pained. And then he smiled, almost tenderly. "I would never do something like that to you. I simply wish for you to rest for the next few hours until we get to where we're going. And you'll be quite comfortable there, where we're going, I promise you." He held out the bottle. "Please, Jessica."

She acquiesced, took the medication and the water from him, and swallowed the pills. Sam would fire her as his sponsee for taking unknown drugs, but surely there were exceptions for kidnappings. She wished she could get over the urge to try to smash this guy in the nose and get away, because she knew if she did try something like that, no doubt he'd blow up Rockefeller Center. Some security measures. She would string that jackass Dirk up herself when she got out of this.

"Thank you," he told her, taking the bottle from her. He led her outside and to the Con Ed truck. He opened the back doors. Inside was a stretcher, lashed to the side, with a pillow and blanket on it. "I think you might want to stretch out there."

It was true, the pills were already starting to take effect. She just felt tired, suddenly, sleepy, and the stretcher looked inviting. So she climbed up into the van and stretched out on it, big black rubber boots and all. "There's a monitor in the cab," he told her. "So if you need anything, just say the word and I'll hear you."

"Okay," she said, yawning. "So you're not going to hurt my friends, are you?"

"No."

"Or hurt anybody else—if I cooperate, I mean."

"I won't hurt anybody," her kidnapper promised. He took the remote-control thing out of his pocket and tossed it with a clatter on the floor of the truck. "That wasn't really a bomb back there. I'm sorry I tricked you, Jessica, but I needed your help."

"Oh," she said. Great, she had cooperated for nothing. Well, maybe for her life.

He closed the truck doors and locked them. There was a night-light so she could see. The engine started up and Jessica vowed to remember the stuff they always did in the movies, like listening for trains and boat whistles and other sounds to figure out where they were going. But all she could hear was the hum of the engine and an occasional squeak of a spring, and feel the gentle rocking of the van as it started to move.

He was trying to wake her and she did come to. Barely. He helped her off the stretcher—she stumbled on something on the floor—and half carried her out of the truck. It was very dark and they were in the country somewhere, on a dirt road. She saw the outline of a darkened house, but he led her away from it, over the grass. Into the woods?

She saw the stars and heard crickets and tried to keep her eyes open. "I'm so tired," she said, but he made her go on. He let her sit down finally and she curled up on her side in the damp grass. She heard him say something and then felt him pull her up to a sitting position. She felt something wet on her forehead.

"You are clean and protected," he whispered.

"Oh," she said, wanting to curl up on the ground again.

He pulled her to her feet and very nearly carried her. She saw stars, the night sky and the silhouette of trees. "It's pretty here," she said, vaguely remembering that she was somewhere strange and with someone she couldn't remember. "I need to take a whiz."

He paused, and then moved her in another direction.

There was the crash of a door and the smell of an outhouse or something. "Can you do it yourself?"

"Sure," she said and went through the routine, her eyes closed. Then he was shaking her and pushing something in her hand. Kleenex? She used it and he helped her up and she pulled up her underclothes. Then she stumbled forward and he kept her from falling. "You are very susceptible to medication, my darling," he said softly, putting her arm around his shoulders and leading her along. "Okay, up." He helped her back into the truck where she tripped on something again and he caught her, gently lowering her to the stretcher.

"Nightie night," she said gratefully, curling up on her side and pulling the blanket over her shoulder.

"Nightie night," he said, closing the truck doors and locking them.

IV

Nightmare

14

Jessica's eyes opened. And then her eyes really flew open and she sat up. *Where the hell was she?*

It was like a scene out of an old Hammer gothic horror movie. She was sitting in a massive mahogany bed with a pink silk canopy and a red velvet bedspread, which smelled vaguely of mothballs. Next to the bed was a round table with red fabric draped over it, and on it was placed an electric hurricane lamp and a glass of water. To the left there was a fireplace with an ornate stone mantel. There was an elaborately carved Victorian sofa across the way, made of mahogany and covered in red velvet. On the floor was a faded Oriental rug. There were three doors—to the left, the right and straight ahead—all made of cypress, stained dark, with large brass plates and door handles. There were carved plaster moldings on the walls, a swirl of carved plaster on the ceiling and a short brass chandelier. The windows on either side of the bed were recessed in brownstone, but Jessica could not look out because behind the red velvet floor-to-ceiling drapes the windows were bricked in.

Bricked in.

She thought of Edgar Allan Poe and tried not to panic. She had been kidnapped by her stalker, a nutcase for sure, and he had brought her to a bedroom with velvet drapes and bricked-in windows. Where was she? Transylvania?

Only then did Jessica realize she was dressed in just her bra and panties.

So he had undressed her.

And she remembered something about this, vaguely, something far away about being undressed, and then she became aware of a pain in her arm. She looked down and saw a bandage taped to the inside of her left arm. She pulled the bandage back. The creep. He had shot her up with medication while she was asleep in the truck. So that's what another vague memory had been about, of an intravenous bag hanging above the stretcher, of being wheeled out somewhere, thinking she was having her wisdom teeth out again. *I had them out when I was fifteen!* she remembered trying to explain. *I better tell them,* she had reasoned, but when she tried to, she had been shushed and she had gone away again, somewhere into the darkness.

The son of a bitch had drugged her on top of the pills. How long had she been out? What day was it? *Was* it day? How the heck was she supposed to know if it was day or night when the windows were bricked in?

Bricked in.

She closed her eyes and did what every good AA member first felt ridiculous doing but always did anyway when in trouble. *God grant me the serenity to accept the things I cannot change, the courage to change the things I can, and the wisdom to know the difference. Help!*

God only knew how far they had traveled. They could have taken a plane, a boat, for all she remembered. Of course, she didn't know how long she had been out, either, so maybe they had not gone far at all. They could still be in New York somewhere.

No. She remembered that outhouse thing, the country darkness, the stars in the sky.

She spotted a letter, folded and taped to the bedpost. *Jessica* it said.

She scooted down to pull it off the bedpost. Then she reached for the glass of water, sniffed it and proceeded to drink it all for she was very thirsty. And then she read the letter.

Dear Jessica,

So what had happened to "Darling Jessica"? Or "Dearest Jessica"? Now that he had her, she was just "Jessica"?

Dear Jessica,
Do not fear. You are safe and nothing will hurt you. I think you will find everything you need for your stay. I cannot say how sorry I am for having had to medicate you, but you will have to trust I have your best interests in mind.
No more medication from now on. I promise. The water is pure and clean and the food in the kitchen is fresh. The microwave is a little temperamental, but if you cook everything on HIGH it should be fine. There are clean clothes in the closet and dresser, clean towels and toiletries in the closet in the bathroom. Everything here is for you to use.
Please, please, PLEASE do not try to leave your apartment, because there are electric fields to keep you safe.
I know you must be wondering what all this is about. All shall be revealed in time. In the meantime, do not fear, for all is well and you are safe.
I love you,
Leopold

"We are doing everything humanly possible to locate her," Alexandra said to Jessica's parents, Dr. and Mrs. Wright. Cassy had asked Alexandra to swing out to Essex Fells to see the Wrights herself, partly out of courtesy but mostly because the police had gotten nowhere with them.

Will had taken one of the DBS cars and driven them out to the New Jersey suburb, and now they were sitting with the Wrights in their living room. The house was one of those lovely 1920s colonials with a big wide porch, Dutch roof, splendid windows and expanses of woodwork and wood shingle. The inside was very nice, too. Dr. Wright had been retired for some time, but had enjoyed an enormous practice. Mrs. Wright's family were distant relatives of the Duponts or somebody, and so she had come to the marriage with money, too.

"I also want to assure you," Alexandra continued, "that the police and FBI are certain the man who kidnapped her will not harm her."

Mrs. Wright looked to her husband and said, "I'm not sure so many people should be so upset over Jessica's disappearance. I'm sure she'll turn up. She always does."

"I'm afraid this is not like the old days, Mrs. Wright," Alexandra said gently. "I'm afraid there's no doubt that Jessica has been taken against her will."

Mrs. Wright's eyebrows arched slightly. "If that's true, then it must be Eric." She turned to her husband. "Don't you think, Mal? That if someone has kidnapped Jessica, it must be Eric." Eric was Jessica's ex-husband of almost nine years.

Dr. Wright made an indecipherable sound deep inside his throat that was apparently an assent of some kind.

"If there's money involved," Mrs. Wright continued, "Eric's involved, you can bet your life on it." Her eyes narrowed slightly. "Received a ransom note, have you?"

"No, no ransom note," Alexandra said. "Not yet. But do you really think Eric's capable of doing something like this?"

"Oh, sure," Mrs. Wright said expansively, just for a split second resembling her daughter. "Those drug people all work together, don't they? He's too unstable to do it by himself. He's too stupid, frankly. And surely he knows you'd pay a lot to get Jessica back, seeing as she is the jewel in the crown of the network."

Alexandra and Will smiled slightly. They couldn't help it. They knew Jessica must have described herself that way to her parents as a joke, paraphrasing the annual report. But clearly Mrs. Wright had absorbed it as a perfectly legitimate illustration of her daughter's position.

Dr. Wright seemed to suddenly wake up, eyes growing large. "Sarah's been kidnapped, you say?"

"Yes," Mrs. Wright said loudly. "Eric's kidnapped her."

Dr. Wright gave an exaggerated shrug, holding his hands out the way a child might. "She's gone back with him before. Don't know why, but she has."

"But that hasn't been for a very long time," Will said.

"Oh, I don't know," Mrs. Wright said vaguely. She touched her cheek with her left hand, showing an older but still elegant hand encrusted with diamonds.

"Not since she stopped drinking," Will added.

"Listen to me, young man, Jessica was into mischief and mayhem long before she ever started drinking. And given the current situation, she's obviously going to remain in trouble for far longer than she ever drank."

Alexandra's mouth parted in astonishment. After a moment, she said, "I'm not sure you understand, Mrs. Wright. Someone has taken your daughter against her will. I was there, I saw it happen. Jessica's in very real trouble and it's not her fault."

Mrs. Wright was silent for several moments. And then she said, "I'd like to think so."

Jessica found slacks and blouses hanging in an orderly fashion in the closet behind the door on the left. On the

floor there was a pair of cowgirl boots from the line she en-
dorsed and also a pair of cross trainers. In the dresser she
found several pairs of underpants and brassieres, and she
stopped herself from wondering how he could know the
right size and brand names to purchase for her.

How could he know this much about her?

The thought made her sick.

Jessica opened one of the other doors and pulled a chain
dangling from the ceiling. An overhead light came on. She
was standing in a dressing-room vestibule that, in turn, led
into a bathroom with a sink, a bathtub, and through another door, a water closet. Literally, a water closet from
some time past. All that was in it was a john, with a long
pipe going up into a big square tank up high, from which a
chain with a wooden handle dangled. Back in the bathroom she surveyed the open shelves and found weeks and
weeks of supplies, everything from mascara to tampons to
deodorant to shampoo and conditioner—

"Hey!" she said out loud. "What's this?" In her hand
was a bottle of conditioner that said it was for color-treated
hair. "Try again, buddy, you haven't stalked me good
enough!" And she threw it into the wastebasket under the
sink.

There were no windows. Anywhere. There was an opening that looked as though it might have been some sort of
ventilation vent, but it had been blocked with a steel plate.

The other door from the bedroom led to a large parlor.
Jessica didn't know what else to call it. The overstuffed
couch and wing-back chairs looked old and smelled
musty. There was an old dining table with two chairs. On
every available seat and seat arm there was a lace doily. On
the walls were several needlepoint pictures in muted col-
ors. Flowers, birds, a hunting scene. Jessica felt as if she had
stumbled into some little old lady's apartment. There was a

small color TV that was not, she discovered, hooked up to anything but a VCR, and she could not bring in any signal at all manually. There was a radio with a built-in tape deck, but like the TV, the radio could not transmit any stations either.

On the bookshelves were about a hundred books, most of them classics, in those inexpensive hardcover editions one usually finds at garage sales. In the cabinets below she found at least thirty videotapes and perhaps twenty cassettes. The movies were old—*Gone With the Wind, Inherit the Wind, Key Largo*—*(Geez, this guy's big on the weather)* and the cassettes ranged from the relatively new to very old: Hootie and the Blowfish to Mozart, LeAnn Rimes to Gregorian chants. There were also some jigsaw puzzles, a deck of cards and a gadget that claimed Jessica could play bridge by herself.

Off the parlor was a little room, an alcove really, which had been made into a makeshift exercise room. The walls were old bare plaster, on the floor was a rubber mat, and there was a mechanically operated Stepper machine, some free weights and a jump rope. There was also something that, on closer inspection, Jessica realized was a freestanding sunlamp. What the heck did she need a sunlamp for?

Unless he was planning to keep her here for a very long time.

God grant me the serenity to accept the things I cannot change, the courage to change the things I can, and the wisdom to know the difference.

Also off the parlor was a little kitchen where she found a sink, microwave, hot plate and refrigerator with freezer. And there was food—an amazingly accurate replica of the food she kept in her own house, everything from Dannon's fat-free vanilla yogurt to Lay's Low-Fat Barbecue Potato Chips to no-fat hazelnut coffee creamer and green olives.

There were several packages of frozen vegetables, pieces of chicken and fish and some kind of red meat wrapped individually in plastic wrap. There were potatoes and garlic and onions. There was a watercooler of Poland Spring water. Lots of pasta, olive oil, tomato paste and sun-dried tomatoes, Pillsbury French bread dough. Vitamins. Canned goods.

And there was a small air vent and fan in the ceiling of the kitchen. She thanked God that, so far, there were no surveillance cameras in this prison.

There was also a clock on the wall that said two-thirty. The only problem was, Jessica didn't know if it was a.m. or p.m. She guessed p.m., making it over eighteen hours since she had eaten anything.

That felt about right because she was starving.

"When was the last time you heard from Eric?" Alexandra asked Mrs. Wright.

"Oh, I don't know. It was around the time our shepherd died, Soupy. I remember because Soupy used to bite Eric when he came here. Dog had a heck of a lot more sense than Jessica ever did."

"And this was around when?" Alexandra asked.

"Oh, eight years, maybe. How old's Poochie Veroogie, Mal?" she asked her husband, referring to the dog that had been locked in the kitchen and hadn't stopped barking since Alexandra and Will arrived.

"Eight. Nine—no seven years." Dr. Wright screwed his face up, trying to think. "I don't know. Six."

"Six years then," Mrs. Wright said. "Because we got Poochie before Soupy died." She watched as Alexandra made a note. "I told Jessica from the very start that Eric was trouble."

"Yes," Alexandra said without looking up.

"Once drugs get a hold of somebody like that, nothing's sacred." She lowered her voice. "He'll probably rape her again."

Will had inhaled sharply. "He's assaulted Jessica in the past?"

"Oh, yes, and it would be just like him to do it again. Get somebody else with brains to kidnap her and get the ransom money, but in the meantime show her he's the big man. He's utter filth, if you ask me."

Will seemed unable to respond to this and so Alexandra picked up the ball. "Mrs. Wright," Alexandra said, "I know you and your husband have no enemies."

"That's right."

"I was wondering about your son."

"Mark is extremely successful and is married and has three children. He lives in Greenwich, Connecticut."

"Yes, I know," Alexandra said. "He's very nice. I've actually met him several times over the years. I saw him last night, as a matter of fact."

Mrs. Wright's expression changed entirely, a light coming into her eyes. "It *was* a lovely party, don't you think? I was so surprised at how many *nice* people were there."

Alexandra cut her off. "Is it possible your son has any business rivals or enemies of any kind?"

"You must be joking," the older woman said.

"What about any strange things happening around here lately?" Alexandra continued. "Can you think of any unusual phone calls? Strangers hanging around? Anything like that?"

"Not that I know of," Mrs. Wright said. "But we've only just gotten home from our place on Sea Island."

"Ah. Yes," Alexandra said. "And when was that? When you came home?"

"Oh, three weeks ago. We came to make sure we'd be

here for Jessica's party." She looked at her husband. "That *was* a good party."

"Does anyone stay here while you're down at Sea Island?" Alexandra persisted. "Do you have a house sitter?"

"Yes, we do. My friend Doris's son, Arno. His name's Arnold but they call him Arno for some ridiculous reason and he seems to like it."

"Do you think I could have Arno's number?" she asked.

"I'll give it to you as you leave," she said, sounding as though this better be momentarily if Alexandra knew what was good for her.

"And what about the family in general, Mrs. Wright?" Will said. "Any bad feelings with anyone, any old family feuds, business misdealings?"

She narrowed her eyes. "Never."

"No jealous rivals? Being so successful—and so attractive—your whole family is very successful and very attractive, Mrs. Wright—perhaps there have been some jealous people?"

"Oh, pooh," she said to Will, rising from her chair to terminate the interview. "I know you have to be going and so we won't detain you any longer."

As Alexandra and Will departed down the front walk, Alexandra glanced back. "Not the most cheerful pair, are they?"

"It's very hard to imagine Jessica being related to them."

"I know." They reached the car and Alexandra went around to the passenger side, saying over the roof of the car, "Jessica always says that whatever her parents did or did not do, they tried their best and now it's her job to make the most of her life."

They got into the car. Will turned the key in the ignition and started the car. He put it in reverse, but then put his foot firmly on the brake and looked at Alexandra. "Is it true what she said? About what Eric did?"

Alexandra nodded. "It happened before she came to New York."

"He raped her."

"He raped her and then he beat her up," Alexandra confirmed.

Jessica thought she heard something. She got up from where she had been sitting on the sofa in the parlor, listened again, and decided it was coming from the bedroom. She walked back in there, standing in the middle of the room, and listened. Nothing.

No, there was something. A scratching?

Oh, God, she wondered, *what if there are rats in here?*

There was definitely some sort of scratching sound. And it was coming from the fireplace. She walked over and knelt down. In the floor of the old fireplace, set on a center hinge, was an ash plate, into which, in the old days, Jessica knew, the fireplace ash would have been swept. There would be a chute down to the cellar of this house where, behind a steel door, the ashes would collect until someone emptied it. Her parents had such an ash plate in their living-room fireplace in Essex Fells.

The scratching sound *was* coming from the ash grate. Ugh. Probably rats. Jessica went into the living room, selected a stack of books and came back to cover over the grate.

15

"What about Will?" Cassy asked Agent Kunsa. "Since he's here and Jessica's kidnapped, I assume you've taken him off your list."

The agent shrugged. "Maybe."

"*Maybe?*"

"You've got to keep an open mind in these investigations."

"Oh, brother," Cassy groaned, walking out of her office.

"You never know," Kunsa murmured to himself.

Jessica resolved to make the best of the situation and ate some yogurt and fruit, showered, washed her hair and dressed in a pair of khakis, a blouse, socks and the cross trainers. She made up the bed, tidied the room and bathroom a bit, went into the kitchen to pour herself a glass of water from the cooler and look at the clock.

The first order of the day was not to freak out. The idea that she could not get out of these rooms could and would give her claustrophobia if she let her mind run wild. And dwelling on the idea that she had no way of knowing if it was day or night outside would only give her the heebie-jeebies. Fire had also crossed her mind, and despite the presence of a fire extinguisher next to the hot plate, the knowledge she would be trapped in the event of one was extremely discomforting. Plain and simple, she would die in here.

She pushed that thought out of her mind.

She had been trying to imagine what kind of dwelling

she was in. One thing was for sure, it was a house, a Victorian house, probably a brownstone—maybe a town house. Since the ceilings were eight feet high (instead of the ten or higher in standard Victorian houses) and the windows were semigabled, Jessica knew she was on the second floor, possibly the third if it was a town house. The strange thing was, she felt no vibration under her feet whatsoever, which led her to believe that not only was she alone in this house, but that it wasn't on a busy street. Which meant, she assumed, that she was not in the city proper. Or any city proper. Or town even.

The walls of the house were very thick, which she could tell from the depth of the windows. She wondered if she might be in one of those abandoned mansions in the Catskills. Leopold had certainly cleaned the place up, but she had still found some ancient cobwebs in the exercise alcove. That seemed to confirm to her that the house was abandoned, or at least had stood empty for quite some time.

On the other hand, there had been lots and lots of hot water in the shower and there had been plenty of power in the spray, which was not likely the case in most abandoned houses. Also, the wiring seemed very good, the current stable.

Except for the scratching in the fireplace grate, she hadn't heard anything. No dog, no Leopold, no telephone or TV or radio. She couldn't hear any birds or cars—she heard nothing but an occasional creak of a floorboard as she walked or the clang of a water pipe in the bathroom after she had used it.

Where the hell was she?

What else did she know? She knew damn well what he wanted from her from his notes.

She banished that thought from her mind as well. He

had shown no sign of that, no sign of wanting to hurt her in any way, either.

She wondered what was happening outside, where they were looking for her, if they might be close by. She knew the gang at DBS had to be frantic. And Will... How could those nights with Will at Alexandra's seem so long ago? How could she *be* in this mess? For once in her life she was in deep trouble that she had not brought onto herself.

She thought about what she could do to send a signal to the outside world. She could somehow blow up the water pipes and cause a flood. (The idea of risking her sanitary comforts while being held captive here, however, made her loathe this idea. And what if the house was in the middle of nowhere?) She could set the place on fire (and burn to death). She could burn something under the exhaust fan in the kitchen and send an SOS, the way Jimmy Olsen and Lois Lane had in an episode of "Superman."

Actually, the latter seemed like the best idea. She could make some good, greasy smoke in the skillet so that if she was caught by her kidnapper, she could claim to have forgotten it on the hot plate.

Or, she could start working on the bricks in one of the bedroom windows. The brickwork that seemed most susceptible to excavation was in the window between the bed and the closet. The trouble was working on it without Leopold seeing what she had done. But who knew when he was coming back? And if she covered the window with the long curtains, he wouldn't even see it. She had two serrated steak knives and some stainless-steel silverware to work with. She could use one of the heavy metal bookends from the parlor as a hammer, and chisel away at the mortar, eventually pushing out the bricks and escaping.

And then there was the locked door in the parlor to consider. Certainly it had to lead somewhere. It didn't rattle, making her wonder if there might not be a sliding bolt on the outside of it. Otherwise the door didn't appear to be anything more challenging than an old cypress door with a brass knob. But then, Leopold's note warned of an electric field.

Decisions to make. How to play this? She had been kidnapped by a man who had murdered Bea. And if he intended on ever letting Jessica go, why had he let her see him? Shouldn't he have worn a mask or a disguise or something? Or maybe he had been wearing a disguise, the glasses and mustache...

On the other hand, if he was going to kill her, he wouldn't have gone to all this trouble to make her comfortable. Would he?

She walked into the parlor. Look at the great lengths he had gone to. The food, the clothes, the bathroom, exercise equipment, books, videos and cassettes. The radio did not work; the TV did not work; there were no magazines or newspapers. So the point was clear, she was to amuse herself without knowing what was going on in the outside world.

But why? What harm could it do?

"Okay, what do we have?" Will said.

"A list of Jessica's old boyfriends," Detective Richard O'Neal of the NYPD offered.

"Table it," Will said. "This guy's someone from the outside. We've got our working profile—it's someone trained in electricity, someone who is or has worked for Con Edison and has access to the layouts of Manhattan buildings. None of Jessica's exes would know anything about that."

"Craig thinks it's someone Jessica knows," Alexandra said, referring to Craig Scholer, the crime-beat reporter who had come up from his paper in Washington, D.C.

"He's tracking that same list, Detective O'Neal, as we speak."

"Rich," said the NYPD detective. "Call me Rich."

"Craig's wrong," Will insisted. "Leopold's someone from the outside. Obsessed with Jessica, yes, but he's not someone at DBS. It's not someone she knows."

"How can you be so sure?" Agent Debbie Cole asked. "Someone she knows may well have hired that stranger to do the actual kidnapping."

Alexandra looked to Wendy, who was sitting quietly in the corner. "I think the possibility that someone involved with the kidnapping knows Jessica is quite high," the private detective said.

Silence.

Will sighed, running his hand through his hair. "Okay, back to the stalker, then, Leopold. Do you agree that he's kidnapped her?"

"Who can say for sure?" Wendy asked, shrugging. "Anybody could have left that note for Cassy."

"Hang on, hang on," Detective O'Neal said. "Let's focus on Leopold for the moment, all right? We've got to start somewhere."

"I think we need to work on the premise that Leopold has kidnapped her," Agent Cole said.

"And I think Leopold is a complete stranger to Jessica," Will said.

"Well, whatever," the detective said, leaning forward over the conference-room table to slide some papers over to Will. "Here's the Con Edison employee lists for the last ten years."

"Good."

"And I've got the list of every outside technical worker who has ever worked at West End," Alexandra said, heaving another pile of paper onto the table.

"Great," Will said. "Dr. Kessler can start cross-checking the lists."

Dr. Irwin Kessler, age seventy-four, was the scientific genius behind the Darenbrook Communications expansion into computer and satellite technology in the early 1980s. He was responsible for the two floors beneath the ground of the West End complex that represented the single largest electronic-information depository in the Northeast. From his organization, the conglomerate orchestrated the printing and distribution of one hundred seventy-six newspapers, twelve magazines, seventeen on-line research companies and united two hundred seven affiliate newsrooms across the U.S. and forty-three in foreign countries to form the DBS News and Information Service.

A refugee from Germany when Hitler took power, Dr. Kessler's most triumphant moment had been returning to East Berlin to cut the ribbon on the DBS News affiliate there after the Wall fell. He was a great man; his health, unfortunately, was not so great. Too much Rhine wine and Wiener schnitzel, Jessica always scolded the roly-poly little man.

"Dr. Kessler's taking a nap," Detective O'Neal said. "Cassy said he's got a heart condition and we're not supposed to wake him up."

"Alexandra?" Will said.

Alexandra, looking at the Con Edison lists, glanced up. "I'll start scanning them in a minute."

"I thought no one else was allowed—" Detective O'Neal began.

"What Cassy doesn't know won't hurt her," Alexandra said, looking up.

"You know how to run that star-wars rig?" Agent Cole said, amazed. The agent had toured West End, including the floors of technical equipment.

"Uh-huh," Alexandra said matter-of-factly, standing up. "Sometimes we need to—well, expedite things." She turned. "By the way, Rich, what was with our mailroom clerk? Cassy said you arrested him, but not for anything connected with this."

"We busted him for dealing dope."

"The guy with the one arm? Stevie?" Will frowned. "He's been here from the beginning."

"Yeah, well, he's made a very nice living on the side here, too," Detective O'Neal said.

"So that's what Jessica meant," Alexandra said to herself.

"Listen," Agent Cole said, "I had another thought about those suspect lists. Someone around here mentioned that Jessica had her apartment renovated not long ago."

"I did," Alexandra said. "It was about a year ago."

"I think we need to check that out," Agent Cole said.

"That's something we can get our guys on," Detective O'Neal offered.

"Alexandra," Will said, looking at his watch, "you better get started on the computers. I'll get started with Detective O'Neal—"

"Rich."

"With Rich on the renovation angle. Wendy, can you help?"

"Sure."

"Okay," Alexandra said, moving to the door. "Let's see, I've got the Con Edison list, the contract workers list—"

"And now you've got the visitors log, too," Agent Cole announced, hefting an enormous stack of computer records and thumping it down on the table.

Jessica set up the old wooden card table she had found in the parlor and opened one of the jigsaw puzzles. She popped in a videocassette—Ginger Rogers and Fred Astaire in *Top Hat*—and sat down at the card table facing the door. About halfway through the movie, she turned it off, went over to the cabinets to get some paper and pen, and sat down on the couch. Using the top of the puzzle as a lap board, she wrote:

Dear Leopold,
    I have a few questions—
    1) Could you tell me which twelve hours are day, and which are night so I can get on some kind of schedule in here?
    2) Are you going to explain why I'm here?
    3) Can you give me some kind of time line for how long I'll be here so I can plan my regimen?
    4) Is there anything I can do to hasten my return home?

                                                    Yours,
                                                    Jessica

She slipped the note under the locked door of the parlor, hoping it would go out to somewhere her captor would find it. Then she went back to her movie and her puzzle, feeling a little bit better.

There would be a regimen in this place, all right. She would eat, sleep, exercise, meditate and pray. And most of all, she'd get ready to do whatever it was going to take to get out of here.

16

Her eyes opened.

Jessica heard something and it was no scratching rat.

It was human. And it was the sound of a human being in terrible pain.

She sat up in bed, pushing the bedclothes to her waist. And listened.

Nothing.

She fumbled to find and turn on the bedside lamp. God. The red velvet and pink canopy and this whole place was like living in a nightmare.

And then that sound. A moan, definitely human, definitely awful. She jumped out of bed and walked over toward the fireplace. It was louder here. She stooped down to move the books and pushed the swivel ash grate.

This time she heard the moan clearly. It was coming through the ash grate. That meant someone was either down in the cellar or in another room that had a fireplace on this same chimney. And that someone sounded like misery itself.

It sounded like a man. It couldn't be Leopold, could it? Sick or hurt?

Now there was a cry and it wrenched at her. Whoever this was, she would have to try to help. Or get Leopold to help. She wished she knew the layout of this house.

Fear started to gnaw at her.

And then there was a strangled cry.

"Pssst, hey!" she whispered loudly into the ash chute. "Hello!"

Silence.

"Are you all right?"

There was a whimper and it made Jessica's flesh crawl. Whoever this was, he was in very bad shape. And then there was a voice, very faint, male. "Help me."

"It's okay, I'm here. I'll find you. I'll help you."

More whimpering.

Could it be a child?

No, it was a man. And he was delirious, and now he was making all kinds of horrible sounds. Jessica stood up and put her ear to the wall. Nothing. She opened the closet, pushed aside the clothes and pressed her ear up against the back wall. She could hear him. She stepped back, trying to look over the wall. She went back out and tried to move the bedside lamp closer so she could see.

The closet wall wasn't plaster like the other walls in the apartment; it was plasterboard. The closet wasn't old, in fact; it had evidently been thrown up in some sort of reorganization of space. Judging by the width of the closet and the plaster molding along the top of the side walls, it appeared as though the closet might have been part of a hallway leading to another room, perhaps a sitting room. And maybe, she figured, whatever room that was had a fireplace backing up to this one.

He cried out.

Oh, this was awful.

Well, she couldn't let the guy die without trying to help.

But maybe it was Leopold. Why shouldn't she let him die?

Because no one knows where you are and you can die in here.

She went back into the bedroom and looked around. Her eyes traveled up to the long velvet drapes over the bricked-in windows. They were hung over a long thin bar of either wrought-iron or black steel (she never knew which was which). She dragged over a chair and climbed up to look. Then she went to the kitchen to get a stainless-steel knife and went on to the parlor for a brass bookend. Back in the bedroom she climbed up on the chair and started working on breaking the seal of who only knew how many coats of black paint on the rod and brackets. She was sweating profusely now; her neighbor's moans had stopped and she didn't know if that was good or bad.

She finally pried the rod out of the brackets, which then came crashing down on her with the enormous drapes. She sat on the floor and slid the curtains off, coughing at the dust. Then she went to the closet, took a running start and javelined the metal rod into the back of the wall.

It broke through.

On Thursday morning, Studio B—Jessica's studio—was packed with the press.

"It hasn't been this bad since O.J.," an ABC camera operator grumbled as a producer from the E Network stepped on his foot.

The group settled down when Cassy, Langley, Jackson, Agent Kunsa and Detective Hepplewhite came out on the hastily constructed dais. There was a dark blue velvet curtain hanging behind them, and a lectern with the DBS logo on the front. To the side of the dais stood an American flag.

"Good morning, good morning," Cassy said into the mass of microphones on the lectern. "Thank you for coming."

The group quickly settled down. There were few in this room who did not know Cassy personally from her years in television and they were perhaps a tad more well behaved than they might have been otherwise. Cassy waited a moment more before speaking. Cleo had done a heroic makeup job to mask the circles under her eyes; Visine had done its best to deal with the red; nobody could do anything about the slight tremor in her hand.

"We asked you to come today not only to tell you what we know about the abduction of our friend and colleague, Jessica Wright, but to implore your audiences for help."

And then Cassy went into a general recap of what had happened, of Jessica's party, of her being abducted through the maintenance tunnel, the Con Edison truck, and the fact there had been no ransom note as yet. At the conclusion of the press conference, she said each member of the press would receive fact sheets on what they knew thus far. Then she introduced Detective Hepplewhite, who gave a brief summary of the manpower on the case. He, in turn, introduced Agent Kunsa, who addressed the cameras and implored the kidnapper to let Jessica go before anything happened.

And then Langley stepped up to announce that DBS was offering a five-million-dollar reward for any information that led to the recovery of Jessica Wright, and he gave out an 800-number.

Then Cassy stepped forward again and asked for questions. She pointed to an unfamiliar face in the second row.

"Mrs. Cochran," the woman said, "there have been reports that Jessica staged this disappearance in order to publicize her new book. How do you respond to that?"

"I respond," Cassy said without hesitation, "that anyone who would believe that must be a stupid idiot and desperate for ratings. Next question."

There were hearty guffaws among the corps and Cassy pointed to another reporter.

The questions were fairly standard, the who-what-when-why-and-where, and Cassy waited for a question that would make a natural lead into the statement Agent

Kunsa said she absolutely had to make at this press conference. Finally, such a question came.

A reporter from ABC was standing. "Cassy, have you
heard from the kidnapper at all?"

"No," she said. "With all the publicity, he—or they—
couldn't possibly contact us without running the risk of
getting caught."

There, she had issued the dare to the kidnapper that
Kunsa said she had to make. Leopold would not be able to
resist it; and they desperately needed to make him contact
them again. The more contact he made, the more they
would know about him, and the greater their chances
would be of finding him.

Jessica knew one thing with certainty—whoever had
constructed the closets between the rooms, it hadn't been
Leopold. Otherwise he would have done something to for-
tify the back wall of the closet. Once she had punched
through the wall a couple times, it was fairly easy to chip
big hunks out of it. All the contractor had done was put up
two two-by-fours, then he'd nailed some drywall up on
one side, stuffed some insulation in there, nailed drywall
up from the other side and slapped on some doors. Voila,
back-to-back closets.

Jessica had donned a pair of rubber dishwashing gloves
from the kitchen and tied a T-shirt around her face as a
mask against the asbestos fibers in the insulation. Over the
course of the morning she set about breaking down the
wall in earnest. The delirium resumed next door and the
sounds were awful. Finally she had a hole big enough to
use. She took the bookend with her as she climbed through
and opened the door of the closet backing up to hers.

If Jessica couldn't see him in the darkness, she could certainly smell where the ill man lay.

*   *   *

"We're down to twenty-three names," Alexandra announced, striding into Cassy's office where the network president was sitting with Agent Kunsa and Detective Hepplewhite at the conference table. "We've got seventeen Con Edison technicians visiting West End in the last three months, five freelance electricians and technicians, and three executives with electrical engineering backgrounds. We've also got four names from the studio audiences that are connected with the power business, but the dates don't jibe at all, so we've put them to the side. These guys, though," Alexandra said, placing a computer printout on the table and pulling out a chair to sit down, "these twenty-three are possible."

"We can check them the fastest," Detective Hepplewhite said.

"It's all yours," Kunsa said, gesturing.

Hepplewhite took the list and dashed out of the office, leaving Alexandra looking quizzically between Cassy and the FBI agent. "What's wrong? Jessica's not—"

"No, no, nothing like that," Cassy said quickly. "No, it's just that we've had some puzzling news." She looked to Agent Kunsa.

The FBI agent sat back in his chair, sliding his thumbs into the waistband of his slacks. "Our lab says Leopold's notes are from two different computer printers. Same typeface, but definitely two different printers. They also say that the paper is the same, but from two different reams. And then the shrink's report says the syntax between the two sets of notes is inconsistent."

"Which means," Alexandra concluded, looking to Cassy, "that Leopold's notes are from two different people." She raised her eyebrows. "So? That would just confirm that more than one person is in on the kidnapping."

"Or," Agent Kunsa said, "it means that the stalker, Leopold, and the kidnapper—who *says* he's Leopold—are two different entities altogether."

Alexandra thought about this.

"Which would mean," Cassy said, "that after the stalker started writing to Jessica, another party started to mimic him."

"But if that's true," Alexandra said, frowning, "who kidnapped Jessica? The stalker or the mimic?"

Jessica moved the bedroom lamp as close to the closet as she could in an effort to throw light into the room next door. She gingerly climbed back through the wall and made her way slowly in the dimness to the body that was curled up on the floor by the fireplace. Her heart skipped and her stomach lurched at what she found; a man whose face had literally been beaten to a pulp, a blood-congealed mess lying on his side by the fireplace, his hands and ankles bound behind him with razor-thin wire.

From the blood-caked Dockers and black rubber boots, Jessica knew that this was the man who had abducted her from Rockefeller Center. *Live by the sword, die by the sword,* she thought. Only she had to push those thoughts aside. No one deserved to die like this, and death, indeed, could have only been the intended outcome.

She needed more light. She couldn't see well enough to undo the wire. And even if she did have enough light to see by, his flesh had swollen over the wire and so the only hope would be to cut the strand that bound his hands back to his ankles.

"What's going on?" Alexandra asked, arriving at her office and finding Wendy slumped over her secretary's desk.

Wearily, the private detective raised her head. "That reporter is the biggest son of a bitch I've ever met in my life."

"Craig Scholer?"

"This guy is not only trouble, but a complete and total jackass. And he's angling to do a major hatchet job on Jessica."

"Leave him to me," Alexandra said, jaw flexing as she looked toward her office. She glanced back. "Could you get Will? And Agent Cole? We might as well all hear what Craig has to say together."

"Sure." Wendy paused. "He's got some pretty tough stuff. I'm not sure Will should hear it."

Alexandra sighed, thinking. Then she said, "Of course he should hear it. He has to hear it." It seemed she was talking more to herself than to Wendy.

The private investigator met her eyes. "You're sure?"

"I'm sure. Go get him." Then Alexandra took a breath and went into her office. "Hello, Craig. What's up?"

Craig Scholer gave a low whistle. "This is some chickee-poo, your Jessica Wright. Jessica *Wrong* is more like it." The fifty-plus investigative reporter sitting on her couch looked like a pile of rumpled laundry. He was smoking a cigarette and using an empty Coke can as an ashtray.

Alexandra took her time sorting papers on her desk before she looked up at him. "Do you have any leads on the kidnapper?"

"Have I got leads," he said.

There was a knock on the door and Will appeared. Behind him was Agent Cole and Wendy. "Come in, you guys, sit down," Alexandra said. "Close the door behind you. Craig was just going to give me his report."

Will pulled a chair over for Agent Cole and then took one for himself. Alexandra came around her desk to sit on the front of it, crossing her legs and leaning forward, resting her hands on the edge.

Craig's eyes traveled the length of Alexandra's legs before he licked his lips and opened his notebook. "Well, I've narrowed it down for you," he announced. He looked up. "How much of that reward money do I get?"

"We'll see, Craig," Alexandra said. "What do you have?"

"What I have is a slew of guys this Jessica's fucked and dumped over the years."

"Watch the mouth," Will said.

Craig looked at him, chuckled to himself, and started again. "Okay, let's put it this way, Jessica has had many, *many* intimate friends and colleagues such as yourself, Will Rafferty."

Will did not blink. "What do you have?"

"I've got a Ronnie Perry," Craig said.

Will glanced down to the clipboard in his lap and started looking though the papers.

"She screwed this guy when she got here," Scholer said, "when she came up from Tucson. He's an electrician and was working on Studio B and she fucked him in the property room. Then she wouldn't have anything to do with him, and friends say he never got over it."

"I don't remember his name on the list of twenty-three," Alexandra said.

"What list of twenty-three?" Craig wanted to know.

"He's on the master list," Will said. "You're right, Craig, he was a master electrician, worked on West End hookups. The only problem is," he said, looking up, "he's dead. Cerebral hemorrhage last year. What kind of friends of his did you talk to that they didn't know he's dead?"

Craig grunted and turned a page in his notebook. "Then there's this black guy," he said. "Sam Wyatt. He's a married guy she'd been seeing on and off for—"

"He's her AA sponsor," Will said. "Next."

Craig looked at him. "Well, she's certainly not going to tell *you* if she's screwing some black guy."

"Craig," Alexandra said sharply. "We all know Sam. Jessica's not involved with him except in the way Will said."

"We checked him out, too," Agent Cole added.

"What else, Craig?" Alexandra said.

"You mean, who else? How about the pill-popping doctor ex-boyfriend? Jessica dumped the guy, he starts hounding her, starts popping pills left and right, has a psychotic episode at his practice, ends up spending three months in a rehab under the threat of losing his license to practice—"

"We know all that," Alexandra said.

"Gets out six months ago to face nearly one million dollars in debts," Craig finished.

"What's that?" Alexandra said.

"The only person to lose his shirt in the biggest bull market in history," Craig continued. "Let me tell ya, this guy's headed for hell in a handbasket. Hasn't paid child support in nine months, lost his apartment, his car, his boat, tried filing for bankruptcy but still has over three hundred thousand dollars in unpaid taxes. He's a mess. On the other hand, he's been to West End many times and the guy did get a degree from Columbia Medical School. Brainy. You know? He could figure out this electricity shit."

Alexandra nodded. "I see your point. I don't think Matt's capable of this, though."

"Would the fact that he seems to have disappeared change your mind?" Craig asked.

"He's in Hazleton rehab in Minnesota," Agent Cole said.

Craig turned to her, looking irritated. "Oh yeah? How do ya know?"

"Insurance claim."

"Aw, that's not even fair. Why didn't you tell me?"

"Because we haven't known where to find you," Alexandra told him. "Okay, so Matt's definitely off the list."

"What about Eric, Jessica's ex-husband?" Wendy asked.

"He's in jail," Agent Cole said.

"That's the guy in L.A. County, right?" Craig asked, making a note.

"Yes," Agent Cole said. She looked up at Alexandra. "Hit-and-run before this started."

"Hit-and-run?"

"Hit an off-duty cop crossing a bar parking lot."

"Oh, brother," Alexandra muttered, making a note. "What about these guys around here? The delivery guy?"

"Clean."

"The maintenance guy?"

"Clean. At least of this."

Alexandra looked at her.

"There was an outstanding warrant for check kiting."

Alexandra raised her eyebrows, looking back at her notes. "Seems our security is a wee bit lacking around here. I'm going to have to talk to Dirk." She looked up. "Okay, Craig, what else do you have?"

Craig was riffling through his pad. "Okay, there's this piece of shit. A charmer they call Keller 'the Snake' Johnson. Jessica was fucking this guy in Mexico some years back—"

"I told you before to clean it up," Will said quietly.

"What's that?"

"I said, clean up your language."

Craig frowned. "Look, boy-toy, I know you've been the one screwing her lately, but what makes you think you're so special?"

"*Craig,*" Alexandra said. "Get on with it." She looked at Will, who only sat there staring at Craig, his face turning red.

"Yeah, yeah, yeah, all right." Craig looked down at his notes. "So anyway, this guy Snake Johnson's workin' for the Dunez cartel now and they're in deep shit with the feds."

Agent Cole's ears had perked up.

"The way I see it," Craig said, "they might have made the snatch to make a trade with the feds for one of their guys."

"Long shot, but I'll check it out," promised Agent Cole. "Give me what you've got." She stood up and held out her hand, which Craig looked at as though it had slime on it.

"No way," he said.

"Give her your notes, Craig," Alexandra said.

"Uh-uh. No fucking way."

"Oh yes you will," Alexandra said, leaning backward over her desk to pick up her phone. "We really appreciate the work you've done, Craig," she continued, punching in some numbers, "and when we get Jessica home we'll give you the story." She put the phone up to her ear. "But for now it's best you get on a plane back to Washington and keep your mouth shut. Oh, hello—it's Alexandra Waring calling. Is this Helen?"

Craig's eyes narrowed.

"Yes, hi, we haven't met. I hope to meet you very soon. Listen, I was wondering if Craig was there... No? Oh, he is? Yes, of course. All right, well, I'll just call his office and leave a message." Pause. Smile. "Thank you, that's very nice of you. Great. Thanks a lot, Helen. Bye-bye." She hung up the phone and looked at Craig. "Nice lady, your wife."

He glared at her. "You bitch."

Alexandra smiled sweetly. "Keep your mouth shut, Craig. Give Debbie your notebook and then get the hell out of here."

"Maybe I don't care," he challenged her.

She shrugged. "I've got nothing to lose by finding out."

"You fucking bitch," he said, struggling to his feet and heaving his notebook across the room. Then he tried to walk out, throwing the door open so hard it bounced off the wall and came back to hit him. He let out a string of oaths and stormed out.

When all was quiet again, Agent Cole looked at Alexandra. "What was that all about?"

"Oh, nothing," Alexandra said lightly, sliding off the desk.

"Well done," Wendy murmured admiringly.

Jessica went into the bathroom with the brass bookend and smashed a safety razor until she could extract the tiny blades. Then she went into the kitchen, searching around for a source of light. Nothing. She searched the parlor. Nothing. Then she had an idea.

She went back into the bedroom and with the stainless-steel knife, unscrewed the hardware holding the mirror in place on the bureau. Once it was removed, she was able to work the mahogany mirror up off the metal rod that held it and carry the mirror into the room next door. She propped it up against the closet door and angled it to reflect the lamplight on the man's body.

She hurried to his side, no longer able to stand the idea of what that wire was doing to him. She worked with one of the tiny blades over and over until, finally, the wire strapping his wrists to his ankles snapped and his whole body straightened out.

Mercifully, he was unconscious. She worked quickly, trying to unwind the wire off one wrist. She got it off, and then started on the other. When that was unwound, she moved down to his ankles and gently pulled that wire out from the folds of his swollen flesh. Then she went back up to gently pat his arms, trying to get the circulation going again.

She couldn't let the horror of what she saw sink in. It would overwhelm her. How anyone could have let someone lie here like this...

She rolled him onto his back, propping his head up on a bundled towel. She went back into her rooms and came back with a bowl of warm water and a clean white sweat sock and gently started dabbing at the clotted blood. Everything on his face was oozing; myriad cuts and slices needed to be stitched. It was hopeless, but she had to try. She brought back a bottle of witch hazel from the bathroom and dabbed it onto his wounds, hoping it would do something toward stopping infection.

She gently patted his lips with warm water. All of his teeth in the front had been broken so that there were just bloody stumps left.

God grant me the serenity to accept the things I cannot change, the courage to change the things I can, and the wisdom to know the difference.

She tried to cut off his shirt, but he regained consciousness and started to cry. She had to get him under proper lighting so she could see what she was doing. She had to get him next door.

She took a deep breath and stood up. She would have to tear out more of the wall so she could get him through.

"Okay, so this is what they have," Alexandra said in the late afternoon, passing the sheets out to Will, Debbie and Rich in her office. "The first sheet are the notes they say are from the original stalker, Leopold. They are numbered in the sequence that the notes were received."

1   Dear Jessica,
        I know how lonely you have been. I have been

lonely too. But now we will have a chance to get to know each other and move on to the kind of intimate relationship I know you long for.

If I may, I wish to suggest you wear less revealing clothing now.

Love,
Leopold

2 Dear Jessica,

You mentioned the other day you needed one of these. I hope you like it. I look forward to seeing you wear it. Perhaps you will tuck it in your bosom. I do not like how much other men can see.

Ever yours,
Leopold

3 Dear Jessica,

I watch your eyes in those unguarded moments and I see the sadness there. You mustn't give up hope. It won't always be this way. We will be together and after that, happy always.

You will be able to wear sexy clothes with me. I do not want you to think I do not find you alluring.

Love,
Leopold

4 Dear Jessica,

It is with great joy I share with you that I am busy working on our future. After so many years of loneliness, the mere thought of you makes everything worthwhile, all pain merely a path to you. I watch you and revel in the love and warmth in my heart. I crave to cover your body with my own. Soon, Jessica, soon.

Love,
Leopold

P.S. Did you like my present? You have not worn it yet.

6 Dear Jessica,

There are people who wish to hurt you. I will do my best to protect you, but you must be careful. Please, please, promise me you will keep a sharp eye out. I'll be there as soon as I can be. Please do not wear revealing clothes. It makes it hard to control myself and yet I must until we are together.

> Love,
> Leopold

#8   I am here, darling Jessica.

> L.

#9   For my precious Jessica,

> With all my love,
> Leopold

#10   Dear Jessica,
Sleep well, my precious. I hold the vision of you in my heart, of your body against mine.

> Love,
> Leopold

#12   Dear Mrs. Cochran,
Do not fear, Jessica will be safe with me. I can and will look after her far better than you can. The danger is there.

> Sincerely,
> Leopold

"And these," Alexandra said, pointing to another sheet of paper, "are the ones the FBI say were composed by someone else."

#5   Darling Jessica,
Beware, for there are enemies around you. But do not fear, love, for no one can keep me away. I will be there soon, love, so close you will feel my protection. I will not let anyone hurt you. I will not let anyone keep us apart.

> Love,
> Leopold

#7   Dearest Jessica,
The time is drawing near for us to be together. I am coming to get you very, very soon. Do not fear, my love, for no one can stop me. I tremble at the

thought of your touch.

> Love,
> Leopold

11   Dearest Jessica,
    She won't hurt you anymore. I'll see that no one else does either.

> All my love,
> Leopold

Will turned to Agent Cole. "Debbie, what do these mean to you?"

"One possibility is someone might have been setting the scene for Jessica to be kidnapped," the agent said, "and setting up Leopold as the fall guy."

"If there is a Leopold," Will said, making everyone look at him. "Look, this Leopold may have been an invention of two or more people setting up Jessica's kidnapping."

"You mean they could be notes written by two different people who are working together," Alexandra said.

"Or more than two people," Wendy offered.

"I tell you," Agent Cole declared, "if we can find out who paid Bea Blakely that ten thousand dollars, we're going to find Jessica's kidnappers."

"And Bea's murderer," Alexandra said.

"On the other hand," Agent Cole said, "it wouldn't be the first time we've had a murderer with multiple personalities."

The room fell silent as they absorbed this possibility.

Jessica held a capful of Mr. Clean with ammonia under the dying man's nose to revive him. His eyes were swollen shut, but he seemed to understand what she was telling him, that he had to help her try to get him up on his feet. He had to get through the hole in the wall to the next room, where there was light, and safety, and where she could bandage his wounds.

It was excruciating trying to move him. She knew she risked killing him—with a beating like this, God only knew what his internal injuries were—but she also knew that leaving him would mean certain death. She ended up taking the bedspread off her bed, laying it out on the floor and then rolling him—who she had come to think of as Hurt Guy—onto it. Then she dragged the bedspread across the floorboards into the closet. Here it became very difficult. She draped one of his arms around her neck—making him cry out—and, half crouching, she tried to drag him through the hole in the wall, but she felt her back starting to give and had to stop.

"You must push with your legs!" she scolded him. "You have to! Now, on the count of three—one, two, *three!*" He tried and she gave it her all, a surge of adrenaline helping her legs, and she pulled him backward, falling down as she did so, but succeeding in getting him through the wall.

He had lost consciousness again. Just as well, she thought.

She took the sheet and blanket off her bed and made a pallet on the floor between the bed and the closet—a view of this side was blocked from the door to the parlor. She elevated Hurt Guy's head on a folded towel, revived him, rinsed his bloody mouth and then gave him some water, which she instructed him to swallow. When he was able to keep that down (for, at first, he could not), she prepared some warm milk, laced with sugar, and spooned that between his swollen lips. After that, she crushed several aspirin, dissolved them in water and gave that to him.

He was burning with fever. Now that they were in the light, as she mopped more blood and dirt off him, she could see purple heel marks all over his rib cage. There was no sign of the mustache or glasses he had been wearing when he'd abducted her. She cut and then peeled off his soiled trousers and underwear, and, trying not to gag, cleaned him. She dabbed more witch hazel on his wounds, wrapped a towel around his middle like a diaper and then covered him with the blanket.

He was asleep and she knew there was nothing more, at the moment, she could do for him. So now to think. First order, she had to clean up, cover her tracks—the most noticeable giveaway was the odor emanating from his soiled clothes.

She did the best she could by cleaning the remains of his clothes in the john, for she had no other place to throw away the excretions. No way to get rid of the smells except with water. And so she turned the hot-water shower on to steam away the smells. Then she stripped and showered herself from head to toe and got dressed again in clean clothes. She hung what remained of Hurt Guy's usable clothing over the curtain rod.

She came back into the bedroom and around the bed to look at Hurt Guy again. Ragged breathing. Out like a light. She knelt to feel his forehead. Fever. She went into the kitchen, wrapped some ice cubes in a dishcloth and came back in to put it on his forehead, praying the aspirin would help.

She had to do something about the plaster and asbestos that was all over the place, and the clothes from the closet that were strewn all over the room. Chances were, whoever had done this to Hurt Guy had left him for dead. If not, and he went in to check on Hurt Guy, he would obviously see that she had pulled him into her room. But, if he had left him for dead, he might not check on Hurt Guy at all. And if that were the case, she might be able to keep the man alive in here until she could get help.

She put the rubber gloves back on and started tossing the debris into the other room. She had gotten the biggest pieces out and was on her knees, moving the dust and dirt and plaster into a pile when she heard a noise. A new one. She tore off the gloves and hurried to the parlor, closing the bedroom door firmly behind her.

The sound she heard was the rattling of the front door.

Someone, evidently, was coming to visit.

Jessica hastily sat down and tried to smooth her hair.

Norm Kunsa knocked on Cassy's door only once before coming in, slamming the door behind him and throwing himself down across her couch. Cassy, who was on the telephone, finished her conversation, hung up and addressed the sprawled body. "Any news?"

"I have personally interviewed every possible suspect working here at West End," he began, looking up at the ceiling. "And you've got the biggest collection of friggin' fruit loops here I've ever seen in my life."

"I'm sure you impressed them, too," she said, coming around her desk to sit in a chair facing him.

He rolled his head to the side to look at her, loosening his tie. "The guys in your research department practically *all* live with their mothers. And the women are more than a little screwy as well."

Cassy frowned. "It's not their fault you don't know what to do now."

"That's where you're wrong," he said, swinging his feet to the floor to sit up. "I know it's time to start praying something comes in over the hot line. I thought for sure Leopold would have contacted us by now."

She was silent for a moment. "We're that much at sea?"

"The trail's getting cold," he said quietly. "Don't get me wrong, we're going to get this guy, and we're going to find Jessica, but unless we get lucky, it's not going to be soon."

Cassy closed her eyes and pressed the bridge of her nose with her hand. "What are Jessica's chances?"

"They're good. Really."

Cassy dropped her hand. "Really?"

"Really." The FBI agent got up. "I'm going to check with the phone banks and see what's come in."

Will was sitting on a bench in Darenbrook Square, staring out at the Hudson. It was like any nice early June evening in New York City; the skies were blue, the trees freshly green, the flowers starting to grow, the air holding a slight chill in the shadows of the sunset. And, behind the wall of firs, cars revved and honked and screeched along in the rush-hour traffic on the West Side Highway below.

"Hi," Alexandra said softly.

"Hi," he said, not bothering to look at her.

"Mind if I join you?"

"No."

She sat down and looked out at the river, too. "You need some sleep."

"You haven't slept either."

Neither looked terribly well; because of his stubble, the absence of an eyebrow and hank of hair, Will definitely looked the worse for wear.

"Wendy's almost talked O'Neal into getting us the hot line call sheets."

"That's good," Will said.

"Denny and Alicia are at the warehouse, sifting through Jessica's fan mail," Alexandra continued. She was referring to the Long Island facility where all fan mail to DBS was taken to be screened and logged. It hadn't been so much a security procedure in the past as one of promotion; the network had accumulated over three million names and addresses of network viewers this way, a database they used to do mailings for special broadcast events. "The thinking is, Leopold may have been writing Jessica for years under his own name."

"It's going to take forever," Will said. "Don't get your hopes up."

Alexandra looked at him. "I have to keep my hopes up. I used to have a field producer who pounded it into my head that I'd never get anywhere on a story unless I combined my brains with a whole lot of hope I was right—and go for it."

Will didn't speak. If anything, he looked even sadder.

After a moment, she said, "It was the meeting with Craig, wasn't it?"

He sighed, eyes still on the Hudson. "It's that I don't know where Jessica is."

"I meant about Jessica's past," Alexandra said. "It was difficult to listen to."

His mouth tightened slightly.

"Do you want to talk about it?"

"I want to find Jessica and bring her back."

"And then what?"

He turned to Alexandra. "Then who the hell cares? What matters is that we find her and bring her home."

"I agree. But I don't think you should try and convict Jessica on other charges when she's not here to defend herself."

He turned away angrily. "You think I believe any of that crap Scholer said?"

"Well, you better," she advised him, "because I'm sure it's not far from the truth."

He glared at her. "How can you say that? I thought Jessica was your friend."

"I'm her *best* friend," Alexandra said, "and she, mine.

But the fact still remains, whenever Jessica drank too much, the first thing she did was debase herself."

Will stood up, jamming his hands into his jeans pockets.

Alexandra looked up at him. "You can't count those years, Will."

He was looking at the water. "Easy for you to say."

"Oh, I see," Alexandra said. "You think I'm just fine with all of Georgiana's ex-lovers. You think it didn't bother me, the fact that she seemed to have something going with every good-looking man or woman who crossed her path? You think it didn't bother me that it seemed like there was a whole fan club out there I had to compete with? But that's the point, Will, there is no competition, there is no real history. What counts is what she's done since then."

"It's not like you and Georgiana."

"No? Well, then, I'm sure when you give Jessica a list of every woman you've had sex with, Will, it's going to make her feel really great too. The problem is, you didn't have a drinking problem when you did it." She stood up. "And how many women might that be, Will? Ten? Twenty? Thirty? Remember Helsinki? Remember L.A.? Remember Mexico City? I was there, my friend, you can't lie to me. You make Jessica's sexual past look like child's play. And just because you've slacked off the last couple of years because you were scared of getting some disease doesn't count. And if it was you being kidnapped, and not Jessica, and she had to sit there and listen to someone go through every woman you've been with, let me tell you something, Will, it would scare her to death because she would think what any healthy person would think that this guy's just about the worst bet for a relationship than anybody in the whole wide world."

When he didn't answer, she moved in front of him so that he had to look at her. "You're scared and exhausted,

Will, but don't be stupid. I've watched you abuse your personal life for over a decade, and I have listened to you bitch and moan that you couldn't find the right woman. Well, guess what? You have. And she is the best God makes." She poked her index finger into his chest. Hard. "So let's find her and bring her home."

He hesitated a moment and then nodded. "Come on," he said, starting back toward the building.

17

Her heart was pounding and she was sweating, and she was sure she must have bits of plaster and insulation in her hair, but what could she do?

Jessica looked up quizzically when the door opened, holding a puzzle piece in her hand.

Her captor slowly peeked around the door. Jessica forced herself to smile. "Hi."

The door opened all the way and he stood in the doorway. Whereas Hurt Guy (in his better days) had been a pleasant-looking fellow, this man was— Well, there was no other way to describe him, *sallow*-looking. It had nothing to do with his clothes; he was wearing a perfectly respectable suit and tie, white starched shirt and shiny black Oxfords. He was not tall, maybe five-nine, with watery blue eyes. His hair was light brown, wispy on the sides and sparse on top. He had thin lips, a recessive chin, not much of a five o'clock shadow and blue-black circles under his eyes. He was somewhere around her age, she guessed. Thirty-five, maybe. He certainly did not look like someone who was capable of nearly beating Hurt Guy to death.

"Hello, Jessica," he said softly.

"I'm glad you've come," she said, friendly enough, lowering her eyes to the jigsaw puzzle. She would play this cool and calm. "I don't suppose you might be Leopold."

"Yes," he said softly.

Her eyes widened in mock delight and she gave him a big smile. "Finally! I'm so glad you've come."

He smiled a little but averted his eyes to someplace behind her. She looked to see what he was looking at—thinking, *Oh, no, the door to the bedroom hadn't swung open, had it?*, but the door was still closed. When she turned back around, she found his eyes breaking away from her face and skittering down to the puzzle.

"I didn't think that guy the other night was you," Jessica said.

His eyes narrowed, hard and cold, and she changed her mind about his ability to beat someone. There was rage simmering behind there all right.

He had clenched his hands. "Was he improper with you in any way?"

"No!" she said quickly. "To the contrary. He was very polite and thoughtful."

"He was evil, Jessica. I saved you."

"Yes, I understand that now. Thank you." She didn't know what else to say. The fact that he had spoken of Hurt Guy in the past tense told her what she needed to know, that he had left him for dead.

Leopold's eyes had darted away again to somewhere behind her. It seemed very difficult for him to look at her. "He won't bother you anymore, Jessica. No one will bother you anymore."

"Well, whatever," she said, reaching for a puzzle piece. "You're here now and that's all that matters." She was beginning to think that maybe she had met this guy before. At least seen him. Maybe in one of her audiences. "So what time is it, anyway?" she asked casually. "Did I guess right by the clock in the kitchen? That it's around six at night?"

He nodded. "Yes."

She felt relieved. She hadn't been sure. Not at all. And it would have been freaky if she had been wrong, having day for night and night for day, completely at odds with, as well as estranged from, the outside world. "And may I ask if it's Thursday?"

"Yes."

"Ah, I guessed right about that, too. Good." She offered him a polite smile. "I, um, I appreciate the quarters. They're very nice. It's very thoughtful of you to make my stay as pleasant as possible."

"You're welcome."

"Did you get my note?"

Uh-oh. She thought she heard a noise coming from the bedroom.

He nodded. "Yes."

"I was just wondering," she began slowly—there it was again. *Oh, God, Hurt Guy must be coming to back there. SHUT UP!*—"If you know how long I will be staying with you?" Making as much noise as possible, Jessica jumped out of her chair and hurried over to the tape player. "You don't mind if I play some music, do you?" she asked, hitting play before he could answer, the sound of Mozart coming out of the speakers. "Great album selection, by the way." She came back to the table. "I really appreciate it. The videos and books and puzzles and the exercise things, too."

"I am glad."

Jessica looked at him, making him avert his eyes again. What was *that* about? She sat back down at the card table, sorely tempted to try to get past him and out the door. He wasn't that big. "So, Leopold, about how long am I staying with you...?"

"I had to bring you here," he said, looking a little upset, eyes down on the puzzle. "They were going to hurt you."

"Who was?"

He dared to look up for a second but suddenly appeared terribly unsure, anxious, as though he was afraid *she* might get angry.

She decided it was best not to upset him one way or the other. What had they told her? As long as his fantasy remained intact, he wouldn't hurt her.

"It doesn't matter," Jessica said. "The point is, you saved me and I'm grateful."

He looked down at her puzzle and his mouth stretched into a wide smile, as a child's might after being praised.

"Would you like to sit down?" she asked him. "And work on the puzzle?" *Because if you don't get out of here soon and Hurt Guy keeps making noises, I'm going to have to hit you over the head with a chair or something.*

He shook his head. "There is a piece or two, though..."

"Please," she urged, gesturing to the puzzle.

Leopold took a step forward, reached across the table to pick up a piece of blue, which he fitted into the framework of the sky. Then he reached to her left to pick up another piece of the sky. And then he picked up yet another piece of sky and fit it in. It was rather startling since the sky was just about the whole puzzle and Jessica had done virtually none of it, having hundreds of blue pieces all over the table. He picked up three more pieces from various parts of the table and fit those in, too, before Jessica laughed and said, "Hey, not the whole puzzle!"

He stepped back, embarrassed. "Sorry."

"Boy, you are a smart guy. I mean, I knew that, but—"

He was modestly shrugging, eyes now darting all over the room in a manner Jessica knew was not normal by any stretch of the imagination. "It's nothing I do consciously," he told her. "It's a gift. Certain things just appear in my mind."

"You have a photographic memory, don't you?"

He nodded, his left hand now starting to flex in some sort of minor spasm.

"I had a whole show on people like that," she said. She smiled. "I should have had you on."

"That's what my mother said." His eyes swung dizzily past her.

"Did you see that show?"

He nodded. "I've seen all your shows. Mother and I watched them every night."

This didn't surprise her in the least; this guy looked like a mama's boy from day one. One benefit—or drawback, depending upon one's point of view—of hosting a talk show was that one came to know a little about a lot of things, and one of the little bits Jessica knew was that strange men always had strange relationships with their mothers. Only, Leopold had said *watched*, past tense, and Jessica nervously wondered what had happened to the mother—or why they had stopped watching her show.

She caught him looking at her—staring at her, actually—with that kind of unnerving beadiness that mentally disturbed people often had. But then he quickly looked away again. He didn't say anything, but his hand continued to flex while he looked somewhere beyond her. That hand was making her nervous. *He* was making her nervous. And knowing that Hurt Guy was in delirium back there was not helping matters.

She thought she might be able to hold her own against him, physically, but then quickly reminded herself that even though only a little bigger, men were almost always miraculously stronger than women. It had something to do with the design of their shoulders—although Leopold, she guessed, had well-padded shoulders in the jacket he wore.

"I didn't know you were coming, Leopold," she said. "If I had, I would have at least put on some makeup."

"I like you this way."

Like me this way? Nervous, sweaty and terrified? Great.

"Thank you," she said. "That's a relief. It's very relaxing not to feel as though I have to be 'on.'"

"I think you are more beautiful without makeup," he continued with a certain note of dreaminess creeping into his voice. And that hand was still doing that thing.

Psycho or not, Jessica knew men and she knew she better get this man off this line of thought. "Leopold," she began, "I am very grateful to you for protecting me from the people who want to hurt me."

He was nodding, evidently pleased that she understood the situation.

"And I was wondering if there's anything I can do to help expedite matters so I can go home."

"I'm taking care of it," he told her. "Two of them are dead." Suddenly he jammed the flinching hand into his suit pocket. "I told Mrs. Cochran the danger is there, not here."

"You've talked to Cassy?" she asked incredulously.

"I sent her a message."

"I see." She bit her lower lip, thinking as she watched his hand continue to jerk in his pocket.

"Where's Alexandra?" Detective O'Neal wanted to know. Will was sitting in the anchorwoman's office, using the computer terminal behind her desk.

"She's taking a nap downstairs in her dressing room. What's up?"

"I've got the first call sheets from the 800-number."

Will was out of his seat like a shot and coming around the desk, hand outstretched. "How do they look?"

"Like thousands of dead ends," O'Neal sighed, handing him the stack of papers.

"But that's always the way they are," Will said, scanning pages. "But it only takes one to break things open."

O'Neal yawned. "Maybe I should take these to Alexandra."

"No, I'll do it," Will said. "I'll scan them into the computer. She really needs a couple hours of sleep."

"Looks like you could do with some too," the detective observed.

"When she comes back up, I'll stretch out," Will promised. "This is great," he added, turning another page. "We've got state and city calls. This is good." He glanced up. "We're working on a particular angle, and this is exactly what we need. Will we continue to get the rest of the call sheets as they come in?"

"Now you are," the detective told him. "Because our manpower on this case has just been cut in half. There's a terrorist bomb threat going on downtown and they're pulling a lot of our guys."

Will wasn't listening; he was reading, walking for the door.

"Did you hear what I said?" O'Neal asked him.

"Yeah, I'll see you later," Will said over his shoulder.

Jessica feigned a yawn. "Oh, excuse me. I'm sorry. I guess I'm just more tired than I knew."

His eyes were focused now over on the bookcase. "Is there anything you need?"

"Well, actually, there is," she said. "But if you can't get any, I'll understand. It's just that I get this recurring sinus infection when I'm indoors a lot, and so I was wondering if you had any antibiotics at home. I'm not even sure what it is the doctor gives me, but I'm pretty sure anything like penicillin or e-miacin might help."

"I'll see what I can do," he promised. "Anything else?"

"Nothing, thank you," she said. "Unless you run across some Alcoholics Anonymous tapes. Of someone speaking, or maybe a collection of Grapevine Articles or something. It would sort of be like a meeting."

He frowned, his eyebrows knitting together. "Of course you would want to hear voices. I was stupid to forget. It would be comforting. It doesn't matter that there is no alcohol here, you have an ongoing spiritual condition that needs daily attention. After all, it's called alcoho*lism*, not *wasm*."

He was paraphrasing a passage from her autobiography.

"You've read *Talk*."

"It is very good," he said, his eyes shooting over to the other side of the room to fix on something in the exercise alcove. He paused, shifting his weight from one foot to the other. "I don't know if I should tell you this, it might make you feel sad because you're here—"

"Oh, tell me. I'm sure you wouldn't think of it unless it was right for me to know."

"Your book is going to be the number-one bestseller next week."

"You're kidding!" And for one split second Jessica forgot everything and flushed with pride and happiness. Number one! But then she remembered the reality of her situation, deflated, and said, "I guess I should thank you for that, too. It's because of the publicity surrounding my disappearance, isn't it?"

His eyes came back to her, and he appeared to be heartbroken. "Oh, no, Jessica. No. It's because your book is very good. I'm your number-one fan. I know these things." And then he turned all the way around to face the door. "I have to go," he said, his back to her. "I will come back tomorrow night."

"Great," she said. "Will you be eating with me? Do you want me to cook something? Or shall we order in?"

He slowly looked over his shoulder to fix his eyes on the ceiling above her.

"I'm serious," she said. "I'd like the company and you must know how much I order in."

"Chinese, Indian, Thai, Mexican, yes, I know."

"So if you know, why don't you surprise me? Bring dinner tomorrow? Say around seven? And bring a candle, will you? For the table?"

He smiled a little and then turned to open the door.

"And," Jessica continued, "maybe we could get a little fresh air. You could blindfold me or something, or just take me to a window."

"I'll have to think about that," he said, moving out the door. "Good night, Jessica."

"Good night, Leopold. See you tomorrow."

He closed the door and she heard a bolt slide across. And then...

Nothing.

She sat at the puzzle for another fifteen minutes, waiting for a cry or a bang or some noise indicating that he had gone into the room next door and found Hurt Guy gone. But the sounds never came.

She turned off the music and sat for five minutes more and heard not a sound.

Then she hurried back into the bedroom.

Egad, it was like a cyclone had hit in here. She really had to clean up.

She knelt down next to Hurt Guy. He seemed to be dozing, and he did not feel quite as hot. She checked inside the towel around his waist. Nothing. Leave him be.

Suddenly she felt very dizzy. She hadn't eaten anything in she didn't know how long. She went into the kitchen and ate some cereal and milk and drank a big glass of water. Then she warmed some applesauce and put it in a sau-

cer, crushed some aspirin in water and went back into the
bedroom. He was still out, so she put the food on the stand
and continued pushing all the debris through the hall to
the other room. Then she swept. Then she hung the clothes
back up in the closet which, to a large extent, hid the hole,
and moved the lamp back to the bedside table. She was
straightening the bedspread on her own bed when she
heard a cough.

One eye was open just a slit in the swollen purple mess
that was Hurt Guy's face. "Uhhh," he said.

She knelt down and looked into the eye. She put a finger
over her lips. "We have to be very quiet," she whispered,
kneeling next to him. "I'm going to take care of you. You're
going to be all right, okay? You just need rest and nourishment, that's all. And then you'll be fine and I'll get you out
of here."

She tried to give him a little water. He gagged a little, but
was able to swallow a little, too.

"I don't know who you are," she whispered, "but someone has beaten you up very badly. And he has me prisoner
here. I'm hiding you in my room. He doesn't know you're
alive. So we must be quiet in case he comes back."

She got a little applesauce in his mouth and he swallowed it. And then a little more. Some water.

God help her, she was going to be as crazy as Leopold
was if she stayed here much longer.

Alexandra came into her office and found Will flat on his
back on the couch, snoring. She looked at the clock on the
windowsill, its brightness contrasting against the night sky
outside: nine. She opened the small refrigerator in her cabinet to take out a bottle of Perrier and a carton of yogurt,
and sat down at the desk, swinging her chair to face the

computer terminal. Taped on the screen was a note from Will.

A—

Check "calls" file. Rich is updating us on the hot line. Dr. K.'s working on-screen for buzzwords. Stuff pops up occasionally, so keep an eye out.

When you love someone, you want to kill anyone who has ever hurt that person. I am not upset for the reason you think. I love Jessica. I love *Jessica*. Her past comes with the package, as does mine.

I love you too, oh bitchy (and wise) friend
W

Smiling, Alexandra picked up the phone and dialed Dr. Kessler.

Hurt Guy slept again for about two hours and Jessica told herself to relax, there was nothing more she could do but pray—which she had, about every fifteen minutes—and try to think about what she was going to do. She thought about stabbing Leopold in the head with the sharp end of the steel curtain rod when he arrived the next night, but then she also thought about getting electrocuted while trying to get out of this house. And what might happen to her if she didn't kill Leopold or disable him.

He'd said, "Two of them are dead."

He must have meant Hurt Guy and Bea. But what had Bea done? Surely he wouldn't have killed her for selling a couple of stories to the tabloids about her. Or would he? Would he perceive that as hurting her?

She better play it safe and try to get this bedroom looking as normal as possible, which meant trying to rehang those red velvet curtains. The second time she fell off the chair with them, she gave up in disgust and went around the bed to check on Hurt Guy. She found that his one good eye was cracked open again. "I'm trying to pick up this room so that nutcase doesn't know anything's happened," she explained. "He's coming tomorrow night and I'm trying to figure out a plan. Until I do, I'll keep you hidden. So don't you worry about anything. I used to be a nurse, you know," she lied, "and I know you're going to come out of this just fine."

"I don't think you should move yet," she cheerfully continued. "I have you wrapped in a towel and I'll change you and clean you up. Don't worry about it, it's okay, seeing that I was a nurse and all." She checked his towel. Her instincts had been right. He needed changing. She had recently signed a new ten-million-dollar contract and here she was changing diapers. Ah, well, poetic justice, she imagined. You do what you gotta do.

She came back with a washcloth, bowl of water, toilet paper and fresh towel.

God grant me the serenity to accept the things I cannot change, the courage to change the things I can, and the wisdom to know the difference.

18

Hurt Guy started moaning about three o'clock in the morning. Jessica turned on the light. Anthony Trollope's *Small House at Allington* was facedown on the bed; earlier she had been reading it aloud. She crawled to the edge of the bed and looked down. Hurt Guy moaned again and Jessica saw that his one good eye had tears in it.

The shock must have worn off and feeling must be coming back to him. His wrists and ankles still had black-purple slashes on them from the wire that had bound them; she was certain he had several cracked, if not broken, ribs; his nose was mush and his mouth was but a swollen gash. His jaw might be broken. His arms and legs did not appear to be broken, but heaven only knew what internal injuries he had.

All she could think to do was keep feeding him aspirin and some kind of nourishment and keep him clean.

She felt his forehead. He was not quite as hot as before. That was good. She smiled. "You're doing much better. I know you're in pain, but that's because your body has started the healing process. Your body is mending itself. What we need to do is try and help your body as much as we can." He whimpered a little, but stopped when she stroked the one square inch of unmarked flesh on the side of his face. "I'm going to get you something to eat," she whispered.

She heated a can of chicken soup and strained out the noodles and meat. It took nearly a half hour, but she got a cup's worth of broth into him. Then she fed him warm milk with sugar. Then applesauce with aspirin. He didn't need changing yet. Jessica picked up the novel and read to him about the perils of Lucy's love life for a while. The lid on his good eye wavered and then closed and he drifted off. Jessica turned off the light and went back to sleep.

Alexandra walked into Cassy's office and found FBI Agent Kunsa sitting behind her desk and Dirk Lawson in the corner at the conference table.

"She crashed next door on Langley's couch to catch a few zzz's," Kunsa explained.

"Good. Will and I got some rest too." She looked at him expectantly. "So, anything new?"

He glanced at his watch and scowled. "What time is it? Damn knockoffs never work."

"Two after six," Dirk called.

"Another night gone," he mumbled, resetting his watch.

There was a brief knock on the door and then Detectives Hepplewhite and O'Neal entered the room. Hepplewhite looked particularly tired and rumpled in the same clothes he had been wearing the day before. "Any word?"

"Fresh coffee's over there," Kunsa said, pointing to the coffeemaker in the corner. The detectives made a beeline for it. "I was just about to tell Alexandra that we've logged more than three thousand calls over the hot line already."

"She knows," O'Neal said. "We've been routing the call lists to her and Rafferty."

"They're not yours to route," Kunsa said irritably.

"Oh, yeah, they are," Detective Hepplewhite countered, turning around. "That's NYPD manning those phones."

"And *she's* NYPD?" the agent asked.

"Might as well be for all the help we're getting from you," O'Neal muttered.

"I heard that," Kunsa said.

"Good," O'Neal said, pouring himself a cup of coffee.

"We're working together, guys," Dirk reminded them.

"So what exactly are you guys up to over there?" Hepplewhite asked, bringing his cup of coffee over to sit with Alexandra. "I hear you're only looking at the hot-line calls from or about New York State."

Kunsa's head jerked in Alexandra's direction.

"No magic," she said, shrugging. "We know that you guys are working every angle, so for the sake of expediency we decided to listen to what our instincts are telling us. We might get lucky—sooner—that way."

"But why just New York?" Agent Kunsa asked. "Why not the tristate?"

"We know that whoever kidnapped Jessica had to have access to the plans of West End, and to Rockefeller Center, the latter of which—Rockefeller Center—had to have been obtained on a moment's notice, since we changed the venue of the party at the last minute. So we're going on the assumption that the person or persons had to be working with Con Edison, or the city, or the state, to have that kind of access at their fingertips. And if he or they are with Con Edison, or the city, or the state, they'd *have* to live in New York State in order to hold that job. And past that point, we're just going on the assumption that he or they are keeping Jessica somewhere close to where they live, somewhere they know well and can easily get to." She shrugged again. "In New York State."

"That's good," Dirk said, nodding.

"Lucky you to have the luxury of working with so many *ifs*," Agent Kunsa said. "If my people worked like that, all of our kidnapping victims would be dead."

"That's what they're on board for, Norm," Hepplewhite said. "To do it differently. And all the power to them since I don't know where the hell we're getting at the moment."

Detective O'Neal sat in another chair and addressed Alexandra, "If your theory's right, and this guy works for one of the outfits here in New York, how do you explain how he bypassed the system at the farm?"

"If he knows the system we use here at West End," Alexandra said, "he'd know what to expect at my house."

"But to get into your house in broad daylight?" O'Neal persisted. "With four of you there?"

"We think he got up there that night, while they were downstairs playing bridge," Kunsa offered. "One bodyguard was with Jessica, the outside guard was watching the house from the front. Whenever Leopold was there, we know he bypassed the alarm system in the circuit box in the barn. A place where he also could have tapped the phone line—the phone line devoted to the alarm system—to place the call to West End that killed Bea Blakely."

Jessica stretched, luxuriating in the size and warmth of the bed, half dreaming she was home. And then she jerked herself awake and sat up. There was no sound from Hurt Guy.

Her heart sank. He must have died. She climbed out of bed and walked around the bed.

Hurt Guy's one eye was open a little wider and he said, "Ahh."

"Good morning!" she cried, relieved, kneeling to touch that one good area on the side of his face. "You look much, much better this morning!"

He groaned and she laughed, because he knew she could understand him. He was telling her that he didn't *feel* any better. And given that some of his wounds this morning were oozing yellow-green pus, she didn't wonder.

"You really can hear me now, can't you? Just say ah."

"Ah," he said.

"Great! Now listen, since I don't know your name, I'm afraid I've been calling you Hurt Guy. I know you're getting better and everything, but I've got to call you something. Is that okay, Hurt Guy?"

"Ah."

"All right then," she said, "close your eye and let me check to see what's going on down here, okay?" He did and she did and found that he needed changing. She went into the bathroom and used the john herself and then headed back to him with the towel that had dried overnight, a washcloth, toilet paper and basin of water, and proceeded to clean him up and change him.

She gave him an ambitious breakfast: half a cup of instant oatmeal with tons of sugar and butter, and aspirin in applesauce. She herself had yogurt and coffee. When he dozed off, she put on her exercise gear and skipped rope for a good fifteen minutes, lifted a few weights and then went to take a shower and get dressed.

He was still asleep. She made her bed and cleaned up the kitchen. When she came back into the bedroom she found him awake, and so she went through the whole routine with him all over again.

"'Morning," Cassy said, coming back into her office at nine o'clock. She had showered and changed into fresh clothes.

As she poured herself coffee, Kunsa filled her in on the track Alexandra and Will were taking, about focusing on calls into the hot line either placed from or regarding sites in New York State. "Huh," she said thoughtfully when he had finished. "They could be right, but I don't know. Has there been anything more on that boat that was seen in the vicinity of the lot where the Con Ed truck was found?"

"Not yet. We're still working with the partial registration number."

"What about the helipad?"

"No, that's a definite no. He didn't take her by helicopter."

Cassy sipped her coffee. "So what do you think? How did he get her out of the city?"

Agent Kunsa looked miserable. "I don't know that he did take her out of the city."

"But if he did, how do you think he did it?"

"By water or by road."

Cassy sighed, walking over to her desk and sitting down. "I can't believe we're just sitting here."

"This is what we do," he said. "Wait until more information comes in from the field."

"I just can't sit here and do nothing," Cassy told him. "For God's sake, Norm, she's been gone for over sixty hours. And you said if I held that press conference, if I dared him to contact us, he would. Well, I held that damn conference, I dared him to contact us and what do we get? Nothing. And we're nowhere. And now you expect me to just sit around here with you and wait."

When he didn't argue with her, Cassy cinched up the side of her mouth in disgust, turned to her computer and punched a button to boot it up.

"Norm," she said a moment later, sounding alarmed. "Norm!"

He jumped up from his seat.

"Get over here," she directed. "Look at this."

He ran around the desk and looked over her shoulder at the screen. "What *is* that?"

Plastered across her computer screen was a head shot of Jessica, looking back at them.

"I don't know what this is," Cassy said. "I don't know where it came from. I just booted up the computer and—"

They froze as the sound of Jessica's voice came out over the computer speakers.

Jessica: And may I ask if it's Thursday? (pause) Ah, I guessed right about that, too. Good.

There was a long pause; Cassy and Kunsa looked at each other. "It's a tape," he whispered.

Jessica: I, um, appreciate the quarters. They're very nice. It's very thoughtful of you to make my stay as pleasant as possible. (pause) Would you like to sit down?

Cassy lunged for a pen and paper and frantically started writing in shorthand.

Jessica: Will you be eating with me? Do you want me to cook something? Or shall we order in? (pause) I'd like the company and you must know how much I order in. (pause) Why don't you surprise me? Bring dinner tomorrow? Say around seven?

When the audio stopped and Cassy had finished writing, she looked back up at Norm in amazement.

"Thursday," he said. "This tape is from last night. She's still alive."

Tears sprung into Cassy's eyes as she reached to her intercom. "Chi Chi, get Dr. Kessler in here immediately, please. Tell him there's something on my computer he needs to preserve."

"Can you save it?" Norm asked her.

"I don't know. I don't know what it *is*." She had

punched in another telephone number. "She's alive, Alexandra, she's alive! We know for a fact that Jessica's still alive!"

"So, Hurt Guy, let me tell you what's happening."

The slit over his good eye was open.

"That nut Leopold is coming to dinner tonight. I figure the nicer I am to him and the more I know about him, the better our chances are of getting out of this alive. Because you will, you know," she told him seriously. "I know you must feel like hell, but the change in you has been miraculous. You're going to make it, no problem," she lied.

It looked like a tear forming in Hurt Guy's eye again.

"So when he comes tonight, you'll have to be very quiet. I'll feed you before he comes and that usually makes you sleepy, so with any luck you'll just sleep through it."

The reality of this man's situation was starting to panic her. There was something terribly wrong with the wounds on his right hand and she wondered if what she saw might not be a precursor to gangrene. And although she kept cleaning his wounds with witch hazel, one of them on his head was oozing horrible-looking stuff, and she knew he had needed something to fight off the infection some time ago.

Then she calmed herself, reminded herself that her grandfather and thousands of people like him had sustained injuries such as this in World War II and had survived. (She sorely wished, however, she could get over the feeling that people today, certainly kidnappers—no matter how polite or thoughtful—were not made of the same stuff as her grandfather's generation.)

"I'm going to start reading *Small House at Allington* to you again," she announced. "I know you missed a lot of it last night, but you'll catch on." And she sat on the floor, leaned back against the bed and began to read to him.

She had the horrible feeling that Hurt Guy was dying.

"This one, this one!" Will cried, pointing with a shaky hand to a call listing on the computer screen.

4:09 p.m. Salt Springs, Pennsylvania. Resident next to park saw Dodge van midnight parking lot. Park closed. Heard voices. Thought kids, but heard male and female voices. Saw man help staggering woman into back of van. Went to see if woman was okay, but van took off. Partial plate, **New York** M4E 8—.

"That's right over the New York State border," Will said excitedly to Alexandra and Agent Cole. "To get there from New York City, they probably took Route 17, and then back roads to Salt Springs."

"So?" Debbie asked.

"So get me the possible plates!" Will cried.

The agent took out her cellular phone and dialed. Then she held out her hand for the call sheet. To Alexandra she directed, "Call up that list of the electric-power people on your computer."

Hurt Guy slept for much of the afternoon. His fever was raging again and Jessica feared what would happen when the aspirin ran out, which, she figured, would be tomorrow morning. She spent most of the afternoon lying on the bed. She needed her rest; she needed to build up her strength. She also knew she needed to get the hell out of here and the only way was going to be through Leopold.

How to play it?

She'd have to kill him.

No way. She couldn't do that.

No, she'd have to tie him up somehow, overpower him and tie him up or lock him up somewhere. If she tried and failed, God only knew what he would do. But if she didn't try, Hurt Guy would surely die and so would she in the end. That twitching hand, skittering eye, turning-his-back thing was not good. She suspected he was going to become sexual very soon. Or try to be. And that she'd probably die resisting him.

She had to find a way out of here.

They came bursting into Cassy's office where Cassy, Kunsa, Hepplewhite and Dr. Kessler were huddled. "We've got him, we've got him, we've got him!" Alexandra cried, rushing in with Will and Wendy. "It's one of two guys and they're both in upstate New York."

Kunsa's mouth dropped open and he looked to Agent Cole, who had piled into the room behind them. "I think they have it," she acknowledged.

"Okay, envision this," Alexandra said, standing in the middle of the office. "Our kidnapper grabs Jessica at Rockefeller Center and threatens her with the fake bomb to get her to go with him. He leads her through the underground passageways to come up by the Sixth Avenue entrance of the NBC building. Wearing Con Edison ponchos and hard hats and boots, they board a Con Edison truck and he drives her to the Twelfth Avenue lot. They leave the truck, he puts Jessica in the back of an unmarked Dodge van and drugs her. He drives up the Hudson River Parkway to cross either the George Washington Bridge or the Tappan Zee, and takes Route 17.

"The kidnapper exits somewhere around Binghamton and cuts down to Salt Springs Park, an isolated place where, he knows, in the darkness he can walk Jessica around a bit. The neighbors see the van and Jessica stumbling around and worry it might be some kind of sexual assault. Just in case, they try to get the license number. Yesterday morning they hear our appeal on the air about Jessica's kidnapping and they call in, not knowing if it could be of any help."

"We were missing two numbers from the plate," Will continued, "but we knew it was a New York combination plate—so it could travel on truck routes and car-only roads. The computers spat out the possibilities and Dr. Kessler narrowed it down to the vans fitting the description and we came up with ten possible vans, all belonging to a fleet owned by the Niagara Power Project upstate. Then we ran a cross-check with our visitor and maintenance logs for West End and we got two hits with the Niagara Power Project—Mark Brewer, forty-three, master electrician with Kraskow Development Corp."

"Kraskow Development Corp helped to build West End," Kunsa said. "So he would have had access to the blueprints."

"Exactly."

"And the other?"

Alexandra's eyebrows went up. "James T. Plattener, deputy commissioner of the department of energy for New York State."

Cassy had picked up the telephone and was dialing a number.

"Zat milquetoast?" Dr. Kessler burst out. Considering that many of Dr. Kessler's best employees in the Nerd Brigade might fall under this loose categorization, this comment got everyone's attention.

"You know him?" Will said.

"Of course I know him," Dr. Kessler said. "Ask Cassy. We haf to deal with him on our power supply and he keeps trying to rescind our tax breaks."

Cassy said something into the telephone and then looked over. "The city and state offered Darenbrook Communications a package of tax breaks for the first twenty-five years if they built the headquarters here in New York City. There were also guarantees about our power supply and the rate for that power. Every time there's a change in government, though, the new guys try to find loopholes to reinstate some of those taxes, and this year they've been on us about surpassing our power projections. I know Plattener too, and the idea that he's our—" She shook her head. And then she paled. "You know—he was just here. The other day. At the sponsor tour."

"The day the marker holder was left in control room B," Hepplewhite said.

"Good God, Dirk was right," Cassy said. "He was here that day."

"A milquetoast, would you say?" Agent Kunsa asked Cassy. "How are his social skills?"

"Pathetic," Cassy said.

Kunsa looked at Debbie. "He could be our man." To Alexandra, "What's his connection with Niagara Power?"

"He was the division head of the technology unit until he was tapped for the department of energy."

"So where are these guys?" Hepplewhite wanted to know.

"Brewer's in Niagara Falls, Plattener's got a house in Buffalo and an apartment in Albany."

"Get on the phone with Niagara Falls, Albany and Buffalo," Kunsa said to Agent Cole. "Tell them we're on our way, but fill them in and tell them to keep surveillance on both of them until we get there."

"Jackson's plane is at your service," Cassy said. "And I just checked. You can get a lift to the airport from the helipad down the street."

* * *

Promptly at seven, Leopold slid the bolt back on the parlor door.

"Come in!" Jessica called. She was back at the card table, working on the puzzle, listening to Hootie and the Blowfish.

The door opened and there he was. Dressed in a suit and tie again, hair freshly washed and combed nicely, chin freshly shaved. She could see a bit of toilet paper stuck on his throat where he must have nicked himself.

"Hi," she said.

"Hi," he said, averting his eyes. He held a large white bag forward. "I brought Chinese."

"Oh, great," she said, standing up. "I'm really hungry." She gestured to the dining table. "I set the table for us."

"Thank you," he said quietly.

"I didn't have any fresh flowers so I took the liberty of using that bowl from the bedroom as a centerpiece."

"It looks very nice." He withdrew a short, round, solitary candle from his pocket. The kind one might use on an altar.

"Oh, that's great. I'll put it here," she said, placing it on the table.

He gave her matches, too.

"Are you hungry?" she asked him. "Would you like to eat right now?"

He nodded, almost shyly.

"Then why don't you sit right down there and just let me go wash my hands. I'll be right back."

She made sure he was settled in a chair before she left. She opened the door to the bedroom, closed it behind her and went over to crouch by Hurt Guy's ear. "He's here." She brought her finger up to his swollen mouth. "Be quiet until I tell you the coast is clear."

She couldn't tell if he heard her or not. The eye through the slit seemed unfocused. She had no choice but to leave him.

As she came out the bedroom door she was startled to find Leopold standing right there on the other side of it. "I need to wash my hands, too," he told her.

"This guy Brewer's a gambler," Dirk said to Alexandra, Will and Wendy. They were sitting in Jackson Darenbrook's plane, still parked on the tarmac at the Marine Terminal, while the FBI agents talked on their respective cellular phones. "From his credit report, it looks like he could use fifty thou just to stay afloat."

Will shook his head. "I don't think he's Leopold. Look at the wife and kids."

"Plattener's got a wife and kids, too," Hepplewhite said.

"But Brewer could be the kidnapper, Will," Alexandra said. "Look at the Niagara Power connection with Plattener. Plattener could *be* Leopold and he could have been in on the actual kidnapping. Maybe they're working together."

Kunsa clicked off his cellular and addressed the group. "Well, this is getting more interesting. One of those Niagara Power vans was signed out to Brewer this week."

"Told you," Detective Hepplewhite said.

"And right now Brewer's sitting at his girlfriend's house in Niagara Falls watching TV," he continued, rising from his seat.

"I thought he was married," Will said.

"The wife and kids are away," Kunsa said, walking to the front of the plane to where the pilot stood waiting. "We're going to Niagara Falls, Captain."

"Hang on, Norm!" Debbie called, holding a hand in the air. She pressed her phone to her chest. "Plattener's been on vacation for the last two weeks, and he's not coming back until the middle of July."

Will and Alexandra looked at each other.

"Our guys are at Plattener's house in Buffalo. No one's home, but it looks like he's been around."

"Tell them to watch for him and let us know if he comes back," Kunsa said. "And make sure Albany stakes out the apartment."

Debbie talked into her phone, while Kunsa continued to stand in the aisle by the pilot, evidently rethinking their itinerary.

"I vote we go to Buffalo," Dirk said. "Plattener's the key. He was *there*, Norm. At West End."

He looked at him. "But the van was signed out to Brewer."

"But Leopold's going to be the one who has her," Alexandra said, "and we think Plattener's Leopold."

"But we need someone to *lead* us to Leopold," Kunsa said. "And if Brewer has the van—"

"I think you should be trying to get a warrant to search Plattener's house," Wendy said.

"Oh, you do, do you? And on what grounds?"

"You're the FBI," Wendy told him. "We *know* you can think of something. Tell the judge he's suspected of having a cache of nuclear weapons. We've got to find her and the answer may be in that house. So let's get to Buffalo—"

"*I'll* get into the house myself, if you can't," Alexandra said. "And you can drive to Niagara Falls if you want. It's right near there."

Kunsa looked to Agent Cole. "Buffalo," she said.

"Buffalo," Will said, raising his hand.

"I'd go to Niagara Falls for you," Hepplewhite offered, "but I've got no jurisdiction."

Pulling his cellular out of his pocket again, Kunsa turned

around. "Change of destination," he told the pilot. "Buffalo, posthaste." He punched in some numbers. "Kunsa again," he said as he walked back down the aisle. "I need an escort to pick me up at the Buffalo airport."

19

"Cass?" Jackson Darenbrook whispered around the door.

Cassy, lying on the couch in her office, opened one eye. Then she smiled and opened both of them. "Hi."

"Hi," her husband murmured, coming over to sit on the edge of the couch. (Actually, with his southern drawl, it sounding more like "Hah.") He brushed her forehead with his fingertips and kissed her gently on the mouth. "Darlin', I think you should come home now and get some rest."

She yawned, covering her mouth, and dropped her hand. "I have to wait. They've all gone upstate." She propped herself up on her elbows. "They've got a lead, Jack. A good one. But Detective O'Neal is all alone here."

Her husband smiled. "I believe he does have the rest of the New York City Police Department to assist him."

"Hmm." She closed her eyes. "I suppose you're right."

"I've got the car downstairs, darlin'. Chi Chi will forward the calls to our house."

Her eyes opened again and she had difficulty keeping them that way. They were extremely bloodshot. "All right." He helped her to get up. "But I need to bring—"

"No, Cass," he said, pulling her back from her desk. "You'll be back soon enough."

"Oh, but Leopold," Jessica said to her kidnapper, who was standing at the door of the bedroom, "it's such a mess in there, can't you give me a minute to pick up a little? I'd be so horribly embarrassed if you saw the rooms the way they are now. Particularly after all the trouble you went to

to make them so nice." She held her breath. While the bedroom was in good shape, the bathroom looked like a field
hospital, with the strips of bloodstained bandages and
towels she had tried to wash hanging in there, and the
witch hazel, aspirin, tissues, napkins, spoons, razor blades
and pans all lined up on the shelf like a small pharmacy.

"I could wash my hands in the kitchen sink," Leopold
offered. "I don't have to—" He blushed scarlet, eyes dropping to the floor. "But it's very important to wash your
hands before eating," he added softly.

"Oh, thank you, Leopold," she said. "Why don't you go
ahead and do that and I'll pick up in the bathroom—just in
case."

"That won't be necessary," he said gallantly.

*It's not necessary, but it gives me an idea. You didn't lock the
door behind you, did you? And you wouldn't have an electric
field on if you had to walk through it to get here, would you? So
if I get you in the bathroom, I could just run out and get away.*

"Oh, but I insist," Jessica said. She touched his arm to
guide him toward the kitchen, but her touch made him
jump. "I'm sorry, I didn't mean to startle you!"

"No, no-no," he stammered, backing away from her,
eyes still on the floor, clamping his right hand over the
place on his arm where she had touched him. "I am all
right," he declared—sounding very uncertain about it,
however—and he went reeling off toward the kitchen.

Oh, man, was this guy whacked-out.

"I'm just going to go in and pick up," Jessica called.

"Th-th-th-that will be no-no-no-not—will not be ne-ne-
ne—" He was back in the doorway, his eyes closed. When
they opened again, he spat out, "Necessary."

Great. He couldn't look at her, couldn't be touched,
found hand washing very important and now stuttered

and stammered. Somehow Jessica did not find this personality profile particularly reassuring.

While Leopold washed his hands in the kitchen, Jessica grabbed all the stuff in the bathroom, shoved it into the shelves and covered it with a clean towel. When she came back out, she found Leopold standing by the table, waiting. He had lit the candle and there was the faint smell of vanilla in the air. He held the chair out for her and they sat down at the table and served themselves out of the cartons.

It caught Jessica off guard when he requested one of the steak knives he had stocked the kitchen with since, at the moment, one of those steak knives was under the cushion of the sofa and the other was under her pillow in the bedroom. The question was, how to gracefully retrieve one without explaining that she had hidden them so to stab him to death in case of an emergency?

"Surely," she said in response to his request, jumping up from her chair. "Oh! There's that puzzle piece!" she cried, feeling a little like a Lillian Gish character in a silent movie as she fluttered over to the couch as if spotting the piece she had been looking for all her life upon the cushion. She slid her hand under the pillow, grabbed the knife, moved over to the puzzle table and put her hand down as if to lay the piece among the pile, and then, whistling, went fluttering off to the kitchen. Then she came back out, handed him the steak knife, and dinner resumed.

Leopold had excellent table manners. In fact, she found the way he effortlessly handled his utensils more than a little unnerving. The only other person she had ever seen use a knife on spare ribs had been a plastic surgeon.

Physically, Leopold seemed to be normal. He was not very manly, and his complexion was sallow, but he dressed well and Jessica knew if he could get the skittering-eye thing under control and was not flustered into stutter-

ing, he could pass for normal. Well, unusual, but not certi-
fiable. He was clearly some sort of genius. And he was
crafty. Still, one would think that someone who had as
many dysfunctions as Leopold did would have drawn notice long before this. Surely someone somewhere must suspect this guy for something.

"Leopold," she began, after bringing him a cup of plain
tea at the conclusion of their meal, "I was wondering if you
could take me out for some air tonight."

"No, I'm sorry," he said quietly, looking down at the table.

"But I promise I'll behave."

He looked at her for a moment and then, as always,
quickly averted his eyes. "No. Not tonight."

"Maybe tomorrow?"

"Maybe tomorrow," he said. His eyes narrowed and
darted over to stare at her breasts for a moment before
darting away again.

"Is it because I might get electrocuted?"

He looked at her again.

"You said in your note that you had an electric field set
up to protect me."

He dropped his eyes and pushed his cup around in the
saucer.

"It's just that my sinus trouble's starting up," Jessica
said, "and I don't want to get sick."

He reached into his pocket and brought out a brown pre-
scription vial and placed it on the table. "I got you these.
Penicillin."

"Oh, bless you!" she cried, reaching for them and standing up. Maybe they could do something for Hurt Guy.
"I'm going to take one right now with some water." She
went into the kitchen, made some noises and came back,
finding him staring at her breasts again. "Oh my, I feel bet-

ter already, just knowing that I have it. Thank you so much."

"Welcome," he murmured, lowering his eyes and sipping his tea with his pinkie extended.

She sat back down. "Dinner was great. Thanks again for that, too."

He nodded.

"And I want to thank you again for saving my life." She was wondering if maybe she should try to kill him.

He smiled, eyes on the table. He had crooked little teeth.

"I was wondering if you could tell me who it is that has been trying to hurt me." How would she do it? With the steak knife? Hit him over the head with a bookend? If he looked at her chest again, she just might try to strangle the son of a bitch.

Watch it, she told herself. Remember, this guy is a real killer.

"Two of them are dead," he said in a conversational tone of voice, as if confirming her thoughts. He sipped his tea.

"And one of them was Bea Blakely."

He put down his cup with a clatter.

His hands were small and soft-looking, the fingernails were clean but bitten to the quick. It was hard to believe these hands were capable of inflicting the kind of beating Hurt Guy had received.

"Yes," he said in scarcely a whisper.

"Who was the other?"

"A man." He was getting nervous now; that hand was starting to do that reflex-jerking thing again.

"What man?"

"He was going to kill you."

She caught her breath. It had never occurred to her that Hurt Guy might have wanted to murder her. That was the easiest way to conceal a kidnapping victim, wasn't it? Just murder them and stick the body somewhere?

Good God, had she been trying to keep her would-be murderer alive back there?

No. She didn't believe it. The man who had taken her out of Rockefeller Center would not have hurt her.

But then, what did she know about killers? Surely people were nice to turkeys too before Thanksgiving.

"Did the man kill my secretary?" When he didn't answer, she asked, "Do you know about that, Leopold? About how Bea died?"

He stood up abruptly, his chair crashing backward to the floor.

"I'm sorry, I'm sorry, I didn't mean to upset you!" she pleaded.

Jessica thought she heard something from the bedroom and so she jumped up too and shouted, "Leopold, I'm sorry!"

He had turned around and was facing the door, his back to Jessica, his arms crossed over his chest like a pouting child.

"I know you're protecting me, Leopold, I know you've saved me from something horrible. And if you had to kill Bea, I know it's because you were protecting me. If you did it, it was because you had to, I understand that. Please don't be upset with me. I'm—" She broke down and started to cry, which, frankly, wasn't very hard to do under the circumstances. "You're all I've got, Leopold," she said, sobbing.

In the next moment Leopold was holding her in his arms and she was crying on the padded shoulder of his suit.

While Alexandra and Will and Hepplewhite dozed on the flight to Buffalo, Agents Kunsa and Cole had been on their telephones. This time when Kunsa hung up he said to Dirk, "You've got to keep a leash on this crew."

"You brought them," he complained.

"They're very helpful," Agent Cole murmured. "I'm happy to take charge of them."

Kunsa glanced over at Alexandra. "If anything happens to her..."

"I'll keep an eye out," Dirk said.

Alexandra cracked one eye open slightly, and then quickly closed it as Kunsa's gaze came her way.

After Jessica calmed down and stopped crying, she backed away from Leopold, apologizing for her outburst, saying she thought it would be best if he left so that she could get some rest. She picked up her paper napkin from the table and turned her back to Leopold to wipe her eyes and blow her nose.

"I don't want to leave you like this, Jessica," he said softly.

She looked at the napkin clenched in her hand. "Will you be coming back?"

"Oh, yes," he assured her in a low tone. "As soon as you wish."

She tried to think. "Are you staying here, too?"

This time he didn't answer and she thought she better let it pass.

"Maybe you'll come for dinner tomorrow? At seven again?"

"All right."

She turned around. "I'll cook for you, if you want."

"No, I'll bring you dinner, Jessica. Something fresh."

She smiled. And sniffed. "Thank you, Leopold."

"Are you going to be all right?"

She nodded. "I just need to rest."

"Good night, then," he said.

"Good night," she said.

He started out the door. "Oh, I almost forgot," he said, sounding like a normal person. He withdrew a cassette from his pocket and walked over to hand it to her.

She looked at it and read the label, "New York State AA Conference, Ben H."

"It's all I could find on short notice."

It was a tape of someone telling his story at a regional AA conference. "You've given me a precious gift. Thank you."

He nodded and went out the door, closing it softly behind him.

She waited for the sound of the bolt.

She didn't hear it.

She wiped the steak knife Leopold had used and stuck it back under the sofa cushion.

Moments later she was rushing into the kitchen to crush penicillin in applesauce to feed to Hurt Guy.

"I thought the warrant would be ready when we got here," Will said, frustrated.

Alexandra didn't even bother answering. Nor did Detective Hepplewhite, who was smoking a cigarette in the corner. They were sitting in a windowless conference room in the downtown Buffalo FBI office.

"It takes time," Wendy said. "And the fact that it's Friday—"

The door opened and they started. It was Agent Cole. "Sorry," she said. "Not yet."

They all slumped back down in their seats.

"Where's Dirk?" Alexandra asked.

"Checking on something with one of our people. He'll be back." The agent moved to the table. "I've got a lot more on Plattener." Heads raised in interest again, and moments later the group had assembled around the table.

"Okay, as you know," Agent Cole began, "Albany says Plattener's on vacation for a month."

"Where do they think he is?" Alexandra asked.

"Europe. With his wife and kids. The thing is, they've gone through the apartment from top to bottom in Albany—"

"They've already gotten in?" Will said. "So what's the hang-up here?"

"Just let me read you the report," Agent Cole begged. She cleared her throat. "In the closets they found almost all men's clothing, with the exception of a few toys—a game called Lie Detector, a Huckleberry Hound stuffed animal and a Lionel train set. They also found three items of women's clothing—a white rabbit-fur muff, a yellow cardigan with lace collar and a Playtex girdle with fasteners, size eighteen." She looked at them. "How does that strike you?"

"It strikes me the toys and women's things are from the 1960s at least," Alexandra said. "A white rabbit-fur muff?"

"The guy is a loony toon," Detective Hepplewhite declared, rubbing his eyes. "God only knows what the wife and kids are like."

"We've got to get into that house," Wendy stressed. "Can't I just—"

"No," Cole said, cutting her off. "And don't worry, we're watching it. No one's going to come or go without our knowing about it."

"But Jessica could be in there," Will said. "Or under there, or—"

"I know, I know," Cole said, "but we have to be patient. Now—" she opened a manila file "—this is what I've got on Plattener. James Albert Plattener. Born Niagara Falls,

1963. Only child of Albert Marcus Plattener, an engineer working on the Niagara Power Project, who died of lymphatic cancer in 1968, age thirty-nine. Plattener was five. Mother, Lillian Ruth Wiesner Plattener, moved them to a house in Buffalo where she worked as a private nurse. Plattener attended public schools, graduated high school at fifteen, Bachelor of Science in interdisciplinary sciences from Buffalo State at eighteen. Started an accelerated Ph.D. program in physics and electrical engineering at Rochester Institute of Technology, but dropped out in 1982 because his mother got sick with asthma and he moved with her to Arizona."

"There it is," Alexandra murmured, making a note on her legal pad.

"Where in Arizona?" Will asked.

"Phoenix. He worked for the Arizona Board of Energy and Resource Management until 1994."

"So he could have picked up Jessica's show from the very first year," Alexandra said, looking up.

"Denny Ladler checked the old program registers," Agent Cole said, "and he confirms it. Plattener and his mother were in the studio audience in Tucson several times while the show was still there."

"Where is that warrant?" Will demanded, getting up to pace the room.

"So when did the mother die?" Detective Hepplewhite wanted to know.

Alexandra looked at him with a question in her expression.

"It's the mother," he explained. "It's always the mother behind these guys."

"She died four years ago," Cole said. "And Plattener came back home to Buffalo, moved back into their old house and then started working for the Niagara Power Project."

"What about the wife and children?" Alexandra wondered. "Where did they come in?"

Cole threw up her hands. "Got me. We're checking on it. Right now, Albany says the wife and kids live here in Buffalo, but here in Buffalo the neighbors are telling us the wife and kids live in Albany."

Hepplewhite visibly winced. "That's not good."

"Oh, God," Wendy said, "I hope he hasn't done something to them."

"How the hell did this guy *get* to Albany?" Will wanted to know. "Who the hell would hire him?"

"Apparently he's a genius," Agent Cole said. "A strange bird for sure, everyone says that, but the guy apparently knows his way around power. Electrical, I mean."

There was a short knock on the door and then Dirk came in. "We were just wondering how this guy Plattener got hired in Albany," Alexandra explained.

Dirk pulled up a chair.

"When Pataki came into office," Agent Cole said, "Plattener's name kept coming up. He was too much of a kook to give him the big post, so the commissioner lured him as a special assistant."

"Ten to one when we look into it," Dirk said, "we'll find that he lured *them*."

"I agree," Alexandra said. "This guy's had a thing for Jessica since Arizona. The state job would get him to the studio in New York."

Hepplewhite was shaking his head. "No, it's too much of a stretch. If he wanted to be near her, why didn't he just move to New York? Try for a job at West End?"

"Who's to say he didn't?" Dirk asked.

* * *

"I don't know jack shit about Jessica Wright's disappearance!" Mark Brewer yelled.

"Suppose you explain to me, then," Agent Kunsa said, "how the van signed out to you from Niagara Power was used to transport Jessica Wright out of New York City after she was kidnapped."

"I told you, I didn't sign out the van!"

"Then how come your name is on the register?"

"I didn't sign it out!" he insisted.

"Have you ever signed out a van before?"

"Of course I have! I transport shit, I *have* to have a van."

"So how did your signature get on the register?"

"I didn't sign the register!" he nearly shrieked.

"Didn't you sign out the van and help James Plattener?"

At the sound of that name, Brewer's face first screwed up in disgust and then expanded into an expression of disbelief. "That wuss? You think I'd have jack shit to do with a wuss like Plattener?"

Kunsa didn't say anything. He only waited.

Brewer's expression had changed again. Now something seemed to be dawning. "Oh, I get it. Hey, look, it's not me you're after—let me tell you about that techno-troll nerd-fuck. He's setting me up."

Hurt Guy was failing. When Jessica went in to give him the penicillin Leopold brought, she turned the corner of the bed and gasped, horrified at what she found. He must have had some kind of seizure while they had been eating dinner, for there was spittle down the sides of his mouth and there was a new gash on the side of his head where, evidently, he had banged it again and again against the sharp corner of the bedpost leg.

"Oh, Hurt Guy, I didn't know," she murmured. She opened his mouth and saw that he had bitten his tongue badly. She cleaned the new wound on his head and bandaged it, made him rinse his mouth and then got the applesauce laced with penicillin down him. Then he went into another seizure.

Alexandra's head was resting on her arms as she dozed on the table; Will was nodding off in a chair, head propped back against the wall; Hepplewhite was curled up around the steam radiator in the corner; and Dirk was poring over papers spread out on the table while Wendy was checking her facial burns in a compact mirror. The overhead light burnt, the clock ticked, and the bureau noises from outside the conference room were picking up.

The door suddenly opened, jerking them all awake. "We've got the warrant," Debbie announced.

Everybody scrambled to their feet.

"And we've got something else on the mother," Debbie added. "Guess what her father's name was?"

"Leopold," Alexandra said, heading out the door.

Jessica snapped on the rubber gloves, jammed a bunch of stainless-steel spoons and forks into the front pockets of her slacks, put the steak knife from the bedroom in her back pocket and went into the parlor. She picked up the round candle from the table, slipped the matches in her other back pocket, took a deep breath and opened the door. Tentatively she stepped out in the hallway.

Where the heck was she?

This was no ordinary Victorian house. She was standing in a huge hallway with an arched ceiling at least twelve feet high. It was a long, enormous space, with wooden and black-steel trusses overhead, and on the floor old-fashioned black-and-white linoleum.

To the right, at the end of the hall, there was a six-foot-high window, but massive wood shutters were spiked over it.

She turned the other way, slowly making her way by candlelight. There was no sound. No sign of life.

Where was Leopold? Moreover, where was that electric field?

There were wooden doors on either side of the hall and Jessica paused at the one next to hers, the room where Hurt Guy had been. Not only was there a big steel bolt across it, but also a large padlock that secured it in place.

Leopold's intentions were clear. He had definitely left Hurt Guy to die.

She stopped at the next door. She took a spoon out of her pocket and tossed it against the door handle. Nothing. The clatter of the spoon on the linoleum sounded horribly loud, but no other sound followed. She opened the next door and peered in. Just a big blank room with a bricked-up window like the two in her bedroom. She picked up her spoon, turning her eyes on the double wooden doors ahead in the hall. The doors met in an eight-foot-high arch and had huge brass handles. Clearly, if anything led to anywhere, these were the doors she was going to have to get through.

20

The authorities were swarming the nice neat property at 23 Old Bridge Road. Curious neighbors had lined the street to watch.

"Got to be drugs, don't you think?" one woman clucked to her neighbor, pulling her raincoat more tightly over her nightie.

"On 'Cops' they always have dogs," her neighbor commented.

"That's the FBI, look at their jackets."

"So what? They still ought to have dogs."

Inside the modest three-bedroom house, Alexandra was watching as Debbie Cole went through the master bedroom with a local policeman. Although clean and tidy, it was clear that no one had actually used this room in some time, and that Leopold—that was, James Albert Plattener—had kept all of his mother's things as if she were still alive. The old-lady dresses and cardigans and sensible shoes were lined up in the closet; the bureau had large old-fashioned bras and panties and girdles and stockings; there was even an embroidery hoop sitting on the padded rocking chair by the window, making it appear as though someone had only paused to go downstairs and get a cup of tea before resuming the project.

The next bedroom was like an embroidery museum. The walls were covered with matted and framed pictures, and there were perhaps a hundred pillows carefully arranged on shelves, chairs and a double bed. Like the agents and the police, Alexandra was wearing a pair of surgical gloves, and she went over to peer inside the double doors of the room's closet.

Glass shelving had been installed in the closet, from floor to ceiling to display what appeared to be hundreds of silver souvenir spoons. Alexandra looked closer.

"Probably the mother's," Agent Cole said over her shoulder.

"She didn't travel much," Alexandra said, bending to check out another shelf. "They're all from New York State or Arizona."

"Let's check out next door," Agent Cole said, leading the way to the third and final bedroom. It was more of a maid's room, it was so tiny. There was a single narrow bed, a tiny window, a narrow dresser and closet. This, evidently, was the bedroom belonging to Leopold. In the closet hung several men's suits; in the bureau there were nice neat piles of underwear, dress socks and laundered shirts. On the bureau was a snapshot of an old lady squinting into the camera. Agent Cole lifted the old green rug briefly to look at the floorboards and then moved on to the bathroom across the hall.

Here everything was pink, the walls, the tile, the rug, the fixtures. There was a large basket of individually wrapped soaps and packets of bubble bath. Samples of expensive perfumes were carefully lined up. There was a sterling-silver brush, comb and hand-mirror set carefully laid out on a pink hand towel. Over the sink, on a small shelf, was a shaving mug, straight razor, an old-fashioned bar of shaving soap and a huge bottle of witch hazel. "Who do you know that uses witch hazel as aftershave?" Agent Cole wondered.

"I think my grandfather did," Alexandra said.

The agent turned around. "Really?"

"On the farm they used it for everything—cuts, burns,

bites. My grandmother used to use it to wash her face. As an astringent."

Downstairs, Agent Kunsa had arrived from Niagara Falls and Will stood by as the FBI agent conferred with members of the local team. In the living room they were surrounded by petit-point pictures, a sofa and chairs with lace doilies carefully placed on them, against the wall an upright piano that was terribly out of a tune, and several cabinets.

"He's been here recently," Hepplewhite said, coming in from the kitchen with Dirk. "He's got milk and eggs and bread in the refrigerator."

Will was looking at the photograph of the young woman and two boys that was on top of the piano. "They look normal enough."

"Considering they have no connection with Plattener whatsoever," Kunsa said, "there's no reason why they shouldn't."

Will turned around.

"The wife and kids don't exist," Kunsa said. "We cracked his tax returns and he's been filing on behalf of a woman who died in Phoenix several years ago, a baby that died in Flagstaff and a child who was killed in Schenectady."

"You mean he—" Will began, horrified.

"No, they died of natural causes," Kunsa said. "The woman had cancer, the baby had a tumor, the other child was hit by a car. But he used them because their ages were about right and he's been filing returns for them under their social security numbers—only he's been filing them as his wife and kids. As for these pictures, who knows who these people are? They don't even match the pictures from his apartment that Albany faxed to us."

"Look at this," Wendy said, straightening up from the crouch she had been in.

Kunsa moved over to the large wooden cabinet and squatted, looking inside. Abruptly he stood back up. "This is our guy, all right."

Will went to look. Inside the cabinet there were four shelves with double rows of videotapes, each one carefully and neatly labeled with five entries. "Jessica 10/14/97 Sarah Ferguson on Princess Diana" listed one, "Jessica 10/15/97 NFL Heroes," "Jessica 10/16/97 How to Buy a Home," "Jessica 10/17/97 Rev. Billy Graham," "Jessica 10/18/97 The Rolling Stones."

"There's more over here," a cop said, stooping to look in another cabinet.

"And in here," Detective Hepplewhite said after lifting the lid on an old mahogany phonograph cabinet.

"Norm?" Agent Cole called, coming down the stairs behind Alexandra. "Central's just called. They've got Plattener's employment records."

"Agent Kunsa?" a female voice called from the kitchen doorway. It belonged to a uniformed policewoman. "You better come downstairs."

Will's expression made her quickly add, "No, sir, it's nothing like that."

Kunsa led the way through the kitchen to the basement stairs. They went down the suspended flight of stairs one at a time, following the flashlight of the policewoman. "The lights are out down here on purpose," she explained. "The wiring's been ripped out."

It was a small basement and the policewoman walked them over to the dusty floor-to-ceiling shelves holding canned tomatoes and pickles and relish. Alexandra audibly gasped when the officer demonstrated how the whole wall swung out on well-oiled hinges, and then they were temporarily blinded by lights. Behind the wall was a very large second room. "This room is hooked into the outside power line."

A police technician was packing several test tubes and vials in his bag while a police photographer snapped pictures. The room was carpeted and contained a large TV, VCR and La-Z-Boy chair, but it was the walls of the room that held their attention. They were covered with pictures of Jessica. There were magazine covers and pictures from newspapers, publicity handouts, fan-club pictures and what looked to be regular snapshots. An agent walked over and pulled down one of several huge volumes in a bookcase and brought it over to Agent Kunsa. Inside was nothing but clippings about Jessica. Then he pulled open a drawer in the file cabinet in the corner, exposing file after file of tear sheets about Jessica. "They start back when she was on-air in Tucson."

"Norm!" came from over Kunsa's walkie-talkie. He unhooked it from his belt and held it to his mouth. "Yeah?"

"The garage," Dirk's voice said. "You better get out here."

Kunsa took the stairs two at a time.

Jessica put the candle down on the floor and tossed a spoon against the handles of the double doors. There was a blue flash, sparks and a horrible searing sound that made her jump back.

Geez.

Now what? The handles of the doors were electrified. The question was, how did she short them out? Or had the spoons shorted them out?

She threw a fork at the door handles and missed. She threw another and she gave out a little yelp as the same blue light and sparks shot off again.

Think, Jessica, think. Okay, electricity could only maintain itself in a closed circuit. She had to break the circuit. Were the brass handles of the door touching? Yes. Okay, so they must be part of the circuit. All she had to do was get one door open and the circuit would be broken.

She had on cross trainers. So she was grounded, right? She had on rubber gloves, very thin ones, but rubber all the same. So she was a circuit breaker herself, wasn't she?

Oh, hell, she wasn't about to experiment.

She ran back to the apartment and looked around. Her eyes traveled to the exercise room. The jump rope. Ah. She took it into the kitchen and cut the handles off and then ran back out into the hall. She carefully snaked the rope through one of the handles, took hold of the other end and transferred it to her other hand so she was holding both ends of the rope with it. Then she reached down to get the candle. After a deep breath, she gave the rope a big yank. The door opened, she slipped through and pulled the rope into the next room with her, jumping back to get out of the way as the door closed again.

Phew.

What the—?

She held the candle high.

She was in some sort of large central foyer. There was furniture, covered in sheets, pushed back along one wall. Otherwise the space was empty and the wooden floorboards bare. Along the far wall, over the furniture, about five feet off the ground were huge recessed windows covered in red velvet drapes like the ones in her bedroom.

As she drew closer to the windows, her heart skipped because she knew what she was seeing was not her imagination. These windows were not blocked over. She could see a faint light coming in from the outside.

* * *

"Look at this," Dirk said, pointing to the clothing sitting in the middle of a crumpled blue tarp on the floor of the single-car garage. "They were stuffed up in the rafters."

Kunsa and Hepplewhite squatted to look.

"The neighbors say he renovated the garage himself about a year ago, sir," a policeman said. "They say he used a cement mixer by himself to pour the floor. We found it out back. It's manual."

Kunsa picked up a piece of the clothing. A red silk cocktail dress. He looked at the label. Size 6. "Not the mother's," he muttered, dropping it and picking up another piece of clothing. A shredded pair of black panty hose, petite. One pair of black panties. A bra (32-D). One black high heel, size 6.

"Norm." It was Agent Cole. Kunsa took one look at her expression, stood up and stepped away to hear what she had to say. Then Kunsa came back to the group. "I want you to tear this place apart," he directed the cops. He pointed to Dirk. "Stay. You know what we're looking for. Alexandra, stay with him. You—" he pointed to Hepplewhite "—with me. Rafferty, you, too." He hesitated and then pointed to Wendy. "You, too. Come on."

Jessica found a library table beneath one of the sheets and dragged it under the first window. She climbed on top of it and, holding the candle in her left hand, reached up to yank on one drape with her right. Besides a billow of dust that fell in a cloud around her, she could see that the window had a wire-mesh door over it.

Damn.

She threw one of the spoons against the wire door, bracing herself for the spark, but it didn't come. She threw another one. No charge. She crawled up on the sill, scraping her knees over the ancient stucco paint in the process. She put the candle down, maneuvered the tips of her gloved fingers into the grille and pulled. The wire door rattled. Behind it, the glass panes in the steel casement window were so hazed and dirty, Jessica could only see a glow of light from the outside. She picked up the candle to take a closer look at the grille.

There was a little latch. She turned it and the wire door swung open.

There was a sound from the other end of the room and Jessica saw a lantern. "Jessica!" Leopold cried.

She gripped the brass window handle and yanked up. Yanked again. It started to give and the window was opening, but Leopold had reached the table below and was trying to climb up. She struggled to open the window, but it was stuck—

She felt his hand clamp onto her ankle. "Jessica!" he gasped.

She kicked his hand off and shoved the window with her shoulder and it gave, and she was just about to jump—

The night air hit, and faraway lights swung dizzily below her. Jessica screamed, grabbing the top of the steel window as her legs kicked at open air. She was at least four floors up; there was a blur of city lights in the distance and a wall of brownstone that sheered down next to her. The window hinges were holding, but the thin edge of the cold steel was cutting into her fingers.

She felt Leopold's hands grab her thigh and yank her toward the windowsill. She managed to swing a foot up onto the sill and Leopold took hold of it. "Give me your hand," he commanded.

She had no choice and flung her right hand toward him, and he gripped it, and started pulling her in. A moment later she was sitting on the windowsill, her back against the frame, panting, Leopold still holding on to her. She closed her eyes against his shoulder, catching her breath.

When she opened her eyes, she saw the steak knife sitting on the sill by her foot. All she had to do was reach down and get it. This madman was not going to let her go;

he had electrocuted her secretary and had nearly beaten Hurt Guy to death. The only way out of here would be to stab him and run. No, wounded, Leopold would be more dangerous. If she were to get out of this, she would have to cut his throat, stab him in the soft part of the neck.

"You could have died," Leopold was whimpering into her shoulder. "You can't leave me."

Jessica reached forward with her right hand to get the knife. "It's all right," she murmured. "You saved me."

"You said you would be good," he cried.

"I got scared," she told him, changing her grip on the knife, holding the blade below her fist so she could just curl her arm around the back of his neck and, in a Frisbee-throwing motion, cut his throat.

"But I'll take care of you," he said. "Aren't I taking care of you?"

"You wouldn't take me outside," Jessica said. "I have to get some air or I'll go crazy."

Do it, Jessica commanded herself. *The guy's a psycho. He watched you on TV with his mother for fourteen years and decided to lock you up in a castle.*

"Love of my life," he said as he sobbed, holding her tighter. "You can't leave me."

Do it.

Jessica sighed. "God grant me the serenity to accept the things I cannot change, and the courage to change the things I can," she said aloud. Then she tossed the knife away; it hit the windowsill and clattered to the floor.

Leopold's head snapped up and he looked down and saw it lying on the floor next to his Coleman lantern. Then he looked back to her.

"I have to get out of here, Leopold," Jessica said, letting her head fall back against the window frame and starting to cry, "I can't stand being locked up."

"Oh, Jesus God Almighty," Kunsa said, reeling away from the plastic storage bin and dropping the top to it.

Agent Cole quickly offered him a handkerchief doused with Noxema, which he quickly took to cover his nose and mouth. He pressed his forehead against the storage-room wall, trying not to gag. "For God's sake, don't let Rafferty see."

Holding a red bandanna over her nose and mouth, Agent Cole looked over the shoulder of the police technician who had kneeled next to the bin with a flashlight and probe. "What do you think?"

"Six months," he said, gently probing the bin with a long rod. "Eight months maybe. The coroner will know."

Agent Cole's eyes traveled back to the rear wall of the storage unit where there were seventeen other large plastic storage bins stacked neatly against the wall, looking obscenely festive in their electric blues and greens.

"The body was badly burnt," the technician observed.

"Could they be electrical burns?" Debbie asked.

"Jesus Christ," Kunsa said through his teeth, banging his forehead against the wall.

The technician looked up at Agent Cole. "Electrical burns would be consistent." His eyes then moved past the agent to a figure standing behind her. Agent Cole turned.

Will Rafferty was standing there, tears silently streaming down his face as Wendy was trying to keep him back.

"It's not Jessica," Agent Cole told him. "Go back outside."

"I've got to see," he insisted. "I've got to know for sure."

Leopold helped her down from the windowsill. "I knew you loved me," he told her, holding her hand.

She knew she had seen him before. He wasn't an employee of West End, she had never worked with him anywhere else, he had never been a guest, but she had seen him. More than once. And the last time hadn't been too long ago, either.

"No more exploring, my darling," he murmured. "Not until we've had a little more time together." He picked up the lantern, leading her along with the other.

He smiled, eyes shining with love. "My precious darling," he murmured, and Jessica was scared he was going to kiss her, but all she could do was close her eyes against the horror.

He pressed his damp mouth against hers and she felt herself getting woozy.

Cooperate, make him feel at ease, comfortable with you, make him think you like him. As long as his fantasy is intact, he won't hurt you.

"Leopold," she said, gently but firmly pushing him back. She gave what she hoped was a womanly-sounding sigh. "You and I have had no time together. And I— well..." she tried to give a maidenly blush. "Well, you know how women are..." *About to puke.*

He was studying her in the lantern light.

"I don't think it's proper to be kissing before...well..." She looked at him shyly.

"You need to be courted," he said.

"Exactly," she said, smiling her best smile. "I need to sit and talk a while, get to know you better. Not that I don't like you already—and care for you," she added quickly.

"I apologize, Jessica," he said in a courtly, gentlemanly voice. "I did not mean to be improper. But I have waited so long. I have loved you for so long."

Jessica wasn't sure where to go from here. "Leopold—" she hesitated "—*dear.*"

His eyes were shining. "Yes?"

"We have met before, haven't we? I mean, not just in our hearts."

He brightened even more. "I went to your show. Mother went to your show, too, several times before she died. When it was a little show."

"You mean in Arizona?"

He nodded.

"Mother loved your show. We never missed any. Not even one. You see," he said confidentially, "Mother loved you, too."

"Oh," Jessica said. "I feel honored."

His expression went very soft. "She is very pleased about us."

She tried to smile.

"You came and visited me at West End, too, recently, didn't you?"

"Yes," he said.

"You work for the state, don't you?"

"Yes."

"I remember you, Leopold."

He beamed. "I knew you would."

"You had glasses on," she said.

"You had makeup on," he said fondly.

She forced herself to smile. "I like you better this way."

He sighed, happy. "Perhaps you could make us some tea now. We can visit more and then we can be together."

"Why, that's an excellent idea," she said. "Some tea and a few cookies." *Be together? What did that mean?* She shuddered to know.

Holding her hand tightly, Leopold led her back to her rooms.

21

"Will!" Alexandra cried, running across the outer-room of the FBI's field office in Buffalo.

"No, she's definitely not there," he said quickly, his voice hoarse. "I looked myself. There's just the one body, and it's from a while ago. We were scared there were more, but there's not."

"Thank God," she said, burying her face in his shoulder. Will put his arms around her. Then Alexandra stepped back, looking up at him, eyes bloodshot and full of tears, chin slightly trembling. "I don't know how much longer I can hold up."

"I know, I know," he murmured, putting his arm around her and guiding her past the front desk toward the back room. "But we're close, Alexandra, I know we are. And if anyone can keep this guy under control, you know it's going to be Jessica." He paused, waiting for her to look at him. "You know that, don't you? That Jessica can take better care of herself than any one of us? That she can talk her way out of anything?"

"I think so," Alexandra said in a small voice. Now she took the lead, opening the door to the conference room. There was a mess of files, papers and computer printouts all over the table. "I've been poring over Plattener's records as they come in."

"Where's Dirk?"

"Hell if I know," she said, sitting down at the table. She gestured to the piles of paper. "Every work review Plattener's ever had says essentially the same thing. He is gifted and works hard, but does not communicate well with his co-workers. In fact, no one has ever felt comfortable working with him, for him, or supervising him. And yet everybody hired this guy and continued to employ him until he quit."

"What jobs do we have?" Will asked, dropping into a chair.

"New York State Energy Commission," she said, passing that file to him. "Niagara Power Project, Arizona Power Authority board, and a series of jobs in graduate school and college—NY Valley Power and Electric, Transelectric Equipment Corp, Erie County Transformer and Condenser Company—"

Dirk appeared in the doorway. "Hi. I heard the news about the storage locker. It's bad news, I know, but it's good news, too, Will. I'm convinced Jessica's still alive."

"Thanks," Will mumbled, looking through the file.

To Alexandra, Dirk said, "The locals are checking out the work addresses."

"Will," she said, "I'm thinking that if all the places he worked around here are as large as they sound, we need to check to see if they have any abandoned or infrequently used facilities. You know, a warehouse, storage facilities, a plant—anywhere he might be hiding Jessica."

There was a quick knock and Agent Cole came in. "Guess what? Plattener attended an energy conference at Hoover Dam in May."

Will looked to Alexandra, not getting it. The anchorwoman's eyes had narrowed. "That's near Las Vegas."

"Exactly," Agent Cole said.

Alexandra turned to Will. "That's where that ten-thousand-dollar cashier's check was drawn for Bea."

"Okay, you sit right there and make yourself comfortable," Jessica told Leopold, practically pushing her captor down on the sofa. "Let me go and put the kettle on and freshen up a little and then I'll be right back. Here, listen to some music," she suggested, turning the cassette player on. "And here's a nice book," she added, handing him a large picture book, *America The Beautiful.*

She went into the kitchen, took off the rubber gloves, filled the kettle and turned the hot plate on medium. Then she went to the bedroom, calling a merry "I'll be out soon!" over her shoulder.

She closed the bedroom door and raced around the bed. In his delirium, Hurt Guy had crawled halfway under the bed, where he now lay, twisted and unconscious, his breathing irregular. If her hunch was correct about how Leopold was going to want the night to go, she had better move Hurt Guy back next door. As for herself—well, there was still the steak knife under her pillow and maybe this time she'd use it.

But how to move Hurt Guy? She tried to turn him onto his back, but he groaned so loudly she had to clamp a hand over his mouth.

Now what?

"You've got to get under the bed, Guy," she whispered to him.

He moaned, totally out of it, spittle oozing from the side of his mouth.

She gave up and let him sleep, pulling the blanket up around him.

She went into the bathroom and took off her clothes. She vigorously brushed out her hair, gave herself a fast wash at the sink and dressed quickly in slacks, blouse and the new cowgirl boots. She put on a little eyeliner, blush and mascara, just enough to make her eyes dazzling. As she emerged from the bedroom, she called to Leopold, "Our tea must be ready." He didn't turn around. "Okay, Leopold? Tea and cookies?"

"Ye-ye-ye-yes," he stammered without turning around.

She prepared a pot of tea and placed milk, sugar, spoons, cups and saucers and a plate of shortbread cookies on a tray and came back out to the parlor.

"Okay, here we go, a nice pot of tea and cookies," she said, rounding the side of the couch.

And there she found Leopold, eyes closed in concentration, his mouth stretched into a hideous grin while he frantically masturbated.

"It's got to be here somewhere," Alexandra insisted, riffling through the papers on the table yet again. "Somewhere he knows that's still around where he could be hiding Jessica."

"The battery factory's gone," Wendy said. "The electrical-equipment corp has been checked. Where else?"

"Exactly," Alexandra sighed. "Where else? We checked the schools, the neighborhood, everywhere we knew he worked."

"Let's try the mother's friends," Kunsa said, jumping up and going to the door. "Debbie!"

In Sun City, Arizona, Agent Yargen, the FBI agent from the local bureau, hung up Mrs. Marcino's telephone and went back to sit with the widow in the living room of her condo. "Can I ask you another question?"

Pleased at the attention, the elderly woman's eyes shone. "Pray do."

"Did Mrs. Plattener ever mention the kind of work James did?"

"Oh, yes, all the time. He was a very important scientist."

"What about when he was younger? Anything about working in a restaurant?"

She looked at him as though he were mad. "He was a very important scientist," she repeated.

"But do you remember anything about James working at an unusual job?"

"All of his jobs were unusual."

"Yes, I understand that, he was a gifted man."

"He was a very important scientist," Mrs. Marcino said patiently, hoping at last the agent would get the party line correct.

"Think, Mrs. Marcino, think back to all those long conversations you had with Mrs. Plattener. Did she ever mention any jobs James did that were different from his other ones?"

"I remember all of Lillian's stories very well," she said. She smiled apologetically. "I just can't remember whether or not I took my pills this morning."

The agent smiled politely.

"She told so many stories about his inventions and how he saved the state so many millions of dollars." She looked out the window at the sun starting to rise over the desert landscape. "Her happiest time, though, I think, was when he was a boy. I think he was a boy—and he solved a problem where she worked. It was an electrical problem, as I recall, and it was going to cost the hospital many thousands of dollars to fix and I believe James fixed it all by himself for nothing." She beamed, looking at the agent. "I think that was unusual. That James worked with his mother that time. It was the only time. When he was fixing whatever that problem was at that hospital."

"What hospital is she talking about?" Kunsa muttered. "The woman was a private nurse. Why would she be working in a hospital if she was a private nurse?"

"What do her records say?" Alexandra asked.

"There are no records!" Kunsa exploded. "The agency's been out of business for twenty-one years and nobody knows where the hell all the records are!"

"Okay, okay," Will said calmly, holding a hand out as if to physically push the frustration level down around the table, "let's stop and think." He paused. "This Mrs. Marcino. Somewhere in her brain she knows. We just need to coax her memory."

"Is this really Alexandra Waring?" Mrs. Marcino exclaimed into the phone.

"Yes, it surely is, Mrs. Marcino. And I am very, very grateful to you for helping us in this special investigation. And as soon as I am at liberty to explain it to you, I will personally fly down to Sun City to thank you myself."

"My!" she said.

Despite her fear and exhaustion, Alexandra smiled. "This is what I need to ask you about, Mrs. Marcino. You told Agent Yargen that James Plattener once worked at the same hospital that Mrs. Plattener did."

"Yes, he was a very important scientist."

"Now, my question is, do you remember what kind of nursing Mrs. Plattener was doing for the hospital?"

"She didn't work for the hospital," Mrs. Marcino said. "She worked for a family. A very well-to-do family."

Alexandra caught her breath. "You mean she was a private nurse?"

"Oh, yes, she was a private nurse to a Mr. Porterly. She was always talking about Mr. Porterly and what a handful he was. And how whenever he went into the hospital, she would go there every day to nurse him."

"Do you remember his first name? Mr. Porterly's name?"

"No, I'm sorry, she always called him Mr. Porterly, with great respect for the name." She chuckled. "But I don't think she respected *him* very much, it was the family, you see. They were very, very wealthy and this was how she was able to take care of her little James. Because the Porterlys paid her very, very well."

Jessica dropped the tray on the coffee table with a clatter and turned her back on Leopold with the excuse of changing cassettes in the tape machine. "Would you pour the tea, please, dear?" she asked. *You filthy pervert.*

He didn't say anything.

Jessica finished changing the cassette—to *The Marches of John Philip Sousa*—and turned around. Leopold had stopped masturbating and was simply sitting there, looking at her, holding his flaccid penis in his hand.

"I like sugar and milk in my tea, how about you?" she said, drawing up a chair and leaning over the tray to pour tea. She looked him square in the eye and she was somewhat shocked to realize that he was now looking back at her just as squarely. Not an encouraging sign, she didn't think. "I asked you how you liked your tea."

He swallowed, eyes looking at the teapot and then coming back to her. "Sugar and milk."

"Just like I do," she said, picking up the teapot. "Oh, darn, I forgot the napkins, we must have napkins," she said, holding the top on the teapot as she poured. "Leopold, be a dear and go into the kitchen and get two napkins. Hurry, please."

After hesitating a moment, he got up, and Jessica saw out of the corner of her eye that he was zipping his pants back up. "Maybe you could bring a pot holder, too," she said.

He moved toward the kitchen and the second he was out of sight, Jessica raced out the front door, slammed it shut and slid the bolt across. Almost instantly she heard a howl of rage from inside as Leopold realized what she had done. His body hit the door in a body slam, the knob rattled and he body-slammed the door again.

Blindly she reached for the wall and headed in the direction of the double doors. She worked her way down, shuddering at each body slam against the door and the screams of rage behind her. He sounded like an animal.

She reached the end of the corridor and felt her way right toward the double doors. She was just thinking that maybe she should test the handles in case Leopold had somehow reactivated—

There was a flash and a loud cracking noise and Jessica fell to the floor.

"She's got it!" Kunsa yelled from a desk in the outer offices of the bureau branch. Will, Dirk, Detective Hepplewhite, Alexandra, Debbie Cole and local staff were all bustling about, but stopped at this announcement. "She's faxing it over—Bruce William Porterly, died 1983."

"It's coming through!" a branch agent called and Debbie Cole raced over to the fax machine to take each sheet as it came through. "Bruce William Porterly," she read from the first sheet, "paranoid schizophrenia."

"Bruce William Porterly," Kunsa was reciting from whoever was on the other end of the telephone in his hand, "was arrested in 1974, 1977, 1978 on child molestation. Released each time for lack of evidence. Arrested and convicted 1979 on multiple child-molestation charges, but found not guilty for reasons of insanity. He was sent to Buffalo State Hospital."

"The Buffalo Psychiatric Center," Agent Cole read from her fax. "June 1972—"

"June 1972," Alexandra repeated. "Yes! So his mother was a private nurse sent to that hospital by the family." She turned to a local agent. "It's maybe seven or eight buildings. It's a historic landmark now."

"Landmark?" Kunsa said, slamming the phone down and running around the desk toward the agent.

"Yeah," the agent answered. "It's empty. The patients were moved out in seventy-four, and the administration building closed down in—oh, I don't know, ninety-four, I think. There's nobody in there."

His words hung in the air for only a moment. And then the group sprang into action.

22

As the car sped down Delaware Avenue and the state insane asylum that had taken from 1869 to 1885 to build appeared on the horizon, Alexandra shuddered. "Good God, can you imagine how people must have felt when they were taken here?"

Rising dramatically from the park lights, the Victorian complex for the insane sprawled some two thousand feet across. But somehow the massive fortress was still emphatically vertical, the central building shooting up into twin towers, the corners spiking up in dark turrets. The outer buildings, spreading back across the horizon, vaulted three and a half floors, from exposed basement windows up to the gabled windows, where the steep, angular roofs began. It was a monstrous mausoleum of Victorian institutionalization.

"Those towers are like—" Alexandra began, searching for a comparison.

"The witch's castle," Wendy supplied.

Alexandra turned to Will. "How are we ever going to find her if she's in there?"

"Kunsa's got heat sensors and nightscopes," Dirk said from the front seat. "They'll find her."

Perhaps a minute later, Jessica came to, coughing on the horrible smell of burnt hair that filled her nose, throat and lungs. Then she cried out, grabbing her right wrist and feeling a totally alien texture. She groped down to touch her hand and screamed with pain. She had been very badly burnt.

"I told you not to go out there!" Leopold shrieked from behind the locked door.

The pain was blinding and yet Jessica knew she had to pull herself together, she had to escape. Her right hand was useless. Burnt. What to do, what to do, *think, think!*

"Open this door at once!" Leopold yelled, pounding on it.

"Oh, fuck you, Leopold!" Jessica yelled back.

"Okay, this is where we are," Kunsa said, pointing to the ancient blueprints on the back of the police car. "We're getting readings here." He was pointing to the fourth floor of the central building, the one with the evil-looking spires. "We're sending three teams in, here, here and here. I think this is the best bet," he said, tapping his finger on one of the staircases. "And I'm leading that group in myself."

"I'm going with you," Dirk said.

"Okay," Kunsa said.

"I'm coming, too," Will said.

"Forget it," Kunsa said. "No argument, Rafferty. Dirk and I have done this before." He waved the policemen on. "Okay, let's hit it, guys. Who's got the keys, where's the tech?"

It had been silent for quite a while now. Jessica, nearly zoned out on the pain in her hand, was lying on her side in the dark, the only light in the hallway coming from the crack beneath the parlor door.

"Jessica," Leopold said through the door in a slightly singsongy voice. "Guess what? I've got company."

"Yeah, right," Jessica said. "You and Jack the Ripper, ya friggin' psycho."

"You better unlock this door."

Then there was a cry at once so horrible and familiar it wrenched her heart. It was Hurt Guy.

"Oops!" Leopold called. "Oh my, I seem to have broken his wrist."

There was another cry.

"Oops! And I just stepped on it by accident!" There was a hideous chuckle. "Oh my, it seems the poor fellow has passed out." A moment later, "I can only assume that you have some sort of attachment to this fellow, Jessica. You certainly have gone to a great deal of trouble to keep him alive." He laughed a high, whining laugh. "You broke down the wall, you silly girl! You amazing girl!"

Jessica groaned, "Leave him *alone*."

"I'm sorry," Leopold said, "but I cannot do that, Jessica. In fact, if you do not unlock this door and come in here now, I am afraid I will have to kill him."

Jessica didn't answer.

"Look at it this way, darling," he continued, "if you don't come in here, you will die out there and he will die in here, and I will eventually get out and go away and will live, I assure you, happily ever after. And nobody will ever know what happened to you."

She was struggling to her feet.

"You have thirty seconds before I spike my knife through his eye socket," Leopold said.

"I'm coming, I'm coming," she said dejectedly. "Hold your horses." She staggered over to the door, felt with her left hand for the bolt, slid it across and threw the door open. "Okay, I'm here, asshole," she said defiantly, tottering in the doorway. "Leave him alone and pick on someone your own size."

The look of horror on Leopold's face was genuine as he staggered back. "Your beautiful hair."

"And I don't color it, jerk-off," she muttered, kneeling to

look at Hurt Guy. "Some stalker you are. You son of a bitch," she said in the next breath, looking up. "You did break his wrist."

"Your hand," Leopold said softly.

Jessica could scarcely see at this point, the haze over her eyes was so heavy, but she managed to get back on her feet to face him. "Stop staring at me, asshole. How the hell would you look if you'd been electrocuted?"

"The-the-the-there must be a mal-fu-fun, uh, function," he stammered. "The-the-the—"

"Fine, whatever, Leopold, you didn't electrocute me," she said, waving her good hand at him in dismissal and weaving past him toward the bedroom. "Just stay the hell out of my way, I've got work to do."

"Come back here!" Leopold demanded.

"I need a splint and some bandages and some penicil-lin—"

"Come back here!" Leopold yelled again, stamping his foot.

"Get a life," Jessica growled, yanking the velvet curtains down with a crash and starting to work the steel curtain rod out of the material.

"I will kill him!" Leopold declared from the doorway, his voice squeaking high. "I will! I will! If you do not bed me, I will kill him!"

Jessica turned around, squinting against the light. "You are so fucking crazy I can't deal with you anymore."

He stood there, blinking, evidently stunned by this pro-nouncement.

She got the steel rod separated from the curtain and turned around. "Now, bandages," she said matter-of-factly, heading for the bathroom.

"I'll kill him!" he raged, running back to the parlor.

Jessica went after him, dragging the steel rod in her left

hand behind her. As Leopold crouched over Hurt Guy and brought up the knife in his hand, Jessica transferred the rod to her right hand and forcibly clamped her burnt fingers around it. "Hey, Leopold!" she yelled, taking a running start.

"Hurry it up!" Kunsa urged at the entrance to the stairwell. Kunsa, Dirk and the local police all had their nightscopes on.

"I can't hurry it up until they shut down the power!" the cop complained. "The meter says there's over five hundred volts in this door."

"Get that power shut off!" Kunsa screamed into the walkie-talkie.

"We're working on it," the walkie-talkie squawked back. "They have to trace the feed— Wait, hang on. Hang on, we're almost there. Hold on, hold on—"

"Damn it, there's not time!" Kunsa seethed. "Come on! Come on!"

Nothing from the walkie-talkie.

"What the hell?" Kunsa said.

"Easy," Dirk said. "They'll get it."

"Found it!" squawked the walkie talkie. "We're disconnecting the power line now."

Kunsa poised himself at the door. "Come on, come on—"

She aimed for the soft underside of his skull, but Leopold ducked and the steel rod glanced off the side of his head. Still, the blow sent him crashing forward into the wall and sent Jessica sprawling.

Then the lights went out.

Kunsa didn't wait for confirmation and shoved the door open, charging up the four flights of stairs to the top. The door on the fourth-floor landing was locked, but Dirk used the master key and it worked.

"Copter 61—we've got a man on the roof, East Tower," the walkie-talkie said. "Can somebody get him in?"

"No go, he's too high," Kunsa said into the walkie-talkie. "He's got to get down to the gables."

"Negative. He says the gable windows are bricked in."

"This is command one going silent," Kunsa said, turning the walkie-talkie off. "All quiet," he instructed the group. He opened the door and waved them to follow. Silently they made their way down a large hallway. Kunsa looked at the screen the police technician offered him; it indicated the body heat of three figures some twenty yards ahead, to the right.

Kunsa led them to a set of double doors. Wordlessly, the tech approached it. Then he quickly put an arm out to prevent Kunsa from touching it. "It's hot," the tech whispered. "Must be on a power pack."

Kunsa gestured.

With one of his heavily gloved hands, the tech extended something to the door. There was a spark, a sizzle sound, a small flash of orange light and then—nothing. He stepped back to let Kunsa lead the way into a large central foyer.

Jessica heard Leopold moving around by the door. She scooted over to the sofa and slipped her left hand under the cushion, looking for the steak knife. Found it.

She put the knife in her left hand and lay down flat on the floor, making her way along the floor on her elbows, pulling her body up behind her. "Hey, Leopold," she whispered. "Come and get me, *darling*." There was a bumping sound ahead and she continued crawling toward the sound.

Then there was an explosion in the building, somewhere near, for the very floor beneath her tremored.

"What the hell was that?" Dirk whispered.

"Don't tell me he's blowing up the building," Kunsa muttered. The tech grabbed him just as the agent reached for the next set of double doors. The tech checked his meter and then gave the okay sign.

The agent slid the strap of his rifle off his shoulder and slowly pushed the door open with it. There was the sickening smell of burnt hair and human flesh. He took a step forward in the darkness and listened. His companions came silently forward, fanning out across the long arched hallway. There was sound coming from somewhere down the hall. To the right. There was an open door.

Kunsa stole silently to the side of it. He leveled his rifle then whirled himself into the doorway, and then stopped in his tracks. He was looking down the barrel of his rifle to see Jessica Wright, with all of her hair burnt off, sitting on the floor, cradling the battered head of a man in her lap, slashing a steak knife blindly through the air at him with her left hand. "You touch him and I'll kill you!" she cried.

"Jessica," Kunsa said. "I'm Agent Norman Kunsa of the FBI. You're safe now. We're here to help you."

"Get away from us, you fucking psycho!" she cried, continuing to slash at the air.

Kunsa backed off and turned to Dirk. "Get Alexandra up here."

Less than two minutes later, Alexandra appeared, huffing and puffing in the doorway. Jessica was still holding on to the injured man, jerking her knife around at every sound.

"Jessica," Alexandra said softly, trying to stabilize her breath. Slowly she came in. "Shine your light on me, would you please?" she asked Kunsa. He did so. "Jessica, look, it's me—Alexandra. We've found you, Jessica. We're here to take you home."

The hand with the knife stopped moving. "Alexandra?" Jessica asked weakly.

"Yes, sweetie, it's me," the anchorwoman said soothingly, coming in and kneeling down next to her friend.

Jessica's head suddenly started swiveling wildly from side to side as she brought the knife back up as if to protect Alexandra, too. "Watch out for Leopold. He's around here somewhere."

"They'll find him," Alexandra said.

Several people were running around the hall now with flashlights, searching.

"Her hand is very badly burnt," Alexandra said over her shoulder.

"The medics are on the way up," Will said softly, stooping down.

Jessica's head cocked slightly. Her face was scarcely recognizable. "Will?"

"Yes, I'm here, Jessica." He leaned forward slightly, holding his hand out. "It's me. We're here to take you home."

Jessica dropped the knife with a clatter and brought her good hand over to make contact with his face. "I didn't let him touch me," she told him. And then she passed out.

23

Two helicopters with their searchlights played over the old Buffalo Psychiatric Center and grounds, and the flashing lights of police cars, rescue vehicles, ambulances and fire trucks made the park grounds look surreal.

Norm Kunsa came striding out the back of the central building and trotted over to the command center. "We've got Jessica on the way to the hospital," Agent Cole told him, handing him a cup of coffee. "They're still trying to stabilize the other guy before moving him."

"What's the verdict?"

"Not great, I'm afraid." She kicked her head toward the building. "So what do you think?"

"I think the son of a bitch is still in there somewhere. He blew up part of the eastern stairwell, so who knows where the hell he is now."

"Can't we get a heat reading?"

"Yeah, like about a hundred of them since we've got a hundred people in there looking." He looked up at the towers. "Thank God she's alive."

The radio of the police car next to them crackled. "Seventy-two. Anyone know where Alexandra Waring is? I've got a TV crew over here looking for her."

"TV crew?" Kunsa said, turning around.

"Waring's still inside," an officer said into the radio.

"Oh, great," Kunsa muttered. "The perfect hostage wandering around in there. Where's Rafferty?"

"I have no idea," Cole said. "He grabbed some of the building plans and ran off."

"What? What plans?"

"I'm not sure," she said, pointing to the back seat of their car. "They were from that box the historical society brought over."

"I specifically told him not to do anything without talking to me first!" Kunsa fumed.

"Actually, he did say something about that," Cole admitted. "But he also said there wasn't time to talk you into it."

The dying man still lay on the floor of the parlor, his head held in a contraption resembling a vise. One arm was in a splint, cold packs were on his hand and a double intravenous bag was hanging next to him. Dirk appeared in the doorway and the medics looked up from their position on either side of their patient. "The police surgeon needs to talk to both of you, pronto, down the hall."

The medics looked at each other.

"Let's go, move it!" Dirk barked.

They got up from their knees and moved quickly and obediently down the hall. Just as quickly, Dirk squatted next to the patient, pulled something out of his pocket and directed it toward the dying man.

"I will happily blow your head off if you move," Alexandra said. She walked out of the exercise room, holding a gun aimed at Dirk with both hands.

Dirk jerked back, instinctively trying to hide whatever it was in his hand.

"And if she doesn't," Detective Hepplewhite added, following Alexandra with his own gun drawn as well, "I will."

"What the hell are you guys doing?" Dirk asked, sounding confused.

"On the floor, Lawson," Hepplewhite said. "Facedown. Move it."

The medics came back and stopped in the doorway, looking from Dirk to Hepplewhite to Hepplewhite's gun and the gun in Alexandra's hand.

"On the floor," Hepplewhite repeated.

"Oh, maybe I should just shoot him," Alexandra sighed, moving closer to Lawson. "Come on, Dirk—flinch. Do something."

Lawson cooperated and stretched out on the floor.

"Hands over your head," Hepplewhite said, gingerly reaching into Lawson's coat pocket. "Ah," the detective said, "a stun gun. Going to finish your friend off, were you?"

"Well, if you can't find Alexandra, you can't find her," Cassy Cochran said, speaking into the mouthpiece of her headset in the control room of Studio A. She listened a moment. "I don't care—we've got to break this story." Pause. "We don't have anybody here, either! It's four fifty-six in the morning, so it's you or me." Pause. "Oh, brother, I knew you were going to say that. Okay, okay. *Okay*, I'm going!" She took the headset off and handed it to Kate Benedict, the acting executive producer of DBS News. "Well, here we go, gang. The unions are going to fine us up the wazoo, so let's make it good."

"All right, Dr. Kessler," Kate Benedict said to the elderly doctor sitting at the technical board, "we're going to make it simple and go with just camera two." She looked out to the DBS News set. "What's happening with those lights?" she called into her mouthpiece.

Moments later, the set came ablaze.

"Thank you," Kate said. "Okay, camera two, how are you doing out there?" She was addressing the member of the Nerd Brigade late shift who was in position behind the camera.

"Piece of cake," he said into his headset.

Cassy was walking briskly across the studio.

"Engineering," Kate said, glancing up at the monitors in the wall, "I don't see the opening yet."

"Coming, it's coming," came the reply.

Kate moved over to flick some switches on the audio board and then she glanced into the studio. "Camera two, tell Cassy to get that mike on."

"Two minutes!" someone called.

The door to the control room crashed open. "We're here!" Denny said breathlessly. "I just got the call in my office."

"Okay, Denny, take the audio board, will you? Alicia," Kate directed, "get a headset on and get out there on the floor. You're floor manager—we've got ninety seconds."

"What about Q-TV, do we have the monitor up?" Denny asked.

"There's no script!" Kate said impatiently.

Cassy was sitting in Alexandra's chair on the set and was putting the earpiece in.

"That mike's screwed up," Denny announced, bolting from the audio board.

"Hey," someone cried from engineering. "I've got a satellite feed coming in from Buffalo!"

"What is it?" Kate asked.

"It's from WBFO," came the answer. "And they've got—they've got Alexandra on a remote. Scratch that. They just have a camera on the scene."

"Let me see it," Kate said, looking to the SAT 1 monitor. There was a flicker, snow, and then a shot of the old Buffalo Psychiatric Center.

"*Fantastic*," Kate murmured.

"One minute!" someone called.

"One minute, Cassy," Kate said. "I've got a feed in from Buffalo, so we'll open with the bulletin, cut to you for the intro and then we'll do a voice-over of the scene, got it? Engineering, where is that opening?"

The DBS News logo appeared in VID 1.

"Good, I've got it," Kate said. "Now what about the cart on Jessica? Do you have that?"

The opening frame of a video about Jessica appeared on VID 2.

"Good." Kate shifted over to the audio board. "Cassy, give me a sound check."

"Testing, testing, one, two, three, after twenty-eight years I can't believe I'm doing this," Cassy said.

"Okay, it's working," Kate said. "Get Denny back in here. Camera two, you've got to close in a little. Yeah. That's good."

"Fifteen seconds!"

In the studio, Alicia gave Cassy the sign for fifteen seconds.

"Okay, quiet on the set," Kate commanded. "Ready to roll video one, Dr. Kessler, and bring up the sound, Denny..."

"Nine, eight, seven, six—" went the countdown.

"Roll video one and bring up the sound." When the sound didn't roll, Kate lunged over to push up a different lever than Denny had and the DBS News music and special-bulletin sound effects kicked in. Kate pointed to individual control pads. "Studio sound—satellite—commercial, okay?"

She came back to stand facing the studio. "Give Cassy the *seven, six, five, four*— Take camera two, bring up sound and cue talent."

"Good morning, I'm Cassy Cochran, here with a special

news bulletin from DBS News," she said into the camera with no trace of nervousness. "DBS talk-show host Jessica Wright has been found in an abandoned mental hospital in Buffalo, New York. Jessica Wright is alive and has sustained some injuries but is expected to make a full recovery."

"There's Alexandra!" Denny cried.

On the SAT 1 monitor they could see Alexandra hastily pushing her hair back off her face and accepting a microphone from someone. She pointed to behind her and the camera shifted slightly, the framing getting her as well as the main part of the hospital scene in the background.

"She doesn't have an earphone," engineering reported. "So she's going blind."

"She's giving the thirty-second signal," Kate said. "Cassy," she said into her headset, "we've got a feed from Alexandra coming over the satellite in twenty-five seconds."

"Ladies and gentlemen," Cassy said over the air, "we have a special eyewitness report from Alexandra Waring, who is on the scene where Jessica Wright was found less than one hour ago. To recap, Jessica Wright has been found, she is alive, has sustained injuries, but is expected to make a full recovery. And now to Buffalo, New York."

"Take satellite one," Kate said. "Bring up the sound."

"This is Alexandra Waring reporting for DBS News from the old Buffalo Psychiatric Center in Buffalo, New York," the anchorwoman said, "where within the last hour kidnapped talk-show host Jessica Wright was found and rescued by the combined forces of the FBI and the police departments of New York City, Buffalo and New York State.

"I have seen Jessica Wright with my own eyes and she is physically and mentally fine. She has sustained some burns, but she is receiving medical treatment as we speak and is expected to make a full recovery." Alexandra looked off camera for a moment and then back into the camera. "One kidnapper is still at large, and one kidnapper is in custody—very badly injured. He is in critical condition and is being taken to a local hospital. A third kidnapper is also under arrest here. His name is Dirk Clifford Lawson, the former head of security at the West End Broadcasting Center in New York where 'The Jessica Wright Show' is taped."

In the studio, Cassy's mouth had dropped open.

"With me is Agent Norman Kunsa of the Federal Bureau of Investigation who has a photograph and description of the kidnapper who is still at large," Alexandra continued, stepping aside and pulling Kunsa into the frame with her.

"Ow! *Damn!*" the rookie police officer said, tripping on a tree root and falling hard on his knee.

"You all right?" Will asked, stopping to look back.

"No offense," the cop said, getting back up and slogging onward, "but do you know where the hell you're going?"

"I'm going to make you a hero, that's all you need to know," Will said, pausing to shine his flashlight on the folded piece of blueprint in his hands. Then he pulled another map out of his inside pocket and looked at that.

"And what if you're wrong?" the cop said.

"Then I'll make you a big TV star anyway," Will promised. He flashed his light ahead. "We have to go over this fence."

The obstruction in question was a ten-foot chain-link fence topped with barbwire.

"Yeah, right," the cop said. "This guy's going to crawl through hazardous waste in a chemical plant?"

"It's not a chemical plant," Will said, bringing out a pair

of clippers from his back pocket. "It's an ore transfer station. The ore comes in on the train and then goes out on the barges."

"I don't know what century you're from," the cop said, "but in this one there's no railroad track here and this is a chemical plant."

Will hesitated and then brought the blueprints out again to look at them. Then he looked at the other map. He showed it to the cop and pointed. "What does that look like to you?"

"A storm runoff."

"And on this?" he asked, showing him the blueprints.

"A sewer crossing under a railroad track."

"They must have converted the old system," Will said to himself. "Built a city sewer and used the old hospital sewer as a storm runoff for the park. Here," he said to the cop, "hold this stuff. We've got to get over this fence."

"Naw, it's okay, I'll do it," the cop said, clipping his flashlight to his belt, shoving the clippers under his belt and leaping onto the fence. He scaled it quickly, clipping the strands of barbwire at the top and twisting them back out of the way. Then he went over the other side and jumped down. Will tossed his flashlight over to him and followed, albeit a little slower.

"Okay," he said, panting slightly after jumping down, "we go straight back this way. To the water."

"Hope a night guard doesn't shoot us," the cop whispered, looking around as they slinked their way around the massive tanks.

Will turned, put his finger to his lips and motioned the policeman ahead. They were approaching a wooden pier. Will went around to the side of it, playing the light underneath. "Down there." The policeman scrambled down the embankment and picked his way over the rocks to go under the pier. Will came down to join him, shining his flash-light at the exposed end of a crumbling four-foot pipe. In-side that pipe was a modern three-foot pipe with a metal grille soldered over it. "They must have snaked the new pipe through the old one," Will said, "so they didn't have to dig it all up when they converted it."

"Looks mighty small to me," the cop said.

Will turned around and gestured to a wet slimy rock.

"What?"

"We sit and wait," Will told him.

The cop rolled his eyes, but nodded and turned off his flashlight. He didn't sit, though, but stood, arms crossed over his chest.

"Jessica?" a female voice called softly.

Jessica tried to open her eyes.

"Jessica, you're safe and amazingly well after your or-deal."

She managed to open her eyes and a figure slowly came into focus. It was a woman in a white coat, and she was standing over Jessica.

"That's right, you're in the hospital. You're here in Buf-falo. And you're safe."

There were nurses there, too, and a man in a white coat. And Wendy.

"Hi," her bodyguard said cheerfully, waving at her from the foot of the bed.

"What happened to you?" Jessica wanted to know.

"Oh, nothing, I'll be fine. And so will you be."

"Jessica," the woman in the white coat said, "I'm Dr. Margaret Stephens. I'm what they call a microsurgeon and I specialize in surgery of the hand."

Jessica nodded, closing her eyes. "I did a show once—

about kids. About doctors victimizing the parents of children born with hand defects."

"Yes!" the doctor said, eyes lighting up. "I saw that. It was an excellent show. And so you know what I do."

Jessica opened her eyes. "It's my hand?"

The doctor nodded. "You've got some pretty bad burns. And if we do a skin graft immediately, Jessica, you have a very good chance of eventually regaining the normal use and look of your hand."

Jessica tried to raise her hand to look at it, but it was in bandages and held in place with a strap of some kind.

"We don't have your next of kin here," the doctor continued, "and so we need to get your permission to operate." She went on, slowly explaining the procedure, the length of the operation, and that she would need to take a small graft of skin from Jessica's thigh.

Jessica couldn't really follow things, except that if she let this gal operate on her now, she might only have to have one more operation later, instead of two or three.

She tried to keep her eyes open. "I have to sign something?"

The doctor nodded, turning to get a clipboard from the nurse. "You have to sign here."

Jessica tried to reach for the pen with her right hand, but couldn't move it; she remembered and took the pen in her left. "You fans will say anything to get my autograph," she told the doctor.

Dawn had broken in Buffalo and a slight drizzle was coming down from the overcast skies. Alexandra, wrapped in an orange police poncho, rapped on the window of the car. Kunsa rolled the window down. "Have you seen Will?" the anchorwoman asked.

"I'd sure like to," the agent said, "because I'm going to wring his neck for making off with my plans to this place."

Alexandra's bloodshot eyes moved to scan the grounds of the hospital. "Still nothing, huh?"

Kunsa threw back the remains of the coffee in his cup. "You can sit in here if you want," he said, gesturing with his thumb to the back seat.

"I can't sit still," she said, shivering.

"Listen, Major News Babe," Kunsa said, "you're going to either die of exhaustion or pneumonia, so get in and wait with me. In the meantime, maybe you can think of where the hell Rafferty went with that map."

The water was dripping off the bill of the police officer's cap. He was looking out across the water at a barge making its way across the mouth of the Niagara River. He looked over at Will, who sat, motionless, eyes glued to the drainage pipe.

"They could have caught him by now and we'd never know," the cop said quietly.

Will covered his mouth with his finger.

The cop looked as though he was going to protest, but didn't. He just sighed, rolled his tongue around in his cheek, shifted his weight from one foot to the other and looked back out at the water.

"Nothing," the voice said over the car radio. "We've gone through every ventilation duct, every chimney, every passage—nothing."

Kunsa snapped up the microphone. "Kunsa here. He's got to be in there somewhere. What about the basements? You guys check the furnaces? Hot-water boilers?"

"Yes."

"Ask them about the water tanks in the towers," Alexandra said from the back seat.

"It's the first place we looked," Kunsa said. He pressed the microphone button. "Double-check the water tanks in the towers, will you?"

"Will do."

"What about drainage pipes? Sewers?" Alexandra said. "What's the sewer system like up here?"

"It feeds into the city sewer—" He looked at her. "No, it's too small. And we checked that out right away."

"We've got to think like him," Alexandra stressed. "He's a government guy, he gets plans, has access. Now, what plans would he have?"

"Same as I have right here," he said, lifting the blueprints. "Except that pal of yours took some other plans and I don't know what they were."

Alexandra was resting her chin on the back of the seat, studying the map in Kunsa's hands. "What's that?" she asked, pointing to a mark on the grounds. "There's another one. And another."

Kunsa got on the radio. "Kunsa here. What are these hash marks on the bottom of the map again?"

"We don't know," came the answer.

Kunsa pushed the button. "What do you mean we don't know?"

"We thought they indicated where the sewer system was, but they don't. The sewers run north to south."

Kunsa sighed. Then he pressed the button. "So find out what they are."

There was a pause, a crackle of the radio and then, "How, sir?"

"Dig, you idiot, dig!" Kunsa yelled, dropping the microphone on the seat in disgust and opening his car door.

Seagulls screeched as they circled over the water. The tide was rising, lapping closer and closer to the men. Will's head had fallen forward to rest on his knees; the cop was listening to the sounds of cars in the distance. He was sitting down now too, on a rock to the side of the drainage pipe.

The cop's eyes narrowed. His eyes looked around, and then he turned his head toward the drainpipe.

He swallowed, then slowly reached down to slide his hand onto his gun. As he pulled it out of its holster, Will's head jerked up with a start, making the cop quickly flash his left hand as a warning to be quiet. He pointed to the pipe.

The seconds ticked by. The seagulls screamed. The water lapped. The traffic noises of Buffalo continued.

There was a metallic clank.

Silence.

Then another.

They saw the grate ease forward out of the inner pipe, a filthy hand grasping the grille in the center. And drop it.

Seconds went by.

One hand appeared on the edge of the pipe. Then another. And then Leopold's head cautiously began to emerge.

"Here, let me help you," Will said, jumping up to grab his wrist.

"*Noooooooo!*" His scream was like a girl's.

The cop had taken hold of Leopold's other wrist and the two pulled him out onto the rocks where he started fighting and flopping around like a fish. The cop finally pushed the small of Leopold's back down flat with a thrust of his foot, reached down to pull the knife out of Leopold's belt and toss it safely away. Then he cuffed him and began reading him his rights.

Leopold struggled against the handcuffs, screaming with rage.

V

Fallout

24

⇒ ⇐

"Hi," Alexandra said, walking into Cassy's office at West End.

"You're back!" the network president cried, jumping up and coming around her desk to give Alexandra a huge hug, and then holding her at arm's length. "You look positively dreadful."

"Yeah, well, you're not exactly fresh flowers, yourself, my friend," Alexandra said, laughing, and giving Cassy's arms a squeeze. "I just wanted to let you know I'm here. I'm going to crash in my dressing room for a couple of hours."

"You should go home, you haven't slept in days."

"It's better I work tonight. Besides, we've got such a big story! Will's already got the gang starting on a special." She smiled. "We're kind of hoping you could clear Thursday night's slate."

"Three hours?" Cassy's eyes were large. "You think we've got enough?"

"We've got fantastic stuff coming in," the anchorwoman said, eyes shining. "Denny and Alicia are pulling great clips on Jessica, and Denny's got tapes from the Arizona days, and Phoenix and Buffalo are working on Plattener's history. I've got Craig researching Dirk down in D.C. with the Bureau, and WST is covering his years here in the New York area—I've got John in Albany on the energy commission, we've got tons of footage of the vans and the trucks and that old mental hospital, and I've got a line on who the dying guy is," she finished, taking a breath.

"Get this," she resumed. "Word is, the guy's fingerprints came up in the system as an old CIA operative. Can you believe it?"

"Cassy?" Chi Chi interrupted, poking her head around the door. "Sorry, but it's Will Rafferty calling from the hospital in Buffalo."

"William Rafferty!" Cassy said gaily into the speaker. "I've got you on the speakerphone. Alexandra just blew in."

"Hi, Will!" the anchorwoman called.

"Hi! I was just calling to let you know that Jessica's out of surgery and the doctor said everything went as well as it possibly could."

"Oh, thank heavens," Cassy said.

"It was pretty funny, though," Will continued, "because they gave her some shots before they brought her to the operating room—Valium and Demerol or something."

"And morphine, probably," Alexandra said. "That's what they gave me when they did my shoulder."

"Well, whatever it was, it was supposed to knock her out," Will said. "But Jessica got high as a kite and was— what was that Alan Greenspan phrase?"

"Irrational exuberance?" Alexandra asked.

"That's what she had," Will said, laughing. "So when they wheeled her to the operating room, instead of dozing she was singing and telling jokes."

They laughed.

And then Alexandra asked, "What's the story on Lawson, what are they doing with him?"

"They've already moved him," Will reported. "Downstate somewhere. I can't find Kunsa or Cole and no one's talking, but they've probably moved him under the federal courthouse in Manhattan, to the holding pens."

"The charges are federal?" Cassy asked, surprised.

"If we're right," Will explained, "and Lawson was trying to kill Jessica's kidnapper to prevent him from implicating Lawson's part in the kidnapping, the feds get the case."

"But it all happened in New York State," Cassy said. "I don't understand how the charges can be federal."

"When someone's part of a kidnapping, he's implicated in everything that follows. So when Plattener took Jessica over the state line to make that stop in Salt Springs, it became an interstate crime and so the feds get it."

"What about Plattener?" Alexandra wanted to know.

"He's here, somewhere, being treated for whatever the hell's wrong with him."

"They don't have him in the same hospital as Jessica, do they?" Cassy said, horrified.

"No! Sorry. And Slim's arrived and is watching over Jessica with Wendy. I meant that Plattener's still in Buffalo somewhere. As to where he goes from here, no one's saying. They've got that woman's body up here, from the storage locker, and then there's Bea's murder down there—Word is the prosecutors in both cities are going for the death penalty, and if that's the case, the feds won't even pursue the kidnapping charges."

"Go to a hotel, Will, and get some rest," Cassy told him. "Jessica's going to be out of it until tomorrow."

"I'll just wait until she comes up from the recovery room, then I'll go. I am fairly wrecked." Pause. "Listen, I'm glad you're there, Alexandra. I know you were counting on me to put the special together, but I'm afraid I really need some time off."

"Take a couple of days," Alexandra said quickly. "That's okay."

He hesitated. "No. It's going to have to be more than a couple of days."

"I see," Alexandra said faintly.

"I had a talk with the FBI psychiatrist up here and she seems to think Jessica's going to have an awful lot to deal with. And I want to be there for her." He paused again. "I think I need to get her away from all of this for a while."

"Well, sure," Alexandra said, sounding agreeable in voice but looking decidedly stricken.

"We'll find someone to pinch-hit," Cassy said. "Don't worry."

"Oh, great, thanks, Cass," Will said, sounding relieved. "Lex, I'm sorry, but—"

"No," the anchorwoman said quickly. "You should be with her—or I should. One of us should be and I'm just glad you're there now."

After they got off the phone with Will, Cassy turned to Alexandra.

"What?" the anchorwoman said irritably, getting up.

"You need some rest."

"I need to get started on this special," Alexandra said, going to the door.

"Have Kate substitute for Will."

"Kate's not Will, nobody is," Alexandra said, opening the door. Then she stopped, closed it again and turned around. "I'm sorry. It's been very stressful. And this is a really important special. It could be unbelievably good and I'm used to counting on Will."

"Then count on me," Cassy said, going over to her chair to pick up her jacket. "I'll get Langley to cover for me and I'll produce your special. What are you looking at? Think I've lost my touch?"

Alexandra looked startled. "No." She blinked. And then shrugged. "Well, okay, come on, we've got work to do."

"He's got a slight concussion and a broken cheekbone," the doctor reported. "A bunch of bumps and bruises, but he'll be okay."

"He doesn't look okay," one cop said dubiously, looking at James Plattener, who was sitting on the end of the examination table in a paper gown, eyes staring vacantly ahead. He had red wounds and purple marks all over his pale body, but his bare legs were nonetheless pressed modestly together and his hands were folded neatly on his lap.

"So, Dirk, would you care to explain these?" Agent Kunsa asked the former FBI agent in the interrogation room, throwing a stapled bunch of papers down on the table. They were reduced photocopies of detailed building plans.

Dirk leaned over to look and shrugged as he made eye contact with his lawyer. "I don't know what those are."

"They're copies of the blueprints for Rockefeller Center," Norm told him.

"So?"

"So you worked with these same plans as an active agent when President Clinton visited Rockefeller Center."

Dirk shrugged again. "I don't remember."

"You personally gave them to the Secret Service to plan security at that event."

"I still don't remember."

"As you can see on this set of the plans," Kunsa continued, pointing, "the maintenance passageways are all carefully detailed."

"If you say so," Dirk said, yawning.

"But the plans you gave out to security for Jessica Wright's book party at Rockefeller Center did not include all of the maintenance passageways. Someone had blanked part of them out."

"You'll have to ask the NYPD about that."

"We did. The copy they gave you had all the passageways marked on it."

"I wouldn't know about that," Dirk said.

"What about this man?" Norm said, sliding a photograph onto the table. It was a head shot of Jessica's kidnapper, the man she had called Hurt Guy. "What is his name?"

"I have no idea," Dirk said, sliding it back across the table.

"That's funny, since you know him very well," Norm said.

"I told you, I have no idea who he is," Dirk said.

"Makes me want to give him a swift kick in the teeth," Detective Hepplewhite whispered to Agent Cole from behind the observation glass of the interrogation room. He was whispering because there were others in the room with them.

"He's been like this from the beginning," Cole whispered back. "And it doesn't look as though Denton's going to make it. And when he dies, so will the link between Lawson and the kidnapping."

Hepplewhite didn't say anything, but stared stonily ahead into the interrogation room.

"You know that we've got you, Dirk," Norm Kunsa was saying, "bang to rights for attempted murder."

"Oh?" Dirk said. "Who is it I am supposed to have attempted to murder?"

"This man," Norm said, pointing to the picture.

"But I told you, I've never seen him before."

"Oh, you've seen him before," Norm said, starting to pace. "In fact, I introduced you to him."

Dirk Lawson looked at Kunsa with the first spark of interest.

Norm took a turn around the room before continuing. "I personally introduced you to this man when you were active with the bureau."

"That's not true," Dirk said.

Norm walked on. "How do you know it's not true?"

"I know because I've never met this man."

"And I'm telling you that you have, Dirk," Norm said, turning to him, "because I personally introduced you to him. He was a CIA operative named Calvin Denton who collaborated with us on the Gedonia drug bust in Miami in 1989."

Dirk looked at his lawyer. "He's making this up."

"Fine, whatever makes you comfortable to think, Dirk," Norm said, resuming his stroll. "I just wanted you to know what I will be testifying to at your trial."

"Then you'll go to jail for perjury," Dirk told him.

"No," Kunsa said. "I don't think I will."

"Did Kunsa introduce them?" Hepplewhite whispered.

Agent Cole didn't answer.

Hepplewhite looked back into the interrogation room. "Why do I get the distinct feeling he's going to get off?"

"Maybe because he set everything up in preparation for this day should it ever arrive," Agent Cole said, sounding bone-tired.

"But we know he had to be in on it," Hepplewhite said. "There's got to be proof somewhere."

"He's a trained agent," Cole said. "He knows everything there is to know about proof and how to get rid of it."

"All right, Dirk," Agent Kunsa said, "let's go back to your attempt to murder Calvin Denton while he lay dying."

Lawson looked bored.

"I've got two excellent eyewitnesses—a highly decorated New York City detective and one of the most revered news anchors in America—who saw you pull out a stun gun, set it on the highest charge and move in to shock Denton with it."

Lawson sighed, sounding put out. "How many times do I have to tell you? I found the stun gun in the mental hospital and had it in my pocket. When I kneeled down to see what the injured man could tell me about the perp's whereabouts, I pulled it out in case the perp was faking and he tried to attack me. If it was set for the highest charge, it was set on that before I found it."

"Why didn't you pull out your gun?"

"I didn't have a gun. I couldn't pack one when I had to fly and you never issued me one in Buffalo."

"Why did you pick up the stun gun? You know not to touch the evidence."

"Given the fact we were in a hostage situation with a known murderer, it was reasonable to annex any weapon of the perp's. Which brings me to a question," he said, following Norm's stroll around the room with his eyes. "What the hell was Waring doing packing a nine millimeter?"

"She's licensed to carry," Kunsa told him. "She's got a permit."

"She always made out to me she was very antigun," Lawson mused.

Kunsa turned to smile. "A very wise policy, don't you think? Given the fact you turned out to be such a fucking scumbag lowlife?"

Trying to sound as though he was attempting to humor him, Dirk said, "I didn't do anything, Norm. You're way off base."

"Too bad Hepplewhite didn't let Alexandra just blow you away," Kunsa sighed, circling the table. "So what were you going to do afterward, Dirk? If you had used the stun gun and killed Denton? What were you going to do when the autopsy showed that he had seven broken ribs, a critical concussion, cerebral hemorrhage, broken wrist, smashed kneecap, massive internal injuries and a blood pressure next to dead? How were you going to explain the danger he presented you—danger that required pumping as many electrical volts into him as you could?"

Lawson just shook his head, as if disgusted. "This is going to mean your career, Norm. You can't go around arresting innocent people. Remember Richard Jewel and the Atlanta bombing."

"This is getting us nowhere fast," Hepplewhite muttered, turning from the window abruptly.

Agent Cole moved close to him. "So do you get a crack at Plattener?"

"That's what they tell me, for the Bea Blakely murder."

"Where are you going to put him?"

"Riker's for now," Hepplewhite said. He looked at his watch. "I've got to get going. Listen," he said, moving even closer, "Rafferty's bringing Jessica back to New York in a few days. If this—" he tossed his head in the direction of the interrogation room "—continues, I think we should pay her a visit and talk to her about Denton. What do you say?"

"I say Norm will have a fit. We're supposed to leave her alone."

"And I think we need to talk to her about Denton. Just you and me—*quietly*. What do you say?"

"I say okay," she replied.

25

"Oh, that's beautiful," Jessica murmured as she came out of her hospital bathroom, spotting the clay pot of white and purple African violets on the windowsill. She was showered and dressed, her arm bandaged and in a sling, and now all they needed was for the hospital staff to bring a wheelchair so she could check out. Her head and face had dreadful bruises on it, and except for a little patch of hair on the back of her scalp and less than a quarter of one eyebrow, she was bald, and so she had a bandanna tied over her head. At first it had taken a great deal of coaxing to allow Will to see her like this ("Even Demi Moore had eyebrows in *G.I. Jane*," she had complained to Alexandra over the phone. "I look a lot more like Uncle Fester after being mugged."), but she was glad she had agreed to see him. The way he had been looking at her ever since told her everything she had needed to know. He did love her, even like this.

"Who are those from?" she asked, referring to the flowering plants. "And how is it I am so lucky as to see them?"

Blanket policy at DBS was that flowers sent to West End from fans were automatically redistributed to area hospitals and nursing homes. As a result, the same DBS policy had gone into effect here in Buffalo and Jessica hadn't seen any of the flowers well-wishers had sent, although she had heard the oohs and aahs up and down the hall from everybody else on the floor who had become their recipients.

"They're from my mom," Will said a little sheepishly.

"Your mother?" Jessica exclaimed, delighted. "Well

then, I'm taking these home!" She walked over to the windowsill and lightly traced the rim of the low clay pot with her left hand. Then she turned around. "Do you really think she'll like me?"

He had to laugh. "Oh, gosh, yes."

"Even after she reads my book?" Jessica winced. "I think if I were a guy's mother, I'm not sure I'd want my son to be involved with a woman who admits to having had so many—" She closed one eye. *"Experiences?"*

"Oh, Jessica," he sighed, coming over to her. "Sit down, darling," he said, quietly, sitting on the corner of the bed and pulling her next to him. "I need to talk to you for a minute."

She waited as Will looked down for a moment, scratching his head. Then he took her left hand in his and looked up. "My father scarcely ever drew a sober breath in all the years I knew him. And yet my mother loved that man like— Well, she loved him like no man who acted the way he did ever deserved. He destroyed my mother's life."

"Not completely," Jessica disagreed. "Because she has you—and your sisters and your brother. You've all turned out so well. And you love each other."

"What I mean is," he started again, choosing his words with care, "she fell in love with a young man and married him. And I don't have to tell you how a lot of our parents took their vows in a much more sacred way than most people do today."

She nodded.

"She was going to stand by him in sickness and in health," he continued, "and after four kids in six years, I don't think she had much choice *but* to stay with him, but by then he had really turned into a son of a bitch. I mean, Jessica, this guy was the meanest drunk. And every once in a while he'd try to go on the wagon and Mom would get so excited and so happy and full of plans and then—" Will shrugged. "You know, then one night, he'd come staggering in and she'd cry and he'd beat the hell out of me because I'd block his way when he tried to take a swing at Mom and..." He shook his head, voice trailing off.

After a moment, he continued. "And you know? I think the thing that bothered me the most was that Mom was from such a good, hardworking family. They weren't rich, but they were comfortable, stable, never really wanted for anything. And then with Dad, she was thrown into the worst kind of poverty. The kind where even if there was money, a lot of it never made it home. Like she knew he had just thrown away the money that would have fed us for the week, or paid the rent, or might have eased things in some way. Like, God forbid, my mother ever had a dime to spend on herself." He looked away, sighing, "Oh, man," in a faltering voice.

Jessica swallowed.

Will brought his eyes back to her. They were moist. "I called my mom while you were missing. I was really upset. But it wasn't just being scared to death about where you were and if you were all right. Jessica—back at West End, they were raking through your past. Everybody was going over your ex-lovers and, well, one-night stands. They were trying to track all these guys down."

Jessica closed her eyes. "I didn't even think of that."

"No reason why you should!" he told her. "It's the past."

The way he insisted that it was the *past* made Jessica know how very much it must be torturing him in the present. He was human. The authorities had probably been pretty thorough, which meant—

Which meant an awful lot of embarrassing and humiliating stories, not to mention downright sick behavior, some of which she had scarcely hinted at in her autobiography because her editor had feared it would alienate readers.

Jessica opened her eyes. "So you called your mother because you realized you couldn't go through with this. That you had rushed into this relationship with me and then discovered you couldn't deal with my past. You couldn't deal with how many men I had slept with."

He looked at her for a long moment, his expression caught somewhere between pain and concern.

"It's all right, Will," she murmured, dropping her eyes. "I can understand that. And I think we should take a step back, particularly now. I mean, you've gone from being a boyfriend to a nursemaid for an invalid, and now you not only have my past to deal with, you've got this mess to wade through. And there's no reason for you to do it."

He shook his head. "You're so wrong," he whispered. He reached over to pull her chin up so she would look at him again. "Jessica, I admit it—I freaked out at one point, because this smarmy son of a bitch from the Darenbrook papers sat there and started saying all this crap—"

She winced. "How much of it has he written?"

"Oh, none," Will said quickly. "Alexandra's got something on him and so he doesn't dare."

Jessica laughed. "Good ol' Alexandra Eyes, my gun-toting, blackmailing friend."

He laughed a little, too. And then he rubbed his eyes, groaning. "Oh, it was bad, Jessica." He dropped his hand. "But Alexandra and I had a long talk about things, and she started talking about Georgiana's past and stuff like that. And then it passed. Because it wasn't real. I mean, yes, those things happened, but to look at the person you are today, and then to look back at the woman who was so ill that she thought drinking was the only thing that was holding her life together—"

He paused, shaking his head.

"I mean, Jessica—God doesn't make them any better than you. And what happened was, after this sort of emotional tantrum I had that one evening, I was so scared that I was going to lose you. It was like I was working through all these imagined difficulties in our relationship, but you weren't there to participate. I can't explain it really, other than the horror started to settle in that I might not ever see you again. That I knew how much I loved you, Jessica, and how, for the first time in my life I knew with all my heart I wanted to settle down and make a home, make a family, our house, our home—I mean, even if it just had a cat, it would be our home. Do you know what I mean?"

Tears were streaming down her face and she nodded.

"And I didn't know what to do! I'd never felt this way. I'd never felt so helpless. And I knew I had never wanted anything more in my life than to have the chance to make a life with you."

She was smiling through her tears; she wiped her eyes with her good hand.

"So I called Mom and I just told her the whole thing, from beginning to end. I'm sorry if that's bad—I mean, talking about you and stuff."

"No, families are supposed to talk," Jessica said, sniffing. "It's only mine that doesn't. So what did your mom say?"

"She was quiet for a long time, just sitting there, listening to me. And then when I finally finished, I realized she was crying on the other end of the phone." He paused, swallowing. "I said, 'Mom, what are you crying about?' And she said, 'I'm crying because my little boy has finally grown up and knows his own mind.'"

Will's eyes were a mess of tears now. "She said she never

had to worry about me anymore, and that she had worried about me for years and years because she knew there was a part of me that would never let me get past what I saw go on between her and my father, and she thought I might not ever let myself love anyone fully." He let out a big breath, trying to regain control. He looked at Jessica and took another breath. "She says only someone like you, who's been through what you have, and who's come out on the other side, could ever really understand someone like me— where I'm coming from." He paused. "Do you think that's true?"

She smiled. "I don't know. But I do know I love you, Will Rafferty, and I know that we've got a very complicated road in front of us."

"But it doesn't have to be."

She blinked. "You think?"

"I know," he whispered, moving forward to hold her. "And I think I know what we need to do."

Outside, in the hall, Wendy and Slim looked at each other. "Are you sure you got what Kunsa said right?" Wendy whispered.

"Yeah. He said to keep an eye on him."

Wendy shook her head. "He's nuts."

"For her sake," he muttered, straightening his tie as an attendant approached the room with a wheelchair, "I hope to God you're right."

26

"No," Cassy Cochran said, sounding tired. "As a matter of fact, the investigation is *not* going well. The evidence against Dirk is only circumstantial, the kidnapper's dying and that murderous creep is in some kind of psychotic trance."

The DBS programming director asked, "How's Jessica taking it?"

"She doesn't know yet, thank God. She's got enough to cope with."

Cassy looked up as Langley Peterson arrived in the conference room, nodded to her and took his seat at the other end of the table. Also present were Denny Ladler, Alicia Washington and the executives in charge of advertising, sales, publicity and promotion, public relations and affiliate relations.

"I've called this meeting today," Cassy began, "to discuss the situation with 'The Jessica Wright Show.' I've had some very long talks with Jessica and also with her agent, and I have just received her final word this afternoon."

Everyone held their breath.

Cassy looked down at the table. "She's not coming back."

"That's it, we're finished," the advertising-sales executive groaned, collapsing on the table.

Alicia's head had dropped forward into her hand, while Denny only looked sadly on.

"I can't believe it," Langley said, blinking several times. He turned to Denny. "Did you know about this?"

He shook his head. "No. I suspected, but—" He shook his head again.

"Denny, Alicia," Cassy said. "She wanted to tell you herself but I wouldn't let her. She's not very strong right now."

Denny waved it off. "I know."

"We've got the number-one prime-time rating sitting there waiting for us with her first appearance back on the air," the affiliate-relations manager said, "and she won't come back. Shit," he added, dropping his hand onto the table with a loud thump.

"What we've got to do," Cassy said, "is select a new host and go with her or him a.s.a.p. Turn the whole publicity focus of the kidnapping into a means of introducing our new host."

"If it's anyone other than Oprah," the ad executive said, "then they'll just be jumping on in time to sink with the whole network."

"DBS does not depend on the success of one show," Langley said.

"Yeah, you keep saying that to us, Langley," the sales executive retorted, "but the reality is, it does. Everything hinges on Jessica. We've known that since the first week we went on the air. She's got the ratings, she's got the international following, and our sponsors support the rest of our lineup only because she continually delivers in her time period. Once in a while Alexandra pulls something out of a hat, but it's too little and too far apart. The long and the short of it is," he concluded, sweeping his hands out, "if we don't have Jessica and her ratings, we don't have a vehicle that the advertisers want."

Silence.

"I can't believe Jessica's just going to walk out on us," the publicity manager finally said.

"Oh, you think she owes us something?" Alicia asked him. "After all we've done for her? Like letting her get stalked, kidnapped, beaten and nearly killed?"

"That's enough, Alicia," Cassy said.

"No, it's not enough, Cassy," Alicia shot back. "These jackasses—" she gestured to the department heads "—don't care about Jessica. They never did. All they've ever cared about is getting their rear end up the next rung of the ladder, and if they don't do it here, they'll just go somewhere else. All talent's interchangeable to them. They don't care whether Jessica lives or dies." She stood up. "You saw them when she was kidnapped—they were ecstatic!" She dropped her arm. "Frankly, I'm glad Jessica's not coming back. She deserves to do something with her life other than supporting these shitheads in the manner to which they've become accustomed."

And with that, Alicia swept out of the room.

After a moment, Affiliate Relations said, "Maybe *she* should be our new host."

"No," Sales said, shaking his head. "There's Oprah and Yolanda and Gayle King already—"

"Oh, shut up!" Cassy said suddenly, losing all patience. She looked at Sales. "And she's right, you know. You really are— Something else." She picked up her pen. "I have to admit, though," she added more quietly, tapping her pen on the table, "I think Alicia's got possibilities myself. But I don't think she's ready."

"She needs to get more comfortable with the camera," Denny spoke up. "But I think she'd be very good in a couple of years. Jessica's been working with her, trying to pull her on stage more and more."

"And don't you ever, *ever*," Cassy suddenly added, pointing her pen back at the sales executive, "start spouting that *crap*."

"I didn't say anything bad!" he protested. "I was just pointing out that there are already a lot of black women—"

Cassy leaned forward and said through her teeth, *"Shut up."*

He opened his mouth, but thought better of it and closed it.

"Cassy," Langley said quietly.

She sat back in her chair, looking back down the table.

"Has Jessica really given her final word?"

"I'm afraid so."

"If we'd been through what Jessica's been through," Denny said, "we'd never want to be in the public eye again, either."

"You mean," the affiliate-relations executive said in astonishment, "she's quitting the business altogether? I thought she was just trying to get out of her contract to get a better deal."

Denny ignored the comment to address Cassy. "Is there any possibility that Alexandra might want to take the show?"

"What?" the publicist said.

"Denny," Langley said, leaning forward, "do you really think, that after all these years of building up the news division, Alexandra's going to want to host a talk show?"

"She might," Denny said. "And it doesn't have to be a talk show per se. Maybe a magazine show. Look at the ratings, all the magazine shows are there—'Primetime,' '20/20.'"

"We can't do a magazine show every night," Cassy said slowly. "But you know, it could just work. Alexandra, I mean. Her TV-Q's off the charts."

"Come on, Cassy," Langley said. "She'll never do it."

"No, Langley, it's not impossible," Cassy said. "Alexandra just might be interested in having a life someday, and anchoring the news division is never going to allow that. At any rate, all she can do is say no, and we might as well ask her before we go to the outside to find someone else."

"But even if she wanted to do it," Langley said, "is Alexandra *warm* enough for a talk show? That steel-magnolia thing of hers works in news, but—"

"She'll never have the body Jessica does, that's for sure," the sales executive said under his breath.

Cassy leaned forward over the table, holding her forefinger close to her thumb. "You are this far from being fired. So you sit up in your chair and pretend like you're a man and say something constructive."

"Maybe it would work with Alexandra doing the show," the sales executive said without drawing a breath, and Cassy looked as though she was going to throw something at him.

"The idea of DBS without Jessica, though," Langley said, shaking his head.

"And while we're talking about it," Cassy added, "I might as well tell you, it looks like we're losing Will Rafferty, as well."

"What?" Langley cried.

Cassy nodded. "He's taking her to Europe for a while."

"What's going on in here?" Georgiana Hamilton-Ayres asked from the doorway. She looked in at Alexandra, who was in her bathrobe, lying on her back on the living-room couch. Georgiana glanced at the clock. "Don't you need to get to West End?"

"Good question," the anchorwoman said vaguely.

Georgiana came in to sit beside her on the couch. Quietly, "What's going on?"

"I'm just thinking about how fast my life's passing."

"Hmm," Georgiana murmured, picking Alexandra's hand up to kiss it.

"And I'm wondering what I'm doing with my life," Alexandra finished.

This took the actress by surprise. "Why? What else do you think you should be doing?"

"Well, for a start," Alexandra said, pulling Georgiana's hand up in front of her and touching the band of diamonds there, "spending more time with you."

"Well, that's a relief," Georgiana said, smiling. "I thought you were going to say 'Make a serious play for Harrison Ford' or something."

"I hate us being bicoastal," Alexandra said suddenly, looking at her. "I was thinking how maybe I could move to California. And buy a ranch, maybe in Napa."

Georgiana looked a little confused.

"I was thinking how nice it would be to start a family."

"Oh," the actress said.

"Well, we're not getting any younger," Alexandra said. "And the one thing I know for sure is that if I keep doing what I'm doing, the rest of it's going to be impossible." She paused, looking back down at Georgiana's ring. "And I was thinking that if I quit, then I could have a child. And maybe you could have a child, and I could stay home and raise them. Or adopt some children, why not? We have plenty of money."

Georgiana threw her head back and laughed. "I'm sorry, darling, but the idea of you being content at home on the farm with a slew of children is rather hard to imagine."

"Why?" Alexandra protested, rising up on one elbow. "I'd run the farm—a proper farm, though, not like in New Jersey, a real farm—"

"I see," Georgiana said. "You'll strap the baby to your chest and go out in the fields..."

"Why not?"

Georgiana kissed her forehead. "Because, Alexandra, somehow it's just not you. I know you like to imagine that it could be."

"It's my heritage," Alexandra pointed out.

"And darling, my heritage is to try and put Mary Queen of Scots on the throne of England, but I'm hardly equipped to do that today."

Alexandra's large blue-gray eyes were studying her. "Do you really love me?"

"Oh, what a question!"

"But I mean, do you? Do you really think we'll be together? Or one day will you just decide that New York's too far and you won't come this time, and then you'll meet someone else who will make a home for you, who will be with you wherever you are—"

"Alexandra, we do have a home together."

"We have four at last count, Georgiana," Alexandra said, correcting her. "And two of them are right here in this city, which is exactly my point. You're there, I'm here, and somewhere in the shadows we live."

"We have the farm," Georgiana said. "And it's been wonderful."

Alexandra sighed, shaking her head. "It's just not going to be the same anymore."

The actress studied her face. "Because Jessica's leaving."

Tears welled up in the anchorwoman's eyes. "Of course it's because Jessica's leaving! It's like my whole family's leaving. The idea of trying to carry on without Will and Jessica—" She searched for the words. "I just don't think I'm going to want to do it anymore, Georgiana. It won't be fun, it won't be—it won't be *ours* anymore. We built DBS together. And now there's not going to be anybody to share it with."

"There's Cassy."

"But that's just it, Georgiana," the anchorwoman said miserably, turning those eyes on her. "I don't think Cassy wants to go on, either."

"Cordelia sends her love," Jackson told Cassy, walking into the den of their apartment after ending a phone call with his sister.

"How's Little El doing?" she asked, referring to his ailing older brother.

"He's about the same." Jackson sighed, and sat down heavily on the couch next to his wife. "I think I better go down. Cordie sounds exhausted."

"I'd go with you, Jack, but—"

"No, I know, there's no reason for you to have to."

Cassy sighed, put her pencil down and slipped off her glasses. Then she leaned forward to dump the load of papers in her lap on the coffee table. "I should be with you in Hilleanderville. My son calls me from Chicago to tell me he's met the girl he wants to marry and I don't even have time to meet her. You and I haven't had more than two hours alone together for the last six months. What's wrong with this picture, Jack?"

"It's not as if we haven't had a little excitement lately."

"And now the excitement's over and I still don't have time to have a life."

"I thought you said Henry was going to bring his girl here this weekend."

"He is, but that's not the point."

"Cassy," Jackson said, putting his arm around her, "Little El's going to hang on for a while. I really don't need you there with me now. Later, but not now. And you're going to meet Henry's girl this weekend. So, sweetheart, what is it really?"

She closed her eyes, letting her head fall on his shoulder. "I'm just so tired, Jack. And nothing's turned out the way it's supposed to."

"You mean about Jessica."

"I mean about hiring Dirk who arranged to have my talent kidnapped—only they can't prove it. I mean this psycho stalker-murderer sitting around in a cell somewhere, not talking, getting his three squares. Jessica's been maimed and is suffering some kind of psychological trauma, our star news anchor is morosely depressed and is on the verge of quitting, my executive news producer won't come back to work, our advertisers are deserting the network and my son wants to get married and I can't deal with it because the last time I had a breather from work he was six years old!"

Silence.

"Is that all?" her husband asked with an understanding smile.

"Oh, Jack. I hate it. I've lost all sense of hope. Or faith that any of this can be sorted out." She looked up at him. "And I'm getting old, Jack. I don't have the energy I used to."

"That makes two of us, but the expression is 'getting older,' not old." He kissed her on the nose. "You don't have to continue, you know."

"That's what scares me," she murmured. "For the first time in my life, I feel sorely tempted to bag the whole thing. I just don't see it anymore. Why I'm doing this." She shrugged. "It's as if after all these years suddenly the wind is gone and I can't remember what the sails were for in the first place or why it was so important to have them. And where the hell it was we were going after we got them up."

"It's hard, babe. There's no doubt about it. Creepin'

crickets, Jessica built the network with you, Cass. And so did Will. It's a tremendous loss."

Cassy closed her eyes again. "It's as though all of our mortality is staring us in the face."

"I know," he murmured. "Langley's feeling it, too."

She opened her eyes. "Is he?"

Jackson nodded. "Belinda says he was up all last night talking about taking early retirement and running a logging camp."

"A what?" Cassy asked, having to laugh.

"I know." Jack laughed. "But you know Belinda, she's all for it. They're going to home-school the kids out in the woods and she's going to write a weekly column about it for *HG* and Lang's going to grow a beard."

Cassy chuckled, nestling in against her husband's chest. After a while, though, her smile died. "The thing is, Jack," she said quietly, "right now, it sounds like the right thing to do."

27

"Really, I'm fine," Jessica insisted to Slim. "You're my bodyguard, not my nurse. Just screen the calls, will you? I don't think I can take the guilt by talking with anyone from West End right now."

"But you've got to eat," the big guy insisted, pushing the bowl of soup on the tray toward her again.

Jessica was sitting up in her own bed in her own apartment, lying back against the pillows, her bandaged hand and arm elevated slightly on a traction gizmo attached to her headboard. Her head and face still had the bruising on them, but a friend of Georgiana's had fitted her with a wig that, along with some eyebrow pencil, made her look something like her old self.

"Thank you, Slim," Jessica said, "but Will will help me, I promise."

Slim put his hands on his hips and looked to Will. "She has to eat to get her strength back."

"You're absolutely right," Will said with a straight face, pulling a chair up to the side of Jessica's bed. "And we'll get right to it."

As soon as Slim left the room, Jessica peered into the bowl, frowning. "What is that glop?"

"It's okra jumbo," Will reported, taking the soupspoon into his hand and stirring it around.

"Big okra soup? What the hell is big okra soup?" Jessica complained. "It's not that slimy stuff, is it?"

"Just taste it, Jess," Will said quietly, holding his left

hand under the spoon as he raised it to her mouth. "Please. A little taste."

Jessica's frown deepened and then she opened her mouth a little, looking very apprehensive. She tasted. And closed her eyes. "It *is* that slimy stuff." Her eyes opened. "But it's not bad."

"That's good, my love," Will murmured, "because Slim's mother made it for you."

"Oh," she said softly, taking the spoon from him and obediently continuing to eat.

"And now the really good part," Will continued, pushing a plate closer to the bowl. "Some garlic bread."

"Mmm," she said, after taking a bite. "You know," she said after swallowing, "even my teeth hurt. Why do you suppose that is?"

"Your teeth hurt because you grind your teeth at night and don't wear your bite guard."

She squinted at him. "You know far too much about me."

"Eat," he directed.

Out in the foyer the house telephone rang and Slim went to answer it. Then he came into the bedroom. "Detective Hepplewhite and Agent Cole are downstairs and wondered if they can come up to visit."

Jessica said yes at the same time Will said no.

"They're not supposed to talk to you until next week," Slim reminded her.

"And they wouldn't be here unless it was important," Jessica said. "Will," she said, pleading her case, "how am I going to get better unless I know what's going on?"

"Darling, you heard what the doctor said. You've had surgery, you're still in some shock from the ordeal, you're running on adrenaline and you have to slow down."

"Collapse, you mean, and forget it's not happening," Jessica said. "Tell them to get up here."

Slim looked to Will. "I suppose," Will said reluctantly.

"Look, sweetheart," Jessica said, taking his hand with her left. "I appreciate you trying to protect me, and taking care of me, but I'm not very good at taking orders from anyone. Not even you."

"Hint taken," he said, lowering his eyes.

Quietly, "I've hurt your feelings."

He looked up and saw Jessica's eyes almost instantly fill with tears. "Oh, Will, I wouldn't hurt your feelings for anything. You've been so wonderful, I'm so sorry."

"*You're* sorry? Jessica, do you know what you've been through? You don't, not really, I know it really hasn't sunk in yet. And Jessica, I'd do anything for you— So hurt my feelings—not that you did—break my arm, stomp on my face, I don't care, just let me help you."

"I'm just not good at being vulnerable."

"Who is? And I know I'm not much of a nurse—I don't know many guys who are, frankly, but I want to do *something* for you. And if I'm playing mother hen, I apologize, but—"

"You tracked me down and saved me! For God's sake, what more can you do?" She smiled tenderly. "You're such a funny guy sometimes."

"I don't want anything more to happen to you, that's all," he said softly, dropping his head in her lap and putting his arms around her. "I don't want to lose you."

"But you won't," she murmured, stroking his hair. "You won't."

Standing in the doorway, Slim cleared his voice. "Detective Hepplewhite and Agent Cole are here."

Will sat up quickly and Jessica cleared her throat, wiping

her eyes with the back of her good hand. "Hi, guys," she managed to say.

"Sorry to intrude," Detective Hepplewhite said, watching Will offer Jessica his handkerchief.

Will stood up to introduce Agent Cole to Jessica.

"Thanks for finding me," she told them.

"Our pleasure, believe me, Ms. Wright," Hepplewhite said. "How's the hand coming?"

"I'm having more surgery next week," she said. "They did a skin graft in Buffalo, from my thigh, which is actually more painful than my hand at this point. Please, pull up a chair. I know you're not supposed to be talking to me yet, so I'm curious about what's up."

Agent Cole grimaced. "We know. And we were kind of hoping this would be off the record."

"Oh, goodie," Jessica said. "Then I'll have something to hang over you. Now, are you, Agent Cole, the one who worked with Will and Alexandra?"

"Yes."

"I've heard many good things about you. And again, thanks for finding me. Now, about you, Hepplewhite," she said, turning to the detective. "What I want to know is, are you or aren't you related to the furniture maker?"

"Not unless he grew up in Harlem," the detective told her.

Jessica laughed. "Darn, and I was hoping you would tell me if my two chairs in the dining room are real or not." She could feel herself getting hyper with nervous energy but she also felt helpless to stop it. "Cassy told me you always hated Dirk Lawson, too, Detective. Is that right?"

"Mistrusted," Hepplewhite corrected.

"Close enough. You and me, that makes a club. So what's going on? Going to put him away for a million and a half years I hope," she said, resettling herself against the pillows.

Neither the agent nor the detective said anything, and Jessica felt a nauseous quease in her stomach. "Now don't sit there and tell me he's gotten away or something."

"No!" Hepplewhite assured her. "No, no, we've got him locked away good and tight. Only—well, frankly, our case against him is not going as well as we had hoped."

"Oh, God," Jessica groaned, letting her head fall back to look up at the ceiling.

"What exactly is the problem?" Will asked, sitting on the edge of the bed and placing his hand on Jessica's arm.

"We're having trouble linking Lawson to the kidnapping. We went through his apartment—"

"What about his ski house?" Will asked. "He's got a place in Vermont."

"We went through that, too," Agent Cole said.

"And found nothing," Hepplewhite said. "We've got circumstantial evidence tying him to the kidnapping, but what we need is hard evidence. An eyewitness—"

"He tried to kill the other kidnapper and you and Alexandra saw him!" Will cried. "What more evidence do you need?"

"We know he wanted to kill him, but we can't prove it. He didn't actually do it, and it wasn't a gun, but a stun gun—"

"And where did he get that from?" Will said. "They're illegal in New York State."

"He says he found it in the hospital during the rescue and until we can prove differently—"

Jessica brought her head back down to look at the detective. "What about Hurt Guy? I bet he could prove Dirk's involvement. I mean, he was his partner, right?"

"His name is Denton, Calvin Denton," Agent Cole said.

"And yes, while what you say is true, that we think he was Lawson's partner, Denton's been unable to speak."

"Who is he? This Calvin Denton?" Will wanted to know. He looked to Jessica. "Have you ever heard of him?"

"No."

"Calvin Denton," Agent Cole explained, "is a former CIA operative. Agent Kunsa, in fact, worked with him once on cracking a Mexican heroin ring in the 1980s. Denton's been retired for a while—he's still young, in his forties, and he started a security outfit down in Atlanta. One of his children—he's got three—has severe epilepsy. Daily seizures, very violent, she's often hurt badly by them, but otherwise she's a hundred percent. Denton and his wife have taken this little girl everywhere, trying to find some treatment or operation that will keep her from having these seizures. Nothing has worked and so this otherwise normal little girl has to wear a helmet and face guard to school and then in front of all her friends—"

The agent gestured with her hand in a way that let Jessica know it would only hurt to hear more details.

"The long and the short of it is, insurance won't cover experimental treatments and that's the only hope for this little girl. So Denton's somewhere around three hundred thousand dollars in debt, he's got three kids under the age of eleven to care for. Somehow, we believe, Lawson knew of his situation and approached him about the kidnapping."

"He was a nice guy," Jessica said. "I mean, I know he kidnapped me and everything, but I could tell. Really, I mean he was courteous, and direct and— Well, whatever. But what about Lawson, what the hell was his problem? I mean what was his motive? DBS paid him very well."

"That's part of the problem," Hepplewhite acknowledged. "There's an absence of motive where he's concerned. He's made good money, he's put some away, has some investments. Now, his wife did divorce him a couple of years ago, and she got the house in Long Island and custody of the kids. He pays very high alimony and we're trying to see if this might have something to do with it."

"Something like the fact he hates women," Jessica said. "I probably remind him of his wife."

The agent and the detective looked at each other.

"I was kidding," Jessica said.

"Yeah, but you never know," Hepplewhite said.

Agent Cole was making a note. "We look into every possibility."

"You're not here to tell me he's going to get off, are you?" Jessica suddenly said.

"No," Hepplewhite said.

"Then what are you doing here? I don't know anything about that idiot Lawson, except he was always obnoxious and a pain in the neck."

"We needed to talk to you," Hepplewhite said, "to bring you up to date on where the case now stands, and also to see if you might know of any detail, or any piece of information that might be of help to us."

"Well, where exactly does the case stand?" Jessica said. "Nobody's really explained to me how this all went down."

"What we think happened," Agent Cole said, "is that Lawson had been toying with the idea of kidnapping you, or perhaps Alexandra Waring if—and only if—the right scenario happened to come up. And when James Plattener—Leopold—started sending his notes, Lawson immediately spotted the possibility of a stalker in the making. So he took the opportunity to compose his own notes—in Leopold's name—to firmly establish the idea around West End that you definitely had a stalker, one who was not only obsessed with you, but obsessed with being with you. Then later, when it became clear that Plattener was a stalker, and did, in fact, successfully penetrate Lawson's own security measures at West End, Lawson knew he had his fall guy. All he had to do was play along, and start planning the kidnapping. But then the real Leopold acted in a way he hadn't anticipated."

"He murdered Bea," Jessica said. "Leopold kept telling me how she was such a bad person and how it was a good thing she was dead."

"Exactly," Hepplewhite said, picking up the story. "That's when Lawson knew he had to make his move, the sooner the better. He had the perfect foil. He lined up Denton to commit the actual kidnapping, he designed an electrical distraction and deterrent that was consistent with the electrical knowledge Leopold had previously displayed, and he even disagreed with the idea of using your publication party as a trap for Leopold, when, in fact, he was counting on us to do it, and counting on him to oversee the security operation."

"But we changed the locale at the last minute."

"Lawson selected the locale at the last moment," Agent Cole said. "He had handled security at Rockefeller Center a few years ago when the president visited, so he had extensive prior knowledge of the layout. So what he did was issue layouts of the complex which failed to include the very corridors he would direct Denton to use to get you out of there."

"But that's proof right there, isn't it?" Will asked.

"It's circumstantial," Hepplewhite said, "because we can't prove where the alterations to the layouts actually happen. But yes, this is, right now, our only real piece of evidence against him—and that it appeared he was about to kill Denton when we stopped him."

"And that's not going to stand up, is it?" Jessica sighed. "So how much was he going to ransom me for, anyway?"

"He wasn't," Agent Cole said. "He was going to have Denton stash you somewhere—"

"Where?"

"We haven't found it yet," Hepplewhite said.

"And then Dirk was going to find you and be the hero of the hour," Agent Cole finished. "And since he was a DBS employee, maybe he'd keep only half the reward and make some grand gesture like giving the rest to charity—"

"How much was the reward?"

"I didn't tell you?" Will asked her. "Five million. And then Jackson was thinking about raising it."

"Hmm," Jessica said, considering this. Then she shook her head, as if to clear it. "Wait a minute, though— What I don't get is, when Denton got me out of there in the Con Ed truck, where was Leopold?"

"Watching," Hepplewhite said. "And waiting for his moment."

The way he said this made her blood run cold. "Did he know I was going to be kidnapped?"

"We don't know," Agent Cole said. "He's not talking yet."

"He kept saying that he had saved me," Jessica offered.

"I'm sure that's what he thinks," Agent Cole said.

"When we found the truck that Denton used to get you away from Rockefeller Center," Hepplewhite said, "we also found bloodstains in the parking lot near it. As Will may have told you, at first we freaked out because we thought it was your blood. Happily, it wasn't. And now we know the blood was Calvin Denton's. And so we're assuming that that was where Plattener overpowered him."

"But I saw Hurt Guy there," Jessica said. "We drove there, he took me to the bathroom and then he made me take some sleeping pills. And then I climbed into the back of the truck, on a stretcher. You know, like an ambulance stretcher on wheels."

"It was after that, we think," Hepplewhite said, "after you were sleeping, that Plattener overpowered Denton."

"Yeah, but—" Jessica frowned, trying to remember.

"You didn't go anywhere else in the Con Edison truck," Agent Cole explained to her. "That truck was left in the lot. Oh, we have your diamond earring, by the way."

"Oh. Good, thanks."

"And that stretcher you mentioned," Hepplewhite said, "was not in the Con Ed truck. That's how Plattener moved you from the Con Ed truck to his van, and then later into the old hospital and up the elevator and down the halls."

"What about Hurt Guy? Where was he during all this?"

"We found a bloody tarp in Plattener's van upstate. We're assuming he just rolled Denton up in it and dumped him on the floor of the van he moved you into, and then brought him along to Buffalo to dump the body in the room next to yours."

She tried to remember. She did remember tripping over something at one point. "When we stopped in the country—"

"That was Plattener who took you out and walked you to the springs."

"I remember tripping over something in the van," Jessica said. "There was a big pile of something. A carpet I thought."

"That was Denton."

Jessica mulled over this for a moment. "So Leopold kidnapped the kidnapper."

"Yes," Agent Cole said.

"And Hurt Guy can't tell you that Dirk was responsible for kidnapping me in the first place."

Looking grim, Hepplewhite nodded. "Unless he regains consciousness."

Reading the detective's expression, Jessica said, "Hurt Guy's dying, isn't he?"

The detective nodded again.

Agent Cole spoke up. "It's a miracle he's lived as long as he has."

"Three kids," Jessica murmured, looking down and absently smoothing her sheets. "What a waste. What a stupid waste of so many lives." She looked at Will. "What's Hurt Guy's family supposed to do?" She looked to Agent Cole. "And Leopold's not talking?"

"No."

"And you're not going to screw this up and let him off on some insanity charge, are you?"

She shook her head. "No. He won't be getting out."

"Good." Suddenly Jessica felt very tired. So dead tired she could scarcely keep her head up. The tears started to come then, and she tried to stop them but couldn't. "I'm sorry," she managed to say.

"It's all right, we shouldn't have stayed so long," Hepplewhite said, quickly standing up. "We've exhausted you."

"You must get him," Jessica said quietly. "That son of a bitch Lawson, you have to get him."

"We will," Hepplewhite promised.

"You can't let him get away with this," she said with new urgency.

"They will, Jess," Will hushed. "It's okay."

"It's not okay," she said, agonized. Will held her tight as she tried to choke back her sobs. "Look at what he's done to me, Will. He's made me a coward. I'm such a mess. I'm so scared of everything now."

"No, darling, shh," Will soothed, rocking her. "No, not for long."

"Should I call the doctor?" Slim asked from the doorway.

Will nodded and Jessica's head came whipping up. "No!"

"But, Jessica—"

"No!" she insisted. "I know what I have to do." And then she pushed Will away and threw back the bedcovers. "Oh, get me unhooked from this thing!" she demanded, irritably swatting at the traction device.

28

The intensive care unit of Lennox Hill Hospital was under heavy guard. Jessica took Detective Hepplewhite's arm as they entered the glassed-in area where Calvin Denton lay. Jessica stood there a moment, assessing the situation, and then drew a chair up next to the bed.

"Hi, Hurt Guy," she said softly. "It's me, Jessica. Can you hear me?"

No response, just the beep, beep, beep of a heart monitor.

"I know you're very weak right now, so you don't have to try and communicate, okay? I just stopped by to see how you're doing." She frowned and spoke more loudly. "And it seems to me you should certainly be doing better than this. After all, now you're spoiled—you've got all these fancy doctors and medicines and everything, and before you didn't have anything except me and a couple of lousy aspirin." She chuckled. "I suppose you've figured out by now that I was never a nurse. I did know first aid, though—well, sort of. But we did get through it, though, didn't we?"

She leaned forward, letting a low, knowing, rumbling laugh roll out. "Remember when Leopold was coming for dinner that night? Remember? When I think back—it was kind of cool, wasn't it? How we snuck you in from next door and he didn't have a clue! And they say he's supposed to be some kind of genius. Well, he's a friggin' psycho, that's what he is. We both know that, don't we, Hurt Guy?"

She sat back, crossing her legs. "So anyway, he's in the slammer now. They've brought him down here to New York, in fact. The feds get him, you know, for the kidnapping—" She stopped here. The feds would be getting Hurt Guy, too, if he lived.

"So listen, Hurt Guy," she said, starting again, "I didn't come here just to see how you're doing. I mean, I did, but, um, I wanted to talk to you about something. The police and the FBI and everybody have been telling me a lot about you— Oh, and by the way, I've told everyone what a nice guy you were. You know, about how polite and courteous and thoughtful you were when you, um— Well, you know, when you picked me up at Rockefeller Center."

Beep, beep, beep of the heart monitor.

"Anyway, what I'm trying to say is, they've been telling me about your daughter's condition, and what a financial bind you got into. They seem to think this is how Lawson got to you—you know, to be part of his scheme. Anyway—" she leaned forward "—I just wanted you to know that we're going to watch out for your daughter. Actually, your whole family. I know you've been through a lot, and they have, too, and the point is, you shouldn't worry about anything except getting better. Because your kids need you. They'll understand why you got mixed up in all this. But they're still going to need you, even if they can't be with you all the time. And sometime they will be with you again, but in the meantime, you have to do father-like things, like boss them around and tell them you love them and stuff."

She paused, looking around at all the medical equipment. "You really have to get better. This is just not your scene. They tell me you were a CIA operative once. So you can't let some wimpy psycho like Leopold get the best of you. I mean, how will it look? The guy is the absolute worst. Mr. Mama's Boy, the sheik of freak." She frowned. "Hey, are you listening to me?"

She stood up to hang her face over his. "Are you? Hurt Guy? Is that one eye I see opening? Is it? Can you open it for me like you used to?"

The eye parted and Jessica beamed, clapping her hands in joy. "I knew you were in there!"

"Easy, easy, Ms. Wright, please," the ICU nurse said as the beat on the heart monitor grew uneven.

"Oops, sorry," she whispered. Then Jessica reached for that little patch of unhurt skin on Hurt Guy's face and touched it with her forefinger. "You're on the mend. And that makes me very happy. If it wasn't for you, you know, I don't think I would have gotten through everything. You gave me something to do, something to think about, a reason to act. And you were good company. I always did prefer people who didn't talk much." She leaned closer and whispered, "I meant that about looking after your family. You just worry about getting better, we'll take care of the rest. And I'll be back, Hurt Guy, to see how you're doing. So rest easy and get some sleep now."

She stood over him a moment more and, sure the eye had closed, she smiled slightly and moved away. At the door, she saw a woman standing by the nurses' station. She was a few years older than Jessica and looked in far worse shape. The woman's eyes were full of fear and Jessica intuitively knew who this was and she walked straight over to her. "It's okay," she murmured, holding her hand out.

"Oh, God," the woman said in a southern drawl, nearly grabbing Jessica's hand. "I just don't know what to say."

"I bear him no ill will."

"They told me you saved my husband's life, even though he— They said you hid him and kept him alive."

"We kind of looked out for each other," Jessica said, smiling. In a moment, Mrs. Denton was sobbing on her shoulder, saying over and over, "I'm so sorry, I'm so sorry."

29

"You don't have to do this," Will whispered to Jessica. "We can just leave right now."

"Tell him to shut up, will you?" she asked Agent Kunsa. "Or he's going to talk me out of it."

"Please shut up," Kunsa begged.

"Now, tell me again, what do you want me to get him to say?"

"Anything," Kunsa said. "But he may well do exactly what he's done thus far, which is to just sit there."

"Not with me he won't," Jessica promised. She took a nervous intake of breath and let it out slowly. "So who else will be in there?"

"We'll all be just on the other side of the glass."

"Cool, like the movies." She took another sharp breath. "Okay, let's do it."

Agent Kunsa led her down a green corridor that smelled like Lysol. They stopped at a heavy metal door with a window. He looked in and then opened the door, holding it open for Jessica. As they had agreed, Jessica came in with no introduction, simply breezing past Kunsa to stand in front of James Plattener, aka Leopold.

He had a bandage on his head and the green prison fatigues made him look clammier than she remembered. Otherwise he looked much the same, neat and tidy and fastidious to a fault. Upon her entrance, however, his eyes had widened and his head had kicked back in blatant surprise.

"Hi, Leopold," Jessica said in one of her more alluring

tones of voice. "It's a wig," she explained, touching her hair. "But it's not bad, is it? Until mine grows back?"

And then Jessica smiled, for Leopold's eyes broke away from her to look at the wall behind her. And so she knew she still had a bead on him.

"I came to see how you were doing," she said, pulling out a chair and sitting down. She held up her bandaged hand. "They say it's going to be all right. I'm having surgery again next week."

Leopold swallowed, eyes still behind her.

"I saw Hurt Guy yesterday," she continued. "You know, the kidnapper you saved me from. I think he's going to live. They don't, but I do. And so you won't have that murder charge to contend with. And it's not like you really kidnapped me, is it?"

His eyes came skittering back to look at the wig again, at her face briefly, before skittering back to the wall.

"I told them that you were, you know, courting me. That you saved me, and then were keeping me safe. And we were getting to know each other while I was there." She looked down to her lap and said almost shyly, "They told me you had gotten your house ready for me."

Now he looked at her.

"Is that true, Leopold?" she asked gently. "Did you have a room ready for me if I wanted to come live with you? A room with all your mother's lovely things?"

He hesitated and then nodded, his eyes moving back to the wall.

"That was sweet, thank you," she said. She gestured conversationally. "But I've got to tell you, though, Leopold, you've got a ton of trouble on your hands about that woman's body in the storage locker." She looked at him. "I told them I didn't know anything about it and I was sure you didn't, either."

Leopold looked down at the table in front of him, his hand starting to jerk.

"I said that the only time you ever hurt anybody it was because that person was hurting me and you were protecting me."

Still looking down at the table, he nodded.

"You don't know who that woman is, do you? The body they found?"

He didn't answer; he didn't look up.

"Are you embarrassed because you don't want me to know that I'm not the only woman you ever loved?"

No reaction.

"I didn't really expect you to have not been with anyone else," she said. "You know, you being an eligible bachelor and all. And you're very smart and you make a good living and you were very good to your mother and everything. I figured there had been lots of girls who liked you before I ever came along."

His eyes skittered up. And then down. And then back up. "Y-y-y-you did?"

"They say she was very attractive, Leopold."

He shrugged, noncommittal, eyes falling back to the table again.

"Well, anyway, I just wanted to tip you off that that's going to be the problem for you, that woman's body they found. But I told them somebody else probably put it there. I didn't think you had anything to do with it."

They sat there in silence a while.

"They are still running reruns of your show," Leopold said quietly.

Jessica looked at him incredulously. "You get to watch TV in this place?"

He nodded, daring to look at her for a moment. "When will you be back on?"

She arched her eyebrows. "But I'm not going back on TV, Leopold. I'm not doing the show anymore."

His eyes widened and he looked at her with a panicked expression. "Wha-wha-wha—"

"What?" she said for him.

"What do you mean?" he sputtered.

"I mean I'm not going on television anymore."

"Bu-bu—bu-bu-bu—"

"But—"

"—yu-you have to!" He held his hands out, jerked back by the chains on them. "You have to, Jessica!"

"Why?"

"Because!" He looked at her, cringing. "How am I going to see you?"

"Mother of God," Will said through clenched teeth in the observation room. "You've got to get her out of there."

"I know it's hard," Kunsa said, holding him by the arm. "Let her do what's she doing. She's knows this guy better than we do."

"Well, let's see," Jessica said. "Maybe I could come and visit you once in a while."

He jumped up and did his facing-the-wall trick, keeping his back to her. "W-w-would you really come?"

"What the hell is he doing?" Hepplewhite wondered out loud.

"He's got a hard-on probably," Kunsa said. "And he doesn't want her to see it. Our shrink says it has something to do with his mother."

"Come on, you guys, get her out of there," Will pleaded.

"The thing is," Jessica was saying, "they're not going to let me see you, Leopold, until you come clean with them.

And we clear you with that body they found. And then there's poor Bea. You and I know how she was hurting me, but you haven't told them your side yet."

"She was a whore," he said to the wall.

Jessica leaned forward. "Excuse me?"

"She was a whore. And she was hurting you, Jessica. She would do anything for money."

"They think you paid her ten thousand dollars to help you stalk me," Jessica said.

"I never stalked you," he said quietly.

"Right. But this is what they think, Leopold. They think you paid Bea ten thousand dollars to help you get into West End."

"She let me set some things up. Like the magnetic field in the control room so I could leave you my present."

Jessica smiled. "That really was pretty terrific, Leopold, I've got to say. Nobody could figure that one out. Did she put the letter on the chair on my set for you? Do you remember? That letter left for me on the set?"

"I never put a letter on the set. I would never break your concentration before a show." He looked over his shoulder. "You know what notes I wrote."

"Yes. I do. But they don't really get it yet, I'm afraid. I mean, they'd like to think someone forged your name on some of those notes, and that someone else masterminded the kidnapping, but right now, Leopold, with Hurt Guy so banged up, they don't have witnesses and they don't have any hard evidence. So right now they're going to try and hang it all on you. And that's why, if we don't sort this out, Leopold, I don't think they'll ever let me visit you again."

"They are so stupid," Leopold told the wall. "You'd be dead if I had not saved you, Jessica."

"They think you just used Bea and then killed her," Jessica continued. "But I don't believe that, Leopold. I believe she must have done something very bad to provoke you. Was it because Bea was selling items about me to the tabloids?"

Leopold wheeled around, furious.

"Look, he does have an erection," Hepplewhite said.

"Oh, this is sick, get her out of there," Will said.

"No, wait, wait, wait," Kunsa said, blocking his way.

"I paid her ten thousand dollars."

"But, Leopold, they say she threatened to turn you in, and that's why you killed her."

Leopold shouted. "I did not kill Bea Blakely!"

Jessica blinked. "You didn't?"

"No!"

"Well, if you didn't kill her, Leopold, who did?"

"The man posing as me. Her boyfriend."

"Her boyfriend? What boyfriend?"

"Her boyfriend. Her lover. She had one at West End. I used to hear them in your office."

"*My* office?"

"At night, late. They did sexual acts in your office. I told you, Jessica, she was a whore, she was bad, she was going to hurt you. I heard them!"

"Who was her boyfriend?" Jessica said.

"I don't know," Leopold insisted.

"What did he look like?"

Kunsa looked at Hepplewhite. "A boyfriend." He said this as though the topic had been previously discussed.

Hepplewhite frowned and looked at Agent Cole.

And then the three of them turned away from the observation window.

"What are you looking at?" Will demanded.

"Nothing," Kunsa said. "What are you worried about?"

"Nothing."

They were all just standing there, looking at him.

"Maybe we should talk for a minute or two, Will," Kunsa suggested.

"Norm," Will said warningly.

"Just for a minute," Kunsa continued. "In the next room." He pointed. "This way."

Will looked at Agent Cole. "Debbie—"

"If you've done nothing, Will, you have nothing to fear."

"Certainly it will be helpful to talk to us before you leave for France," Hepplewhite added.

"How do you know what Bea was doing in my office?" Jessica was asking him. No response.

"Leopold," she said more sternly, "come away from that wall and sit down here at the table and talk to me."

Amazingly, he did as he was told, chains clinking as he moved.

"Now, tell me how you know about this boyfriend of Bea's."

Leopold was looking dejectedly down at the table. "I could listen in. In your office. She didn't know. I put it in there one of the nights she let me into West End." He dared a quick look at her and looked back down, turning beet red. "The first time I thought it was you. I am so sorry, Jessica, I knew better, but for a moment I was very upset, but of course it was not you. I knew it was she, Bea Blakely, doing those things in your office."

"Who was Bea's boyfriend?"

"I did not know his voice."

"You have to tell them about this, Leopold. They're blaming you for Bea's death."

"I did not kill her," he said. "I did not lay a hand on her," he added, a mysterious shudder running through him.

"We're going to have to think this through, Leopold," Jessica told him seriously, "or else they're never going to let you see me again."

"The microphone should still be there," Leopold said. "In your office. It's voice-activated. And there's a laser-disc recorder in the air vent. There must be hours and hours of recordings on it."

"Where in my office is the microphone?"

"Inside the electrical socket near your big bookcase. I could get a radio playback from down on the West Side Highway. I just had to pull over and I could hear what was going on, or I could replay new parts from the recording disc."

"You were fantastic, Jessica," Agent Cole said when Jessica emerged from the interrogation room.

"Thanks. Where's Will?"

"He's gone with Agent Kunsa," Cole said. "We've got a lot of new information to check out, thanks to you. They asked me to see you home and he'll call you later."

"I'm glad you've given him something to do," Jessica said, looking around. "He's been so anxious to do something to help. Is there a drinking fountain?"

"Down here," the agent said, escorting her. She glanced over. "You're shaking."

She held up her good hand to show the agent how, yes, obviously she was shaking. "Casualty of the profession. You sit there chatting with a murderer like he's any old interview for DBS, and then later it sinks in what you've been doing—hell, yeah, I'm shaking."

She leaned over to take a long drink of water and then straightened up. "But I've got to tell you, I don't think he killed Bea."

"We're already checking out what he said. About Bea having a boyfriend."

"Good. Where's Slim? I need to go home and lie down."

"We'll pick him up on the way out," Agent Cole told her.

30

$\longrightarrow \longleftarrow$

"Why do you need your lawyer?" Agent Kunsa asked him.

"Because you're crazy!" Will yelled.

"Am I?"

"*Yes.*"

"Then why don't you just have a seat and relax while we wait for those tapes to be retrieved."

"Because I want to see Jessica."

"Oh, I don't think that's a very good idea at the moment, do you?" Kunsa said. "Why would you want to upset her?"

"Kunsa, you are so off base—I'm telling you, you're going to owe me big time, buddy."

"So when did it start?"

Will glared at him. "What?"

"You and Bea Blakely."

"It never started. I scarcely knew her."

"Were you doing her all along?"

Will was shaking his head.

"You were getting it on with her, weren't you? And then later, when it looked like Jessica was finally coming around, you tried to dump Bea."

Will's mouth twisted in contempt.

"You must have gotten a real charge doing it on Jessica's desk. We know you were obsessed with Jessica for years. I guess this was the next best thing to getting into her pants."

Will rubbed his eyes with one hand and then used the

same hand to point at the agent. "Fuck you, Kunsa. You leave Jessica out of this. You don't know what you're saying."

"Oh, I know what I'm saying all right," Kunsa said.

"You have no idea how much I love Jessica. And you have no idea what I would do for her."

"Well, obviously, we're beginning to, now. You'd write her notes, you'd engineer a crisis, you'd even murder someone so Jessica would never know that you were screwing her secretary."

"Forget it," Will said, abruptly crossing his arms over his chest. "There's no point in trying to talk to you. Get your stupid tapes and listen to them, knucklehead."

But Kunsa would not stop with the questions and kept at him. And at him. For three hours.

"Alexandra Eyes," Jessica said over the phone, "have you heard from Will?"

"No."

"He's somewhere with that Agent Kunsa, but I don't know where."

"I don't, either."

"Oh, come on, Waring, you're killing me with enthusiasm here. I haven't left yet, you don't have to be so cold."

"I'm not being cold," Alexandra said. "I'm trying not to cry."

"What's interesting," Kunsa said, looking at a sheet of paper, "is rereading this police report about how you caught Plattener coming out of the runoff pipe. Knowing what I know now, your actions could be interpreted as something far from heroic, Rafferty. In particular," he said, looking at Will, "I'm still very interested in how you stole those plans so that we didn't know about that storm sewer."

"I didn't steal your plans. I took them because you weren't using them and there wasn't time to discuss it."

"The point is, Rafferty, we had over one hundred law enforcement officers at the scene, and you decided that you—and only you—could catch this guy."

Will shook his head. "Not true."

"We had one hundred law enforcement officers there. Federal agents, state police, Buffalo SWAT, and you choose a local rookie less than a month out of the academy."

"He was the only one who would come."

"If one reads this report carefully," Kunsa continued, "one can see how you were setting up an execution. That you were counting on the officer to shoot Plattener as he came out of the pipe and thus, could let Plattener take the rap for murdering Bea Blakely." He paced the room. "Which would leave you free to play hero with the object of your obsession." He paused. "And marry her." He paused again. "And take her to Europe, far, far away."

"I took the plans and the cop because you guys had it in your heads Plattener was holed up in the complex—wedded to the ghost of his mother or something, and there was no time to try and disabuse you of your theory."

Kunsa looked at his watch. "It's not going to wash, Will."

Agent Cole popped her head in. "They've got the disc, Norm. It'll be here shortly."

"Thanks." After the door closed, Kunsa turned to Will. "You might as well start talking. In the end, it's the only thing that's going to help you."

"Can you believe that psycho Leopold expected to sit in prison for the rest of his life and watch me on TV every night?" Jessica demanded of Slim.

"Yes," the big man said. "And he'd probably enjoy it."

"Yechhh!" Jessica said, throwing a couch pillow across the room to bonk Slim on the head. "Some conversationalist you are." She looked at the clock. "Where the heck is Will? I'm beginning to think he's found another girl."

"He'll be here," Slim said. He lofted an eyebrow. "How about some popcorn?"

"Who's making it?" she asked suspiciously.

"I will," he offered, standing up.

Jessica turned her attention back to the TV. After a moment, she leaned back and called, "You know, we haven't discussed yet if you want to go to France with me and Will. Wendy says she'll go."

"I don't speak French," Slim called back.

She shrugged, turning back to the TV. *"Bonjour, Monsieur Slee-mah."*

The FBI technician plugged the laser recorder into the wall socket of the interrogation room. Kunsa's eyes moved over to watch Will.

Will's eyes were on the recorder. He swallowed. His breathing picked up.

Kunsa's eyes moved to Agent Cole.

Her eyes were on Will Rafferty, as well.

"Okay, all set," the tech said. "Press Play. Do you want me to do it?"

"No, that's okay, thanks."

The technician left the room.

Silence.

Kunsa sat down across the table from Will. "This is your last chance to cooperate. And I tell you this for one reason and one reason only. I believe you love Jessica Wright. And I honestly believe that you helped us to find her before it was too late. And that without you, we might not have gotten there in time."

Will looked at him, jaw tightening.

"But that doesn't let you off the hook for murdering Bea Blakely. I'm giving you this chance to help yourself. And I wouldn't be giving it to anyone else."

"Will, he's telling the truth," Agent Cole said. "If you talk to us now, we can say that you came forward and confessed."

Will shook his head. "No."

"When I turn this tape on," Agent Kunsa said, "and I hear you and Bea Blakely going at it, my friend, that's it. There's no turning back. They'll go for murder one."

Will only looked at him.

"Last chance," Kunsa said.

Will shook his head.

Kunsa glanced at Agent Cole, then to the observation window, and then back to the laser-disc player. He punched the Play button.

"No, no, this is what I want to do," a woman's voice said. It was Bea Blakely's, low, hoarse, in a rush. "I want to do it right here on her desk."

There was a male grunting sound and the rustle of clothing.

"Mmm, that's good," Bea panted. "Right there. That's goooood. Yeah." She sucked the air in between her teeth. "Yeah."

"Oh, this is good, baby," the man said. "Oh, yeah, this is good. Right on that bitch's desk—fuck her."

Bea giggled.

"Yeah, like that, baby, good, good—" the man panted. "That's good, fuck me, fuck me—"

Kunsa hit the Stop button and the room was silent. Slowly the agent raised his head. "That's Dirk's voice," he said in amazement.

"Knucklehead," Will said, pushing his chair back to stand up.

Epilogue

31

The DBS News three-hour special, "The Kidnapping of Jessica Wright," was predicted to be the most watched program across the U.S. for the week of June 22.

"This is one of the best psycho-thrillers produced in recent years," the *New York Times* wrote in a preview. "The special has everything: sex, psychos, love, loyalty, betrayal, pain, violence, romance." The *Daily News* reported, "The fact that it was the DBS network's own talk-show host, Jessica Wright, in the center of it all, is now only a dramatic accident of television history that has resulted in one of the finest documentary projects of the decade."

"With the full cooperation of almost all the players in the game," the *Washington Post* wrote, "from Jessica Wright to the FBI and NYPD and the members of the special investigative unit of DBS News that helped to find her, the documentary also includes actual footage of the rooms where Jessica was held hostage and the eventful rescue itself."

"In the beginning, right after the kidnapping, the authorities were confused," host Alexandra Waring related into the camera during her opening monologue. "But of course, at that point, they didn't know it wasn't just one stalker-murderer-kidnapper they were after, but *three* different men involved in two different kidnappings, and not one, but *two* different murderers."

She explained how the story began some thirty-five years before in Niagara Falls, when an electrical engineer with the Niagara Power Project lay dying of cancer, and how in desperation and grief, his young wife came to believe in curative powers of water, and began strange cleansing rituals with her young son, James.

"How could I forget?" an older man who had been their neighbor in Niagara Falls said when Alexandra questioned him about the Platteners. "It was maybe thirty years ago, but I remember it like yesterday. I went outside to get our dog and saw that she had that little boy outside in the cold. Stark naked he was, shivering on the ground in their backyard. I said, 'Mrs. Plattener, your little boy's going to catch pneumonia,' and she glared at me, yanked the boy off the ground and hurried him into the house. Later that night, my wife woke me up and said she was back outside again with the boy. Naked, with candles going, the little boy crying. This time I called the police." The old man shook his head. "She didn't do it again, at least not where we could see. Because we kept a sharp eye out."

Shortly after that, Albert Plattener died, the young widow, Lillian, moved her son to Buffalo where she worked as a private nurse to Bruce Porterly, a diagnosed schizophrenic who had been suspected of molesting children. Unfortunately, Porterly's parents were multimillionaires who had succeeded in keeping their son on the loose for years.

"Oh, my, my," an old lady with a faint Irish brogue said gravely, shaking her head, "it was a very sad situation for the little Plattener boy, if you ask me. I was the Porterly's housekeeper, you see, but I made it very clear I would have nothing to do with that son of theirs, that madman, Bruce, they kept in the guest house in the back. I should think the fact they had iron bars over the windows of that little house would have told the police everything they needed to know about the creature who lived in it. But she, that Lillian, the nurse, she spent whole days and weeks back there with him, and the little boy was there too." She shook her head again. "We knew that no good could come of it. We knew what that creature liked to do to little boys and little girls. But *she* didn't seem to care."

The camera cut to Alexandra. "Didn't anyone say anything?"

"Aye and indeed," the old lady said, "but it was my job at stake, you see, and a good one it was, and that Lillian Plattener was the only nurse the Porterlys could get to stay. They had a man come at night. But he wasn't any good—the creature would get out. And then finally they put him away. If you ask me, they should have taken him out back and shot him the first time it happened."

"The first time what happened?"

"He attacked the little girl down the road—Mother of God, he did things that no human being could do to a child."

"And it happened again?"

"It happened and it happened and it happened. And don't imagine the little Plattener boy escaped it. I don't see how he could have."

And so it seemed that young James Plattener had been sexually molested by Porterly from the time he was six to thirteen years old, possibly longer. And it was possible the mother even encouraged it as a means of controlling her charge.

The Porterlys paid Mrs. Plattener handsomely for her services. When Porterly escaped a prison sentence for child molestation by pleading insanity, he was placed in the high-security ward of the Buffalo Psychiatric Center, and Mrs. Plattener continued there as his private nurse. As for young James Plattener, he was already demonstrating a genius in the sciences, and often hung out at the insane asylum with his mother after school.

"What was he like back then?" Alexandra asked an attractive woman in her late thirties who had been a classmate of Plattener's.

The woman made a face. "I don't want to be unkind, but he was— Well, he was weird. He was little—he was, I don't know, three or four years younger than everyone in the class. And he was physically little. Stooped. He used to crouch over his desk, like an old man. I mean he was *weird*. He never spoke if he could help it. The guys used to taunt him unmercifully. I don't know what used to happen in the showers after gym class, but more often than not James' clothes would end up on the flagpole in the front of the school." The woman thought a moment, looking very grave. "If I felt bad then, I feel horrible now. I guess we made a monster out of him."

Plattener graduated from high school at fifteen, got his bachelor's from Buffalo State at eighteen, and began his doctorate at the Rochester Institute of Technology.

"He was brilliant," a retired professor said defiantly. "He could have been one of our great scientists."

"What held him back?" Alexandra asked.

He paused, as if debating what answer to give.

"He was not good with people. He was, I think, afraid of them."

Before he finished his degree, Alexandra explained that his mother, Lillian, became ill with severe asthma.

The story then moved to Phoenix, Arizona, where the lonely, sexually confused, socially retarded young man dominated by his invalid mother became enamored with a talk-show host out of Tucson named Jessica Wright. Lillian, it seemed, shared his enthusiasm for the show and he drove her down to Tucson several times to be a part of Jessica's audience.

"Once I saw pictures of him," Denny Ladler, Jessica's

longtime producer recalled, "I remembered him right away. In those days we were syndicated, but the audience was still very small, and his mother needed oxygen close by, and so Plattener would wheel this cylinder into the studio. And then of course we'd see his mother outside smoking, and we wondered what the—" Denny shook his head. "Anyway, he was on our mailing list and used to come to all the audience appreciation days."

"It took me a long time to recognize him," Jessica said. "I had been held prisoner in that old mental hospital maybe three days before I remembered." She narrowed her eyes slightly as she looked into the camera. "I realized I had seen him at West End a few times—but then, as soon as that sunk in, I knew I had seen him before. I knew he had been down in Arizona." She looked sad. "I think that was the thing that scared me the most in the whole ordeal—the moment I realized this guy had been watching me for years and years." She grimaced slightly. "After that, frankly, I didn't care what I had to do to get out of there."

They showed how Plattener carefully videotaped each of Jessica's shows, and the elaborate archive of files and scrapbooks he would accumulate over the years. As the health of his beloved mother declined, his obsession with Jessica Wright increased.

James Plattener, as described by his colleagues where he worked in those years—the Arizona Board of Energy and Resource Management—was neat, polite and a genius, but he was also described as a geek and a freak and a loner. Nobody, however, would underplay the contribution he had made to overhauling the redistribution project of electrical power in the state.

"How can you deny the contribution of a single individual who saved Arizona residents over a billion dollars in power costs?" his former supervisor asked helplessly.

"And I gotta tell ya, the idea that the guy who kidnapped Jessica Wright was the same guy that worked for us—" He shook his head in amazement. "No way we'd make the connection." He squinted. "The guy had a lace doily on his office chair. Does that give you the picture?"

After his mother Lillian died, Plattener packed up and moved back into the same house he had shared with his mother in Buffalo, and took a job with the Niagara Power Project, where his father had worked for so many years. Now his obsession with Jessica Wright, who had now become a national media star, accelerated into a full-fledged fantasy world, where Plattener "knew" he and the talk-show host would be together forever, and he began in earnest to plan how to make this happen.

"This is a notebook of his plans," FBI Agent Norman Kunsa related. "As you can see, it's hundreds and hundreds of pages. I can't read any of the contents until after the trial, but I will say he planned their every moment together for years."

Then Plattener landed a job with the New York State Energy Commission, a position that necessitated an apartment in Albany, but which also afforded him frequent trips to New York City, and a few to the West End Broadcasting Center itself.

"He vas a milquetoast, vat more can I say?" Dr. Kessler was shown saying. "Ve had to deal vith him on our power requirements at Vest End. And the idea that he vas the vun stalking Jessica..." He threw his hands up.

In a parallel story, the special chronicled how an FBI agent stationed in New York City had left the agency under an undocumented cloud. "Oh, I can tell you what Dirk Lawson was up to," his former wife said. "He was drinking and sleeping around with other women and hitting Atlantic City three times a week to gamble, that's what he

was up to. I have children to protect, so I threw him out."
Evidently the former Mrs. Lawson had to get a restraining
order during their divorce proceedings to stop the agent's
midnight raids on the house. He ignored it and was arrested several times. When his superiors told him to clean
up his act, he opted to resign with—what amounted to—
an honorable discharge.

The sad reality of celebrity, Alexandra then explained,
was that it often created a target of obsession for mentally
unbalanced people. "I myself perhaps know this better
than most." They rolled footage of Alexandra being shot
on the steps of the Capitol building eight years before by a
crazed fan. Then they showed footage from the TV studio
in Detroit where another crazed man had tried to shoot her
seven years ago.

"After that," Cassy Cochran said when interviewed,
"we had to get a top flight security person in here to design
our system. Our first security expert was great. He was a
retired NYPD captain, but then he developed heart disease
and had to retire from here as well." She sighed heavily
then, shaking her head. She bit her lower lip a moment and
then looked up into the camera. "That's when I hired Dirk
Lawson. The Federal Bureau of Investigation told me he
had handled all the security for visiting dignitaries to New
York. Who better than he? I thought." She closed her eyes,
shaking her head again. "Good Lord."

What went wrong with Dirk Lawson was hard to pin-
point. "The best definition I've heard," Agent Kunsa explained when questioned, "is an overblown ego trying to
compensate for low self-esteem. He has a grandiose vision
of himself, a craving for power over those around him, particularly when it came to women. One thing we know
about Lawson is that he and Jessica Wright did not like
each other at all—and from the very start. And that Jessica,

in fact, actually resembles Lawson's ex-wife, in force of personality, even a little bit physically. Their hair color, for example."

Lawson began to dream about a big score, a way of winning the recognition he deserved and money and power and glory. Very soon an idea began to form in his mind about kidnapping one of the DBS stars—Alexandra Waring or Jessica Wright—and then playing the hero by finding them. "Evidently he thought Alexandra was the toughest to get to," Kunsa said, "because Ms. Waring had such high security around her from the beginning. Jessica, on the other hand, had been relatively unscathed by her fame, and she simply didn't believe that people presented a possible danger the same way Alexandra knew that they did."

Lawson, fifty-one, started an affair with Jessica's new secretary, the lonely, somewhat troubled Bea Blakely. "I knew something was funny," one of the West End custodians said. "They were acting funny. At night, I'd see them around, together. I figured they were working on something for Miss Wright."

When James Plattener began writing to Jessica, writing her under the name of Leopold, Lawson realized that a perfect fall guy—or at least a very good screen—was in the making if he were to actually kidnap Jessica. "We know that Lawson then got in touch with a former CIA operative in Atlanta, Calvin Denton," Agent Kunsa said. "Denton was in a vulnerable position and Lawson knew just how to play it to draw him into his scheme."

At this point the documentary briefly detoured to profile Calvin Denton's family, focusing on the long struggle of their second child, little Alyson, and her cruel battle with violent epileptic seizures and the failure of the Dentons' insurance to cover experimental treatments and the Dentons' subsequent descent into hundreds of thousands of dollars in debt.

Lawson had found his man. The deal was, twenty thousand in cash up front to Denton to make the snatch, and a four-hundred-thousand-dollar "contribution" from Lawson to the Dentons' little girl when the reward money was paid. No violence or force would be used; it would be a well-thought-out, humane kidnapping of Jessica Wright.

"Denton felt he had little to lose," Kunsa's voice said, superimposed over movies of Denton with his young daughter. "He was confident he could pull it off. And most of all, he was confident he could keep Jessica Wright safe and calm throughout the whole ordeal. He had actually done some work in this area before, overseas."

And so Dirk Lawson decided to mimic Jessica's obsessed fan, and composed a note in Leopold's name that promised he and Jessica would be together soon. The note worked very well, making everyone nervous that Leopold was about to appear and do something. But then Leopold did do something. Leopold got through Lawson's own security system to stage an elaborate gift-giving scenario—the present hanging in midair in the control room to Studio B—that demonstrated a fantastic knowledge of both electrical engineering and the detailed internal layout of the West End complex.

"It must have freaked Lawson out," Kunsa said. "Here he had just written a note in Leopold's name saying he was coming and then the guy appears. And Lawson had not a clue as to how he had gotten in. The irony was, it was Lawson's own girlfriend, Bea Blakely, that had let Leopold in."

To complicate matters further, Lawson discovered that Bea Blakely was making money on the side by supplying secrets about Jessica Wright to the tabloids. Lawson told her to stop. She said maybe he better start paying her to stop, particularly since she knew a lot of other stuff that would get Lawson in big trouble. Whatever Lawson told her, evidently Bea Blakely thought everything was well between them, for she then dyed her hair like Jessica's in anticipation of satisfying a particular sexual fantasy of Lawson's concerning Jessica and one of the property rooms.

"In her journal," Detective Jefferson Hepplewhite said, "Ms. Blakely had detailed a lot of their sexual encounters. One of the fantasies they had often played out involved her pretending to be Ms. Wright, of him surprising her in her office or in her dressing room. Now, in this case, Bea Blakely had gone the whole nine yards and dyed her hair and set up the property room the way he had described it in his fantasy. Only they didn't have sex this time." He paused, swallowing. "Instead, he electrocuted her, burning her practically beyond recognition."

As a diagram of the crime scene filled the screen, the voice of Agent Kunsa explained, "Lawson killed her with over a thousand volts of electricity, diverted from a major power line into the telephone line Blakely was using. The sophisticated setup was consistent with the knowledge demonstrated by Leopold in his magnetic field gift-giving scenario, and so Lawson successfully threw all suspicion for the murder onto the invisible stalker, Leopold."

In the aftermath of Blakely's death, it came to light that she had actually known Leopold and, in fact, had accepted ten thousand dollars from him to help him beat Lawson's security system. "It was an extraordinary piece of luck for Lawson when that ten thousand dollars turned up in her bank account," Alexandra related. "Because the authorities then assumed that Leopold had simply killed her when he had no further use of her."

The thing was, Alexandra reported, not even Bea Blakely

had known that Leopold, on one of those visits to West End, had bugged Jessica's office.

When the authorities failed to track down Leopold and began looking at Jessica's book publication party as means of attracting him, Lawson feigned objections to the plan. "This is the part that burns me up most," Agent Kunsa said. "I had worked with Lawson before, when he was with the Bureau, and it honestly never occurred to me that he could go bad. He was a good agent. But, man oh man, what a scumbag he turned out to be."

The authorities of course had no idea that the former FBI agent they were relying on to coordinate security for the event was, in fact, coordinating with a former CIA operative to set up a successful kidnapping. The last-minute choice of Rockefeller Center as the site of the party was not last minute at all, but was the very site Lawson had selected months in advance.

In another ironic twist, the party *did* attract the stalker, Leopold, and he had known exactly where it was going to take place because he had been listening in when it had been explained to Jessica in her office. "Contrary to everyone's belief," Alexandra said, "Leopold had not gone there to stalk or kidnap Jessica, but to protect her from the danger he knew was present at West End. Someone had murdered Bea Blakely, and Leopold didn't know who."

So on the Monday before the party, Plattener hacked into the Niagara Power Project system to sign out a truck in master electrician Mark Brewer's name and went up to Niagara Falls to pick it up. He drove down to New York City and waited to hear where the actual site of the party would be on Tuesday. As an assistant commissioner, Plattener had high-security clearance and access to the electrical plans of every major building and building complex on file with the state. When he heard where the party was to be, he simply called up the Rockefeller Center plans on his computer to familiarize himself with the layout and decide on the best vantage points to watch.

Leopold was there early that afternoon, surveying the area. "What caught his eye," Agent Kunsa said, "was a Con Edison work project roped off in front of the NBC building on Sixth Avenue. There was only one worker there, and he knew that they were always assigned in pairs. So he called and checked and found out there was no work detail assigned to the site, and so he knew the guy had to either be a part of the security effort for the party or the guy was a potential threat.

Leopold was outside the party, on the upper level over the rink, listening in on the security walkie-talkies. (The security cameras had caught him several times, and it was eerie, watching him, knowing what was to come from this very nondescript, mild-mannered man.) When Leopold heard over the walkie-talkie frequencies that Jessica had been nabbed and pulled through the maintenance door, he had a very good idea where the kidnapper was taking her, and he was waiting in his own van when Denton and his hostage came out of the NBC building and took off in the Con Edison truck.

He followed them to the downtown lot and watched as Denton walked Jessica into the tool shack. Leopold went to the front gate to close it, affixing the open padlock hanging there and locking it. Then he hid.

He watched Denton help Jessica into the back of the truck and then drive to the front gate. Looking baffled, Denton jumped out to examine the lock, at which time Leopold hailed him, asking if he could help. Denton asked him if he had the key to the gate. Leopold said yes, walked over, and instead of taking the key out, struck Denton in the face with a wrench. When the former CIA operative fell to the ground, Leopold proceeded to beat him almost to death. Then he took Denton's keys and unlocked the back of the Con Ed truck and found Jessica sound asleep on the stretcher. He brought his van up next to the Con Ed truck and rolled the stretcher with Jessica on it into his van. Then he dragged Denton's body into the back of his van, leaving Denton on the floor. Finally, Plattener used the lock cutters from the Con Ed truck to cut the lock off the gate and head out of town.

Then the documentary took a moment to introduce Salt Springs, an idyllic park located just over the New York state border in Pennsylvania. For centuries Indians had associated magical powers to the waters that bubbled up from the earth here, which Plattener's mother, Lillian, so many years ago, had also come to believe in. "And so this night, under the cloak of darkness," Alexandra said, as the screen showed the strange beauty of the spot, "Leopold had veered off Route 17 to Salt Springs, where he endeavored to cleanse Jessica with the magical waters, and to make her his."

"I saw the van pull in," the witness who had called the hotline said. "I had gotten up to go to the bathroom and I saw the lights. I didn't think much about it—there's always kids parking there. But then I couldn't sleep. I— There was just something that bothered me. It was a school night, you know? And it was very late. And so I got up again and looked out and I saw this woman stumbling around with this guy and I thought maybe she was drunk or drugged or something. And I thought, gosh, I better get down there. This doesn't look good, what is he doing to her? So I went downstairs and hurried outside, but when I called out, the guy slammed the door and took off. I saw most of the license plate and came back in and wrote it down on the pad in the kitchen." He shrugged. "Then I saw the press conference about Jessica Wright being kidnapped, my wife and I looked at each other, and then I ran to the phone to call in."

"And now you're a multi-millionaire," Alexandra said.

He beamed. "Well, yeah."

"Which just goes to show, it pays to get involved."

He grinned. "Well, yeah."

In the van, Alexandra continued, Leopold injected Jessica with a sedative to knock her out for the rest of the night. He drove her to Buffalo, to the now abandoned mental hospital where his mother once worked. He moved Jessica up to the suite of rooms he had prepared for her, and locked Denton's body in a room next door, leaving him to die.

The documentary now focused on how the FBI, NYPD and DBS News worked together to profile Leopold, track the van to Niagara Power and put all the information together to zero in on James Plattener. Meanwhile, at the network, when the authorities were preparing to race upstate to find Plattener, Dirk Lawson was genuinely frantic. "Only now did Lawson realize," Alexandra paused for effect, "that Calvin Denton, the kidnapper he had hired, did not have possession of Jessica, but that the real Leopold did. As to what had happened to Denton, he had no idea, but he knew that he needed to find out before anyone else did—for Denton was the one person who could tie Lawson to the kidnapping."

After a commercial break the documentary resumed with a clip from one of Jessica's shows where she bemoaned her essentially useless nature and "inability to hold a real job." Then Alexandra and Jessica took viewers through the rooms where Jessica had been kept captive. Jessica detailed how she had heard the moans of the dying man next door and had tunneled through the wall to find

Denton. In a re-creation, they showed how she had dragged him through the wall, how she had made up a bed for him on the floor, hiding him in her room, and had not only attempted to nurse him to the best of her ability, but had demonstrated extraordinary kindness. "You would have done the same thing," Jessica responded when Alexandra questioned her compassion. "When you hear that certain pitch—animal or human—you know you have to try and help. You just can't let someone die."

Alexandra then detailed Jessica's relationship with Leopold in her captivity, her attempt to simultaneously win his trust and make him relax, and her ongoing attempt to keep him away from the man Jessica called Hurt Guy, who was lying under her bed moaning in the next room. When Leopold's attentions turned overtly sexual toward her, however, she frankly admitted "I bolted for daylight and nearly got volted to never-never land. But I'll tell you, anything was better than being touched by that guy."

The drama of the rescue assault on the old Buffalo Psychiatric Center was illustrated through film footage from that night. It highlighted how, after Jessica's rescue, Detective Hepplewhite and Alexandra Waring had stood by to witness Dirk Lawson's attempted murder of Calvin Denton.

Then Alexandra showed how Will and the local rookie had made the mad dash for the end of the runoff pipe and how they had waited hours and hours for Leopold to finally crawl out at dawn. "We knew that if the perp were to use that old runoff pipe as a means of escape," the rookie cop said, "that we had to act fast. The hospital grounds are so massive, I knew the others would be tied up for hours. And so I thought I just better go with Mr. Rafferty. I was pretty confident I could handle the situation, and fortunately, that's how it turned out."

Then the documentary went into the arrests, Plattener's silence, the cocky denials of Dirk Lawson, and the frustration of being unable to obtain the evidence that was dying with Calvin Denton. "But then Jessica really came through for us," Agent Kunsa said. "She marched right in there and confronted Plattener, face-to-face. I've never seen any kidnapping victim demonstrate that kind of strength before. But she did, by golly she went right in there and got enough information so that we could retrieve the bug he had planted in her office. And we also got the recordings that linked Dirk Lawson to Bea Blakely."

"I still don't know what to say," Mrs. Denton said with tears in her eyes. "We owe our family's existence to this woman. To Jessica Wright." She blinked rapidly in an attempt to keep her tears at bay. "Not only did she risk her life to keep my husband alive, but I saw her go into the intensive-care unit later and literally talk my husband back to life." She swallowed. "And now she's getting help for our little girl, and she's trying to help my husband, and help us to maintain hope as a family." She broke down.

Alexandra chronicled the gradual stabilization of Calvin Denton and the miracle of his being able to testify against Dirk Lawson. (He had to type his testimony with his one good index finger on his right hand, attached, happily, to his only unbroken limb.) Denton also sent the authorities to the intended hideout—the basement of an abandoned warehouse in Newark—and to evidence physically linking Lawson with the site. Denton would be going to prison and would be a cripple all his life. "I know better than anyone else what Calvin Denton was going to do to me, and how he intended to treat me," Jessica said. "And I know that I will be testifying on his behalf, because I will tell you something—that man has suffered hell itself. Not just with this situation, but for years, with his little girl. Not just with him knowing how much his family is suffering over this. But think about what it must be like for a man who always prided himself on being fit and athletic, to now be barely able to walk. Ever."

"The most condemning factor in a kidnapping is demanding a ransom," Agent Kunsa explained. "Once kidnappers do that—that's it. But in this case, there was no ransom demand, and that lessens the charges against Denton. And with Ms. Wright pushing so hard for his cause, that certainly can't hurt his situation."

Then they cut to the Manhattan district attorney. "In Dirk Lawson's case?" he said. "Oh, yes, we'll be going for the death penalty for the murder of Bea Blakely."

Lawson, Alexandra explained, was being held in Riker's Island, awaiting trial.

James Plattener's plea of insanity was struck down by the courts and he was transferred upstate to Attica Prison, where he is awaiting trial for the murder of a Niagara Falls cocktail waitress named Bambi Sharp, with whom he had tried to practice his social sexual skills with before meeting Jessica in person. (Unfortunately Ms. Sharp had evidently said something unkind and Plattener had slashed her throat and later dismembered her in his garage in Buffalo, packing her remains in three plastic storage containers and tucking her away in a storage locker with other family heirlooms.) Other charges were pending for Plattener in the courts—in Manhattan, the attempted murder of Calvin Denton, and in the federal, the kidnapping and assault of Jessica Wright.

"Interestingly," Alexandra said at the conclusion of the special, "James Plattener has had to be isolated from the general prison population in Attica. Because, you see, when it was announced that Jessica would not be returning to the air after her ordeal, several inmates promised to murder him."

Alexandra smiled and said, "And that's the report from all of us here at DBS, and DBS News. We'll see you tomorrow night for our regular news hour. Good night."

It was a remarkable television event and DBS was flooded with congratulations from newspeople around the world, not only for the special, but for the personal participation of Alexandra and Will in helping to track down and rescue their friend and colleague. And in the ratings war, "The Kidnapping of Jessica Wright" scored a 22.8 Nielsen rating, beating all competition.

32

On Saturday night, June 27, Langley Peterson threw an official farewell dinner for Jessica Wright at the Waldorf Hotel. Included among the guests was the whole Monday-through-Friday cast and crew of "The Jessica Wright Show" and "DBS News America Tonight." Following the sophisticated tradition established by Betty Ford, waiters and waitresses at this black-tie affair carried not only champagne glasses of Moët on silver trays, but champagne glasses of Perrier water, each with a piece of lime to clearly signal its nonalcoholic content. Trays of sumptuous hors d'oeuvres were passed. It was a giddy group, excited by the food and drink and finery, but it was also an unhappy group, one nervously dreading that final goodbye.

Dinner was served. Filet mignon or chicken or vegetarian. At the head table, Langley and his wife, Belinda, played host and hostess, Jessica, Will, Cassy, Jackson, Alexandra, Agent Kunsa, Agent Cole, Detectives Hepplewhite and O'Neal, Denny Ladler and Alicia Washington chatted on, looking out over the room, waving to colleagues and friends.

Jessica had gone crazy with a long green silk dress and spiked sandals, and between yet another new auburn wig and Cleo's makeup, she looked very much like her old self. Because her right hand was still healing, she also wore long white dress gloves. Will was wearing his tuxedo (standard gear for TV executives). Alexandra was in a long blue-sequined gown. Cassy was in a pale yellow one. Agent Kunsa kept fussing with his black bow tie (a real one) and white dinner jacket that he had been loaned from the DBS wardrobe. Hepplewhite was aglow in a tux, and Agent Cole surprised everyone with a black silk dress and daring neckline. Slim, in his rented tuxedo, had chosen a seat off-stage, and so had Wendy, who frankly looked fantastic in a long black dress.

After dinner, as the dessert wagons were being rolled out, Langley got up to make a toast. First it was to the safe return of Jessica and the people who had found her—Hepplewhite, Kunsa, Cole, Rafferty, Waring, Cochran, Mitchell and gang—and then to the making of the documentary, "The Kidnapping of Jessica Wright," which had earned DBS their first number-one rating.

"This is the part I hate to get to," Langley said then. He paused for a long time, looking down at his note card, blowing air out of his cheeks. He looked up sadly to the group. "How do you say goodbye to someone who, it feels, gave birth to us? This is not to say, Jessica," he added quickly, "that you're our mama, but I think there are some who might say that you are some kind of mother."

The group burst into laughter.

"Seriously, I don't even know what to say. I was talking to my wife last night, and I said, what do I say? What can I say? And she said, just tell them how you feel. Well..." He took off his glasses and dabbed his eyes with his handkerchief. He put the glasses back on. "I feel heartbroken. I feel like we're all wondering, 'How are we ever going to go on without that crazed woman in Studio B?'"

A little laughter, but people had also started to tear up.

"If Alexandra is the shaping intellectual force of DBS, certainly Jessica is the heart—" His voice broke and, annoyed, he scratched his head and tried again. But stopped, took a breath and said, "There's no way we can ever thank you, Jessica. You've given us careers, you've given us a network, you've given us a pain in the neck, a pain in the ass—"

Laughter.

"And now a very bad pain in our hearts. Anyway, kiddo, we got you something. All of us. We took up a collection and then Cassy yelled at me that four dollars wasn't enough—"

Laughter.

"So we had to kick in a little from the emergency fund. And so, Jessica, from your friends and family here at DBS, I give you this present with our deepest gratitude, our love, and our best wishes—forever and ever."

The side doors of the ballroom opened and a group of employees rolled in a brand-new Mercedes convertible coupe. There were excited oohs and aahs, and when Jessica stood up to speak, everyone vaulted to their feet and the entire room went into thunderous applause that lasted almost five minutes.

By the time people stopped clapping, Jessica was completely in tears. She kept blinking, trying to dab her eyes; Cleo ran up to do some repairs, and when the room finally grew silent, Jessica smiled. "Wow," she said softly.

Laughter.

Jessica shook her head. "Where do I begin? I guess by saying that when I arrived at DBS, that very first day, I was drunk. I was drunk because I *was* a drunk—"

"You still got great ratings," Langley quipped, making people laugh.

"Yes, well," Jessica said, "at a price. A *high* price. But now it's seven years later, I'm seven years sober, and I owe a great deal of everything good and wonderful in my life to you people at West End. You were kind to me, supportive, protective— And a lot of you were good role models. And what a life I've had these past seven years! You gave me a hit TV show, hundreds of new friends and family and the best kind of life possible. And then, as if that were not enough, you gave me my future husband, as well."

Cheers and applause.

"Yep. Me and playboy Rafferty are getting married. And you're *all* going to be invited to the wedding!"

Cheers and applause.

"The only thing is," she continued, "it may be kind of boring—because Dirk Lawson will *not* be handling the security."

Winces and oohs and laughter.

"Anyway, tonight we're blessed to have some very special guests here, FBI Agents Norman Kunsa and Debbie Cole, and Detectives Jefferson Hepplewhite and Richard O'Neal of the NYPD. I owe them my life. Um, this time, anyway. I've always owed my life to a great extent to Alexandra Eyes and Cassy and all those guys, but these outside people really went all out to find me and to help me put away the bad guys—something that really has helped me in getting closure on this whole ordeal.

"Um—" she stopped to think, looking at the back wall of the room, then, "It's interesting how love works and I wanted to tell you a little bit about it. Um, as most of you and the rest of the whole wide world knows, I've had a fairly horrible love life—"

Laughter.

"I mean, it wasn't—I didn't, you know, sleep with animals or anything. I mean, *animal* animals—there were some guys that—" She cut herself off, clearing the air with her hand. "Let's just move on, shall we?"

Laughter.

"Anyway, I really never expected that I would ever fall in love. One of the great joys has been to realize, year by year, how emotionally shut down I've been. Not the hysterical emotions being shut down—I think we all know I still have more than my share of hysteria to offer—"

Laughter.

A wince. "Remember when I smashed my office window with the phone?"

Laughter.

"Anyway, now that I am perfect—"

Laughter.

"I realize that not only had I not ever fallen in love before, but that I had no idea that loving someone could be so simple. I always thought falling in love meant euphoria followed by depression and anger and conniving, and lots and lots and *lots* of tricking and trapping—"

Laughter.

"—followed by guilt and remorse, and then passion turning quickly into loathing and hatred." She shrugged. "So falling in love was not something I particularly felt I was missing in sobriety."

Laughter.

"I'm not going to go into details, but after seven and a half years of us saying, 'Hi, how are you?' in the halls of DBS, I fell in love with Will Rafferty. Of course, he fell in love with me, too, basically because I hit him in the head with a golf ball at the affiliates convention and he hasn't been the same since."

Laughter.

"What's been most interesting to me these past weeks, with the ordeal of my being stalked and kidnapped, was that Agents Kunsa and Cole, and Detectives Hepplewhite and O'Neal seem to belong to the same school of love that I used to. In that when something or someone seems too good to be true, then they *must* be too good to be true. And since they could see how devoted Will was to me, and how very much he loved me, they naturally assumed, then, that

Will had to be a murdering, stalking psycho—which says what about me I'm not exactly sure."

Gales and gales of laughter, whoops and whistles.

"And so, I wish to thank them in particular, because, you see, they've done all the tricking and trapping and conniving with Will for me— So I don't ever have to do that. I can just marry him and love him with all my heart."

Everyone vaulted to their feet again, clapping and cheering. Jessica made Will stand up and wave at everyone. He remained next to her, holding her hand, blushing to the roots of his hair.

"Thank you, thank you everybody," Jessica said. "And just think of what we can name our children! Cole, Hepplewhite and Kunsa!" She stooped over, as if addressing a small child. "That's right, Kunsa sweetheart, you were named after the nice man who wanted to put Daddy in the electric chair."

Everybody laughed.

"Anyway," Jessica said, straightening up, waiting until the noise died down. "I've got to tell you, I've been in tears over my departure from DBS ever since I made the decision. It is just about the hardest thing I've ever done. And yet it seems to be what I need to do." She gestured to the car. "You guys got me the car, the benefits department said we could keep our pensions vested in DBS, Langley threw this big dinner, on and on— Everybody's been really wonderful and extremely generous. Particularly emotionally, for letting us go in the first place.

"And so," she continued solemnly, "I want to finish by thanking you, from the bottom of my heart, for everything—my life, my career, my husband, my happiness. And I want to tell you how much I love you all, how much I respect you and how terribly I will miss you." She turned to look at Alexandra and Cassy and the rest of the gang.

"You guys are the best friends I have in the entire world. You're my family."

Everyone was in tears.

Jessica turned around, and with a very sad face concluded with, "The only problem is, I'm not leaving. I've got too many things left to do in this job, too much to say."

At first no one reacted. And then Alicia said, "Are you dissing us?"

"Yes, I'm dissing you, Miss Jive Talk!" Jessica taunted, waving her finger and then her fanny at her head writer. And then she grabbed the mike and belted, "THAT'S RIGHT GUYS, I'M NOT LEEEEEA-VIIIIIIIING!"

"What? What?" Cassy said, stunned, looking around.

"So take the car back, Langley, and roll out some dough for a new set. 'The Jessica Wright Show' goes on!"

People were cheering and dancing around their tables. They had jobs again, they had a network.

In the chaos that ensued, Alexandra went up to put her arm around Jessica, whispering, "You are in big trouble, my friend. You really had us going."

"I thought I was going," Jessica said. "But I can't. There's just too much left I want to do on the air."

"Did you know about this?" Alexandra asked Will.

"Well, let's put it this way," he said, "I'm telling you now that I think we need to get to West End so you can break this news on the air yourself."

"Oh—right. You're right!" Alexandra turned to Jessica. "Well—" She shrugged and kissed her on the cheek. "Welcome back."

"Come on, hustle," Will directed the anchorwoman. He kissed Jessica. "Bye, darling, see you at home."

Alexandra leaned over the head table to tell Cassy, "Well, I guess I'm staying."

Cassy smiled and turned to Langley. "Well, I guess I'm

staying, too." She stood up. "And I'm going to go offer Wendy and Slim those security jobs we talked about."

Langley leaned forward to look at Jackson. "So, Jack, I guess I'm not leaving, either." He looked at his wife. "Sorry, Belinda."

"It's all right, darlin'," she assured him. "I don't think I was really up to home schooling and giving up Bergdorf's anyway."

"Somehow I had a feeling none of you would really leave," Jackson said to himself, sipping his wine, smiling at the scene in front of them.

People had surged around Jessica, and she was laughing and hugging people and accepting congratulations.

And, of course, Jessica was talking.

Always talking.

Making the world just a little bit better.

About the Author

Laura Van Wormer grew up in Darien, Connecticut, attended the University of Arizona in Tucson for a year, but then graduated from the S.I. Newhouse School of Public Communications at Syracuse University. Starting as a secretary to the editor-in-chief of Doubleday & Company, she worked her way up to editor before leaving to pursue her own writing career. She worked with the creators and producers of "Dynasty," "Dallas" and "Knots Landing" to write the official books of the shows, and in 1988 published her first novel, RIVERSIDE DRIVE (in which the characters Cassy Cochran and Alexandra Waring first appeared). Since then she has written WEST END (in which the character Jessica Wright is also featured), BENEDICT CANYON, ANY GIVEN MOMENT, JURY DUTY and JUST FOR THE SUMMER.

Laura divides her time between Manhattan and a 1920s English-style farmhouse in Meriden, Connecticut.